From as far back as she can remember **Michelle Conder** dreamed of being a writer. She penned the first chapter of a romance novel just out of high school, but it took much study, many (varied) jobs, one ultra-understanding husband and three gorgeous children before she finally sat down to turn that dream into a reality. Michelle lives in Australia, and when she isn't busy plotting she loves to read, ride horses, travel and practise yoga. Visit Michelle: michelleconder.com

When Canadian **Dani Collins** found romance novels in high school she wondered how one trained for such an awesome job. She wrote for over two decades without publishing, but remained inspired by the romance message that if you hang in there you'll find a happy ending. In May of 2012, Mills & Boon bought her manuscript in a two-book deal. She's since published more than forty books with Mills & Boon and is definitely living happily ever after.

Jennie Lucas's parents owned a bookstore and she grew up surrounded by books, dreaming about faraway lands. At twenty-two she met her future husband and after their marriage, she graduated from university with a degree in English. She started writing books a year later. Jennie won the Romance Writers of America's Golden Heart contest in 2005 and hasn't looked back since. Visit Jennie's website at: jennielucas.com

Royal Scandals

Royal Scandals: Royally Wed

MICHELLE CONDER

DANI COLLINS

JENNIE LUCAS

MILLS & BOON

First Published in Great Britain 2022
By Mills & Boon, an imprint of HarperCollins*Publishers,* Ltd
1 London Bridge Street, London, SE1 9GF

www.harpercollins.co.uk

HarperCollins*Publishers*
1st Floor, Watermarque Building,
Ringsend Road, Dublin 4, Ireland

ROYAL SCANDALS: ROYALLY WED © 2022 Harlequin Enterprises ULC

Their Royal Wedding Bargain © 2019 Michelle Conder
Cinderella's Royal Seduction © 2020 Dani Collins
Chosen as the Sheikh's Royal Bride © 2019 Jennie Lucas

ISBN: 978-0-263-30463-3

MIX
Paper from
responsible sources
FSC™ C007454

This book is produced from independently certified FSC™ paper to ensure responsible forest management.

For more information visit: www.harpercollins.co.uk/green

Printed and Bound in Spain using 100% Renewable electricity at CPI Black Print, Barcelona

THEIR ROYAL WEDDING BARGAIN

MICHELLE CONDER

To Heather – for years of love and friendship and for always being in my corner. I'll always be in yours too.

And to my dad. There just wasn't enough time in the end. I miss you.

CHAPTER ONE

TONIGHT WAS GOING to be a total disaster. Alexa could *feel* it.

The Annual Santarian Children's Charity ball, one of the most prestigious events on the international calendar, would commence in under an hour, and she felt sick with apprehension.

'He's here, Your Highness,' Nasrin, her assistant-cum-lady's-maid-cum-devoted-companion, murmured as she closed the bedroom door, a ripple of excitement evident in her quick steps as she returned to Alexa. 'One of the chambermaids confirmed that the Prince of Santara has just entered the Summer Palace.'

Retrieving the hairbrush from the old-fashioned vanity unit, Nasrin picked up a skein of Alexa's long dark hair and met her wide-eyed gaze in the mirror. 'This is so exciting. I can't believe you're actually going to do it.'

Alexa couldn't either; releasing a measured breath at the thought of what she intended to do, followed swiftly by the seizing of her stomach.

Known for her cool, unflappable poise under pressure, she felt as if she was about to throw up the grilled cheese sandwich she'd had for lunch all over her custom-made designer gown.

He was here. He was really here.

Prince Rafaele of Santara, the King's younger brother,

had actually arrived. There had been whispers that he might not attend tonight, given that he'd created a scandal at this very event last year, embarrassing the King. But apparently nothing stopped the Rebel Prince of Santara from following his own path, and that was a trait that could work in her favour tonight so she should see it as a positive. Being a determined rule follower, she found that somewhat difficult, adding to her massive sense of self-doubt.

How was she going to do it? How was she going to ask a prince with the reputation as a consummate playboy to marry her, even if she was a princess herself? Because that was what she intended to do. What she *had* to do if she wanted to appease her father.

She and Nasrin had hatched the crazy eleventh-hour plan to propose a fake marriage—or engagement because, as she would explain to the Prince, she had no intention of actually going through with the wedding—two weeks ago when she had realised that her father was deadly serious about seeing her married as soon as possible.

Of course she'd tried to argue with him. Tell him that she wasn't ready, that she needed more time, but he had shaken his head and informed her that nothing she said would change his mind. As the Crown Princess of Berenia, and only remaining heir, he would not rest until she was settled.

To be fair he had given her six months to create a list of possible marriageable contenders, but Alexa had dragged her feet, hoping he would forget all about it. On the night he'd told her he hadn't forgotten at all, she and Nasrin had sat down to commiserate over a glass of Sauterne and a completely unrealistic rom-com at the end of a long working day.

According to Nasrin the main actor looked like the dreamy Santarian Prince, his character replete with arrogant, bad boy tendencies and a super-hot body, and the idea had been born. In the film the hero had not wanted to marry the heroine, but love had won out in the end.

Alexa knew from past experience that love rarely won out in the end, but fortunately that wasn't what she required from the Prince.

'It's going to be fine, Princess Alexa; he'll do it,' Nasrin murmured, accurately reading the panic in her eyes for what it was. 'Then you'll have everything your heart desires.'

Everything her heart desired?

What she desired the most was time to make her own marriage match, and for her older brother to still be alive.

Sol had been the true heir to the Berenian throne but since his tragic death three years ago that duty had fallen to her. And she wasn't up to it, not yet anyway, and deep down she wondered if her father believed that she wasn't up to it either, especially after the serious lapse in judgement she'd made when she was seventeen. Perhaps that was one of the reasons he was pushing so hard for her to marry right now. Why he was so determined to have it done.

That, and to remove the stink of shame that still hovered over her after the King of Santara had abruptly ended their betrothal twelve months earlier. The ink hadn't even dried on their marriage contract before he had pulled out and immediately married another woman—an outsider, no less—his actions stirring up centuries-old animosity between their nations and giving the BLF—the Berenian Liberation Front—just the excuse they needed to re-engage in hostilities with Santara.

Her and King Jaeger's brief, ill-fated betrothal hadn't been a love-match by any stretch, but his rejection had still felt like yet another kick in the teeth for Alexa because she had *liked* him. She'd developed a massive crush on King

Jaeger when he had saved her from an embarrassing experience on her first official engagement as her father's consort. At thirteen, she'd been so nervous, decked out in a white tulle gown that had made her feel like a beautiful fairy, that she'd accidentally upended a full jug of cranberry juice all over herself. She'd frozen to the spot as the cold, sticky red liquid had drenched the front of her beautiful gown and chilled her skin. Before she'd been able to respond the newly crowned King of Santara had stepped in behind her and enveloped her in his jacket and whispered that everything would be okay.

Mortified, Alexa had buried her scalding cheeks against his chest, allowing him to draw her from the room without anyone really noticing them. He'd instructed a servant to find her lady's maid and then melted back into the party. Alexa hadn't drunk cranberry juice since, and nor had she forgotten the King's kindness. As she'd matured he'd become the epitome of her dream man: kind, loyal, compassionate and strong.

His brother, by contrast, couldn't be more different. The consummate good-time guy, Prince Rafaele moved from one lissom blonde to the next as if he was doing nothing more important than choosing a new tie to wear with his suit.

'Having your hair up was a good choice,' Nasrin said as she twisted the last of Alexa's waist-length tresses into place. 'It shows off the sheer panelling at the back of your dress to perfection.'

'It's not too revealing, is it?' Alexa murmured, twisting on her padded stool to get a better view. She'd chosen her nude-coloured off-the-shoulder gown to attract as much attention as she dared, but she wasn't used to wearing clothing that revealed so much skin.

'Not at all. It's perfect.'

Alexa stared at her carefully made-up face with critical indifference. Perfect would be to have the task ahead of her put behind her and sorted to her satisfaction.

'And you're sure he doesn't want to get married?' she asked, her outward calm slipping ever so slightly. One of the things that made the Prince so perfect was his reported disinclination to marry. If he didn't want to marry he would never want to make their union permanent and interfere with her chance to do things her way.

'Absolutely.' Nasrin nodded. 'He's been on record as saying he never intends to marry. Not that the women seem to be listening. They throw themselves at him like lemmings off a cliff, hoping to be the one to change his mind.'

So why did she feel so sick?

Probably because actually attracting the attention of a man like the Prince was completely foreign to her, thanks to her father's strict rules and regulations, and her own sense of inadequacy with men. Not that she'd always felt that way. Once, when she was seventeen, she'd believed a man—Stefano—had found her beautiful. But what he'd really found was that she was gullible. Gullible enough to be seduced by a man who was more interested in her title than her as a woman. The mistake had hit her budding confidence hard, pushing her to focus on her degree in business management, and her royal duties, to the exclusion of all else.

Not that she wanted to *attract* Prince Rafaele. No, she only wanted his cooperation in a scheme that, in the end, would serve him as equally as it would her by restoring cordial relations between their two nations. A scheme that had seemed a lot easier to follow through on when she'd gone over it late at night in her bed than in the cold light of day.

Trying to remain positive, Alexa slipped on her heels

and smoothed her hands down her bespoke gown, ignoring how the clever creation made her feel both elegant *and* naked—which, according to her exuberant assistant, was the whole point of the design.

'You will feel sexy and alluring,' Nasrin had assured her when she'd first set eyes on the dress. 'And every man in the room will look at you and want you.'

Right now she felt as sexy and alluring as a tree. And she didn't want *every* man in the room looking at her. She was nervous enough thinking about *one* man looking at her.

She picked up the dossier Nasrin had put together on Prince Rafaele last week, rifling through photo after photo of him attending parties and movie premieres every other week. Vastly wealthy in his own right, he owned an empire of nightclubs and bars across Europe that, once opened, became the only place to be seen. *'Dens of iniquity*, her father had once disparaged.

An unwanted shiver shot through her as she gazed at a shirtless photo of the Prince holding onto a sail line on the deck of a yacht. His white trousers were flattened against his muscular thighs by the breeze, his dark shoulder-length hair streaming out behind him, his broad chest deeply tanned to the colour of the teak deck. His face was turned towards the camera and the lens had lovingly captured his perfect wide smile, hawkish features and startling blue eyes as he laughed at something in the distance.

The caption underneath read: *The Rebel Prince in search of sun, fun and adventure.*

Alexa studied his image. Despite his relaxed pose there was something about the way he held himself that said *Danger…beware.* A jaded slant to his lips that indicated that he had seen everything there was to see in life, and was surprised by none of it. Which would be a good thing if he went along with her plan because their break-up would seem inevitable: the Playboy Prince and the shrinking violet could never have lasted. Not that she *was* a shrinking violet. She just chose not to make waves if she didn't have to.

'Hot, isn't he?' Nasrin said as she glanced at the photo before running a practised eye over Alexa. 'You look stunning, Your Highness. The Prince won't be able to resist you.'

While Alexa appreciated Nasrin's optimism, she knew from personal experience that men found her all too easy to resist. 'More likely he'll laugh in my face.' She closed the file. 'And if he's that opposed to marriage he might not even go for a temporary engagement.'

'But you have an ace up your sleeve. If he agrees, it could help settle all the bad blood between our nations. Of course he'll go for that. And the engagement would only be temporary. Unless...' Nasrin's pretty eyes sparkled mischievously '...you fall in love with each other.'

Alexa shook her head. Nasrin had a romantic nature that no amount of rational conversation could extinguish. And while Alexa might have once craved love and a happy-ever-after too, she'd been disappointed enough in the past not to wait around for it.

Love wasn't as important as dignity. Self-respect. Objectivity. And imagining the Prince of Santara falling in love with her, or her with him, was frankly hilarious.

'That's as likely to happen as the moon is to turn blue,' she said dryly.

'If you wish hard enough, Your Highness, you'll get whatever you ask for.'

Alexa knew that rarely happened either.

'Fortunately, I don't want the Prince's love. Just his co-operation.'

'Then go get it,' Nasrin urged with a flourish.

Alexa smiled. Nasrin had been like a gift when she'd come to work for her after Sol had died, organising her life and making her smile again with her chatty, easy nature. Everything else had felt so oppressive at the time, oppressive and overwhelming, during those dark days.

Not that she begrudged her role as the future Queen of Berenia. She didn't because she loved her country, and her countrymen, and she wanted to do the best job for them in Sol's stead. She wanted to make her father proud. And if the Prince went along with her plan she could do that. She could help rebuild relations between Berenia and Santara, and buy herself the necessary time to make a marriage that not only pleased her father but herself as well.

The decider would be whether or not she could implement a plan that had seemed perfectly logical at inception, but now felt desperately naive.

But if the Prince turned her down she'd just have to find someone else. Because the alternative—marrying the man who was on top of her father's list of eligible suitors—didn't bear thinking about.

Rafe gazed around the ballroom of the Santarian Summer Palace, a place he'd spent many formative years, with mixed emotions. As a general rule he tried not to return here very often, not only because it didn't hold the best memories, but because when he'd left Santara as a disaffected teenager he'd cut all ties with his nation.

And he wasn't sorry that he had. He didn't miss the life here. He didn't miss the sun that was hot enough most of the year to blister paint, and he didn't miss the endless round of lacklustre royal duties his father had expected him to carry out as the second son of Santara. The less important son. He didn't miss having his ideas shot down in flames by a man who had never understood his drive and ambition to forge his own path in life.

'It's lucky you're a prince, sibi,' his father had often snarled. *'You'd amount to nothing if you weren't.'*

Hard-nosed and narrow-minded, his father had treated opposing opinions as little more than ripples on a quiet pond.

Rafe had learned not to care, disconnecting from his father, and rubbing his nose in it any chance that he got. And despite—or perhaps because of—his father's convictions that he wouldn't amount to anything he'd made a success of his life.

He'd broken free of the constraints of royal duty and lived life on his own terms. Not that his father was around to see it. His death when Rafe had been eighteen was the very thing that had set him free. Or rather his brother had set him free when he'd stepped into the role of King at nineteen and given Rafe permission to spread his wings.

Returning from studying in the US at the time, Rafe knew that Jag could have used his insider knowledge and support, and it was only now, looking back, that he understood the sacrifice his brother had made for him, shouldering the burden of a troubled nation on his own and never asking anything of Rafe in return.

Once sharing what he would have said was an unbreakable bond, their relationship had grown strained with distance and Rafe was never sure how to bridge the gulf without losing himself in the process. Still, he owed Jag a debt of gratitude, even if his brother didn't think so.

Catching the direction of his thoughts before they progressed any further, Rafe shook them off with well-practised ease. This was partly the reason he hated returning home. The memories, the choked feeling of constraint and the heaviness that came over him that wasn't a part of the life that he lived now. A life based on unsurpassed pleasure, beauty and freedom. A life he lived predominantly in England, where he'd used a stellar investment in technology while attending Cambridge to purchase his first bar and nightclub. He had 'the touch' some said, an innate ability to tap into what his clientele wanted and to transform any venue he took over into the hottest place in town.

Which often made *him* the hottest *property* in town, pursued again and again by women looking to change his mind about remaining single. Something he had no intention of doing. Ever. In his experience the novelty factor rarely lasted beyond the bedroom and, even if it did, his parents' tumultuous relationship had cured him of ever thinking marriage was an institution he wanted to be part of.

Much better to have fun while it lasted, and move on before anyone got hurt. And if the tabloids wanted to paint him as a playboy prince to get foot traffic on their websites, that was hardly his problem. Something Jag didn't understand.

But then Jag was still a little aggrieved about the whole French heiress debacle at this event last year. Having grown bored early on in the night, Rafe had taken her to his hot tub upstairs, only to have her post photos of the two of them to her social media account. If he'd known Jag was in the middle of important negotiations with her father at the time he would have insisted that she leave her phone downstairs.

An oversight that had led him to promise his brother that he would stay out of trouble this evening. Which wasn't exactly fair because Rafe rarely went looking for trouble any more. More often than not it found him.

As if on cue, he saw his sister making a beeline for him

as she wound her way through the throng of impeccably groomed guests at the ball.

'I take it the ostrich lost?' he teased, his eyes going to the brightly coloured feathers covering her skirt. 'Or do you have plans to return the outfit to the poor creature at the end of the night?'

'Laugh all you want,' Milena challenged with narrowed eyes. 'But I love the dress and every feather had already been shed before it was collected. Is that what you were grinning at before? Or was it something else? I swear you had that glint in your eye that said you were up to no good.'

'Just remembering a certain French heiress I met at about this time last year.'

'Oh, please.' Milena rolled her eyes. 'Don't let Jag hear you say the words "French" and "heiress" together in a sentence; he'll blow a gasket.'

'He needs to loosen up. He got the deal with her father through in the end so it was a win-win for both of us.'

'No thanks to you,' she retorted. 'When are you going to start dating women you respect *and* want to—'

'Don't say it.' Rafe shuddered. 'I like to imagine that you're still innocent of such matters. And anyway, I promised our esteemed brother that I'd be on my best behaviour tonight, so don't worry.'

He gave his sister his trademark grin, knowing that it wouldn't work one bit. She might be six years younger than his thirty years but she'd always had his measure.

'That only makes me worry more.' She groaned. 'And, speaking of Jag, you need to cut him some slack. He's got a lot on his plate right now.'

'Like?'

'The Berenian thing.'

'Still?' Rafe arched a brow. He knew Berenia was causing problems but he'd thought that would have died down by now. 'So he didn't marry their revered Princess last year. They need to move on and get over it.'

'There's more to it than that. Santara has advanced much further on the world stage than Berenia, which brings its own set of resentments.'

'Yes, but still their incompetence can hardly be our problem.'

'I don't know the ins and outs of it but… Oh, there's Jag, looking for us. I was supposed to find you so we can get the official photos out of the way.'

'Lead on,' Rafe said with amusement. He'd smile and play nice so his brother would have nothing to grumble about at the end of the night. Then tomorrow he'd fly home and resume his normal life, which wasn't dictated by pomp or protocol.

'Rafa.' Jag greeted him with a hint of stiffness. 'I wasn't sure you were going to make it this year.'

'Never miss it. Especially if there's a French heiress to be had.'

'Rafa!' Milena scolded under her breath. 'You promised.'

Rafe laughed. 'Don't worry. Jag knows I'm joking.'

'Jag hopes you're joking,' his brother muttered. 'And just because you made a career out of annoying our father don't feel that you have to carry the tradition on with me because I'm King.'

'Wouldn't dream of it.' Rafe grinned. 'I hear you're having some issues with the Berenians.'

'Don't mention that word. I swear they're the most stubborn people on earth.'

A photographer stopped in front of them. 'The lighting is probably better over by the far column, Your Majesty; do you mind moving in that direction?'

'Not at all,' Jag said, casting his eyes across the sea of

chattering guests until he spotted what he was looking for. He crooked his finger, a small smile playing at the edges of his mouth, softening his face in a way Rafe had rarely seen before. Following his line of sight, he watched as Jag's new wife made her way towards them. Clearly pregnant, in a slim-fitting gown, she looked beautiful and only had eyes for his brother.

When she reached his side, Rafe could have sworn the rest of the room dissolved for both of them. Bemused, he wondered what it felt like to want someone that much, and then decided he didn't want to know.

'Good evening, Your Majesty,' Rafe greeted his new Queen. 'You're looking as beautiful as ever.' He took her hand and raised it to his lips. 'Should you ever tire of my stiff-necked brother, you only have to—'

'Rafa—' Jag began warningly.

Queen Regan laughed softly and placed her hand on his brother's arm. 'Always the devil, Rafaele.' She smiled at him. 'It's a skill to make a pregnant woman blush. But where is your date tonight? I understand you're seeing a Spanish supermodel. Ella? Or Esme?'

'Estela,' Rafe corrected.

'My apologies.' She glanced around curiously. 'Did you bring her with you?'

'Unfortunately, we had a difference in priorities and parted ways.'

'And you're clearly crestfallen.' Regan arched a brow, a playful glow in her eyes. 'Do I want to know what those priorities were?'

'If you two are quite finished flirting,' Jag said with an edge of menace in his voice, 'the photographer is waiting.'

'Sorry.' Regan threaded her arm through his. 'But I'm a married woman now. I have to live vicariously and Rafaele always has such *interesting* stories.'

'I'll give you an interesting story later on,' Jag promised throatily. 'For now just smile and imagine it.'

'Whatever they have, I don't want it,' Rafe grouched, lining up on the other side of his sister.

'It's called love,' Milena said impishly. 'And I can't wait to experience it.'

'Just don't fall in love with anyone I haven't checked out first,' Rafe warned sternly.

'Oh, fiddle.' She waved him away. 'You and Jag are as bad as each other. You're more alike than you might think.'

She was wrong. It had always been easier to be the bad to Jag's good. But he didn't offer an objection. Instead he pasted a smile on his face and pinched his sister's side just as the photographer clicked the shutter. Milena kicked his ankle in return and it was their usual game on to see who could make the other break first.

Two hours later, bored to the bone, Rafe thought about heading to his hot tub—alone—when he saw her. A vision who appeared to be nude at first glance but who, unfortunately, wasn't. But she was breathtaking, with her dark hair, smooth caramel skin and elegant cameo-like profile. Her delicate features were complemented by slender curves and long legs.

They'd fit, he realised with a jolt, somehow already knowing just how good they would be together though he'd never even spoken to her. Instantly intrigued by the notion that he wanted to know the colour of her eyes and the taste of her lips under his. He wanted to feel her warm silken skin and feast his eyes on her sweet curves as he stripped that clever gown from her body with aching slowness for the very first time.

As if sensing the heat of his thoughts, she turned her head, her eyes instantly finding his.

She blinked, as if she felt the caress of the erotic images coursing through his brain, a flush touching her high cheekbones. Or was that just his imagination going overboard? It certainly couldn't be because of the fool standing in front of her. Count Kushnir wouldn't know what to do with a woman like that if he had a set of instructions and an accompanying magnifying glass.

Rafe let a slow grin curve the corners of his lips, noting the way her eyes widened with alarm as if she too already knew that they were destined to become lovers.

Because they would become lovers. Tonight, tomorrow night—for Rafe it was already a forgone conclusion. He only hoped she wasn't one of those women who liked to play hard to get, imagining that if he had to work for it he'd be more interested. He wouldn't. Because he couldn't be more interested in this woman if he tried.

CHAPTER TWO

ALEXA FELT PRINCE RAFAELE'S gaze on her as if it were a tractor beam.

This was it. The moment she'd been waiting for. The moment he'd notice her so that they would meet and she could introduce herself. Not that she'd probably need to do that because he would surely know who she was but still, it was the polite thing to do. She'd introduce herself, make small talk and…and…

'Choo-choo…choo-choo!'

'I'm sorry?' Forcing her attention back to the man in front of her, with a noble Russian lineage dating back before Peter the Great, she tried to smile. 'I don't think I heard you right?'

At least she hoped she hadn't. But no…there it was again. An obnoxious, high-pitched noise as he mimicked the sound his toy steam engine made as it trundled around an apparently life-sized track. It reminded her of the stories of sybaritic kings of old who set up lifelike warships in large lakes and watched them battle for supremacy. If she had thought this man might be a possible candidate for a fake engagement should Prince Rafaele turn her down, he'd just convinced her to look elsewhere. The only thing she could fake in this man's company was a smile. And even that was growing old.

'May I interrupt?' A smooth deep voice beside her thankfully broke off the man's description of yet another steam engine.

Expecting the voice to belong to Prince Rafaele, she breathed a heavy sigh of relief intermingled with disappointment when it wasn't. Immediately her eyes cut to the place she had last seen him but he wasn't there any more.

'Your Royal Highness?'

Somewhat perplexed that the Prince had simply walked away after staring at her so openly, Alexa smiled at the newcomer beside her. What had he asked her? To dance? 'Yes. Thank you.'

She didn't actually want to dance but maybe movement would help settle her suddenly jangled nerves.

It had been the look the Prince had given her. That all-encompassing male glance that had raked her from head to toe and then pierced her with heat. It had completely thrown her. Of course she'd known he was good-looking. The mouth-watering photos Nasrin had dredged up on the Internet were demonstration enough of that, but in the flesh... In the flesh he was something more. More charismatic. More powerful. More sensual. More *physical*.

Taller than those around him, he'd been wide-shoul-dered and lean-hipped, his body exuding the kind of ani-mal grace that drew the eye of anyone in his vicinity and held it. His dark brown hair was cut in longer layers, fram-ing his chiselled jaw and well-shaped lips to perfection.

In many ways he'd reminded her of King Jaeger but this man had a laconic, laidback sense to him that was powerfully sexy, and strangely she'd never once thought of the King as sexy.

Powerful, yes. Intimidating and regal, yes. But she'd never looked at him and felt her blood pump faster through her veins, as had happened from one long, wicked look from Prince Rafaele.

Feeling guilty that she was completely ignoring the man who was currently holding her at a respectful distance on the dance floor, she tried to dredge up something interesting to say to break the silence between them. God knew she had years of banal small talk rolling around inside her head but, for the life of her, she couldn't seem to recall any of it, her brain stuck on the strange lethargy that had entered her body at Prince Rafaele's heated stare.

'I hate to cut in, Lord Stanton, but you need to contact your office. Something about a paternity test being carried out with your name on it.'

'Pardon?' Her dance partner instantly dropped her hand and frowned at the man she'd been waiting all night to 'run into' with horror. 'That can't be true.'

Prince Rafaele gave an indolent shrug of one wide shoulder. 'Don't shoot the messenger.'

Alexa frowned as Lord Stanton mumbled an apology and carved a purposeful path through the crowded dance floor as if the devil was on his trail.

'Allow me,' the Prince said, taking her into his arms and holding her much closer than Lord Stanton had done.

It took her only a moment to realise that he'd done that deliberately, and that there was probably no paternity test in the works at all.

'Was any of that true?'

'Not a word.'

Alexa didn't know whether to laugh or frown at his candour. 'That wasn't very nice. I think you really scared poor Lord Stanton.'

'Only because it's happened to *poor* Lord Stanton before.'

'It has?' She blinked at him. 'How do you know that? Is he a friend of yours?'

'I know everything. But no, he isn't a friend. Not even close.'

'He's not going to be happy when he finds out you lied.'

'Probably not.' The Prince raised an eyebrow as if to say he couldn't care less, his gaze skimming her face. 'But first things first. That soft accent I can hear in your voice isn't French, is it?'

'No.'

'Good.' Before she could think too much about his question he manoeuvred her closer, distracting her. 'Now I can just enjoy how good you feel in my arms.'

Incredibly aware of the warm male chest mere inches from hers, Alexa's breath caught. One of his hard thighs was pressed ever so slightly between her legs, keeping her slightly off balance, so that she had to grip onto his hand to stay upright. Aware that she'd never felt such a powerful response to anyone like this before, she automatically drew back, her reaction causing a slow masculine grin to curve his lips. 'Too fast for you?'

'I…' Completely unprepared to be meeting him like this, let alone be plastered up against his hard body, Alexa frowned. 'Yes. I don't like being crowded.'

Truth be told, she wasn't used to being touched like this. Her father had never been overly tactile and, as her mother had died giving birth to her, she'd been raised by a procession of nannies, each one leaving before she or Sol could become attached to them. It had been her father's way of training any neediness out of them, his methods intended to instil in them both a sense of objectivity and distance befitting a monarch of their realm.

She still remembered the day her beloved Mrs Halstead had left. At five, Alexa had cried herself into a stupor, thus proving her father's point. After a while she had stopped crying when people left but, given the mistake she'd made with Stefano, the lesson in objectivity had taken much longer to master. And sometimes she worried that she still hadn't got it. Especially now, when she was struggling to remain objective in this man's arms.

'By all means I can do slow,' he said with a grin, his mesmerising eyes flicking over her with sensual intent.

Even though she had dressed to attract attention she was so unused to men flirting with her it took Alexa a moment to assimilate his meaning. When she did, heat curved up the side of her neck. She hadn't fully worked out what she was going to say to him when they finally met so she found herself at a loss for words. It was only her love for her country, and a desire to placate her father, that had her still considering going ahead with her plan.

Because ordinarily she wouldn't go near a man like the Prince. And not just because of his bad boy reputation but because he was too big and too male—his level of testosterone swamping her and making her way too aware of him. It was like being confronted by an enormous, sated wolf; even though you knew it was well fed you still couldn't relax in its presence for fear that it might pounce just for the fun of it.

The orchestra music changed tempo and she realised that the Prince danced very well, his movements fluid and graceful as he moved her in time with the beat. Wondering how to gain control of the situation and suggest a place for them to sit down and talk, she was completely unprepared for his enticing all-male scent to swamp her as he leaned in closer.

'You're exceptionally beautiful,' he murmured, bringing her left hand up to his lips in one smooth move, smiling against her fingertips. 'And unmarried. Two of my favourite attributes in a woman.'

His earlier question about her being French came back to her and she pulled back to stare up at him.

Did he not know who she was?

She'd received so many sympathetic glances during the night from those who knew her to be the jilted Princess of Berenia that her teeth had wanted to grind together.

For him not to recognise her... It didn't seem possible but...perhaps it was. After all, he'd been off doing his own thing for a decade now, where her life had remained incredibly small by comparison. A bolt of inspiration shot through her. If he didn't know who she was it would give her a chance to find out how amenable he would be to her plan without having to embarrass herself by asking outright.

His eyes watched her, confident and direct. Sapphire blue surrounded by inky black lashes, they drew her in with the promise of delights she had probably never even dreamed of, drew her in as if he could read every one of her secret wishes and desires and had the power to answer them all. The notion was both terrifying and utterly irresistible.

The prince's heavy-lidded gaze held an amused glint as if he knew exactly how he was affecting her. Only she didn't plan to become one of his worshippers so it was best to set the scene early.

'Are you always this direct?' she asked, meeting fire with fire.

'I'm not one to waste time on trivialities.' His fingers brushed the inside of her wrist, sending an unexpected trail of goosebumps along her arm. She fought off another tremor as she thought about what those fingers would feel like stroking other, more intimate, parts of her body. 'State what you want and go after it has always been my motto.'

She didn't doubt it.

But ever since her brother had died her life had been mapped out for her and stripped of any real choice so she rarely, if ever, stated what she wanted, or went after it.

He swung her in a tight circle, the hand at the base of her spine covering the small of her back. 'It hasn't failed me yet.' The smile he gave her was one hundred per cent lupine in nature. 'I hope it's not about to.'

'Are you propositioning me?'

The words were out before she could stop them and she only just managed to stop herself from cringing. No doubt none of the sophisticated beauties he was frequently photographed with would need to ask such a gauche question.

Even white teeth were revealed by a frankly amused smile. 'I do believe I am.'

'But you don't even know me.'

'I don't need to know you to know that I want you.' His tone lowered to a sexual purr. 'But if names make you feel more at ease I am Prince Rafaele al-Hadrid. Rafe to my intimates, Rafa to my family.'

'I know who you are,' she said, blinking hard to defuse the sensual spell he was effortlessly weaving around her. 'And I also know of your reputation.'

His smile widened. 'Which one?'

Not sure how to handle the fact that he seemed completely unperturbed by her revelation, Alexa pushed on with her plan to gain information about him. 'The one that says that you're not marriage material.'

'Very true,' he drawled. 'I am good at many things but being a husband would not be one of them. And I believe in playing to my strengths.'

So did she. 'Why wouldn't you be a good husband?'

'According to many of the women I've seen, I'm emotionally stunted, closed off from genuine affection, afraid of true intimacy and utterly selfish.' His eyes twinkled down at her with amusement. 'I did take exception to the "closed off from genuine affection" comment as I happen to think I'm very affectionate when the mood strikes.'

'I'm sure she was way off base.' Alexa laughed despite herself.

'I'm glad you agree.' He grinned charmingly. 'But you haven't introduced yourself,' he reminded her softly.

'No, I haven't.'

His dark brow arched with quicksilver interest. 'And you're not going to,' he surmised accurately. 'Do you want me to guess?' His gaze roamed her face, heating her up as it went. 'You do seem vaguely familiar. Should I know you?'

'I would say so.'

'Have we ever—'

'No.' She stumbled as his meaning became clear, causing him to bring her into direct contact with his warm body again. Heat that had been simmering away inside her exploded low in her pelvis.

Sensual amusement curved his lips as if he had her right where he wanted her.

Danger, her brain signalled once more, only stronger this time, with the added instruction to retreat. Only she couldn't because she couldn't remember why she should. Not with those intense blue eyes lingering on her lips and turning her mouth so dry she had to fight not to moisten it. Her heart felt like a trapped bird trying to break out of its cage, her whole body assailed with a kind of sweet lethargy she'd never felt before.

The drawn-out notes from a violin signalled the end of the musical score they'd been dancing to, and then someone on the end of a microphone announced that the silent auction was about to take place.

Clusters of murmuring guests started making their way

towards one of the anterooms, and Alexa was startled to find that she hadn't moved an inch out of the Prince's arms. Scrambling to get her brain back on line, it took her a moment to realise that he had taken her hand and was leading her in the opposite direction to everyone else.

'Where are you taking me?' She pulled up, digging her spindly heels into the marble floor and gaining no traction at all.

'Somewhere we can talk.' The Prince's enigmatic gaze swept her from head to toe. 'I made a promise that I wouldn't cause any scandals this evening and I'm very close to breaking it.'

He steered her through a set of open doors and along a wide corridor before she had the wherewithal to stop him once more. 'Wait.'

Instantly coming to a halt, he looked back at her.

Alexa blinked as she tried to regulate her thoughts— and her breathing. At some point she would need to get him alone to go over her proposition with him but, with her body sending a whole host of mixed messages to her brain, she knew she wasn't ready for that now. Plus, he wasn't taking her anywhere for them to talk. She might be relatively inexperienced when it came to men, but she already knew that they could be unscrupulous when it came to getting what they wanted.

He looked down at her, amusement lighting his eyes as she gently tugged her hand free of his.

'I'm not going to kiss you.' The bold statement slipped out before it had fully formed in her mind and she knew she'd never felt as tempted to do exactly what she said she wouldn't in her life before.

His sinful lips curved into that devilish smile and a blush stained her cheeks. 'You don't like kissing?'

Not particularly, but that wasn't the point, was it? 'I don't kiss strangers.'

'But I'm not the stranger here; you are,' he pointed out. 'And fortunately I have no such reservations.'

His tone was teasing but she sensed his hunger in the coiled strength of his body and the heat that radiated from every pore. The earlier image of a wolf about to pounce returned. This time it was definitely hungry and she was in its crosshairs. Rather than scare her as it probably should, it sent another thrill of sensation down her spine. She shuddered with unexpected anticipation and of course he noticed, his blue eyes darkening, his nostrils flaring slightly with his next breath.

Something exciting and wickedly enticing wound between them.

'Come with me,' he invited huskily. 'I get the impression that your life could do with a little excitement in it.'

She wanted to deny it but his assessment was so accurate she couldn't. Every hour of her day was usually accounted for with paperwork or meetings and she rarely took time out to just have fun. A roar of laughter from nearby guests broke into her reverie as if to drive the point home.

Those serious doubts she'd had about going ahead with her plan returned tenfold.

Prince Rafaele was much more lethally male and charismatic than she had anticipated, and the blatantly sexual way he looked at her awoke every one of her senses. She hadn't expected him to have such an uncontrollable edge beneath the civility of his custom-made tuxedo but it was there—primal and dangerous and totally untameable.

'Come,' he coaxed once more, his hand raised towards her. 'Take my hand.'

It was more command than invitation, the silken gravel

of his tone making her forget that her future was on the line this weekend. Making her forget how much she had at stake: the ability to fulfil her royal duty to Berenia *her* way.

Against all rational thought, Alexa gave into temptation and placed her hand in his, allowing him to lead her through a solid door and into a beautiful, softly lit reading room. Glancing around, she noted that it was empty, the soft furnishings and gauzy curtains in the windows giving the room an odd sense of intimacy that was heightened when she heard the door click closed behind her.

'I'm not sure this is wise,' she said, knowing by the wild hammering of her heart that it definitely wasn't.

He grinned with mischievous intent. 'Probably not.'

Completely absorbed by the animal grace of his stride as he pushed away from the door and came towards her, Alexa was unprepared for him to invade her personal space and bumped the low table behind her as she unconsciously retreated.

Fortunately, he caught her around the waist, his fingertips spanning her hipbones with blatant possession.

'Your Highness!' Alexa exclaimed on a breathless rush, her mind as unbalanced as her body. 'I told you I'm not—'

'Kissing me. I know.' His head lowered to hers, the warmth of his lips ghosting across the line of her jaw as he inhaled her scent deep into his lungs.

A shiver of awareness bolted down Alexa's spine, turning her knees to water. Her hands flattened against his hard chest as if to hold herself steady, her senses logging the hard heat of his body and the strong beat of his heart through the thick fabric of his jacket.

Despite her four-inch heels, their height difference put her only at eye level with his chiselled mouth and she couldn't look away, her fingers curling of their own accord into his dinner jacket.

The prince's hands firmed on her hips. 'You've got exactly three seconds to step out of my arms before I kiss you properly.'

His tone was low and husky with need and Alexa flushed as an answering need flooded her lower body with silken heat. Completely out of her depth, her knees almost too weak to hold her upright, she leant against him in a move that perfectly signalled her desires to a man well versed in reading the play.

'I'm pretty sure that's five,' he murmured, his head bending as his mouth found hers. This kiss was firm, warm, his lips capturing hers with consummate skill and drawing a response from her she didn't even know she had in her to give.

When she didn't resist a soft groan left his mouth and one of his hands rose to cup the nape of her neck, his body moulding to hers as he took control of her very will.

Alexa knew she shouldn't be doing this but she couldn't seem to organise her thoughts when the desire to taste him was so strong. The prince's heat and scent surrounded her and soaked into her, his mouth driving out any thought of resisting.

'That's it, sweetheart,' he whispered, 'open for me.'

Having never been kissed with such carnal expertise, Alexa felt a rush of burning heat as his tongue entered her mouth and licked at her own. The unexpected eroticism of the move made her hands grip his shoulders, her body arching towards his, seeking more. Craving more.

The sensations were so wickedly enticing that when his fingers curved around one of her breasts she moaned, no longer concerned with what she was here to do. This was all that mattered. This man's mouth fused with hers, his hands caressing her all over and making her burn.

She slid her fingers into his hair, tugging him closer,

and he groaned again, his hands moving lower to cup her bottom and bring her in closer against his body, his callused palms snagging on the tiny crystals covering her dress.

'You taste like honey and nectar,' he murmured, his lips trailing a heated line along her jaw towards her ear.

'You taste like heat and mint,' she panted, her neck arching to accommodate his lips, her nipples painfully tight against the fabric of her dress.

He laughed huskily as if she delighted him. It was quite the aphrodisiac after her previous sexual encounter had obliterated her burgeoning self-confidence.

'Come upstairs with me.' The Prince's kisses continued down her neck and she felt him shudder as he gently bit down on the tendons that joined her shoulder. 'I can't take you here; we'll get caught.'

Alexa didn't know which part of that statement permeated her stunned senses more, but suddenly her hands were firm on the hard balls of his biceps as she pushed him back. Memories of her teenage mistake tumbled into the space between them, tripping up her thoughts as she fought to draw oxygen into her lungs and clear the haze from her brain. 'We can't... I'm not... Let me go!'

As soon as the words were out he released her, his chest heaving like bellows as his breath rasped in and out of his lungs.

His dark hair was in disarray around his shoulders and she realised with a mortified groan that her fingers must have done that.

'What's wrong?'

'What's wrong?' Her eyes widened at his ridiculous question. 'We nearly... I just... I didn't come in here for that.'

Struggling to even out his breathing as much as she

was, the Prince's brows drew together. 'Why did you come in here then?'

Still experiencing the drugging after-effects of being in his arms, Alexa blurted out the first thing that came into her head. 'I came in here to ask you to marry me.'

CHAPTER THREE

'You should have gone with that as your opening line, sweetheart,' Prince Rafaele drawled. 'It would have smothered the chemistry between us faster than a Santarian sandstorm.'

Unsure how to handle him as well as her rioting emotions, Alexa frowned. 'I didn't expect you to pounce on me as soon as we got here.'

'Pounce?' He gave an amused look. 'I gave you a chance to pull back.'

'Three seconds?'

His grin deepened. 'It ended up being five.'

'You don't even know my name,' she said, flabbergasted that he could so quickly switch from arousal to amusement when she was still struggling for composure.

'I've never found that to be all that important when I want a woman.'

Well, that stung. No woman wanted to be just another notch on a man's bedpost. But what had she expected? This was the exalted Rebel Prince who had attempted to seduce her. Attempted and nearly succeeded! 'Why?' she felt compelled to ask. 'Because you don't plan on seeing the woman again?' she challenged.

'Now that depends on the night. And the woman.' His eyes narrowed on her face as if he was trying to work something out. 'So who are you? Because I have to admit you're damned familiar, although I know I've never touched you before.'

She didn't know whether to be flattered by that statement or not and went with not. 'My name is Alexa, Crown Princess of the House of Berenia.' She gave her tone just the right amount of haughtiness to signal her displeasure with him, and was pleased when his eyes widened.

He raked a hand through his hair. 'You might have mentioned that sooner as well.'

'I did plan to when we got inside the room, but you kissed me before I could come out with it.'

Rafe's gaze dropped to her lips and he cursed under his breath. She was right. He'd never acted on his attraction for a woman faster. His only excuse being that he'd felt her hunger run as deep as his own and he'd been unable to resist testing that hunger when they were alone. And he'd been right. She'd gone off like a firecracker in his arms. Another few minutes and they both would have been naked and horizontal.

Thank God he'd had enough sense to suggest they go to his room, and the restraint to release her when she'd asked. But he hadn't wanted to. The inferno that she had lit inside him had been ready to explode. It still was, but this time partly with recrimination. He should probably apologise for pouncing on her as she had accused him of doing. It wasn't his usual style, which leant itself to more finesse and a small measure of self-control!

And she was his brother's cast-off, dammit, the daughter of the man who was currently making his brother's life hell. Jag would just love it if he had witnessed this near blunder. It had been one thing to piss his father off deliberately, but he'd never do that to his brother.

'Well, I'm not kissing you now, Princess, so I suggest we leave and forget this ever happened.'

If he could. He had a feeling he'd be dreaming about the taste of her mouth and those soft kittenish sounds she'd made as he'd cupped her bottom in his hands for a few nights yet. Even now he wanted to reach for her again.

'But I was serious about what I said before.' She drew in a long breath, her lovely breasts straining against the fabric of her gown. 'And I'd really like to make a time to speak with you about it.'

Rafe sent his mind back and focused on what she'd said that had halted him in his tracks. 'Marriage?'

'Well, engaged more than married.'

He shook his head gently, unable to believe that she was actually serious. 'I don't do marriage. You'll have to find someone else to fulfil that fantasy.'

'I know you don't do marriage. That's the point. I don't either.'

He frowned at her earnest expression. She was either crazy or… 'How much have you had to drink, Princess, because you're not making any sense?'

'I've hardly had anything to drink,' she retorted as if he'd insulted her. 'I'm perfectly sober.'

'Then that response before was all you?' He gave her a lazy smile as her cheeks coloured. 'Good to know.'

'I'd rather not talk about that.' Her lips pinched together. 'And, given what just happened, now probably isn't the best time to discuss my proposal. Could we meet tomorrow?'

'Tomorrow isn't going to change my mind. Neither will the day after.'

'Look…' she held her hands up as if to placate him '… I'm not talking about a real marriage. I'm talking about a temporary engagement that works for us both. We won't even have to spend that much time together. We just need to put out a joint statement, go to a couple of events together and break up amicably at a time that suits us both.'

'As far as proposals go, this one is definitely novel, but marriage—sorry, *engagement*—doesn't work for me at all. Temporary or not.'

'I know.' She gave a heavy sigh, tucking a strand of thick silky hair that had come loose back behind her ear. She looked gloriously mussed from where his hands had been and that reminded him of how much he'd like to put them there again. Unwind all that magnificent hair and find out how long it was.

As if they had a will of their own, his eyes followed her as she paced the mahogany-decked reading room, her gown hugging her heavenly curves as she moved. 'That's why I chose you.'

'Chose me?' He blinked to get his brain back on line.

'Yes,' she said with the patience of a mother speaking to a recalcitrant child. 'I need to get married—or at least engaged—and you have all the attributes I want in a fiancé.'

Curious, Rafe found himself extending the conversation, if only for the amusement factor. 'Such as?'

'You follow your own rules, you're completely disinterested in marriage, and your values in life are questionable.'

'Questionable?'

'According to everything that's said about you, you're quite the hedonist.'

Rafe leant against the back of a sofa. 'Really?'

'I'm paraphrasing. But the point is we're completely incompatible so it won't surprise anyone when we don't go through with the marriage, and no one will be blamed for it not working out.' Unlike when his brother had called off their engagement and everyone had thought it was her fault. That she hadn't been woman enough for the King of Santara. 'It will just seem obvious.'

'I have to confess,' Rafe drawled, 'I've never had those reasons put forward by a woman wanting me to put a ring on her finger before. Usually it's more along the lines of: *You're rich, powerful and a prince.*'

'Oh, the prince part is important to me too. At least that you're from Santara.' She frowned as she perched on the edge of the sofa. 'Women actually say that to you?'

'I was paraphrasing.' His eyes glinted mockingly. 'So why is my being a Santarian prince important to you? I would have thought it was the last thing you would want.'

'My father is convinced that seeing me happily settled will ease the current tension between Santara and Berenia and help our people move forward from your brother breaking our betrothal. He gave me six months to find someone, but I didn't realise he was serious. Now he's planning to take matters into his own hands and arrange a marriage that I don't want.'

'Ah, I'm beginning to see the picture.'

She let out a slow breath, her narrow shoulders slumping slightly forward. 'When my father is like this he's immovable, and I need more time.'

'Hmm…' Feeling a little sorry for her, Rafe offered up the only solution he could think of. 'You know you could always say no.'

'No isn't a word my father understands.'

'Is doormat a word *you* understand?'

Her eyes flashed up at him like deep pools of jade backlit by fire. 'Are you implying that I'm a doormat?'

Rafe shrugged, enjoying her display of defiance. 'If the shoe fits.'

'The shoe does not fit,' she said a little too vehemently. 'The fact is my father has been through a lot in recent years and I'm not going to add to his problems. And this is partly your brother's fault. If he had gone ahead with our marriage as he had agreed to do then none of this would be an issue right now.'

'But nor would you have got to kiss me quite so passionately, so there is that.'

Her feathers well and truly ruffled, the Princess pushed to her feet. 'You either have a colossal ego or you're making fun of me.'

'Let's go with the ego theory. A lot less volatile.' Rafe crossed to the booze cabinet between two arched bookcases and poured himself a whisky. 'Drink?' he asked, holding the crystal decanter up for her to see.

She set her top teeth into her plush bottom lip, reminding him of how exquisite her mouth had felt under his, and surprised him with a terse nod.

'Dutiful does not equal doormat, you know.' She moved towards him, careful not to touch his fingers as she took the glass. He gave her a small smile that said he knew exactly how nervous he made her and watched her chin come up in response. 'Not that I expect you to understand that.'

'I understand it,' he said curtly. 'I just don't adhere to it.'

'Well, you're lucky. I don't have that choice.'

Rafe clinked the ice in his glass, wondering what it was about her he found so enthralling. Because he did find her enthralling—from the way she moved to the feminine lilt in her voice, and definitely in the sexy lines of her body. He suspected that she took life far too seriously, and for some reason he wanted to change that.

'You're an intelligent, beautiful woman,' he began, watching her closely. 'And a future queen. How hard can it be to find a husband?'

'It's not hard at all.' She sighed. 'But finding the *right* husband is.'

'Do I even want to know what the right husband looks like?'

'Someone kind, compassionate, caring.' She took a delicate sip of his brother's hundred-year-old Scotch, shuddering delicately as it hit the back of her throat. 'Someone I can respect and who will put Berenia first. Someone who has a similar outlook to me.'

'Not looking for someone with a sense of humour?' he enquired lightly.

Alexa frowned. 'That would go under "similar outlook to me".'

'So none then.' He grinned as her eyes widened. 'What about love?'

'I have a sense of humour, thank you very much,' she defended hotly. 'And love is not essential.'

Rafe's eyes widened at that. 'I think you're the first woman I've ever heard admit that.'

'Love complicates things and who even knows if it exists? I think it's made up by Hollywood executives and songwriters trying to make money.'

'And I thought I was cynical.' Her brow furrowed and his grin widened. 'That was a compliment, by the way. But what about passion? Surely that's on your list.'

She wrinkled her nose. 'Not essential either. I'm not the most passionate person on the planet, and respect far outweighs passion.'

Contemplating what had put her off passion when his body still throbbed at the memory of her mouth opening under his, Rafe gave her a smile that was pure sex. 'You felt pretty passionate to me before.'

She moved to sit again on the sofa, unable to meet his gaze. 'That wasn't me. I don't know who that person was.'

'Whoever she was, she was intoxicating.'

She wrinkled her nose. 'So will you consider it? I'm not sure how long I have before my father takes the decision completely out of my hands. And, frankly, I'm desperate.'

'I can see that.' He was actually sorry he had to turn her offer down. If life hadn't taught him that he needed to steer clear of matrimonial entanglements at all costs he might even have considered it. But marriage had the potential to inflict pain on the unwary and the innocent. Why would any man deliberately buy into that? Temporary or not. 'Sorry, Princess, but I'm not that desperate.'

'You won't even consider it to help improve relations between our nations?'

Rafe blinked away the dark memories of his past and found himself pinned by a pair of gorgeous green eyes that, if he wasn't careful, had the potential to suck him in deep and never let him go. 'See, the problem with that part of your argument is that I don't care about the issues between Santara and Berenia.'

She blinked as if he'd just said *Down with world peace.* 'But how can you not?'

'I live in London and have done for a decade. I have as little to do with Santara as I can.'

'Then what about to improve your reputation? Being engaged to me would stop some of the gossip. For a while at least.'

Princess Alexa, he realised, was a real fighter. He liked that. Not enough to agree with her hare-brained scheme, but enough to find that he was enjoying her company. A lot.

'Who said I wanted the gossip to stop?'

'But surely some of the things written about you must bother you.'

'Not particularly.'

'Why is that?' Her brow pleated as if his attitude was something she couldn't contemplate. 'Because it's all true?'

Rafe wondered which particular piece of gossip had widened her eyes to the size of dinner plates. Hardly any of it was true but denying the many claims made about him would only give them energy so he rarely bothered. Still, he knew that Alexa didn't think much of his supposedly 'hedonistic' lifestyle and he couldn't help teasing her a little. 'Only the really bad ones.'

Watching the wings of colour heat her cheeks almost made him want to rescind his words so that she'd think better of him. Then he wondered why he cared and remained silent. He didn't like that he'd already delayed this conversation for the pure pleasure of listening to her speak. Adding to his uncharacteristic behaviour would only make things worse.

'So your answer is no?'

'My answer is no.'

She blew out a breath and set her glass on the table abutting the sofa. 'Then there's nothing more to say.'

There was plenty more to say, starting with enquiring which room she had been allocated so they could revisit that kiss, the sensations of which were still echoing inside his veins. But instead he said, 'What are you going to do now?'

She raised her chin and gave him a look he imagined she gave international dignitaries she had no further use for. 'Find someone else, of course.'

Find someone else? Rafe scowled at his fogged-up reflection as he stepped from the shower the following morning. *Just how many men did she plan to approach with her absurd proposal? And, more importantly, had she found someone who had taken her up on her offer last night?*

He didn't want that question running through his head but he was unable to banish it. After she had walked away from him he'd spent another hour at the party looking for her, to no avail. Presumably she'd gone to bed, so he had done the same, thinking about her all night as he'd known he would.

Even though he had no intention of countenancing her proposal himself, he knew that someone would eventually agree to it. What sane man wouldn't? With that face and body...

Rafe dropped his towel on the floor and padded back to his room to dress. *He'd* turned her down, hadn't he, and he was a sane man.

Yes, but he was sane and *smart*. Smart enough to know that her problems were none of his business and that he should let it go.

And he would. As of now.

His jet was waiting to fly him back to London and he planned to stop downstairs long enough to grab an espresso, wish his sister-in-law well in her pregnancy and tell his siblings he'd see them some time in the future.

What he wouldn't do was think about the beguiling Alexa any more today.

Pleased to be back on track, he pulled a clean shirt over his head, stepped into his jeans and shoved his feet into his boots.

Women just shouldn't go around proposing to men who were basically strangers and expect that it would all work out exactly as they wanted it to. Especially not future queens who looked like cover girls. Alexa was asking for trouble.

Trouble that had nothing to do with him.

And why was she back in his head again? So she'd surprised him when so few people did any more—so what? At the end of the day she was just a beautiful woman he'd wanted to take to bed. And she'd wanted to be there too. The way she'd caught fire in his arms...her response to his touch... Grinding his teeth, he zipped his overnight bag closed. What she'd done was drive all rational thought from his head, and kept him up way too long last night.

But it wasn't just the chemistry that had kept him awake. It was the puzzle she represented. She'd gone up like a flame in his arms but then claimed that she didn't have a passionate nature, dismissing the desire between them as an anomaly. And what about her belief that love might not exist? Presumably something, or someone, had put that in her head and he'd like to know who or what. Not that he disagreed with her. He didn't. He didn't believe in love either, but something about the way she'd said it made him think that she was either lying to him, or lying to herself. And yet she'd seemed so honest…so sincere…

Scowling at the procession of questions that wouldn't say die, Rafe grabbed his phone. Time to push Princess Alexa from his mind and think about something else. Because thinking about her made no sense. She wasn't someone he planned to pursue—not with marriage on her mind—and added to that she was his brother's ex, for God's sake.

Assailed by a sudden wave of jealousy he'd never before felt for his brother, Rafe nearly put a hole in his pocket shoving his phone into it. He didn't share his women. Ever.

And since when is a woman yours after one kiss?

Leaving that ridiculous question unanswered, he slammed out of his room and made his way to breakfast. He needed coffee before his mood deteriorated any further.

Refusing to wonder if he'd meet up with the beguiling Alexa, he heard a message arrive on his phone and homed in on it like a drowning man reaching for a life vest. Unfortunately, it was only a stock commodity update and he was in the process of closing it when he nearly barrelled into Jag as he rounded the corner of his private hallway.

Instantly alerted by his brother's taut, exhausted expression, Rafe frowned. 'What is it? Is there something wrong with Regan?'

Rafe might not have much to do with his brother any more but he could still read him and he couldn't think of anything else that might put that ragged look on his brother's face other than his wife, or all-out war.

'No, Regan's fine. I've just come from a meeting with King Ronan and Princess Alexa.'

Rafe felt himself instantly tense. 'They haven't declared war, have they?'

'Not yet.' Jag's scowl deepened. 'But last night a firebomb was thrown into a building site near the border in a show of protest at King Ronan and Princess Alexa attending the charity ball last night. Two of our workers were injured.'

'That's insane,' Rafe growled. 'Why did the King even attend if things are that volatile?'

'We believed it would be a display of unity between us but the Berenians didn't take it that way. They see my slight of their Princess as the highest insult.' He smiled faintly. 'Sorry to burden you with my problems. It was nice seeing you mucking around with Milena. It's a pity we don't see each other more often. I know Regan would like it if we did. I would too.'

Rafe swallowed the lump that suddenly lodged in his throat. He loved his siblings but he wasn't like either of them; he was a loner. He didn't require the same level of closeness, or connection, that drove others to forge unbreakable bonds. He didn't need someone, or something, special and neither Jag nor Milena understood that about him.

'Let's focus on one thing at a time. What can I do to help sort out the Berenia thing?'

Alexa's proposal of the previous night came into his head and he instantly shelved it. Marriage—or becoming engaged—was not the answer here.

'I thought you needed to head back to London?'

'I do. But if there's something I can assist you with while I'm here then I will. I'm not so obtuse that I can't see how much you have on your plate right now.' Not that he expected that Jag would need him. Their father never had. The important issues he'd gone to Jag for counsel. Rafe had been relegated to the lesser duties of opening flower shows or attending state dinners where he was expected to be on his best behaviour to prove what a great parent and leader his father was. Rafe was pretty sure they hadn't fooled anyone on that score.

'I appreciate the offer but, as I said, I've just had a meeting with King Ronan and Princess Alexa. We've come up with a diplomatic response to ease the tension.'

Rafe had a feeling he wasn't going to like the response. 'What was decided?'

'You really want to know?'

Yes, for once he really did.

'Why not? I'm here and I am still a Santarian.'

'Princess Alexa has agreed to a union with Lord Alec Richton of Urbana. I'm not sure when the wedding will take place, but the plan is for Lord Richton to fly into Berenia later in the week for a formal announcement.'

Rafe's whole body went still. 'You've got to be kidding me?'

'No, why would I do that?'

'Because it's barbaric and I can't believe you'd allow Alexa to be bandied around like a box of chocolates everyone can take a pick at.'

Jag frowned at his harsh tone. 'That's hardly what's happening here.'

'Isn't it?' Rafe felt unreasonably livid. 'You were betrothed to her.'

'When King Ronan approached me early last year I said
I'd consider the idea,' Jag said evenly. 'It was never a done
deal, and it should not have been made public.'

'So now Richton gets a go at her?' Rafe swore under
his breath. 'What if he pulls out? Do you and Ronan have
someone else up your sleeve for her?'

Jag's gaze sharpened. 'Someone else…?' His tone
turned thoughtful. 'That's the kind of question a jealous
lover might ask.'

'Hardly.' Unable to remain still under his brother's per-
ceptive gaze, Rafe paced the floor.

'Richton won't pull out,' Jag said. 'Apparently he's been
in talks with King Ronan for some months about a union,
but regardless, the Princess is an incredibly lovely and
intelligent woman. Most men would jump at the chance
to marry her.'

Rafe knew how lovely she was, and having his brother
notice only made his aggravation deepen. 'But what about
what she wants?'

Jag sighed. 'I really don't understand what's got you
so het-up about this but she does want it. We all want to
end the hostilities between Berenia and Santara so we
can move forward. If Alexa's marriage is able to promote
peace in the minds of the Berenians, then I'm all for it.' He
frowned as Rafe continued to pace. 'Come on, Rafa. You
know that arranged marriages have been happening here
for centuries. They've worked out in the past, and they'll
work for a while to come yet.'

Too agitated to argue with his brother any further, Rafe
headed for the door. 'We'll see,' he said, slamming it closed
behind him.

* * *

He found Alexa in the breakfast room, speaking to another of the guests who had stayed overnight at the palace.

The smell of coffee made his saliva glands go into overdrive but he bypassed the silver pot on the sideboard and headed straight for Alexa.

As he neared he realised she was speaking to Lord Graham, the son of an English earl. Had he been another one of her candidates?

Not that it mattered any more.

'Princess Alexa?' He stopped beside her, completely ignoring Lord Graham. 'We need to talk.'

Clearly startled by his abrupt tone, her green eyes widened. 'Your Highness?'

'I told you last night, it's Rafe. I rarely use my title.'

'Prince Rafaele…' Lord Graham frowned at him. 'Princess Alexa and I are in the middle of—'

'Nothing.' Rafe turned his most cutting gaze on Graham. He knew he could be intimidating; he owned nightclubs and had been called upon to throw more than one drunken patron out onto the pavement, so he wasn't surprised when the other man's eyes flickered warily. 'The Princess and I have…unfinished business to settle.'

Not at all as intimidated by him as Graham, Alexa frowned. 'What unfinished business?'

Unprepared to stand around explaining himself in the middle of a room full of people, Rafe raised a brow. 'Have you forgotten the proposal you made last night? Perhaps you were drunk after all.'

'I was not!'

'Then you haven't forgotten.' He cut his gaze back to Graham, who had foolishly remained rooted to the spot. 'And unless you want Lord Graham here to be privy to our chat I suggest we take this somewhere private.'

Clearly unimpressed with his high-handed tactics, Alexa's mouth tightened. 'Fine. Please accept my apologies, Lord Graham. Prince Rafaele obviously has a bee in his bonnet about something.'

A bee in his bonnet?

Rafe shook his head and reached for her elbow. 'You don't have to be nice to everyone, you know. Graham will survive without your company for a while.'

Rafe directed Alexa through a nearby door to a small private terrace, which was thankfully empty.

'You need to stop doing that,' she complained, glaring up at him. 'I am not a horse to be led around at will.'

She brushed past him as she moved out of the direct line of the sun and the subtle scent of her perfume drew his muscles tight.

Irritated that he was affected by a woman who wasn't even trying to win his favour, Rafe met her icy stare with one of his own. 'All evidence to the contrary.'

'What does that mean?'

'It means I've just spoken with my brother, who informed me about your impending nuptials with Lord Richton.'

'He had no right to do that.'

'Why not? He didn't reveal anything I wouldn't know in a week or two anyway.'

'Then you also know why we reached the decision.'

'Because a group of hot-headed Berenians went about a hundred steps too far? Yes, I heard. Did you ever think of just calling in the army for protection?'

'Oh, that would really work,' she scoffed. 'Make a show of aggression and give the BLF even more of an excuse to start a war. Maybe you could lend us a few of the bouncers who work the doors at your nightclubs for extra muscle.'

'It seems a damn sight better than marrying someone to reach an outcome it might not even achieve.'

Her eyes narrowed at his disparaging comment. 'Diplomacy is always better than might.'

Not in his view. 'I take it this marriage isn't of the fake variety,' he said, an edge in his voice he was struggling to control.

'No.' She paused, as if what she was about to say was distasteful, staring out over the expanse of green lawn surrounded by potted roses and gardenia bushes. 'It won't be fake.'

Silent fury made his voice gruff. 'Is that what you want? To marry Richton?'

She gave him a fulminating look. 'You know it isn't.'

'But you'll do it anyway.'

'If my country needs me to do it.' Her chin lifted, as if daring him to contradict her. 'Then yes, I'll do it.'

'The dutiful little mouse.'

Jade fire flashed from her eyes at his mocking tone but what did she expect, that he'd ignore the obvious?

'I am no more a mouse than a doormat,' she said icily.

'You're doing something you don't want to do. I'd say that makes you one or the other.'

'Sometimes sacrifices have to be made,' she said with regal fortitude. 'Why do you care?'

'I don't like injustice. And I know how it feels to be trapped by circumstance.' He knew how it felt to be bullied into doing something you didn't want to do. His father had made an art form out of it, and it seemed her father was doing the same to her. 'It's why I left Santara.'

'So you're trying to help me? Very chivalrous, Prince Rafaele,' she mocked softly. 'But I don't have the luxury of choice. I have to marry at some point.' She swallowed heavily and turned her gaze out over the elaborate garden once more. 'It might as well be Lord Richton.'

Watching how controlled and closed-up she was only made Rafe's temper hit a new high. 'Richton might seem like an upstanding citizen, but word is that he has a dark side. One you don't want to meet.'

'How would you know that?'

'Because he's been blacklisted from at least seven clubs that I'm aware of, including mine.'

A grimace crossed her face as she shook her head. 'I'd prefer not to know that.'

'Dammit, Alexa. That's not even the point here.' He stepped closer, deliberately crowding her. 'Stop being a martyr.'

'My, you have a lot of names for me, don't you?' she mocked, her eyes cool enough to freeze lava.

Yes, he did have a lot of names for her, utterly beautiful being one of them.

'My brother died three years ago,' she said, a note of sadness replacing the iciness of moments ago, 'leaving all of us utterly devastated and me the only heir to the throne. When you add in the problems with Santara, combined with the corruption my father has just weeded out of our government, that has set back our modernisation plans and given the BLF even more to gripe about, you can see that something has to be done. And quickly.'

'I'm sorry you lost your brother, and I'm sorry you're facing political challenges, but that doesn't mean you just give up.'

'I'm not a quitter!' she denied hotly. 'I'm not giving up. I'm giving in. There's a difference.'

'I don't see that.'

'You don't have to. And I'm sorry if asking you to marry me last night made you think that you have the right to question me. In hindsight, the whole fake engagement idea was a mistake. It probably wouldn't have worked anyway. I was desperate for an alternative but now I don't need one. If by marrying Lord Richton I can ease the political tension between our two countries, and prevent more violence, then I'll consider that a win.'

He saw the line of her throat move as she swallowed. She was putting on a brave face but he'd bet that she wanted to marry Richton about as much as a person wanted a root canal. She was just too nice to say it. Too nice to demand her due. And that bothered him. Almost as much as it bothered him to imagine Alec Richton putting his hands on her. His mouth.

'Have you even met Richton?' he grated.

'Of course.'

'Have you kissed him?'

'That's none of your business.'

It wasn't difficult to read that she was furious with his question. As she had a right to be. He was behaving entirely out of character, getting involved with a woman beyond the bedroom, especially with a woman he had already made off-limits. He didn't bed women who were looking for marriage—either temporary or permanent. Especially not princesses from politically hostile neighbouring countries.

And yet thinking of her married to some other man when she'd kissed him as she had the night before left a nasty taste in his mouth. And that was strange in itself. He'd kissed—hell, he'd made love to—plenty of women and never given a thought to who they might end up with. The notion had never entered his head before.

But then he'd never been as attracted to a woman as he was to this one. It was something he wasn't sure how to handle. Because he still wanted her. In fact right now he wanted to take her into his arms, press her back against the wall and challenge her to ignore the sexual chemistry that pulsed between them.

'I'm making it my business,' he said, noting how her eyes widened at his tone.

'You can't.' She made to move past him and her body brushed his. Raw, unparalleled desire arced between them, making a mockery of her words. Frowning in consternation, he knew she would have put more space between them if she hadn't found herself neatly trapped between him and an outdoor table. 'Marriages in our part of the world have been arranged for centuries,' she continued, raising irritated eyes to his. 'It's a tradition.'

'That's what my brother said. But I'm a bit of an anti-traditionalist unless both parties are in agreement.'

'Not all of us have the freedom that you do. And I have a duty to uphold.'

'A duty that will lead you into a worse situation than you're already in.'

'That's your opinion, not mine. An opinion you have no right to offer since you very clearly turned down my proposal last night.'

'And the chemistry between us?' He hadn't realised he'd moved closer to her until she made to move away from him again. Irritated, he reached out and clasped her wrist in his hand. It was fine-boned, delicate, so small. His body hardened as memories of how she had felt in his arms coursed through his veins. Of how her nails had dug into his shoulders through his clothing. He wanted that again, but directly on his skin this time. 'You're just going to walk away from it? You're going to pretend that you didn't dream about me last night?'

Her breath left her in a soft rush. 'I did not dream about you last night.'

'I dreamt about you.'

Her eyes widened at the admission, her sharp inhalation setting every one of his nerve-endings on fire.

'What would you have me do?' She shot him a wary look, as well she might, given the nature of the questions and the answering thoughts currently running through his head.

What a pity that he couldn't give into any of them.

'I'd have you stand up for what you want,' he bit out. Which was true enough. Being dutiful was one thing, being foolish another thing entirely.

She shook her head as if that wasn't even a possibility. 'Sometimes the only way to win is to retreat. It's called strategy.'

'It's called insanity.'

'To you,' she said curtly. 'To me it's my duty. But I still don't understand why you're so interested in all this. Apart from wanting to play the white knight, that is.'

'I don't play the white knight,' Rafe growled. He'd done that as a boy, stepping in between his parents during their more vitriolic arguments to protect his mother from his father's rages. Neither parent had appreciated the conciliatory gesture—his father thinking him insubordinate, and therefore worthless, and his mother too caught up in her own pain to notice his.

The memory was a timely reminder as to why he steered clear of emotional entanglements. Entanglements like this.

'And you're right. This isn't my business. If you want to marry Richton and commit to a life of unhappiness then have it.'

'I didn't say I *wanted* that.'

'Then what do you want?'

Already charged with emotions he was unused to feeling, Rafe's jaw clenched. She must have read his tension accurately because her gaze dropped to his mouth, her tongue darting out to moisten her lips. The air between them went from volatile to explosive. The pulse in her neck throbbed and her eyes widened as if she sensed danger. But she didn't move away.

Instead she went still, her whole body taut as if she was waiting for something. As if she was *wanting* something…

Rafe told himself not to do it. Not to reach for her. Not to touch her. But he might as well have told himself to cut off his own foot while he was at it.

'Ah, to hell with it.' Without giving either of them a chance to think, and completely disregarding any consequences, Rafe lowered his mouth to hers.

If she'd shown any form or resistance or hesitation he might have stopped, he might have pulled back and reminded himself that she was not only 'off-limits', but that he didn't go around kissing women just to prove a point. But she didn't resist. Instead she gave a low moan of assent, wound her arms around his neck and pulled him in closer.

This. *This* was what he'd woken up craving today. The soft velvet feel of her mouth under his again, the sweet taste of her on his tongue and the long length of her warm curves moulded to the hard planes of his body.

Shock waves of pleasure shot through him as her fingers gripped his hair, her tongue caressing along his, filling his mouth as she shyly tasted him in return. Rafe groaned, curving his fingers around the slender nape of her neck, his thumbs firm against her cheeks as he deepened the kiss. He couldn't seem to get enough of her. Her taste, her touch. He wanted more, he needed—

'What the devil is the meaning of this?'

Rafe knew instantly that the deep voice that thundered behind Alexa was her father, and from the way her body instantly stiffened so did she.

He could have kicked himself. Never before had he become so lost in a woman, so lost in his own senses, that he'd forgotten his surroundings the way he just had. The way he nearly had the night before.

Cursing softly, he raised his head to see the shocked fury on her father's face, followed by the shocked disbelief on his brother's.

Alexa's stricken gaze rose to his. 'Please tell me it's not as bad as I think,' she whispered unevenly.

'Worse,' he murmured, his gaze firmly fixed on her father.

'Well? Are you just going to stand there and ignore me?' the King thundered. 'I want to know the meaning of this! Alexa? Explain yourself.'

Straightening her shoulders, Alexa moistened her kiss-swollen lips and turned to face her father's wrath, smoothing her hands down over her hips. 'Father... Your Majesty...' Her face flamed anew as her gaze landed on his brother, a fresh wave of mortification turning her cheeks rosy. 'I was... That is to say we were...'

'Celebrating,' Rafe said, knowing that there was only one way out of this mess and taking it.

'Celebrating?' King Ronan's face became almost mottled.

'Rafe—' Alexa's worried gaze met his as if she had already guessed what he was about to say, but Rafe ignored the look.

Taking her hand in his, he raised it to his lips. 'That's right,' he confirmed, his eyes never leaving hers. 'Alexa and I were celebrating our betrothal.'

CHAPTER FOUR

'BETROTHAL?'

Her father's voice was imbued with such a note of incredulity that Alexa knew immediately what he was thinking—that this man would never do as her future consort.
It was only Rafe's rank as second in line to the throne of
Santara that kept complete scorn from his voice.

'That's right,' the Prince drawled lazily.

Alexa nearly groaned out loud at the Prince's antago-
nistic tone.

'Is this true, Alexa?' Her father's voice sliced like a
filleting knife. 'Did you accept Prince Rafaele's hand in
marriage?'

No, *she* had asked *him*. And he'd said no. But, that aside,
how was she to answer his question diplomatically when
she had no idea *how* to answer it at all? Rafe had thrown
her in at the deep end with his charged announcement
and she wasn't at all sure why he had done it. An outright
denial seemed implausible given that she'd been caught
with her arms wrapped around the Prince like a vine, but
agreeing seemed just as problematic.

Fortunately her father was too incensed to notice that she
was struggling to come up with an answer and didn't have
the patience for her to formulate one. 'After we had already
agreed that you would marry Lord Richton this morning?'

Oh, dear. Lord Richton. She had completely forgotten about him. If the floor were to open up and swallow her whole right now, she wouldn't mind.

'Lord Richton is no longer in the picture,' the Prince declared, his hard-packed body lethally tense beside her.

Alexa frowned at the way he took control of the situation, at the way he took control of her, as if he had every right to do so.

Just then a flutter of movement caught her eye and Alexa was appalled to note that they were no longer alone. Some of the King's other overnight guests had also come out to the terrace to view the stunning gardens.

'Why don't we take this discussion inside?' King Jaeger offered smoothly. 'The terrace is hardly the place to discuss something of this magnitude.'

Her father looked like he wanted to argue but gave a curt nod.

Rafe settled his hand in the small of her back, causing a jolt of fresh awareness to race through her.

'After you,' he said politely.

Hanging back from her father and his brother, Alexa glanced up at him from beneath the fringe of her lashes. 'Why on earth did you tell them we were betrothed?' she whispered hoarsely, absently noting that Rafe had matched his stride to hers.

'Because I could hardly tell your father that I wanted to take you to bed, and that you wanted to be there. I do value my life,' he countered.

Not nearly enough, she fumed silently at his cavalier answer.

'Just because I kissed you does not mean that I want to sleep with you!' she hissed, wondering if she would have had the wherewithal to deny him this time if it had come to that.

'My apologies, Princess. I assumed you wouldn't want a scandal any more than I do, and you did ask me to marry you. I thought it was what you wanted.'

It had been. Last night. Last night, before he had kissed her and brought forth a whole host of emotions she didn't want to feel. Before she had dreamt about the two of them in bed together. Naked.

Easing out a choked breath, Alexa nodded at King Jaeger as he held a door open. She reluctantly followed her father inside, with Rafe so close behind her she could feel his body heat through her clothing.

At least she understood his thinking now. He'd promised his brother that he wouldn't create a scandal and so he'd improvised by taking up her proposal. Something she should feel much better about, given that it *was* her idea and it *had* been what she wanted.

Only the purpose of asking the Prince to marry her was to *gain* control of her life, and she somehow felt that she was about to lose it altogether.

She surreptitiously placed a finger against her temple, which had started to throb. She supposed there was no other option but to go along with it now because Rafe was right; she didn't want to marry Lord Richton, and she had always viewed a fake engagement as a better option.

King Jaeger offered her father a seat but he refused, choosing to stand beside an oak dresser, his arms folded across his corpulent chest.

Rafe planted himself in the middle of the room, his legs braced wide on the silk rug, facing his brother. Not wanting to be the only person in the room seated, Alexa chose to remain beside him, even though her legs felt as capable of holding her up as matchsticks.

'Well, now that we're all standing,' King Jaeger began

with a resigned note in his voice, 'would someone mind explaining what's going on here?'

'There's nothing to explain,' Rafe began. 'Alexa and I share a certain *chemistry*, and have decided to take things further.'

Wondering why he hadn't led with the political advantages their union would bring, Alexa was only grateful that he hadn't chosen to reveal how she had approached him the night before.

'When did this happen?' her father asked suspiciously.

'We spoke about it last night,' Rafe answered, throwing her a heated glance that told her exactly which part of last night he was thinking about. 'At length.'

'If you spoke about it last night, Alexa—' her father's gaze pierced hers '—why did you agree to marry Lord Richton during the meeting this morning?'

'Last night I got cold feet,' Rafe interjected smoothly, placing his arm around her waist. 'It put Alexa in an awkward position. After thinking things through however, I now know what I want. Do you think we could ring for coffee? I'm parched.'

'I was addressing my daughter,' her father snapped impatiently. 'Alexa can speak for herself.'

Yes, but nowhere near as eloquently. She was almost in awe of how the Prince could reveal so much and yet so little at the same time.

'Prince Rafaele is correct, Father,' she said, trying to ignore the heavy warmth of Rafe's hand against her hip. 'We did speak about it last night and I'm… I'm still coming to terms with his change of heart.' She glanced at the Prince with a look just short of panic, hoping that King Jaeger had indeed rung for coffee—or perhaps something stronger.

'Sometimes a man doesn't know what's important until it's about to be taken away.' Prince Rafaele gave her an indulgent smile. 'When Alexa informed me of your plan to marry her off to Lord Richton, I couldn't let that happen. If Alexa marries anyone, she'll marry me.'

Alexa swallowed at the possessive note in his voice. What would it be like if he truly meant those words? If he actually wanted to marry her for real? And why had that thought even entered her head? She wasn't looking to turn this into a love story. No matter how well he could kiss, Prince Rafaele was completely the wrong kind of man for her.

'This is all very surprising,' King Jaeger said reasonably. 'Why don't we take some time to think about it and agree to meet next week to—?'

'No.' Her father cut the King's offer off before it was fully formed. 'If your brother wants to marry my daughter then the wedding will be held at the end of the month.'

In three weeks!

Her father's words sounded like a death knell in the quiet room. Alexa swallowed hard. This was only meant to be a temporary engagement, not an actual marriage.

'That's not possible,' she choked out. 'I…that is to say, we…'

'This isn't a game, Alexa,' her father interrupted tersely. 'Of his own admission, Prince Rafaele has already experienced cold feet and I will not have another Santarian royal make a fool of you by pulling out at the last minute.' He turned to square off against the Prince. 'If you want my daughter, those are the terms.'

Fully expecting Rafe to run from the room like a man with the devil after him, Alexa wasn't surprised to hear him say, 'The end of the month doesn't work for me. I have a new club opening on that weekend and I have to be there.'

'There you go,' she said, breathing a sigh of relief. 'Now why don't we—?'

'The weekend before then,' her father challenged.

Alexa felt Rafe go dangerously still beside her. Her father didn't move either; his chin jutted out at an angle she knew meant that nothing would get him to back down. They were like two stags facing off against each other over unclaimed territory. Only she was the piece of precious veld they were fighting over.

Deciding she had to do something to defuse the tension in the room, Alexa stepped towards her father, only to have Rafe's hand firm on her hip to hold her in place beside him.

'Tight,' he murmured, his hard gaze flicking from her father's to hers. 'But so be it.'

'So be it? *So be it?*'

Somehow Alexa had convinced her father that she needed a moment alone with her *fiancé*. She moved out of his arms now, and rounded on him.

'Are you completely mad? Why did you say that to him? Why did you agree with his terms?'

'Breathe, Princess,' the Prince ordered curtly, 'before you pass out.'

She wasn't going to pass out. She was going to… Alexa groped for the edge of the sofa behind her and all but fell onto the cushioned seat. She was going to pass out.

'Here.' A glass with amber liquid in it, not unlike the horrible Scotch she'd sipped the night before, was thrust in front of her face. 'Drink this.'

'It's too early for alcohol.'

'It's five o clock somewhere in the world. If you don't drink it, I will.'

'Have it.' Alexa took a deep breath, her palms against her belly to settle the pitching sensation inside. 'I'm too much in shock to drink it.'

'Why are you so shocked? You're the one who asked me to marry you in the first place.'

'I asked you to cooperate in a fake engagement, not enter into a real marriage.'

'And why *was* that?' His eyes were like blue granite when they met hers. 'You weren't surprised when your father initially disapproved of you marrying me. Was this just an act of rebellion on your part? The perfect, pampered little princess, lashing out against authority by becoming engaged to the Rebel Prince?'

'No!'

Rafe gave a mocking stare. 'Your face gives you away, Princess. Don't ever play poker. You'll lose the bank.'

'Okay, yes, in some small way I was rebelling, but not because I'm perfect, or pampered. Far from it. I don't want to marry anyone right now, and because I knew my father didn't approve of you I never imagined he would push us both to the altar the way that he has.'

'Appears you were wrong.' He paced away from her to stare out of the window. 'It seems the bad brother is just as good for his Princess as the good one.'

Alexa frowned. 'You mean King Jaeger?'

He turned back, his brow lifted in a cynical arch. 'I do only have one brother.'

'I… I've never compared the two of you like that.'

'Like I said, don't play poker.'

'Okay, fine,' Alexa conceded. 'But you can't deny that you're totally different from each other. By your own ad-mission you're not interested in duty and commitment, and you don't care about Santara or politics. Honestly, your life is completely alien to me.'

'Because it's based on pleasure?'

'Because it's hedonistic.' Her face flamed as his eye-brow arched again. 'What I mean is, you do what you want, whenever you want, regardless of what others think of you. You live by your own rules, and I don't know anyone else who does that. Frankly, I envy it.'

For a moment he didn't say anything. Then he sighed and dragged a hand through his overlong hair. Alexa didn't want to remember how thick and soft it had felt beneath her fingertips but she couldn't help it. Her gaze drifted over his unshaven jaw and paused on his well-shaped lips. Lips that were skilled and warm.

Suddenly aware that he was watching her just as closely, she lifted her chin and forced her gaze to remain steady even though she was quaking inside.

'Well, regardless of how this all came about, your father has effectively checkmated us both.'

'So it would seem.' Unable to sit still with so much energy coursing through her body, Alexa rose from the sofa, her mind in a whirl. 'And now we have to un-checkmate ourselves.' Not that she had any idea how to do that. Her father was more stubborn than a mule when he chose to be.

'That won't be possible.'

Alexa frowned as the Prince stared moodily into the glass he was holding.

'It has to be.'

'Not without seriously angering and embarrassing both our Kings.'

Feeling trapped, Alexa absently reached for the glass in his hand, taking a fortifying gulp before handing it back with a grimace. 'So what do we do now?'

'We do what your father wants. We marry. You get to appease your father and help your country and, if you're right, the violence between our countries ceases. I get to pay off a long-standing debt I owe to my brother and ease his load.' He tossed back the remaining contents of the glass and placed it on a low table. 'But nothing else changes. You live in Berenia. I live in London. At a time that is convenient to us both we'll agree that the marriage isn't working and end it.' His gaze sharpened. 'Six months should be long enough.'

'I don't know if that will work. My people will expect you to move to Berenia.'

'I expect billion-dollar deals to fall into my lap every day but unfortunately that doesn't happen either.'

Ignoring his sarcasm, Alexa paced away from him. 'You really think this will work?'

'Why not? I have stories written about me that aren't true all the time. Only this time I'll be the one in charge of creating the story. I find I quite like the idea.'

Alexa gnawed on the inside of her lip in consternation. 'I still think we can find a way out of this if we try.'

'Fine. If you find one, you let me know. As long as it doesn't make things worse for my brother I'll be all over it.'

'And what if six months isn't long enough to convince everyone that this is real?'

'Six months will be plenty. But if you're worried you can just gaze at me adoringly from time to time.'

'That would only feed your ego.'

'Something I'm all for.' His gaze settled on her lips, and heat spiked deep inside her. Suddenly she was thinking about kissing him again and, as if he knew exactly where her mind had gone, his gaze lifted to hers, amusement highlighting the dark blue depths.

Embarrassed, and not a little disconcerted by the strength of her reaction to him, Alexa lifted her chin. 'It will be expected that we're seen together at some point, you know.'

'Perhaps.' His eyes were a hot and watchful brand as they locked with hers. 'But let's cross that bridge when we come to it, hmm?'

* * *

If Alexa had wondered over the course of the last two weeks how Prince Rafaele felt about their impending nuptials, all doubt evaporated when she caught sight of his grim expression at the end of the aisle.

He hated it.

Something Alexa would probably have been more aware of had they not delegated every aspect of the wedding planning to their respective assistants.

Not that she'd wanted to plan it. The thought of it had been so challenging she'd deliberately thrown herself into horrendously long working days so that she'd be too exhausted by the end of the day to think about anything at all, least of all the wedding.

The down side to having been so busy was that the time had seemed to rush by. And now she was about to trust her future to a man who liked to be in charge, and whom she hardly knew.

One she was incredibly attracted to.

The unwanted thought entered her head entirely without her permission. For two weeks she'd been trying to avoid thinking about the way he had kissed her and touched her and the way she had responded, but she hadn't been completely successful, her dreams often so erotic she had woken sweaty and embarrassingly aroused on more than one occasion.

Because sex with Prince Rafaele would be unforgettable.

And thinking that way would lead to trouble. They had struck a marriage bargain with each other for political purposes. It was nothing more than a marriage of convenience; the Prince might kiss like a dream but she couldn't have sex with him. Not only would it not serve any long-term purpose but she was very afraid that she'd like it too much. That she'd like *him* too much. And if he were to find her lacking… If he were to find her inadequate… A horrible queasiness settled in the pit of her stomach before she swallowed it down.

No. As tempting as the Prince was the key to making their temporary marriage work was to focus on her objectives—freedom to make her own marriage match in the future, as well as the restoration of political peace between their nations. The latter of which already seemed to be working.

The people of both Berenia and Santara had greeted the announcement of her impending marriage to the Prince with unmistakable enthusiasm, treating it as the love story of the age. That was thanks, mainly, to a photo that had been taken of the two of them dancing at the charity ball. In the photo the Prince was holding her far too close, the smile on his face shockingly sexual, while her own expression was one of stunned stupefaction. At least that was how it looked to her!

But their respective PR departments had loved the photo, adding it to their marriage announcement for the entire world to see.

Alexa eased out a steadying breath as she came to a halt in front of the Prince, her long white gown settling around her ankles in a rustle of silk. If ever there had been a stony-faced groom, he was it.

She swallowed the lump in her throat. If she'd been hoping for some other reaction from him, and maybe deep down she could admit that she had been, then she would have to get over it.

Gone was the devil-may-care seducer she had met at the Santarian Summer Palace just over two weeks ago. Gone was the charming rebel who didn't let anything bother him. This version of the Prince couldn't be more bothered if he was being swarmed by angry wasps, his face carved in stone, his muscles taut as if he were fighting the urge to run.

Join the club, she thought as the celebrant spoke the first words of the service.

As if in a dream state, Alexa barely followed the proceedings, her senses leaping with surprise when the Prince placed his hands on her shoulders and turned her towards him, his fingers sure and strong, his expression unreadable.

Before Alexa fully understood that they had reached the end of the service his head bent to hers, his lips covering her own in a searing kiss. She didn't mean to close her eyes at the contact but she did, and it only heightened the riot of sensations inside of her.

A tremor went through her as his fingertips brushed the nape of her neck in a feather-light caress and Alexa swayed, barely catching herself at the last moment before she completely melted against him.

Fortunately she was able to recover herself as the wedding guests clapped and whooped, and the *qanun* and *oud* struck up a lively tune as they proceeded back down the aisle.

Everyone seemed happy as they ate and danced and mingled during the lavish reception. Everyone except Alexa, who grew more and more miserable as the afternoon wore on. Prince Rafaele had behaved like a polite stranger during most of proceedings and Alexa couldn't wait for him to return to London.

Guilt and nerves ate away at her. Guilt that she had somehow caused this whole debacle with her wretched plan to find a temporary fiancé, and nerves because she had a strange premonition that her life would be changed for ever by marrying him.

Which, of course, it would be—but only temporarily.

And what was the shortest marriage on record? If it was two hours she'd surely beat it because she'd like nothing more than to pretend it hadn't happened at all and end it now.

Badly needing a distraction, she caught sight of King Jaeger, now dancing with his heavily pregnant wife, Queen Regan. Alexa had tried not to like the Queen when she'd first met her, but Regan's compassion and understanding of how she had felt to be jilted by the King had shone through from the start. It was embarrassing now how Alexa had become tearful when she'd first met the Queen, having had to sit through a dinner watching the man she'd had a teenage crush on stare at a woman he clearly adored.

It was strange watching them now because none of those old feelings she'd had for him seemed to exist any more. She could appreciate his good looks and strong masculine presence but she could no longer see herself by his side. As his wife. Instead she found herself comparing him to her new husband. They both had dark hair and similar eyes and they were both incredibly well built but, as suitable as the King had been as a marriage prospect, he had never drawn her gaze the way Prince Rafaele did.

Alerted by a tingling sensation along the back of her neck, Alexa's eyes cut across the room to find her new husband watching her closely, his face devoid of emotion. She couldn't hold the intensity of his gaze, her face flushed as she found herself admiring the cut of his suit that moulded perfectly to his wide shoulders and lean physique.

It was embarrassing how attractive she found him and the only saving grace was that he'd be returning to London some time in the evening. She couldn't wait for that to happen.

As if reading her desperation for distraction, the King of Santara and his wife approached her.

'May I have this dance, Princess Alexa?'

Alexa swallowed hard as she gazed at the man she had once thought she would marry. While the awareness of what might have been between them was gone, she was still embarrassed by how easily he had cast her aside.

'Please,' Regan encouraged when Alexa automatically turned to her for permission. 'The wedding was beautiful and I hope we can one day become friends as well as sisters-in-law.'

They were sisters-in-law *for now,* but not for ever. She was sure the Queen knew, because Rafaele had told her that he intended to explain the situation to his brother so that he could prepare for when their marriage ended. Alexa had only told Nasrin that their marriage was a sham, not wanting her father to know in case he tried to interfere with her decision.

Ignoring the curiosity of nearby guests as they took to the dance floor together, Alexa pinned what she hoped was a convincing smile to her lips.

'I hope you're having a good time,' King Jaeger murmured as they fell into an easy waltz.

'I am, thank you,' Alexa returned, keeping her misgivings about the wedding to herself. 'I only hope this isn't all for nothing at the end of the day.'

'I have a feeling it won't be,' the King responded enigmatically. 'Although I must confess my surprise in finding my rogue brother in the position of being forced down the aisle so neatly.'

'But you know how that came about,' Alexa said, her voice slightly husky as she gazed into blue eyes that were almost the exact shade as Rafe's, but which didn't make her breath catch at all when she looked into them. 'My father demanded it.'

'True,' he mused softly, a knowing glint in his eyes. 'But

not even our father could force Rafa to do something he didn't want to do if he *really* didn't want to do it.'

'Then he met his match in my father,' she said dryly.

'I wonder…' The King smiled. 'My brother is not his usual easy-going self today, and he didn't seem to try all that hard to get out of the wedding.'

As far as Alexa was concerned Rafe had definitely tried to get out of their wedding, and as to his lack of ease… well, that was easily explained. The man had been forced to get married. No doubt that would have wiped the smile off any confirmed bachelor's face.

'My dance, I believe.' Rafaele suddenly cut in, his eyes riveted to where her hand held the King's.

'I was just about to tell Alexa how beautiful she looks,' the King said smoothly. 'Don't you think she looks beautiful?'

'Extremely.' Rafe's eyes narrowed on his brother's, his tone anything but convincing. 'But perhaps if you devoted this much attention to your own wife she wouldn't appear so unhappy,' Rafe prompted lazily, his brow arched.

At that moment a joyous giggle rang out from across the room and they all turned to observe Regan, hand protectively over her baby bump, having a great time with a small group of guests.

'Yes, I can see she feels terrible,' the King drawled, his eyes just as mocking as Rafe's.

The tension between the two men, while not aggressive, was palpable, and again Alexa wondered at the state of their relationship. For two brothers who looked so much alike and who were so close in age they didn't seem overly bonded, the way she had been with Sol.

Alexa gave Rafe a curious look as King Jaeger strolled from the dance floor in the direction of his wife. 'What was that all about?'

'What was what all about?' He gave her a too-innocent look.

'You were rude.'

'Maybe I was jealous.'

'You? Jealous?' Alexa nearly snorted at the prospect. 'Have you ever been jealous before?'

'Not so far.'

'I didn't think so.'

'But then I've never married a woman who was once betrothed to my brother and who gazes adoringly at him every chance she gets. Are you sure nothing ever happened between the two of you?'

The coolness behind his question took Alexa by surprise. 'Of course not.' Her incredulous gaze met hostile blue. 'Your brother is an honourable man.'

'And I'm not?'

Sensing that his emotions were barely leashed beneath the facade of civility, Alexa moistened her lips. 'I didn't say that. But I was unaware that honour was so important to you.'

'It isn't.' The Prince gave her a benign smile that belied the tension emanating from his large frame. 'As you pointed out previously, I have very different priorities to my brother. That aside, I believe it's time for us to leave, dear wife.'

It took a moment for her mind to process his words but then she frowned. 'What do you mean, *us*?'

'Generally it denotes oneself and the person one happens to be speaking with.'

'Don't be smart,' she retorted. As far as she had understood, Rafe would head back to London alone, claiming that they would take a honeymoon later on, when time permitted. 'I'm not leaving with you. That was never part of the plan.'

'Alas no, but then nor was our actual marriage. But one must improvise.'

'I'm not big on improvising. And we agreed to delay our honeymoon so that we didn't have to have one.'

'Once the international press bought into our *love* story, I thought you'd realise that we would have to present a united front. You were the one who first mentioned that our people would want to see us together, if I remember correctly.'

'Yes, but I was projecting into the future. I can't leave with you now. I have people to see next week. Meetings to take.'

'It's not negotiable, Alexa. I'm not leaving here without you.'

The way he said her name sent a frisson of sensation skittering along her nerve-endings, flustering her. 'Why can't you stay here instead?'

The Prince arched a brow. 'Because it might be a bit hard to open my club from here next weekend—considering it's in Chelsea.'

'Oh.' She hadn't thought of that. 'Well, I need more time to think about this.'

'You have an hour.'

Feeling as if her life was spinning out of control again, Alexa tried to hold her ground. 'Maybe I can join you in a few days.'

'Fine. You do that. And while you're at it you can explain the delay to the press *and* your father, who happens to be watching us closely.'

Knowing she was defeated because she did not want to face her father right now, Alexa groaned. 'But I haven't packed.'

'Throw an overnight bag together. Anything else you need can be sent on.'

'How long do you expect me to be gone?'

'Allow for two weeks. That's the usual time allotted to a honeymoon, isn't it?'

'Honeymoon?'

Her startled gaze met his and something sizzled in the air between them, making it hard to breathe. The room seemed somehow oppressively hot and all Alexa could think about was that blisteringly short kiss at the altar. Her heartbeat picked up and she really wished she knew what he was thinking.

'Not a real honeymoon,' he drawled gruffly. 'Unless that's what you want, of course.'

For a moment Alexa nearly said yes, and the shock of that realisation was enough to have her vigorously shaking her head. 'No, no, it's not.' She hated how she sounded like a frightened rabbit, but it was exactly how she felt.

'I didn't think so.' He gave her a tight smile. 'Which is why we'll spend two weeks in my London apartment. I'll meet you at the palace airstrip in…' he checked his watch '…fifty minutes.'

Fifty minutes?

That was nowhere near long enough for her to work out how she was going to survive two weeks holed up in an apartment with a man who tempted her like no other, but who couldn't be more wrong for her.

CHAPTER FIVE

RAFE GREW MORE and more agitated the longer he had to wait on the tarmac for his new wife, his usual cool deserting him. Not that he had to wonder too hard to figure out why that was. He was married. A state he'd thought he'd never find himself in. And okay, it wasn't a real marriage—but it damn well felt like one, with the ceremony, the two hundred plus well-wishers and the stunning bride.

His heart had all but leapt into his throat when he'd first caught sight of Alexa holding on to her father's arm at the end of the aisle. Covered head to toe in a lace gown that had outlined every slim curve, her floor-length veil hiding her face, she had been a vision in white.

Over the last couple of weeks he'd told himself that he'd imagined how sensually alluring she was. Exaggerated how potent his response to her was. Then she'd walked towards him with a smooth, graceful stride and he'd known that he hadn't exaggerated any of it. If anything, he had underestimated her appeal.

A shocking realisation for a man who had decided long ago that he would never let himself be trapped into matrimony under any conditions and now found himself desperately attracted to his wife!

A wife he didn't want, but who he would neatly use to repay Jag for the debt he'd incurred when his brother had been forced to leave his studies and return to Santara to become king after their father had died. At the time Rafe knew the ins and outs of the palace like no one else and could have smoothed the way for his brother, but he'd been desperate to leave and make his own mark on the world and Jag had seen that.

He'd told him to leave, to go find himself, and so far he'd never found cause to call on Rafe to help out. Something that was a little galling, because he'd told Jag that should he ever need him he'd be there.

But Jag had never needed him. However, his brother *had* needed a way to repair the relationship between Santara and Berenia and Rafe had seized the opportunity to repay his debt of gratitude by marrying Alexa.

And he didn't regret it. He hated being in debt to anyone more than anything and doing this for his brother— for his country—would ease his conscience whenever his siblings got up in his face about the way he lived his life.

But that's not the only reason you married her, a sly voice reminded him.

It was a voice he'd ignored over the past two weeks, burying himself in his latest business endeavour to the point of exhaustion. Now, though…now it was hard to deny that perhaps he'd also been under the influence of a shocking sexual attraction when he'd decided to marry Alexa that had exceeded anything he'd experienced before. That, and a deep-seated need to keep her from Lord Richton.

And who's going to keep her from you?

Rafe exhaled roughly. Nobody would keep her from him because nobody would need to. He might want her in his bed but that didn't mean he'd follow through on it. Alexa was not a woman a man toyed with. Not only was she the future queen of Berenia, but she was ultimately looking for something long-term, something permanent, and the last thing he wanted was to sleep with her and give her the impression that he was the right man for her.

Because he was most definitely not that man.

A truth that bothered him, though why it should he couldn't fathom. He'd never wanted to be any woman's 'right' man. Ever. His life was just fine as it was, even if Alexa believed it to be 'hedonistic'.

He shook his head. A Buddhist monk probably had a more exciting life than he had of late. Even the Spanish supermodel hadn't inspired him enough to take her to his bed while they'd been dating.

But Alexa did. Alexa, with her potent combination of steel and sweetness. Alexa who he couldn't seem to get out of his head. Who lit a fire inside of him that made his body throb with need.

Alexa who he wasn't going to touch.

And no doubt she'd be happy with that decision if the horrified expression on her face when he'd raised her veil at the altar was anything to go by.

He exhaled a long breath and rechecked his watch. Realistically, he'd only been waiting on her for twenty minutes. It felt like twenty years.

And then finally she appeared from the side door of the palace, looking extremely tantalising in a casual pair of jeans and a lightweight jacket held closed with a zip that begged to be tugged downwards, the cool desert breeze teasing the long strands of her ponytail.

For some reason the tension inside his chest eased at the sight of her. Had he been worried she wouldn't show?

Irritated at the very idea, he scowled down at her. 'I hope you have a thicker jacket than that. March in London isn't exactly warm.'

Jewel-green eyes blinked up at him and he reminded

himself that this situation wasn't exactly her fault so he needed to calm down.

'I believe Nasrin packed one, yes.'

Her assistant, who stood behind her, nodded enthusiastically. 'I did, Your Highness. I also know that you stowed your laptop into your satchel before you left.' She gave Alexa a firm look. 'No matter who contacts you, your father specifically told me that you are on your honeymoon and therefore not to do any work.'

Alexa stiffened at the mention of their 'honeymoon' but then gave her assistant a warm smile. 'Duly noted.'

Nasrin made an unconvinced sound in the back of her throat, piquing Rafe's interest in their relationship. Alexa had a reputation for being cool and remote, and yet it was clear that she and this woman shared a strong connection that went beyond simple employee and employer. There weren't many things Rafe admired more than those in positions of power treating the people who served them with respect and kindness.

'Ready to leave?' he asked, aware that as he spoke her body went stiff with tension. Which irritated him even more. How were they going to convince anyone that their union was more than a marriage of convenience if she turned to stone every time he spoke to her?

Forcing his eyes away from her jeans-clad butt as she preceded him up the stairs, Rafe stopped to speak with his pilot while Alexa buckled herself into her seat. No doubt she wouldn't be impressed by his plane. He might be a prince, but he wasn't a king. He couldn't offer her anything that she didn't already have.

And why was he even thinking like this? Their marriage wasn't real. It wasn't even damned convenient when it came down to it. It wasn't anything. They were two people who were doing each other a favour. So why did something that wasn't supposed to be monumental feel as if it was?

The circular nature of his thoughts warred with the constant need to put his hands on her and did little to restore his usual good humour. He wasn't sure anything could.

Using work to distract himself, he opened his laptop to go over the latest specs on a building he'd just purchased in Scotland. It was a grand old edifice that had once been a cinema and his COO was urging him to tear it down rather than restore it because the cost would be exorbitant. There was something charming about it though and, while he was all about the bottom line, he had an inclination to go in the other direction this time.

He wondered what Alexa would make of it and then scowled at the thought. It wasn't as if he was going to ask her. He might have to live with her for the next two weeks but that didn't mean they had to interact. In fact the less they saw of each other the better. Because wanting her was driving him to distraction.

Perhaps he could discreetly settle her into a hotel, then he wouldn't have to see her at all. Which would work right up until the press got hold of the information and blew their whole 'love story' out of the water.

'Sorry.' She gave him a small smile. 'I feel sort of responsible for all of this honeymoon palaver, and I know you're not happy about it.'

'You're not responsible.'

'Well, at least you didn't try to make me feel better by pretending to be happy.' She gave a strained laugh. 'But I know you didn't want anything to change and it clearly has.'

'That was a bit short-sighted, given the monumental interest in our wedding.'

'Yes. It seems that my father was right about our marriage moving everyone's attention from problems to pleasure. Do you know they even have a mug and tea towels with our faces on it?'

'Quaint.' He noticed the purple smudges beneath her eyes that he hadn't seen before and wondered if she'd had as little sleep as he'd had over the past fortnight.

'I know. My people went all-out. I think after your brother ditched me no one thought I'd ever find anyone else to marry.'

At the mention of his brother Rafe was reminded of the way she'd gazed at Jag only hours earlier. It had appalled him to think that she might still have feelings for his brother, and he didn't like it.

'Why would anyone think that you wouldn't get married? You're the heir to the throne of Berenia.'

'Thanks for pointing out my most saleable quality.'

Her self-deprecating tone made him frown. 'That is not your most saleable quality.'

He'd say her lips were definitely high on the list. Along with her legs, and the keen intelligence that shone from those magnificent green eyes. 'My brother fell in love with someone else. That was hardly your fault.'

'Some saw it differently.'

Noting the way her shoulders had tensed, Rafe's eyes narrowed. 'Define "differently".'

'I can barely remember.' She waved her hand between them as if the whole thing was inconsequential. 'Something about me not being womanly enough to keep hold of him.'

Rafe made a rude noise in the back of his throat. 'I've never heard anything more ridiculous.'

Or wrong.

'Anyway.' She made another flicking gesture with her hand. 'I was thinking that if your apartment isn't big enough for the both of us, then I could stay in a hotel.'

Even though Rafe had come up with the same idea only

moments earlier, the fact that she would prefer a hotel to his home chafed. 'My apartment is big enough.'

'Still, I could—'

'It's big enough.'

'You didn't let me finish.'

'I didn't have to. How do you think it would look if I set my beautiful wife up in a hotel straight after our wedding?'

'I suppose.' She fidgeted with her phone so he knew there was more coming. 'And your staff? Will they think it strange when we have separate bedrooms?'

Rafe lazily leaned back in his seat, relaxing now that he knew what her angle was. 'Is that your way of telling me that sex is off the table, Alexa?'

As he expected, her eyes flashed and turned frosty. 'Of course sex is off the table. It was never actually on the table.'

'Really?'

Hot colour poured into her cheeks and he knew she was recalling every hungry kiss they'd shared, just as he was. 'That wasn't the impression I got.'

And no way would he let her paint it any other way.

'I'm sorry you got a different impression,' she said stiffly, refusing to meet his eye, 'but I'm not interested in meaningless sex.'

Meaningless sex?

He regarded her steadily. 'Who said it would be meaningless?'

She shifted in her seat, unwittingly drawing his gaze to her body. He could see the outline of her rounded breasts beneath the fitted jacket and his body clenched as he recalled how perfectly she'd fitted into the palm of his hand.

'What else could it be?' she said, bringing his eyes back to hers. 'And, regardless, it would only blur the lines between us. So there's no reason for us to become intimate.'

Her voice was matter of fact, her reasoning completely logical. So logical that he agreed with it. Unfortunately he didn't care. This thing between them pulled at his self-control and her ready denial of its existence only made him want to prove her wrong.

'I can think of at least one.' In fact right now he had about one hundred and one filtering through his brain. 'Pure, unadulterated pleasure.'

'Oh.' The soft catch in her voice fired his blood. It made him want to reach over and haul her out of her seat and into his.

As if reading him correctly her face flamed. 'I'm not that...*physical*...but, since you obviously are, I don't mind if you seek...*relief* elsewhere. I only ask that you be discreet about it.'

It took Rafe a moment to fully understand what she meant and then he didn't even try to hide his incredulity.

'You're giving me permission to cheat on you? What kind of wife does that?'

'The non-real variety. Obviously.'

'Princess, while I'd love to live up to this wild image you have of me as some sort of sexual deviant, not every relationship I have with a woman ends between the sheets. And, to answer your earlier question, I only have one full-time housekeeper, apart from my security personnel, and she won't ask any questions.'

'Good to know.'

What was good to know? That he didn't sleep with every woman he met, or that his housekeeper wouldn't care about their sleeping arrangements?

His mouth thinned. She was driving him crazy and when she coolly turned her attention to her phone he decided to drive her a little crazy in return. 'Alexa...' He waited for her eyes to reconnect with his before leaning toward her to whisper throatily. 'Sex between us wouldn't be meaningless at all. It would be mind-blowing.'

It was nearly midnight when the plane touched down in London and Rafe ushered Alexa into a waiting limousine.

She had spent most of the flight vacillating between being mortified that she'd told Rafe about the rumours pertaining to her lack of femininity and growing hot at the thought of what mind-blowing sex with him would feel like.

She knew better than to air her dirty laundry in public and what had she wanted him to say? That she *was* womanly enough to hold a man?

Wishing she could just curl up and sleep for the next two weeks, Alexa did her best to ignore the man beside her and take in what she could see of the city.

She'd been in London once before for a state dinner but she'd had no time to explore at all, flying in and out within twenty-four hours, due to work commitments.

It must have rained before they arrived because the streets were shiny and black, the twinkling lights outlining a world that was miles away from what she was used to.

In no time at all, it seemed, the big Mercedes pulled into the underground car park of an impressive plate glass ten-storey building.

Yawning, Alexa barely noticed the high-tech layout of the garage, or the impressive array of luxury cars parked in personalised bays.

She did, however, notice the state-of-the-art glass-encased lift that whisked them to the top floor and opened out into a polished marble foyer lined with a dark wood finish.

'The building is patrolled by Chase Security,' Rafe informed her, 'a high-level security firm, and all the windows are bulletproof. Two of your secret service detail will be arriving later on tonight. I've organised for them to have a lower level apartment while you're here. A concierge is on duty twenty-four-seven if you should need anything and I'm not here.'

He walked through to a living area with twelve-foot ceilings and enormous windows on three sides that gave an incredible view over the park and the city beyond. An ultra-modern monochrome chandelier hung from the high ceiling, perfectly setting off the sectional furniture that was both homely and state-of-the-art.

Even though she lived in a palace, the architectural elegance of Rafe's home took her breath away. 'It's beautiful,' she said reverently. 'Like a castle in the clouds.'

Glancing up from checking mail that had been neatly placed on a display table, Rafe gave her a mocking glance. 'The ceiling chains are in the bedroom.'

'Ceiling chains?'

'It's par for the course with being a *hedonist*. Isn't that the word you used?'

Alexa groaned as he threw that back in her face, but really, what did he expect her to think when he made so little effort to refute any of the wicked claims made about him? In fact, he'd basically told her they were all true!

'Are you saying I've got it wrong?'

His mouth twisted into a cynical line. 'I'm saying I had a good time in my twenties. Make of that what you will.'

Alexa thought about everything she'd read about him, and everything she knew to date. So far he didn't seem all that self-absorbed at all, and he *had* stopped kissing her in the library when she'd asked him to. In fact, he'd given her fair warning that he was going to do so, thereby giving her enough time to say no. Not that he'd given her fair warning the second time. The second time he'd taken her in his arms on the terrace she'd all but swooned at his feet.

'Here's the thing, Alexa.' His voice sounded all soft and growly. 'I like sex, but I like straight up bedroom sex. Sometimes I like shower sex or spa sex. I've even been known to enjoy table sex and floor sex. I leave kinky sex for those who enjoy it more.'

Knowing he was trying to shock her with his litany of sexual venues, Alexa ignored the jolt of pleasure from just hearing him say the word. 'Does that mean that the whips are in the bedroom too?'

Clearly surprised by her comeback, his mouth twitched. 'No.' Heading for the doorway, he gestured for her to follow him. 'I keep those in the safe.'

She couldn't help laughing, and it relieved some of the tension that had plagued her since she'd walked down the aisle towards him.

'I've asked Mrs Harrington to prepare one of the guest suites for your use down this hallway. If you want to use the pool or gymnasium they're on the lower level and the library is on the mezzanine above to your right.'

'I thought apartments were small,' Alexa said, admiring the artwork on the walls as she passed. 'You like the Impressionists?'

'I like all art as long as it's not a landscape. I prefer the real thing to a painting.'

'I feel the same.'

Alexa couldn't hold back a smile as she took in the gorgeous honey-toned bedroom with a view of glowing city lights that spread for miles. Her eyes darted to the ceiling with impish humour, but she wished she hadn't because now he was looking at her lips and she couldn't breathe properly.

Sexual awareness pulled at her insides, worse than it

had done all day, and the quiet of the apartment highlighted that for once it was just the two of them. Alone. Together.

As if feeling the same pull she did, Rafe stepped back. 'Your private bathroom is through the walk-in closet. Stevens will be up with your bags in a moment.'

Trying to steady her breathing so he didn't see how badly he affected her, Alexa dropped her handbag onto the king-sized bed that faced the wall of windows. 'I probably won't sleep tonight anyway. This view is incredible.'

'That's up to you. I intend to sleep very well. Goodnight, Alexa.'

Watching him leave through the reflection in the windows, Alexa let out a slow breath. She couldn't deny the effect Rafe had on her. Especially after he'd listed off places where he liked to have sex.

Good lord!

But being intimate with a man like the rebel Prince of Santara would be like driving a Formula One racing car on a suburban road.

Deadly at every turn, but, oh, so much fun.

And why was she even countenancing such a thought when she'd already made her position on intimacy clear? But she knew why, didn't she? She was attracted to him. Incredibly attracted and no logical reasoning or denial made a difference to how she felt.

And it was something she needed to work on. Because even knowing that he was the most unsuitable man on the planet, and that there was no chance she would ever imagine herself in love with him, she couldn't deny that just looking at him made her body crave something she had no experience to deal with.

At least not objectively. And she could not afford to fall into her old ways and get *emotional* over him. Because he certainly wouldn't get emotional over her. No one ever had and it hurt, knowing that men found it so easy to walk away from her.

And Prince Rafaele would definitely walk away from her; it was what he did with all women. It was why she had married him in the first place. She wanted him to walk away from her in the end.

Restless, she moved to stand in front of the tall windows, trying to figure out why she felt so unsettled.

Was it just the pomp and ceremony of the day? Was it exhaustion from lack of sleep? Or was it that tonight was her wedding night and she was spending it alone? Alone, overlooking a picturesque night sky in a beautiful room with a bed the size of a swimming pool, and an ache deep inside her that longed to be satisfied. An ache to have Rafe touch her again, kiss her again…

'Your Highness?'

A voice outside her door broke into thoughts that were rapidly spiralling out of control. Ushering the chauffeur into her room, she thanked him for delivering her luggage and immediately set out to find her nightwear. All she needed was a good night's sleep. She only hoped it didn't elude her yet again…

Fortunately it didn't and she woke feeling more refreshed than she had anticipated. After a quick shower she donned her yoga gear, stretched on her yoga mat until she felt all the kinks leave her body, then went in search of coffee.

Following one hallway to the next, she eventually found the kitchen, a beautiful room of shiny stainless steel and polished wood. The state-of-the-art coffee machine took almost as long to locate. It was set into the wall above the oven, and the various buttons and dials looked like they belonged on a flight panel rather than on a coffee machine.

Having only ever fixed herself a coffee from a small machine in her private suite, Alexa had no idea how it worked.

Still, how difficult could it be to operate? She opened a few cupboards until she located a mug and set it under the central cylinder that looked like it dispensed coffee.

Gnawing on the inside of her lip, she hoped that if she started pressing buttons she wouldn't blow the thing up.

Before she could decide which one to push, however, she felt Rafe's presence behind her.

'What are you doing?'

Alexa glanced over her shoulder to see her husband standing in the doorway. He was dressed for business in a pale blue fitted shirt buttoned all the way to the wide column of his tanned throat, and a royal blue silk tie that turned his eyes the same shade.

Beautiful. He was utterly beautiful and Alexa did her best to calm the spike in her heart rate.

'I'm studying your coffee machine and trying to figure out how not to break it,' she said, giving a tentative smile.

Probably the best thing going forward would be for them to become friends. Anything would be better than the sense of awkwardness she currently felt. 'You don't have an instruction manual, do you?'

His eyes narrowed even more as his gaze swept over her with cool indifference. 'What type of coffee do you want?'

'A soy latte. If it does that.'

'This thing could probably reboot NASA,' he growled, coming up behind her and reaching over her shoulder, stabbing his finger at the buttons. 'Let me show you how it works.'

He started going through the various options and Alexa tried to concentrate but his heat and clean woodsy scent were doing crazy things to her brain. The urge to turn her face into the crook of his neck and sniff it was incredibly powerful and it took every lesson she'd ever learned in how to be objective to prevent herself from actually doing so.

By the time she'd mastered the urge the lesson was over.

'Then you hit Start.'

Great, she hadn't learned a thing.

Moments later the machine hissed and gurgled and Rafe handed her a perfectly made coffee.

Breathing the aroma deep into her lungs, Alexa groaned gratefully, her sexual awareness of the man in front of her immediately superseded by the need for caffeine. Which lasted right up until she opened her eyes and saw his dark gaze fixed on her mouth. Heat and desire swept through her at a blinding rush but, as if he hadn't felt a thing in return, he stepped back from her and fetched an espresso cup from an overhead cupboard.

Seriously disturbed by how easily he made her want him, Alexa racked her brain for something to say that would ease the tension between them.

'So you're off to work then,' she said, silently cringing at the obvious statement.

'It pays the bills.'

'And do you work at your nightclubs or an office?'

'Both.'

Okay, then. So he wasn't going to make this easy.

Unperturbed, Alexa leant against a glossy cabinet, watching him reset the machine. 'You know I'd really love to come to the opening of your club this Friday night. I've never been to a nightclub before.'

'No.'

Alexa blinked with surprise at his curt tone. 'No?'

'That's what I said.'

'Why not?'

'You're too straight.'

'Too straight?' She scowled at him. 'What does that mean?'

'It means what it means,' he dismissed in a way that only ratcheted up her annoyance. 'And I have no intention of arguing with you about it. It's too early in the morning, for a start.'

'Then don't be obnoxious.'

'I'm not being obnoxious.' His brows drew down, matching the set of his mouth. 'You're not the clubbing type. If you want to do touristy things like shopping or going to the West End or the ballet, just let me know and I'll have Hannah arrange it.'

'Hannah?' She was completely miffed at his condescension. 'One of your old girlfriends?'

'She's my assistant.'

Oh, right. She remembered Nasrin mentioning Hannah now that she thought about it, but she'd been too incensed by his attitude to place her. 'I'm nowhere near as straight as you seem think I am,' she said, wondering what he would say if she told him about how she had gone behind her father's back to be with Stefano.

'Yes, you are.'

He retrieved his coffee and turned to face the kitchen windows as if that was the end of the discussion.

Infuriated, Alexa glared at his wide back. 'You're as immovable as my father,' she snapped, her temper spiking. 'And you think you know everything, just as he does.'

'Alexa—'

'Are you usually this grouchy or is it having me here in your space that's making you so unreasonable?'

'I'm not a morning person.'

'You don't say. Well, I am, and when you walked in before I thought maybe we could find some common ground between us, maybe even become friends, to make the next two weeks easier, but you're really making me rethink that strategy.'

Rafe let out a rough breath as if the very sight of her annoyed him. 'Good. It's best if we're not friends.'

Not having expected such a brutal response, Alexa blinked. 'Then what would you suggest?'

He paused, his blue eyes as stormy as the Atlantic as he stared at her. 'Nothing. I suggest nothing.'

Alexa's brows shot up. 'So you want me to come up with all the ideas?'

'No.' He pushed a lock of hair back from his forehead, clearly frustrated. 'I meant that we literally do nothing. This isn't a forever thing, Alexa. We're here because I mucked up and let chemistry get in the way of rational thinking. That won't happen again.'

'By chemistry you mean—'

'Sexual attraction. Biology.' His eyes pinned her to the spot and all she could think about was sex. Something hot and dark passed between them before he blinked, deliberately severing the connection. 'I'm referring to this thing between us that you'd like to pretend doesn't exist. Fortunately, it will fade soon enough. In the meantime I don't need to know if you're a morning person or a night person and I don't want to know if there is any common ground between us. If you want this to go easier you'll stay on your side of the bed—metaphorically speaking—and I'll stay on mine.'

Shaken by the harshness of his tone, and her own hurt response at how little he wanted to do with her, Alexa hid her emotions behind an arched brow. 'Okay, well, that does make it easier. Now I don't have to rack my brain trying to make small talk while I'm here. Thanks for the heads-up.'

'Alexa—'

'You know, if you ever get sick of women falling in love with you, just show them your grouchy side. It will cure them of any fantasies straight away.' She kept her tone deliberately light but she could tell by his frown that he wasn't buying it. Still, she didn't care. She was close to tears because, after their brief moment of camaraderie the night before, she'd thought he liked her, if only a little.

But that was what came from being too needy and she'd thought she'd learned that lesson a long time ago.

And suddenly she was assailed by a feeling of loneliness she hadn't felt since Sol had died, old feelings of inadequacy threatening to swamp her.

'Alexa—'

'Sorry, I have to go.' Knowing that her emotions were way too close to the surface and refusing to cry in front of another man who didn't want her, she quickly dumped the cold remains of her coffee in the sink and rinsed the mug. 'I'm all sweaty after my yoga workout. Thanks for the coffee. Have a nice day.'

Escaping down the hall, she headed for her bedroom, her ears straining to hear if he followed her. Of course he hadn't. Why would he?

She released a breath she told herself was relief, an ache in her chest she didn't want to acknowledge. What did she care if he didn't want to be friends? She didn't need his friendship either. She didn't need anything from him.

Grabbing her laptop from her satchel, she set it on the bed and typed in her passcode. Two weeks stretched before her as endless as two years, and she pulled up the files she'd been working on before the wedding.

If she did nothing else, these two weeks she could at least work. There was plenty of it, and she had to prove to her father that she could do this. And to herself. Besides, anything was better than this horrible hollow feeling of rejection inside her chest that she had never wanted to feel again.

CHAPTER SIX

A MAN'S HOME was usually his castle, but right now Rafe's castle—his 'castle in the clouds'—felt more like a prison. Only it wasn't a prison keeping him locked in; it was a prison keeping him locked out. This past week he'd found it safer staying at the office for as long as possible rather than risk returning home, where he might run into his delectable wife.

But even for a man who kept long hours, this routine was exhausting, especially since it was past midnight for the fourth night this week and he still wasn't home.

It was either stay away or be rude to Alexa again, as he had been that first morning. Finding her in tight-fitting yoga gear, frowning at his coffee machine like a cute disgruntled kitten, had nearly had him lifting her onto the counter, stepping between her legs and telling her that the only instruction she needed was in how to pleasure him.

Just thinking about it was enough to make his body burn. So instead he'd been rude and hurt her when he'd dismissed her invitation of friendship. And he hadn't liked hurting her. Hadn't liked dimming the light in her clear, green eyes.

Normally he was laid-back and calm. Normally he'd come home from a hard day at work and put on some rock music, maybe play a little jazz or classical Chopin depending on his mood. Sometimes he'd grab a cold beer from the fridge and turn on the football, catch up on some of the highlights. Other times, if he was tired after a night networking at one of his clubs, or being with a woman, he'd grab whatever Mrs Harrington had left for him in the fridge, wash it down with an accompanying Burgundy and head straight to bed.

Simple. Easy.

He rarely questioned his routine, and if he ever felt a little lonely, or restless, he hit the gym.

Now he found himself looking for signs of Alexa in his home. Like the sweater she'd left over the back of a chair last night, and the hairband she'd left in the kitchen the night before that. He probably owed her an apology for being so distant all week, but that would involve speaking to her and the last thing he wanted to do was to encourage her to want to be 'friends' again. Friends didn't want to tear the other person's clothes off at just the sight of them, so that was out of the question.

'We're here, sir,' Stevens said, alerting him to the fact that he was sitting in the back of the Mercedes and the engine wasn't even running.

'Great.'

He gave Stevens a curt nod and headed for his lift, thankful when he found his apartment shrouded in darkness because it meant that Alexa would be once again in bed.

Placing his computer bag on the sofa, he noticed a pair of socks sitting on the side table, along with an empty mug of herbal tea and a scattering of magazines.

Shaking his head, he wondered how he was supposed to forget she was living with him when she left tiny reminders of her presence lying around. Not to mention the sweet scent of her perfume that lingered in the air.

Gritting his teeth, he dumped her mug in the sink and her socks in the laundry before heading to his room.

Strangely, keeping people at a distance and compartmentalising his life had never been one of his issues before, but he had to admit that he was struggling with Alexa.

Nine days.

That was all he had left of her stay in his home. If he survived it with his sanity intact he'd deserve more than a gold star.

He'd deserve her.

Biting back an oath at the ridiculousness of that thought, he decided to ignore his hollow stomach and head for bed. God knew he didn't want to tempt fate and run into the woman in his kitchen again. Which was when he noticed a light glowing from beneath his library door.

Hoping Alexa had left the light on by mistake and wouldn't be inside, he was pulled up short when he opened the door to find her slumped over the antique desk in the corner.

With his heart in his mouth, he strode towards her, hoping with every breath in his body that there was nothing wrong with her.

'Alexa?'

He reached out and gently shook her shoulder, relieved beyond reason when she made a small snuffling sound and buried her face against her arm.

Thank God. She wasn't unconscious, or worse, and his heart rate steadied once more.

She looked angelic in sleep, her glorious hair piled on top of her head in a messy topknot. Rejecting his body's immediate reaction to the sight of her, he frowned as he took in the mountain of paperwork scattered over the desk.

Work, he realised as he studied the papers, remembering how her assistant had told her she wasn't to do any.

She must have printed the documents from the laptop that was on sleep mode beside her.

'Alexa?' He tried again to rouse her but she gave another grumpy little whimper and tried to flick him away. Presumably, since she was a morning person, she wouldn't be chirpy at being woken in the middle of the night.

He found he quite liked seeing her all rumpled and sleepy, and then cut the thought off at the knees.

'Alexa, you need to wake up.'

Coming to with a start, she blinked up at him, and it was all Rafe could do not to reach down and kiss the sleepy pout from her lips. To distract himself he jerked his glance in the direction of the papers spread around her. 'Have you been at this all day?'

'Oh, hello.' She yawned and stretched her arms above her head. 'Mostly. It took longer than I thought. I did go for a walk in Hyde Park, but I had to put the sightseeing I planned on hold— Oh, sorry, I didn't mean to bore you.' She glanced away from him and when she spoke next her tone was decidedly frosty, as if she'd recalled their last interaction and hated him. 'What time is it? No, don't answer that. I'll find out for myself.'

'It's after midnight. And you don't have to treat me like a villain.'

'I'm not,' she said coolly, stacking her papers together.

Rafe scowled. 'Have you been at this all night? You'll wear yourself out if this is the pace you keep in Berenia.'

'That's not your concern.'

'Okay.' He held his hands up in front of him. 'Will it help if I apologise for being a first-rate jerk the other morning?'

She glanced up at him from beneath long sooty lashes, and Rafe's jaw clenched against the punch of instant attraction.

'Perhaps.'

'Then I'm sorry. I wasn't in a great mood, but I don't want you to feel uncomfortable around me.'

'I don't. I've had work to do.'

Which brought him back to how tired she looked. 'Work you're not supposed to be doing.'

She shrugged. 'Someone has to do it or it won't get done.'

'Delegate.'

'It's not that simple. We need to hire new staff, and—'

'Duty called.'

'Yes. Something I would have thought you would understand even if you don't like it.'

'I understand it. I even lived it for a time, particularly when Jag was studying in the US. Unfortunately, I didn't live up to my father's expectations as a suitable fill-in.'

She blinked at his harsh tone. 'How could you not?'

Rafe's jaw hardened. 'I wasn't Jag.'

A slight frown marred her forehead, her eyes fixed on his as if she saw more than he had intended her to see. 'But that's—'

'Irrelevant.' He cut off her sympathetic response. He never talked about the past. Not even with his siblings. 'If the people of Santara should ever need me I would be there for them, but this isn't about me. This is about you needing to find balance.' He perched on the edge of the desk, his fingers itching to push back the strand of hair that curved over her cheek. 'I told you before that you need to say no more often.'

'I'm not good at no.' She gave him a brief look. 'I suppose that makes me the dutiful little mouse in your eyes but—'

'I should never have said that,' Rafe interjected. 'You're

dedicated and focused and that will make you a great queen, but you should stand up for yourself more.'

'Well, thanks. For the compliment.' She huffed out a breath. 'As to the rest... I do try to say no, but there's so much to learn. And it's so easy to make a mistake.'

'Mistakes are *how* we learn.'

'They're not how *I* want to learn.' She shook her head. 'They cost too much.'

Rafe frowned at the vehemence in her voice. 'You're speaking from experience.' And not a good one, he guessed.

'Yes, but we all make mistakes, don't we?' she replied defensively. 'Even you.'

'I don't deny it. Most of mine get splashed across the Internet. But I doubt you've ever made a mistake worth talking about.'

She narrowed her eyes and took the bait as he hoped she would. 'I told you the other morning that I'm not as straight as you think I am. I nearly caused a scandal once.'

Rafe raised an eyebrow. 'I doubt that.'

'You think me so boring?'

'I don't think you're boring at all.' He thought she was the most beguiling woman he'd ever met and, to his surprise, he wanted to know her secrets. Especially this one. 'Tell me about your scandal.'

Her lips twisted distastefully and for a moment he thought she'd tell him to mind his own business again.

'I was seventeen and naive.' She arched a brow as if daring him to mock her. 'He was Italian with nice arms and he worked in the stables.'

'Ah, I think I see where this is going,' he said, hoping he was wrong. 'Pray, continue.'

'It's not that ground-breaking, actually... He told me that he loved me and took me to bed. Then he went straight to my father and used my virginity as a bargaining chip so we'd be forced to get married.'

She was right; the story wasn't ground-breaking, just totally humiliating for the one who had been used so callously.

Knowing how bad it felt to be judged out of hand, he kept his tone as light as hers. 'I take it that your father didn't exactly jump for joy at the information and welcome him into the household with open arms.'

Alexa gave him a wry grin. 'I still don't know how much he paid Stefano to leave and never contact me again, but sometimes, when I'm feeling particularly low, I like to imagine that he put the country into debt because of it.'

Rafe laughed at her dryness, but it didn't stop him from wanting to shove this Stefano's teeth down his throat and bury him beneath the blazing sun with just his head showing, as his ancestors would have done.

'If you give me his full name I could find him and have the Chase brothers beat the cretin to a pulp.'

Unless he got to him first, of course.

'You'd do that for me?' She blinked at him in surprise, as if no one had suggested it before. 'Not even my father said that, and you're the ultimate heartbreaker. You leave women crying all the time.'

'That is not true,' he said curtly, for the first time wishing that his playboy reputation didn't exist. 'I only enter relationships with women who know that I won't fall in love with them, and I'm upfront and honest about that from the beginning. If they cry when it ends it's not because I duped them.'

Her green eyes grew thoughtful. 'How do you know you won't fall in love with them?'

'Because I don't need love. And I make sure to never confuse emotion with sex.'

She paused as if that information required some effort to digest. 'I need to be more like that. But at least Stefano taught me what to look out for when it comes to choosing a life partner. Or what *not* to look out for.'

'What he should have taught you was how good it can be between a man and a woman in bed.'

He saw her throat constrict at his words and suddenly his hands itched to touch her. That Italian idiot might not have been able to show her a good time, but now Rafe couldn't stop thinking about how much he wanted to re-place her bad memories with good ones that he'd person-ally created.

Needing to stop himself from reaching for her and doing something he'd later regret, he pushed away from the desk.

'We should go to bed.'

Alexa blinked at him, her eyes as wide as a baby owl's. 'Together?'

The muscle in his jaw clenched tight as his brain easily conjured up an image of her naked on his sheets. Before he could figure out how to respond to that, a streak of hot, mortified colour scored along her cheekbones. 'Forget I said that. I'm clearly more tired than I thought.'

Wanting to defuse the situation, Rafe nodded. 'I get it. My club is opening tomorrow night and I could use a few hours myself.'

'Right.' She blinked up at him from beneath long silky lashes. 'About that. Am I still banned from your club?'

'Yes.' No way did he want her at one of his clubs, dis-tracting him constantly.

'Won't that look strange?' she persisted. 'As your wife I would be expected to go to support you.'

'I don't need support.'

'Everyone needs support. But, regardless, the media

will expect to see me there. I take it you are having a media presence.'

'Only for a couple of hours. No one will know you're not there.'

She mulled that over and then tilted her chin up at a belligerent angle.

'I'd like to go.'

Not wanting to get into a debate with her when his brain and body were mutually stuck on images of her naked and wanting, Rafe sighed. 'Alexa—'

'You've just told me I should stand up for myself more. Not to take no for an answer.'

'I believe I said you should start saying no more often.'

'Something you're really good at. But it amounts to the same thing. Taking charge of my needs. And I'd like to see your club. So I'm taking charge.'

Rafe ran a hand through his hair, a frustrated growl leaving his throat. 'I didn't mean for you to start "taking charge" with me.'

Her sudden smile made his heart kick against his ribs.

'For some reason I feel safe with you.'

'The last thing I am is safe.' Especially with the visions currently going through his head. When she didn't respond, or back down as he'd hoped, he shook his head. 'Fine. I'll arrange a car to pick you up at ten.'

'Ten? Isn't that a bit late?'

'That's early by London standards. Nothing happens before then.'

'Ten. Okay, got it.' Her eyes sparkled like clean-cut emeralds, her happiness making his heartbeat quicken.

'If you need anything before then, or change your mind, I'll have Hannah on standby to help out.'

'I won't change my mind. And you won't regret this.'

She was almost vibrating with excitement. 'You won't even know I'm there. Promise.'

Rafe groaned silently at the enormous smile on her face. He should have left her asleep at the desk.

Pacing the upper floor office suite at Bound, Rafe watched on a bank of security monitors as guests continued to pour through the front door of the club, each one wide-eyed with delight as they took in the chrome and glass chandeliers and the Dalí-inspired decor.

'So far, so good,' Hannah, his assistant, ventured beside him. A pocket rocket, Hannah had the energy of a race-horse, which was probably why she hadn't quit on him like so many of his other EAs had done over the years.

Rafe grunted in acknowledgement. At this point he didn't much care about the success of the club. He just wanted to know where Alexa was.

'Oh, relax,' Hannah admonished as she saw him check his watch again. 'I organised Chase Security to travel in with her as well as her own security detail, as you in-structed. Between the lot of them, you'd think she was bringing the heads of state of fifty nations with her. But she should be here any minute.'

'Since when do I worry?' Rafe said, not bothering to hide his irritation.

Hannah's grin widened before she checked a message that popped up on her tablet. 'Since you got married, it seems. But I can see why you married her. We had a great time shopping. She's truly lovely. Not at all stuck-up, as one might expect from royalty, but then you're not stuck up, so I don't know why I thought she would be. And she looks incredible in her new dress. We had a lot of fun choosing it. Oh, I better go. The Duke and Duchess of Crenshore have arrived and I need to show them to their private table.'

Not hearing a word she'd said after 'new dress', Rafe's mind was now obsessed with exactly what this new dress would look like. Would her hair be up or down? He still had no idea how long it was. Another unwanted obsession he'd suddenly developed.

Glancing once more at the display showing the entrance, Rafe saw one of the Chase Security guards he'd organised to shadow Alexa walk through the door.

Not realising he was holding his breath, he waited for Alexa to appear and exhaled at seeing her.

Her hair was down. And it was long. Almost waist-length and as straight as an arrow.

Wearing a trench coat and stiletto heels, she looked regal and calm except for the glitter in her eyes that gave away her excitement as she scanned the foyer.

A similar feeling went through him now and he did his best to douse it. There was no reason he should be 'excited' that she was here. He'd agreed to let her come because he felt sorry for her, stuck in his apartment working. She worked too much, trying to prove herself, as he had once done. Only she was perfect as she was.

Stopping those thoughts dead in their tracks, he noted with satisfaction how her security detail scanned the crowd before allowing her to move further inside. It was guests only at the club tonight, and Rafe had personally checked over the list and given it to her team to cross-reference, but he didn't want to take any chances with her safety.

For some reason I feel safe with you.

A muscle ticked in his jaw. She'd been talking about taking charge of her professional needs, but his mind was still stuck on her 'taking charge' in a much more pleasurable capacity.

Cursing at the single track his mind had been on ever

since the Santarian charity ball, he refocused on making sure Alexa made it into his club without incident.

A member of his staff approached her, indicating that he would take her jacket, and Rafe's gut tightened as she slowly pulled at the belt, shrugging her shoulders so that the fabric slipped down her arms.

Rafe nearly choked on the air he'd just sucked into his lungs.

The dress she was wearing was black, tight and minimal in the extreme. It was as if the manufacturer had run out of fabric, shrugged and sewn it together anyway. Sheer gossamer tights covered legs that looked impossibly long in stiletto heels. Her waist looked tiny, her breasts full and voluptuous.

Nearby, men gave her covetous looks and Rafe found himself moving towards the lift that would take him to the ground floor before he'd even thought about it. She would cause a war in his club if he didn't immediately bundle her back into that coat.

'I feel so alive. Almost electric.' Alexa's eyes sparkled with pleasure when she spotted him. 'This place is fantastic. Dark and mysterious—it's as if something magical could happen around any corner. But it's also a touch romantic with the effect of the mauve and blue lighting on the wall murals. And the music—'

Hannah interrupted her excitement with a glass of champagne. 'It's French, of course. You look brilliant. That dress is perfect. Don't you think so, Rafe?'

'Perfect.'

Alexa raised a brow at his droll reply. He was going to have to pull himself together before he sank his hands into all that lustrous hair and said to hell with the club—they were going back to the apartment to have the kind of sex he was always reputed to have.

'Thanks to you, Hannah.' Alexa grinned happily. 'I had the most amazing afternoon.'

'My pleasure,' Hannah replied. 'I'll swap the office for Bond Street any day of the week.'

'Are you okay?' Alexa finally remembered he was present and frowned. 'You seem angry.'

'I'm not angry. But I suggest you don't bend over in that dress.'

'Is it too short? Hannah assured me that it wouldn't stand out in the crowd.'

Rafe gave Hannah a look that promised she'd be missing her bonus next Christmas. 'Hannah was wrong.'

'Okay, well… I think I see a fire I need to put out,' Hannah said tactfully. 'You two have fun.'

Alexa smoothed her hands down the slightly flared hem of her dress. 'It's no shorter than some of the other dresses being worn tonight. I have to confess I didn't think you'd mind, given the photos of some of the women I've seen you with.'

Yes, but none of those women had been his wife, and he had never even noticed if anyone had thrown them admiring glances. Now he couldn't stop noticing the men who cast covetous glances Alexa's way.

'Let's go to my table.'

That would be a safe place to stash her for a while. She could watch everything that happened from the third-floor balcony that overlooked two split-level dance floors before he sent her home.

She pressed in closely behind him, grabbing the sleeve of his shirt so she didn't lose him in the crowd. Rafe thought about placing her in front of him but there was only so much his control could handle, and having her pert derrière so close at hand just might tip him over the edge.

'I know I'm not familiar with nightclubs,' she said as he led her up the circular glass staircase, nodding to one of the ground staff monitoring the third floor, 'but I doubt there would ever be one out there to top this. You must be really proud.'

Exceptionally pleased by her praise, he smiled. 'I'm glad you like it.'

Reaching their destination, he ushered her into the velvet-upholstered circular sofa. Her slender legs were partially concealed by the small central table, but that left her cleavage and her wide, happy smile for him to focus on and that wasn't much better. Forget working out how much time they had left in days, he needed to work out how much time they had left in hours; it would at least give his mind something to do.

One hundred and ninety two.

Not helpful.

Trying to ignore how tense Rafe was wasn't easy, but by her second glass of champagne Alexa was managing it. Berenia didn't have anything like this and while she was used to being the centre of attention she'd never been completely comfortable with it. But here, in this club, she felt as if she could be anyone. She didn't feel as if she had to be the proper Crown Princess. She felt as if she could let her hair down. And she had. The feel of it against her bare back heightened her senses and made her feel so different from her usual self. So did the loud music flooding her body with its throbbing beat.

She glanced across at Rafe, who was speaking to someone who had stopped at their table and who was more interested in him than in her. This was his domain and she liked seeing him in it. She liked taking a back seat. Like this, she could just be any one of the women he took out with him. A woman he would later take home. To his bed.

Her gaze roamed his wide shoulders and silky dark hair. She'd always imagined that her dream man would be someone upstanding and good. Someone like his brother, whom she'd built her secret fantasies around, based on his chivalrous actions when she was younger. But really, the King of Santara, as handsome as he was, had never made her feel the way Rafe did. Never made her want to climb into his lap and straddle his hard thighs the way she wanted to do now.

As if she'd actually reached over and touched him, Rafe turned his head away from the man leaning on their booth seat, his smoky gaze connecting with hers as if he knew every one of her sinfully erotic thoughts. Instinctively, her eyes moved to his sensual mouth and the stubble that had grown in over the course of the day. In a black shirt, his hair falling in thick waves, he looked like a modern-day pirate.

Alexa casually picked up her champagne glass and tried to pretend that her heart wasn't racing. What would he say if she vocalised her desires? What would he say if she slid along the raspberry-coloured bench seat and whispered that she wanted to change their bargain? That she wanted sex with him whether it was meaningless or not.

'I see everyone agrees that this club is sensational,' she said as the man Rafe had been conversing with strolled away from their table. 'You must feel proud.'

'It takes an army of people to create something like this. It's not all my doing.'

'But it takes a visionary to conceive of it, and then someone to take the risk and actually execute it.'

He swallowed a mouthful of champagne and Alexa felt transfixed by the movement of his throat. She felt breathless and the cavernous room seemed to shrink as he sat there watching her with an intensity she wanted to interpret as sexual.

Because this man might be wrong for her on so many levels but that didn't stop her from wanting him. He was so easy to talk to, so easy to be with. It was sexy to be able to say something to a man and have him actually listen to her. And she did feel safe with him. Safe and sensual. Especially when he kissed her.

'Alexa, if you don't stop looking at me like that I'm likely to do something we'll both regret.'

His deep growly voice flowed through her body like hot caramel. 'Like what?'

His blue eyes turned as hot as a flame, his body going so still at her words she knew he was holding his breath. 'Like things you don't want to know about.'

Alexa's tongue slipped out to moisten her dry lips. 'Maybe I do.'

'You don't.' The blunt words were edged in steel and made all the insecurities left over from Stefano, and King Jaeger's, rejection come storming back to her. What was she doing? She wasn't some femme fatale! She was the woman that men walked away from.

But you already know he's going to walk away, a little voice reminded her. *It's why you chose him.*

Emboldened by that voice, her slinky dress and the hard, hot man beside her, Alexa decided she could either give into her inadequacies or throw caution to the wind and see what happened. With her heart in her mouth she embraced the latter, slowly crossing one leg over the other and gathering her hair in one hand to bring it forward over her shoulder. 'Why don't you let me be the judge of what I want? I'm not a child, Rafe.'

'I know you're not a child,' he bit out. 'Nobody looking at you in that dress could mistake you for one.'

'You don't like my dress?'

Before he could respond a laughing Hannah stopped by their table. 'Everything okay, boss?'

'Everything is fine, Hannah. You can officially clock off duty now and have a drink.'

'Oh, thank goodness.' She gave Alexa a wide smile. 'I've been desperate to hit the dance floor. Have you had a dance yet, Your Highness?'

'Please, just call me Alexa. A title seems so inappropriate tonight. Tonight I just want to have fun.'

'Then let's dance. Do you want to come, boss?'

'No.'

'Mind if I drag Alexa along?'

'Yes.'

But Alexa was already sliding from the booth seat. 'Don't listen to him, Hannah. I'd love to go dancing. It's what I'm here for.'

Hannah laughed. 'I like this one. Make sure you don't do anything to lose her.'

Weaving her way down the stairs, Alexa could feel Rafe's gaze on her the whole way but she refused to turn and glance back at him. Somehow she knew the steps to the timeless game he had started playing with her at the Summer Palace, which had stalled when her father had forced them to get married. Well, no one was forcing him to do anything now, and if he didn't want her she'd find someone else who did. After all, that had been the point of her initial mission—to buy herself some time to find a man she *did* want to marry.

Unfortunately, her mind seemed inconveniently stuck on one man right now. *Her Prince.*

'This club is going to be on everyone's list of where to

go for years,' Hannah stated, raising her voice above the upbeat music. 'I love my job!'

She waved her hands in the air, her enthusiasm catching, and Alexa found herself loosening up as she gave up any semblance of self-consciousness and moved her body in a way that felt sexy and liberating.

'So you like working for Rafe?' she asked.

'Oh, he's amazing. The best boss in the world. And I'm not just saying that because you're his wife—it's true. He's generous and disciplined and so kind. Last month he asked me to organise an all-expenses-paid holiday to the Caribbean for a month, along with six months off with full pay, for one of our accountants whose wife is ill. He's a dream boss.'

A dream boss? Hannah had just described her dream man. She certainly hadn't described someone Alexa had believed to be self-centred and hedonistic.

'You're a lucky woman to have captured him,' Hannah continued. 'I think a thousand women lay heartbroken in their beds on the day you married.'

'You can stop talking now, Hannah.'

Alexa turned at Rafe's droll tone to find him standing stock-still in front of her, the gyrating bodies of the other dancers surrounding him like caricatures in a stage play. She slowly dropped her arms from over her head, unable to take her eyes from his.

'I thought you didn't want to dance?' Hannah laughed.

'I don't.' Rafe's gaze slid down over Alexa's body with such searing heat she turned liquid inside. 'Go get a drink, Hannah. Your duty is done here.'

'I can see that.' Hannah grinned and melted into the surrounding dancers.

Alexa didn't notice Hannah disappear; she only had

eyes for Rafe, who was looking at her as a wolf might look at a helpless deer.

'I do like your dress. But I like you even more.'

'You do?'

His hands moved to the sides of her waist. 'Too much. I've been trying to avoid giving in to this all week, but you've defeated me.' His voice turned low and growly. 'But this won't just blur those lines between us, Princess, it will completely obliterate them.'

'I don't mind.'

A serious glint entered his dark eyes. 'And if it's another mistake?'

'Are you trying to warn me off you? I'm not that naive young girl any more, Rafe. I've grown up a lot since Stefano. I know this isn't about love, so if you're worried that I'll fall for you like every other woman, I won't.'

'That's not what I'm afraid of.'

'Then what are you afraid of?'

His hand came up to the side of her face, his fingers stroking through the heavy strands of her hair. They could have been alone for all the notice they took of the energetic dancers around them. 'I'm afraid I won't want to stop once I've had you. I'm afraid I want you too much.'

His words were thrilling, a balm to her wounded feminine soul. 'Then take me,' she whispered, moving a step closer so that her body was flush up against his. 'Take me and show me what pure, unadulterated pleasure feels like.'

A harsh curse left Rafe's mouth right before his lips crashed down over hers. It was like a match meeting a firecracker. Alexa's body caught alight, her mind empty of everything else but this moment. This man.

Too soon the kiss was over, Rafe lifting his head and tucking her in tightly against him. 'We can't stay here. We'll get arrested.'

All but dragging her from the dance floor, Rafe stopped briefly in front of her security detail before clamping his hand over hers and leading her along a series of narrow hallways until he opened a heavy door and ushered her through.

Glancing around, she realised they were in an underground garage beside a shiny black motorbike.

Rafe pulled out a leather jacket from beneath the seat and fed her arms into it. The jacket swamped her and smelled of him.

'What about you?' she asked when she noticed that there was only one.

'I'm hot enough.'

There were many responses she could make to that but she didn't have the experience or confidence to banter with him in that way.

Rafe pulled a helmet from the handlebars and turned back to her. One of his hands went to her hair and he breathed deeply. 'Your hair is beautiful.' He twisted the strands in his fist and brought her mouth to his in a fierce kiss that set her on fire all over again.

Alexa moaned softly as he released her.

'Home first,' he said, plunking the helmet on her head and buckling it.

Taking his hand, Alexa slid her legs over the back of the bike and settled on the seat, futilely tugging at her skirt. 'Ignore it and hang on tight,' Rafe instructed. 'I won't be going slowly.'

It was a rush to know that she affected him like this and she did what he asked, sliding her arms around his lean waist as the bike started to move.

CHAPTER SEVEN

THE RIDE HOME was as fast as he'd warned it would be. Alexa felt as if she'd just got used to the vibration of the engine between her legs and the thrill of being on a bike for the first time when he was zooming down the slope that led to his underground garage.

Moments later they were in the lift and heading skyward. Rafe watched her from across the small cubicle but didn't touch her. She used the time to catch her breath, her senses completely alert to his every breath.

Stepping out of the lift, Alexa smoothed her skirt and wondered what to do with her hands. Now that she was here, now that they were doing this, she felt a moment's hesitation.

'Alexa?'

Standing before her, all tall, dark and dangerously male, he made her heartbeat quicken. He was so beautiful,, his jaw clenched with the intensity of his arousal.

The knowledge was as intoxicating as it was scary because, for someone who always thought about the consequences of her actions, Alexa knew she hadn't thought this through completely. She also knew that she might never experience a feeling like this again and that she wanted this man. She wanted him more than was good for her.

'You still with me, princess?'

Rafe smoothed his hands over her shoulders, his touch electric. Alexa's eyes sought his and although she knew this would likely mean more to her than it would to him she couldn't bring herself to care. After she and Rafe ended their marriage she would always have this memory, this moment, and she shoved any remaining inhibitions and concerns aside and took the extra step needed to bring her into his arms.

'Yes,' she husked. 'I'm still with you.'

Taking her at her word Rafe took command, pressing her back against the door and eradicating the last of her doubts with an erotically charged kiss.

It was like a brand, a claim that said 'mine', and Alexa opened her mouth to the demand of his tongue. Her arms went around his neck to hold him close, her fingers buried in his hair as she pulled him closer.

'You smell like sugar and…leather,' he groaned, his lips working their way along her jawline as he swiftly stripped the jacket down her arms and let it drop to the floor.

Excitement poured through her at the hunger in his eyes, her legs suddenly giving out so that the only thing holding her up was his arms, banded around her waist.

He moved his hands to cup her bottom and Alexa moaned indistinctly into his mouth, her body craving his.

Needing to touch his skin, her fingers tugged at his shirt until she had it free, a frisson of desire racing through her as she stroked her fingers over lean male flesh.

Her touch unleashed something primal inside him because his mouth turned greedy and hot, his hard body pinning her to the door as his hands roamed, bringing her core up against his hot hard erection.

'Rafe?' Alexa wrenched her head back as everything inside her softened to yield to that hard male presence between her legs.

Swearing softly, he scooped her into his arms and carried her into his bedroom.

Momentarily breaking the kiss, he slid her body down his until she was standing in front of him. With sure, practised fingers he found the invisible zip in the side of her dress and deftly divested her of both her dress and her bra, holding her hands to the side so that he could look at her.

'You're beautiful,' he breathed, bringing one hand up to cup her breast while the other went to the back of her head to bring her mouth back up to his.

The kiss was fierce and sweet, the sensations of his fingers teasing her nipple sending sparks of need through her body that obliterated everything else except the man touching her.

'Oh, please...' She didn't know what she was begging him to do but when his mouth closed over the tip of her breast and he flicked her with his tongue she thought she might expire from pleasure. Shifting to her other breast, he let out a low chuckle at her soft pleas and then she felt the coolness of the mattress at her back as he lowered her onto it.

Aroused and aching, Alexa fumbled with the buttons on his shirt, desperate to expose his body to her view. Helping her, Rafe shrugged wide shoulders until the shirt slid down his back and her hands roved over his naked chest and back.

The sheer size and power of his corded body was breathtaking and even though part of her knew it was dangerous to want him this much she couldn't help it. She had no control over her body or her senses and she didn't want any. She was a willing captive to the fever raging through her body, and she would have flown into the centre of the sun if he had asked her to.

His lips returned to hers, commanding and potently

male, his fingers hot against the inside of her thighs as he swept them higher until he was cupping her through her panties.

A small whimper escaped her and she bit gently into the hard ball of his shoulder as his finger stroked and teased until she was a writhing mass of nerves and sensation.

'Rafe, please…'

Smiling against her neck, he nuzzled at her breast, flicking his tongue against the rigid peak at the same time as his fingers teased.

'Please what, my sweet?' He continued to stroke and torture as he slowly, so slowly, shifted the silk aside until finally he was touching her, his fingers finding and parting her flesh before plunging inside her hot, wet sheath.

Gripped in a fever of desire, Alexa wasn't sure who groaned the loudest and then she didn't care as Rafe expertly flicked a finger across the bundle of nerves nested at her apex and sent her spiralling into an earth-shattering orgasm that made her scream.

She must have lost consciousness because suddenly her panties were gone and Rafe had cupped her bottom and raised her to his lips, his tongue lapping at her and bringing her body to another mind-numbing climax.

Spent and gasping, she couldn't move as Rafe crawled back up her body, kissing every inch of skin he came into contact with.

'You,' Rafe growled, coming down over her with lethal male grace, 'are incredible.'

Alexa felt incredible but she wanted more. The space between her legs felt hollow and empty, her eyes widening as Rafe rose to his knees and unzipped his trousers. With bated breath she watched as he lowered the fabric down over his hips, his thick, gorgeous erection springing free.

Unaware that she'd licked her lips until he made a low growly sound, she pushed to a sitting position and ran her hands down over his heated torso, the dark hair on his chest soft like a wolf's pelt beneath her fingers. Moving downwards, she couldn't stop herself from reaching out to touch him. As she gripped him her eyes flew to his. He'd sunk his teeth into his lower lip, his eyes hooded as he watched her, and it made her more daring.

Stroking firmly, she felt one of his hands softly grip her hair and she hadn't even realised she'd brought her mouth closer to the swollen length of him until she felt him against her lips.

The earthy taste of him burst across her tongue, the flavour so deeply male. She opened her lips and took him into her mouth, a heady sense of power filling her when his fingers gripped harder in her hair and a groan tore from his throat.

Loving the silky hard length of him against her tongue, Alexa increased the pressure of her lips until she heard him swear, and then she was being pulled up and stretched out beneath him like a feast.

A thrill raced through her as he parted her thighs and looked down at her. Grabbing a condom from the side table drawer, he rolled it on and then braced himself with his hands either side of her face. Mesmerised, Alexa couldn't look away from his hungry gaze as he slowly pushed into her.

Something in the way he watched her almost tenderly made her unable to tear her eyes from his. Rafe must have felt the force of the connection too because his lips came down to claim hers once more as his body thrust hard, filling her and driving her to the heights of another pulse-pounding climax before he followed her over the edge on a hoarse cry of completion.

* * *

Waking up from what might actually have been the best
sex of his life, Rafe glanced at the woman curled up in his
arms, her dark hair spread out on his white sheets like a
waterfall of black silk. She was asleep, her head nestled
in the curve of his shoulder and her sweet breath warm
against his chest.

Waiting for the usual need for space and privacy to
overtake him, he was surprised when it didn't come. Instead he felt replete and relaxed, and more complete than
he'd felt in forever.

Complete?

The alien concept entered his head then was gone just
as quickly. Sex didn't make him feel complete. That wasn't
what he was feeling. What he was feeling was... It was...
He frowned. It was pure, unadulterated pleasure after a
week of being tied up in the tightest sexual knots he'd
ever experienced.

No woman had ever made him want so much or had
satisfied him so fully.

Had he really thought he'd be able to ignore her, with the
level of sexual chemistry they shared? Well, if he had, he
couldn't now. Alexa had been responsive and giving and
so sweet that just the memory of her hands and mouth on
his body was turning him surprisingly hard again.

His hands stroked down over the silky skin of her arm,
his fingers finding and twining with hers. She breathed out
a sigh and relaxed more deeply against his side.

He remembered that she'd been up working late last
night and was probably exhausted. She worked hard and
took her job seriously. Which he supposed she had to. Just
as seriously as he took his. When you had the amount of
staff he had relying on you to provide their wages it was
important to perform well. He supposed they were similar

that way. Only he no longer sought the approval of others the way he suspected Alexa did. He'd given up on needing to please a long time ago. She would need to do that too once she became Queen or she'd work herself into the ground. But why was he thinking about Alexa's future?

Usually he didn't concern himself with a woman's life after sex. He'd already moved onto his next task or his next project. It didn't matter where he was, or who the woman was, Rafe always liked to be on the move, rarely staying still long enough to feel trapped. It came, he knew, from always having to toe the royal line when he was younger. From having a father who'd demanded that he behave a certain way, and then giving him grief if he missed the mark.

But why waste time thinking about things that weren't important when he had a warm naked woman he knew would be receptive to his advances if he were to wake her with a soft kiss on those delectable lips?

At least he assumed she'd be receptive. Every other woman he'd ever been with would be, but Alexa wasn't like every other woman. She didn't play the same games, acting coy to try to attract his attention, or turning girlish when she had it. Alexa was far too straightforward and earnest. But then she had no need to play games with him because they were already married. She already had his ring on her finger and he had hers on his.

He held his hand up to the moonlight that spilled in through the gap in the curtains. The room was too dark for him to see the gold, but he could just make out the dull shape of the band. When she'd first slipped it on his finger the weight had felt foreign and unwanted. Funny how it didn't feel like that any more.

It felt right and good.

Right and good?

Something stirred behind his breastbone, some unwanted emotion that caused his ribs to tighten around his chest.

As if sensing his unease, Alexa shifted her knee higher across his thigh. A shot of lust raced through him, a primitive hunger that bordered on need.

Not that he did need. Need had a serious edge of permanence about it. Want? Now want was something he understood. It came and went and put a smile on his face, and his body stirred at the way he *wanted* to wake Alexa now with a line of slow kisses starting at her slender shoulder and encompassing her whole body.

Shifting again, she made a cute little sleep sound that made him lose his train of thought.

He felt her body tense as she awoke and he gently gathered her closer, stroking his hand down the silky skin of her spine.

'Stay asleep, Princess,' he murmured, even though sleep was the last thing on his mind. 'I know you're tired.'

'Sleep?' She raised her head and blinked at him. 'I...' She looked flustered, her eyes uncertain in the dim light as she stared at his face, his chest.

Her tongue came out to lick her lips and before he was even aware that he'd made the decision he rolled her onto her back and kissed her.

After a split second of hesitation her arms went around his neck, her body rising to his.

Hunger ripped through him at the soft sound of pleasure she made when he stroked his tongue into her mouth, his body primed to take her immediately.

But he also wanted to savour her. He wanted to taste her body again, her sweetness.

Loving the way she clung to him, Rafe kissed his away across her face. First her cheeks and the soft skin below her ears, then her eyelids and her nose. Feeling her completely relax beneath him, he slowly moved down her body, laving her neck and licking at her collarbone.

Her gorgeous breasts pointed skyward, her nipples achingly beautiful, and he took first one and then the other into his mouth. Then he positioned her so that she was beneath him, her long legs moving restlessly on the outside of his own.

He used his knees to open her to the hard throb of his erection and he sank into her softness with unerring accuracy. She sobbed his name as he slowly filled her, sweat beading his forehead as her body took him in, her inner muscles gripping him tight.

'Alexa...' he groaned, remembering at the last minute that he wasn't wearing a condom. She arched beneath him, her lower body straining for his thrust.

Seriously perturbed at just how close he had come to forgetting protection, he reached into his side table and sheathed himself before thrusting back inside her tight body.

She came almost instantly, the hot pulsing sensation of her climax shattering his self-control in a maelstrom of pleasure.

Opening her eyes to find herself wrapped in Rafe's arms for the second time that morning, Alexa felt herself tense at the overwhelming vulnerability of being naked in his arms. Not because she regretted what they'd shared, but because she liked it a little too much. The feeling left her somehow defenceless, and her instinct was to pull back because, while she had anticipated the pleasure, she hadn't counted on the emotional connection she'd feel when he joined his body with hers. Only she was quite sure Rafe would have experienced no such thing in return.

Undoubtedly last night had been par for the course for a man of his experience, and she had to keep that front and centre in her mind at all times. Because while she had experienced something monumental in his bed, she knew she'd be alone in that line of thinking.

But it had been monumental. The way he had worshipped her body, the tender kisses he'd lavished on her, the powerful thrusts of his body... It had definitely been mind-blowing, but not in the way that he had meant it would be. It was mind-blowing in that it was so lovely. So beautiful. So everything.

Deeply asleep, he was sprawled on his side, one arm above his head, the other draped over her waist. Shifting slightly out from under his hold, Alexa took advantage of the moment to take her fill of him.

Naked, he was utterly superb. The swell of his biceps and muscled shoulders, the broad chest and trail of hair that bisected his flat belly, the lean line of his hip that made her want to put her lips on his skin again.

He'd lost none of his power or authority in sleep, but he did look more peaceful. More rested.

She thought about the things she had discovered about him the night before. His generosity with his employees, his strong work ethic and the way his employees treated him with such deference and respect. Hannah had sung his praises and not because he was a prince. She truly liked and admired him for the man that he was.

A man, Alexa was starting to suspect, was decent and kind, even though she doubted he'd admit to it. And why was that? Why did he hide that side of his nature? And why, if he wanted her so much, had he stayed away from her all week?

Was it out of deference to her wishes? Because he was afraid she'd fall in love with him? Or something else?

Whatever his reasons, Alexa accepted that she'd been very short-sighted in believing everything she'd read about him. And really she should have known better, but then almost everyone believed what had been written about him and he didn't help that by not defending himself.

Still, there was no doubting some of the stories. He was a notorious playboy, and he'd definitely been a rebel when he was younger—the story of him stealing his father's favourite sports car and cruising through the mountains with a girl, and another of him winning a dangerous cross-country horse race his father had forbidden him to enter, and the stories of his wild parties at the Summer Palace were the stuff of legend—but there was another side to him. A deeper side she longed to explore further.

Her eyes drifted to his mouth and her body flushed with remembered pleasure at all the ways he'd satisfied her throughout the night. He'd certainly delivered on his promise of unadulterated pleasure and in one night he'd completely obliterated her first bumbling sexual experience with the treacherous Stefano.

Recalling how easily she'd fallen under the Italian's spell all those years ago, even knowing that she was older now, still made her throat constrict with unwanted emotion.

The earlier vulnerability she'd felt on waking in Rafe's arms returned full force, along with the sense that she'd never felt such a soul-deep connection with another human being before.

And that was exactly the kind of thinking she needed to avoid at all costs.

Driven out of bed by the knowledge that she was at risk of history repeating itself and creating meaning where there was none, Alexa quietly made her way to her room and jumped in the shower.

Once there she groaned softly as the soapy cloth moved over the sensitive marks left behind by Rafe's love making. He'd been both tender and demanding during the night, and a smile curved her lips as she thought about the way one particular mark had been formed. Warning herself again not to get hung up on what had happened between them, she pulled on her kimono-style robe and went in search of a much-needed coffee.

Determined to figure out how to work the machine on her own this time, she'd just tried her fourth combination of buttons when she heard a deep chuckle behind her. 'For a smart woman, that machine seems to have defeated you.'

Alexa glanced over her shoulder to find six foot three of hot muscular man leaning against the doorframe watching her. He'd put on baggy sweatpants, the rest of him completely bare, his biceps bulging as he folded his arms across his chest, amusement shining from his sexy blue eyes.

She gave him a droll look, unable to stop her gaze from falling to his naked chest. 'For a man with a huge wardrobe, you seem to have forgotten your shirt.'

A sensual grin curved his mouth as he sauntered towards her. 'Why cover up what you like to look at so much?'

'So arrogant,' she accused, catching her breath when he wrapped his arms around her from behind and nuzzled her neck.

'Why didn't you wake me before you got up?' he murmured, his hot breath making her melt.

'I didn't want to disturb you,' she said. Nor had she wanted him to spot the panic that had galvanised her out of his arms.

His lips grazed her ear and he gave it a light nip. 'Next time you wake me, okay?'

'But you were sleeping so peacefully.'

'Wake me so I can kiss you good morning.'

Cupping her jaw, he turned her face so that he could demonstrate and Alexa sighed as she leant into him, a sharp pang darting through her as she wondered if he always insisted on morning kisses from his women.

Reluctantly breaking the kiss, he reached around her to change the coffee settings before pressing Start.

'Does this mean you haven't had coffee all week?' he asked, grinning down at her.

'No, it means your very helpful concierge has brought me one from the café next door every morning.'

He turned her in his arms and linked his arms around her lower back. 'Now you have me.'

The tender words made Alexa's heart beat faster. If she could stop time this second she would, with his strong arms enfolding her body and his hot gaze pinned to hers.

The tone signalled that her coffee was ready, and severed the connection between them. Alexa rubbed her hands over her arms and gripped the mug he handed her in both hands, inhaling the heavenly aroma with a sigh.

Rafe's fingers sifted through her hair, making the mass tumble down around her shoulders.

'This should never be restrained,' he murmured, winding it around his hand.

'It's not practical to wear it down.'

'Practical is boring.'

He dropped a kiss on her mouth before stepping back to grab his own coffee. Alexa watched the play of muscles over his back from beneath the sweep of her lashes, heat curling through her.

When he turned back and saw her a pulse of raw sexual energy arced between them. Watching his eyes darken, a thrill of excitement wound through her right before her stomach announced that it was empty, the loud rumble echoing off the polished angles of the cabinets.

Mortified, she clamped her hand over the offending area and gave him a startled look.

Rafe laughed. 'Aren't princesses allowed to make bodily noises?'

'Not in company.'

'Company?' His eyes narrowed. 'I'm not company.' He dropped his empty espresso cup in the sink and leant back against it, reaching for her and tugging her between his splayed legs. 'I'm your husband.' He massaged the nape of her neck and she moaned as she leant into his touch. 'And your lover. I get special privileges.'

She knew she liked the sound of his words more than was good for her but for some reason she couldn't bring herself to pull away. Being with a man like this was new and intoxicating, and somehow being with *this* man quadrupled the sensation.

'Like hearing my stomach growl?' she said dubiously.

'Like taking you out for breakfast. In fact, let's make it the whole day. We can start with this great place I know that does a mean English breakfast, and play tourist for the day. Go to those places you didn't get to during the week.'

'Really?' Her eyes sparkled like a child standing in front of Harrods' window display at Christmas. Then she remembered that she'd promised to email HR with the report she'd been working on the last few days. 'I would love that but I can't. I have work to finish up.'

'No, you don't. Not only do you need to rest, but it's Saturday.'

'Oh, so it is.' She grinned at him. 'I've lost track of time, and I *never* lose track of time.'

'You work too hard. And while I respect your dedication, you also need to know when to take time out for yourself.'

'And you're going to tell me that now is that time?' Not waiting for his reply and having thrown caution to the wind once already, she decided that she might as well go all-out. 'Okay, fine. The report I have to finish up isn't all that urgent and this...' she opened her eyes wide '...being here with you, is a rare treat. Will we go there on your bike?'

He laughed at the hopeful note in her voice. 'You liked the bike, huh?'

She gave him a wicked grin. 'I loved the bike. Especially when you did that corner thing where it dipped low.'

'The lean-in.' Setting his hands to her waist, he pulled her closer. 'I love that you love my bike.' He kissed her long and deep, making her body quicken.

Desire consumed her in a flame of need and she moaned, threading her fingers into his hair and flattening her body against his. Rafe made an indistinct sound that was somewhere between pain and pleasure, his hands on the sash of her robe. 'If this goes any further we won't make it out of the apartment.'

'Oh, then we have to stop.'

Stepping back, Alexa retied the sash on her kimono and smoothed her hair.

Rafe shook his head. 'Tossed aside for a hunk of metal. Nice to know.'

Alexa gave him a teasing smile. 'It is a really big hunk of metal, though...'

He reached for her to give her a punishing kiss but she danced out of the way, laughing as he threatened retribution for her impudence.

Breakfast was as large and decadent as he'd promised and afterwards Alexa didn't think she'd be able to eat for a week.

Rafe teased her for her measly attempt and hoovered

up her remaining eggs and spinach as if he hadn't just devoured a plate twice the size of hers.

The café he'd taken her to was warm and low-key, like she suspected he liked to live his life. Exactly the opposite to how she lived hers, which was all polished silver service and structured decorum.

Tossing money onto the table, Rafe took her hand and led her from the café as if they were just a normal London couple enjoying a springtime weekend on the town.

Throwing his leg over the big black bike, Rafe kicked the stand up and helped Alexa settle herself on the back, her body automatically moulding to his. He'd given her his leather jacket again and she curled her fingers into the over-long sleeves for extra warmth and tucked them against his stomach. The cool spring temperature wasn't so bad with the visor covering her, but she didn't really care about the cold anyway. She was just enjoying being with Rafe.

'Where to now?'

'I don't know. You decide,' she said, wrapping her arms around his waist as the bike moved off from the kerb.

Rafe was an exceptional driver, his movements smooth and confident as he navigated his way through the congested city streets. But then he was exceptional at most things. His business enterprises, his coffee-making—okay, that was mostly the machine, but still—his dancing, and most of all his love-making...

Hugging him tight, she stopped daydreaming and tuned into the world-famous landmarks that dotted the city. Rafe was clearly enjoying his new role as tour guide, but her attention was more on the man she was wrapped around than anything else.

Until the bike zipped past a relatively normal-looking building bursting with pedestrians and shoppers. Tapping him on the shoulder, Alexa indicated that she wanted him to stop and when she saw that it was a bustling market she clapped her hands with glee.

Ever since she was a young girl she'd been enthralled by the sights and scents of a busy market, loving the combination of old and new, and the anticipation that came with finding a hidden treasure. She still had the pair of lurid green sunglasses her father had once given in and purchased for her on a trip she had tagged along on and, much to Sol's disgust, she'd worn them constantly for months afterwards.

Rafe groaned good-naturedly when he realised how keen she was to explore, swapping their helmets for two caps and tucking her hair out of the way.

'Don't make eye contact with anyone and don't leave my side. I don't feel like getting into a fight.'

Alexa rolled her eyes. They might have left their security detail behind for the day but she'd never felt safer— or happier. Shelving that unsettling thought, she rolled her eyes. 'As if.'

'Sweetheart, with those exotic green eyes of yours I'm almost tempted to keep you indoors.'

Alexa grinned at him; she couldn't help it. 'Compliments like that will get you kissed.'

'In that case, you're not only beautiful inside and out, but when you slid down my stomach earlier and put your mouth on—'

'Rafe!' Knowing exactly what he was about to say, Alexa laughed and reached up to kiss him. His mouth immediately turned hungry and desire coursed through her with unnerving force.

Moaning into his mouth, she extricated herself from his arms and stepped back. Being with him like this, so relaxed and natural, had a freeing effect on her. It was as if all her fears and inhibitions had been washed away and she didn't have to worry about what the future might bring. It was just the two of them here and now.

'Come on.' She broke the kiss and hooked her arm through his. She'd stashed some pounds in her pocket on her way out of the apartment and she wanted to spend the lot.

Wandering past various vendors, Alexa soaked up the Reggae music and the delightful fragrance of the multi-cultural food on offer, stopping first to buy some exquisite chocolates and then to stand behind a crowd of onlookers to watch a curly-haired Australian juggler ply his trade.

Later, pleasantly exhausted and dressed in one of Rafe's shirts and a thick pair of socks, Alexa wandered into the kitchen to find Rafe putting the finishing touches to their evening meal.

'He cooks, he rides a motorbike *and* runs a multina-tional corporation.' She took a glass of Sauterne he held out for her. 'Is there anything you can't do?'

'Concentrate for any length of time when you're in the room.'

'I can live with that.' Alexa laughed because she was meant to, but a pang of longing she didn't expect to feel pierced her heart.

Careful, she warned herself. *You only have seven days left.*

'So what are we having?'

'Steak with pepper sauce, potatoes and salad.'

'Wow, now I'm even more impressed.'

Rafe smiled across the bench at Alexa, unsure if he'd ever enjoyed a woman's company as much as he was enjoying hers. She was bright, funny, beautiful... His eyes took in her clean face and laughing eyes. He liked being with her like this, relaxed, natural, just the two of them without any outside interruptions. And as much as he enjoyed making love with her, having her in his space filled him with a sense of wellbeing he would be hard pressed to explain. Maybe it was knowing that he could take her to bed any time he wanted. Because he did want to. All the time.

'I know that look,' she said huskily, her eyes growing heavy.

'You should.' Rafe told himself to pull it together before she accused him of having a one-track mind.

'So how is it you can cook?' she asked, reaching for a carrot stick.

Glad to be focusing on something else other than the way he was *feeling*, Rafe sliced vegetables and answered her question. 'When I moved to Cambridge I shared a house with a few other guys who could barely reheat beans. Since I had developed a penchant for fine dining, thanks to the palace chef, it was either learn to cook or starve.'

'I'm sure your brother would have provided a chef if you'd asked.'

'He would have, but I was determined to make my own way. Which I did. Partying, drinking, studying...playing darts. You do realise that your lover is a Cambridge darts champion?'

'Darts?' Alexa grinned. 'Be still my beating heart.'

Rafe arched a brow. 'Some respect, please. It's more difficult than it looks.'

Alexa grinned and sipped her wine. 'It sounds like fun. By contrast, I had private tutors and then I studied at Berenia University, surrounded by security.'

He looked up from chopping herbs for the vinaigrette. 'No partying for the future Queen?'

'No.' She gave a wistful sigh. 'I was accepted into an American university, actually. Sol helped me apply and then, when I got in, he managed to convince my father to let me study abroad, but then I made the mistake with…'

Rafe stopped chopping, noting the way the smile had died on her face. 'The Italian with the arms?' he prompted softly.

'Yes. Him. My father decided that I was too young. Too *vulnerable* to be that far away from home. He was probably right.'

'He wasn't right, Princess, and you need to stop feeling guilty about it. What happened wasn't your fault. You're entitled to make mistakes, and you have to live your life.'

'Yes, but I should have known better. I should have been prepared.'

Hearing the subtle anguish in her voice, Rafe reached over and took her chin gently in his hand. 'How could you? You were seventeen years old. I bet your father kept you under a tight leash when you were young—there, I see I'm right—so what previous experiences could you have had to prepare you for being conned by a man like that?'

She looked at him for so long he wondered if he had offended her when her lips twisted into a faint smile. 'Do you know, when I was in my teens I used to be a champion horsewoman and I always trusted my judgement. Then Stefano happened and *bam*—it's like I've second-guessed myself ever since. I've blamed myself for what happened for so long. Trying to be good and to do the right thing…' Her smile hit him like a sunbeam. 'Why did I never look at it the way you just did?'

Rafe leaned over and gave her a quick, deep kiss before handing her another carrot stick. 'Too hard on yourself, perhaps.'

'Maybe. It's something I've never been able to talk about with anyone else before.' She palmed her glass of wine and watched him cook. 'You're a good listener. And a good person, you know that?'

Rafe placed the steaks on the grill. 'Careful, I'll get a big head.'

'You don't like me saying that.' She tilted her head as she studied him. 'Why not?'

'I suppose I'm not used it. It wasn't something I heard growing up.'

'Your parents never told you that you were a good person?'

'My father and I never saw eye to eye. He told me he'd disown me if I didn't follow his rules.'

'But that's awful.'

'He was hard on all of us. We got used to it.' Rafe shrugged off her sympathy. He never let himself indulge in weak emotions like sympathy and need. 'Do you eat mushrooms?'

'Yes.' She frowned thoughtfully. 'I do remember hearing he was often upset with you, but you were always blamed for any issues that came up.'

Rafe laughed, turning the steaks. 'Often I deserved it.' He gave her his trademark smile, but somehow it felt false. 'I enjoyed riling my father by getting into scraps I shouldn't have.'

'At least he didn't actually follow through on the threat. I can't imagine how you would have felt if he'd actually disowned you.'

'I have no doubt that he would have, had he lived. Do you want your potatoes salted?'

'Yes, fine,' she dismissed with a wave of her hand. 'And your mother? She didn't tell you that you were a good person either?'

Wondering how the topic of conversation had turned from her to him so neatly, Rafe frowned. He had already told Alexa more about himself than he'd told anyone else and now he was flooded with memories he'd rather forget.

'My mother had her own problems,' he said tonelessly. 'Namely my father. They were always at each other's throats about something or other and I'm not sure she noticed any of us most of the time. She left when I was ten.'

He placed the steaks and potatoes on a plate and dressed the salad.

'Ten?'

He saw the sympathy on Alexa's face and his gut clenched. He still remembered waking up the morning after his mother had stolen out of the palace like a thief in the night, never to return. He'd come to terms with his childhood loss a long time ago. Come to terms with the fact that his mother lived the life of a recluse now, and rarely saw anyone.

'Did you see her often after she left?'

'No. She moved to Europe and Jag, Milena and I stayed in Santara. She didn't want us to go with her. She wanted a clean break, to be able to make a fresh start with her life.'

'But how could a mother do that?'

'Not all women are maternal, Princess.' He held two plates up with a flourish. 'Let's eat.'

Alexa was so shocked by Rafe's revelations about his childhood that she didn't know where to put the information.

According to stories she had heard about her own mother, she had been kind and compassionate, and Alexa would give anything to have memories of her, whereas Rafe sounded like he'd give anything *not* to have memories of his.

Her heart went out to him as a young boy stuck in a

volatile household. Hers hadn't been overly warm, her father often a distant figure, but she'd never doubted his love for her.

'But what about Milena and Jaeger?' she asked, following him to the table. 'Did it bring you closer to them?' Because she had always run to Sol when she'd felt down, and she missed him terribly now that he was gone.

'Yes and no. Milena was extremely young when our mother left and she needed a lot of support. Jag was away at boarding school.' He set their wine glasses on the table. 'I hope you're hungry.'

She was starving but she didn't care about food. 'Do you ever talk about it with Jag or Milena?' she prodded.

The look he gave her was one of surprise. 'Why would I do that? They have their lives, and I have mine.'

'It might be healthy,' she offered. 'How do you know they're not suffering in some way?'

She saw a muscle pulsing in his jaw as if she'd hit a nerve, his eyes suddenly remote. 'Jag and Milena both have my number if they need me. And you—' he said with silky emphasis '—do not need to concern yourself with any of this. I'm fine, Alexa. There's nothing missing from my life.'

What about love? she thought.

He didn't have love, but nor did he want it. As soon as the thought entered her mind a deep sense of misery filled her whole body. Misery for the boy whose parents had cared more about their own needs than those of their children. And misery at the wounds their behaviour had inflicted—inadvertent or otherwise. But at least now she had some understanding as to why he was the way he was.

Where she had always craved connection to others as a result of the lack of warmth in her own childhood—often to her personal detriment—Rafe had been let down by the very people who should have had his back, so he didn't let anyone close. He didn't try at all.

And she would do well to remember that because he didn't want that to change, and she'd be a fool to want it to be otherwise.

CHAPTER EIGHT

SOMETHING TICKLED HER ribs and Alexa swatted at it. 'Don't wake me.'

'I thought you were a morning person.'

She rolled over and groaned when she saw the clock. 'I am when I've managed to get some sleep.'

Rafe sat down on the bed beside her. 'I have coffee.'

'Coffee?' Alexa sprang up and blinked the sleep from her eyes. She breathed deeply and there it was, that delicious aroma.

Rafe laughed and handed her a mug. 'So predictable. But drink up. I have a surprise for you.'

'You do?'

'How do you feel about going on a road trip?'

'Don't you have to work?'

'Hannah's been nagging me about taking time off so I've cancelled my appointments for the next couple of days. If you need any further incentive, the road trip involves my bike.'

'It does?' Feeling helplessly happy and knowing it was dangerous to keep indulging in an emotion that had everything to do with the man creating it, Alexa shelved the voice in her head that said she was letting herself feel too much and nodded. 'Give me five minutes.'

Rafe laughed, leaning in to give her a lingering kiss. 'Now I really am jealous of my bike.'

A couple stretched into five days of exploring the English and Scottish countryside, as well as each other.

Rafe had taken her to Cambridge and the pub he'd frequented during his student days. From there they'd spent an afternoon climbing the ruggedly green Old Man of Coniston in the Lake District, before skipping over the border to explore Scotland. They'd stopped at Glasgow for a few nights where Rafe had checked out the nightclub scene and a couple of buildings he said he was thinking of investing in. One in particular, a grand old Art Deco cinema, Alexa had fallen in love with, totally on board with his vision of restoring it to its former glory rather than tearing it down.

Now they were by Loch Ness, standing under a cloudy sky and staring at the inky black waters of the lake.

'I've always wanted to see the monster,' Alexa said, her eyes searching for a tell-tale ripple or sign of an arched neck.

Rafe slipped his open coat around her body and hugged her closer against the sudden drop in the temperature. 'There is no monster.'

'Don't ruin the fun of it.' She burrowed even further into him against the cold. 'I've decided I'm going to do this every year.'

'Look for the Loch Ness monster?'

'No.' She jabbed him playfully. 'Take off for a week where no one knows who I am or where I am. I might even get my motorbike licence.'

'The Princess who rides?'

'Absolutely.'

She tilted her head up to gaze into his amused blue eyes. They stayed like that for what felt like an eternity, the connection between them so deep it took her breath away more than the scenery.

Suddenly feeling something damp on her face, Alexa shifted her gaze to the sky. 'Rafe! It's snowing!'

He smiled at her indulgently, stroking a flake from her cheek. 'So it is. Rare for this time of year, but damn cold enough!'

She started laughing and turned out of the circle of his arms to spread hers wide. 'I've never seen snow before. It's glorious.'

'You're glorious.' He pulled her back to him and crushed her lips beneath his until she forgot all about the snow.

When they finally parted to draw breath Rafe reached down to brush the wetness from her cheeks. 'Happy?'

Alexa could have melted into a contented puddle at the way he was looking at her. 'So happy.'

The following morning, their last on the road, Alexa relaxed in the quaint bedroom of a traditional English pub somewhere in a picturesque valley in the Yorkshire Dales.

It was dreamily quiet and she had woken to the faint sound of birds outside her window, and a crisp layer of snow covering the valley. Snuggled up in bed, she realised that she hadn't practised her normal yoga routine or thought about work all week, and she didn't even care. This trip with Rafe was a break from real life and she'd embraced it much more heartily than she would have thought possible.

Out here, they were just Mr and Mrs Nobody, taking a week off and travelling together. Last night the publican and his wife hadn't batted an eye as they'd pulled up late and asked if they had a room. A week ago Alexa would never have thought she would ever be in such a situation. She'd never thought she'd feel this magical, and all because she'd decided to 'take charge', as he'd suggested, and embraced uncertainty.

She could only imagine Nasrin's face when she told her how sexy the Prince really was. Or would she tell her? She'd certainly grown close to Nasrin over the last three years, but perhaps this experience was too private to share with anyone. Because she had no doubt that Nasrin would have her romantic hat on and interrogate her with a litany of questions about what had happened and how she felt about him. No doubt expecting Alexa to have fallen in love with him or something equally absurd.

Fortunately she wasn't at risk of that happening. She was having a good time with Rafe. A wonderful time, but that was all it was for both of them. The public might have bought their romantic love story but Alexa knew the truth, and this time she was determined to remain objective.

Wondering why she felt so unsettled all of a sudden, she nearly fell on the phone beside the bed as it started to ring. Out of habit she picked it up, checking the display before she realised that it was Rafe's phone and not her own.

Regan's name flashed across the screen and Alexa glanced at the bathroom door, where she could hear the shower running. She'd been too drowsy to join Rafe when he'd tried to cajole her into shower sex, promising to go in search of a soy latte for her as soon as he was out.

Regan's name flashed again and Alexa sat up, pulling Rafe's discarded T-shirt over her head to ward off the chill, and swiped the screen to answer the call. The Queen might be calling because of a family emergency and she didn't feel comfortable letting it go through to voicemail when she had the chance to answer it.

Delighted to hear her voice, Regan was keen to find out how Alexa was enjoying her time in England with Rafe and, before she knew it, Alexa found herself drawn in by the other woman's natural warmth. It was clear why the King had fallen in love with her. Even on the phone she was animated and sincere, so opposite to Alexa's own tendency to be closed down. Not that she'd been closed down this week. In fact the way she'd been with Rafe shocked the life out of her. Reminding her that she could be fun and relaxed when she wasn't so worried about the future, and how everyone perceived her.

Maybe a little bit of Rafe's capacity to let things go had rubbed off on her. Not that she'd go as far as he had in letting things go. Like letting go of his country, and his family.

'So I've organised a surprise birthday dinner for Jag in London tomorrow night,' Regan said in a hushed tone as if she half expected her husband to sneak up behind her. 'And I haven't heard yet if Rafe is coming. It's not that big a deal because I've booked the whole restaurant, but I'd really like to know. It would mean so much to Jag and me if you were both there.'

'Of course we'll be there,' Alexa said, not really thinking about the ramifications of that statement until she hung up and Rafe strolled out of the shower a couple of minutes later, a white towel draped around his lean hips, another draped around his shoulders, the tips of his hair glistening with wet drops from the shower.

'She lives.' He grinned at her. 'I was hoping you'd join me.'

'I was thinking about it,' she murmured, automatically opening her mouth for his kiss. 'But then Regan rang.'

Given that he'd said that he liked things just the way they were between him and his siblings, she wasn't sure how to tell him she'd accepted Regan's invitation. She would give anything to be able to go to another birthday dinner for Sol but she knew that Rafe didn't feel the same way about his family.

Rafe dropped the towel from around his shoulders, going still. 'Is everything okay?'

'Everything's fine. She told me she's throwing your brother a surprise birthday party tomorrow night and that you haven't RSVP'd.'

Rafe nuzzled a path down the side of her neck. 'I've been so distracted I forgot. I need to let her know that we're busy.'

Alexa braced her hands on the balls of his shoulders to shift him back.

'Are we busy?'

He frowned as she thwarted his attempt to rid her of his T-shirt. 'Yes. Tomorrow is our last night before you return to Berenia and I plan to make love with you the entire time.'

Their last night together? How had it come about so quickly? And how had she forgotten?

'Would you mind terribly if we had a slight change in plan?' she asked, arching her neck as he resumed his teasing kisses.

'How slight?'

'Well…' She winced, some sixth sense warning her that this might not go as well as she'd originally hoped. 'I sort of accepted Regan's invitation on your behalf.'

As predicted, Rafe drew back, frowning at her. 'How do you sort of accept an invitation?'

'You say yes.'

'Why would you do that?'

'Because it's a *really* nice idea, and she *really* wants you to be there. She said it would make Jag's night.'

Rafe shook his head, moving further away from her. 'I just saw my brother at our wedding two weeks ago, and then at the ball two weeks before that. I've seen him more this month than I did the whole of last year.'

'Surely that's all the more reason to go.' Sensing his physical and emotional withdrawal, and hating it, Alexa touched his arm. 'What are you afraid of?'

'Afraid of?' Rafe barked out a laugh. 'Fear isn't what's keeping me from wanting to go.'

'Then what is? Because it's important to make time for family.'

'Not all family members are best friends, Alexa.'

'I know. Which is why it's so vital to forge strong bonds. The more you see someone, the more you want to see them.'

Rafe gave her a look. 'Sometimes the opposite occurs.'

'It doesn't count with family because, as annoying as they can be, they're the only ones who will rush to your side when the chips are down.'

'I don't plan to let my chips go anywhere,' he drawled. 'Especially not down.'

Alexa returned his look of a moment ago and pushed a skein of her hair back behind her shoulders. Rafe's eyes darkened, the air between turning from frigid to molten in a matter of seconds.

'You did that deliberately,' he accused softly.

Dragging air into her lungs, Alexa blinked. 'Did what?'

'Doesn't matter. It won't work.'

Their eyes locked and then he vaulted off the bed, turning his back on her to stare out of the small window.

The morning had brightened and the sunlight drew shadows across his muscular shoulders and biceps, the white towel riding low on his lean hips. Alexa knew she had crossed a line in accepting the Queen's invitation on his behalf; she'd known it at the time, and she should never have done it. Not that she had expected his complete withdrawal or the hollow feeling inside her chest as if someone had carved out her heart and left an empty cavity behind.

'I'm sorry.' She moved towards him and placed her hand in the centre of his back, enthralled with the play of muscle that bunched beneath the surface of his skin at her touch. 'That was incredibly arrogant of me to impose my ideas of family onto you. I absolutely hate it when people think that they know better about my life than I do and I should have spoken to you first.'

Rafe swung around, his eyes full of an emotion that was somewhere between pain and anger, and she couldn't move. In the distance she heard the tread of someone's footsteps as they walked past their room and the sound of crockery clinking together, but all she could focus on was Rafe standing before her like a Greek God come to life.

He made a rough sound in the back of his throat and then his hands were in her hair, tugging her up onto her toes so that her lips were inches from his. 'How can I resist you when you look at me like this?' His voice was rough, his mouth hard and insistent when it met hers, his kiss eradicating everything else in the world for her but him. This man who gave new meaning to her life.

Alexa moaned, her mouth opening beneath his in an emotional onslaught of need that seemed never-ending, her hands clinging to his wide shoulders as if she might tumble over a cliff and be dashed against jagged rocks if she were to let him go.

Finally Rafe raised his head, leaning his forehead against hers, his breathing ragged.

'I'll go to my brother's party. This time. But, even though I know you mean well, I don't want you to ever interfere with my relationship with my family again. It is what it is, and I can't change that. I don't *want* to change that.'

'I hear you.' Alexa gulped in a few deep breaths to

steady her heartbeat. She did hear him and even though she might like to fix things for him that wasn't her role.

The following night Alexa smiled at Stevens as he opened her car door and waited for her to exit onto the damp London street.

An avant-garde restaurant loomed ahead, illuminated by a single bright light; the black door and grey brickwork looked as if it hid an illegal gin joint rather than a Michelin star restaurant.

Rafe's security team moved ahead of them, clearing the way and entering the building first.

Trying to lighten the mood between them that had shifted since she'd accepted Regan's invitation, Alexa chatted as if nothing was wrong.

'I've heard of this restaurant. The chef is some sort of food maestro. I read that he creates new recipes in a laboratory rather than a kitchen.'

'He's innovative,' Rafe agreed. 'And good at what he does.'

'Something you admire.'

'I admire lots of things.' His gaze slid down her body as the maître d' took her coat. 'Like you in that dress.'

Relieved that he no longer seemed upset with her, Alexa smiled. 'I believe you said that back at the apartment.'

'No, I nearly stripped it off you back in the apartment. Somehow I've convinced myself that anticipation will make the pleasure worth waiting for and didn't want to disappoint you by cancelling tonight.'

As usual the explosive chemistry that was never far below the surface when they were together ignited, stealing her breath.

'I'm glad you didn't cancel,' she murmured. 'I think it's going to be really special. And this dress deserved an outing because I'll never be able to wear it in Berenia.' Alexa adjusted the shoestring straps over her shoulders. The dress was low-cut at the front, even more daring than the one she'd worn to Bound, and it made her feel sexy and confident—exactly how Rafe always made her feel.

Buoyed by a mixture of renewed happiness and lust, Alexa glanced at him from beneath the sweep of her lashes. 'But I look forward to what anticipation looks like later on.'

'I can tell you what it will look like.' Rafe placed his hand against the small of her back and leant close. 'A tenth of a second.'

Alexa gave a husky laugh and suddenly she was plastered up against Rafe's hard body. She gasped at the unexpected contact and the doorman discreetly glanced at his feet.

'Stay an extra week,' he said gruffly.

'What?'

'Don't leave tomorrow. It's too soon. Stay an extra week. You can work from my place if you need to. I've hardly scratched the surface of what I want to show you.'

Dazed by the forceful nature of his request, Alexa's mind blanked of everything but him. She was sure there were a hundred good reasons why she should say no, not least because she wanted to stay with him in London a little *too* much, but she couldn't utter any of them. 'I'd love to.'

'Good.' A satisfied smile curved his lips just before they connected with hers for a brief searing kiss. 'Now let's go and get tonight over with.'

Giddy with delight that Rafe wanted to be with her as much as she wanted to be with him, Alexa floated through the sliding steel door into a large room that had once been an old warehouse. The designers had kept many of the original features, including industrial lighting suspended from black cables and exposed beams along the walls.

Long tables dressed with pristine white tablecloths and sparkling silverware filled the space, with a brushed metal bar running along the back wall.

Most of the guests seemed to already be present, about forty people standing in small groups holding champagne flutes and chatting animatedly.

A waiter in a white coat stopped in front of them, holding a tray full of coloured drinks.

'Mimosas,' Rafe murmured, obviously reading her perplexed expression correctly. 'Chilled juice and champagne. You might like it.'

Alexa accepted the pink drink, her eyes wide with appreciation at the sweet taste. 'I do like it.'

Rafe's eyes gleamed, but he had no chance to respond as Regan carefully crossed the room to greet them. She looked amazing in a gold three-quarter-length dress that cleverly hid her massive baby bump.

'I don't know much about pregnant ladies,' Rafe said, bending to kiss his sister-in-law on the cheek, 'but you look ready to pop.'

'Rafe!' Alexa admonished. 'You don't say that to a pregnant woman. You look amazing, Your Majesty. I hope I look as beautiful as you when I'm eight months pregnant.'

'Thanks. But please call me Regan.' Her eyes sparkled with merriment, her hand cradling her stomach. 'I'm not due for a month yet, but the sooner this little darling comes out the better. I feel like a hippopotamus.'

'My thoughts exactly,' Rafe deadpanned.

'I'll make him pay later,' Alexa promised. 'Where's the birthday boy?' She held out a silver-wrapped gift Rafe had organised earlier in the day.

'I'll take that,' Regan offered. 'And Jag is with a good friend who is plying him with some sort of whisky that was created in a cave five hundred leagues below the sea, or some such. You should join them, Rafe, while I introduce Alexa to the other guests.'

'Love to.' Rafe gently touched Alexa's jaw. 'You okay with that, Princess?'

Alexa's heart bumped behind her chest at the sweet endearment she'd come to love. 'Of course,' she said, watching as he walked away.

'Wow,' Milena said by way of a greeting as she stopped beside Alexa. 'I never thought I'd see the day my brother looked at a woman like that.' Quirky and exuberant in an orange dress and bright blue stockings, she grinned delightedly at Alexa. 'But it had to happen one day, right?'

Alexa knew she thought Rafe was in love with her, but that was because Milena had no idea that they'd married for political purposes. Alexa hated lying to her, but she knew that the less people who knew their relationship was staged the better.

'We're having a good time together,' Alexa supplied, which was true enough. They were having a very good time together. Or at least she was. She frowned a little as she gazed over at Rafe, greeting the men beside the bar. She was pretty sure Rafe was too. At least she knew he was in the bedroom. Just as the thought formed in her head, Rafe glanced back at her, his blue eyes finding hers with unerring accuracy.

'Can you both excuse me?' Regan said. 'I need to remind the caterers about the cake.'

'I'll take care of Alexa,' Milena promised, snagging a champagne flute from a passing waiter. 'You know my brother can't stop looking at you,' she mused happily. 'And whatever you've done to soften him, I'm glad.'

'Soften him?'

'Yeah, he actually listened to me the other day when I called him to complain about the amount of security Jag was insisting I have with me when I move to New York next week. He even promised to speak with him about it to see if he could reduce it.'

'He's worried you'll get taken advantage of. And there are a lot of toads out there,' Alexa said. 'Believe me, I know.'

'I suppose you're right,' Milena conceded. 'But I'm not thinking about that. I believe in destiny so whatever happens, happens. I'm just happy for my two brothers. One about to become a father, the other so in love he'd walk over hot coals for you. I still find it hard to believe, and I can't wait until you become Queen and Rafe has to walk two paces behind you at all times.' She gave Alexa an impish look. 'Given that he likes to always be in charge, I plan to tease him shamelessly about his subservient position every chance I get.'

Alexa knew that Milena meant well with her sisterly digs, but her comment struck a chord deep inside Alexa. In Berenia the spouses of a monarch didn't walk two paces behind; they walked ten paces behind.

And Rafe would never do it.

Moreover, she'd never ask him to do it.

And she'd like to be able to tell Milena that. Tell her that, actually, she didn't love Rafe at all. But even as the words formed in her mind she knew that not only could she not say them for reasons of confidentiality; but because they were no longer true.

She had gone and done the inconceivable and fallen in love with him, she realised with a sickening jolt. She didn't know when, or how, her feelings had changed, but she knew that they had, and the need to protect herself, to hide herself away from prying eyes threatened to overwhelm her.

She'd been so careful to keep their relationship in context. Tried so hard to remain objective and not to make more of their connection than was actually there, even embracing Rafe's ability to separate emotion and sex, and yet…at the end of the day she found him as utterly irresistible as most other women he'd dated. Because underneath that layer of sophistication and rebellious charm was a man who was caring and loyal and strong. A man who was worth keeping.

Her dream man.

Only she wasn't his dream woman. And she never would be because, although he clearly enjoyed spending time with her, he didn't want anything more from her. He didn't want that from any woman.

'Are you okay, Alexa?'

Milena placed a hand on her arm, her exotic eyes clouded with concern. 'You look a little dazed. Do you need to sit down? I hope it wasn't something I said. I know Rafe won't mind walking behind you. I should never have joked about that.'

Rafe was right, she thought with self-disgust; she really did need to work on her poker face if Milena had picked up on her distress so easily.

'I'm fine,' she automatically assured the other woman. 'I think this mimosa has gone to my head.'

'You need food,' Milena said. 'If I drink without eating I get lightheaded too. Let me find you some of the delicious canapés the waiters have been passing around.'

Alexa knew that an empty stomach was hardly enough to make her feel so dizzy. But realising she was in love with a man who would never love her back would do it.

She sucked in a deep breath. She was going to have to develop a new poker face and fast because this wasn't information she could ever reveal to Rafe. Everything would instantly change if she did. He'd see her as some lovesick fool like the women in his past who couldn't control their feelings for him. He might even withdraw from her like he had the day before, feel sorry for her, look at her with sympathy or, worse, worry that she would try to cling to him when it was time to end their marriage.

Right now she was his equal in and out of the bedroom. Right now they were having a good time, a wonderful time, but all she would have to do to ruin that would be to utter those three tiny little words and it would be gone. He'd probably send her home immediately, making up some excuse to avoid seeing her again. It would be awful.

And it was her fault. She'd become attached when she'd promised him that she wouldn't. When she'd promised *herself* that she wouldn't.

But she wasn't a dreamer in need of a fairy tale ending. She was a strong woman in charge of her own destiny.

Destiny.

There was that word again. And the irony of how her destiny had yet again interfered with her love life wasn't lost on her. Because even if Rafe did—by some miracle of the universe—have feelings for her it would never work out between them. While Stefano had wanted to marry her for who she was, Rafe *didn't* want to be married to her for who she was. He had made it clear on multiple occasions that he had no wish to return to Santara. That he hated all things to do with duty and royalty, so it stood to reason that he'd never want to move to Berenia. And while she could abdicate and pass the crown onto her cousin, it wasn't ideal because—

Abdicate?

Stumbling into a chair, Alexa threw her hands out to stop herself from falling when she was grabbed from behind and pulled up against a hard male body that sent tingles to her toes.

'Whoa.' Rafe reached for the half-empty champagne flute she'd nearly upended all over herself, grabbing it in time to prevent any of the pink contents from spilling. 'Careful, Princess.' He nuzzled her neck indulgently. 'You have a habit of spilling brightly coloured drinks all over yourself. At least this time you're not wearing white.'

Distracted by his lips against the tender skin of her neck, it took Alexa's dazed brain a moment to realise what he'd said. When it sank in she spun around in the circle of his arms and stared up at him.

'You?' Her gaze collided with his sparkling blue eyes as her brain rearranged the events of her past into a new world order. 'It was you. It was *always* you.'

Her heart lurched inside her chest and she didn't know whether to laugh or cry at the realisation that he had been the one to save her from embarrassment all those years ago, not his brother.

Her heart gripped tight inside her chest as she stared at his beautiful face. Him. It had always been him.

Destiny, whispered through her head again and she could have burst into tears on the spot. Because he wasn't her destiny at all. He wasn't her anything.

Bemused, Rafe cocked his head to the side as if he hadn't heard her right. 'Always me?'

'Yes.' How had she mistaken him for his brother all those years ago? How had she *not* known?

But then Rafe enjoyed playing the bad boy so much, how could she have ever thought that it would have been him? Who would have thought that the Rebel Prince would have possessed the empathy to prevent a young girl from embarrassing herself in front of a room full of dignitaries? But he'd always been that person deep down. It was why women fell over themselves to have a piece of him. Rafe was charming and debonair and handsome as the devil, but he possessed a deep sensitivity that eclipsed everything else. It was why his father's continual rejection had hurt him so much that the only way he'd been able to survive it was to pretend that it didn't hurt at all. It was why he reacted so strongly whenever he felt judged. He cared about those he loved, she realised, perhaps a little too much.

'Stop monopolising your new bride, Rafe,' Milena teased. 'She needs to eat!'

Feeling raw and exposed, Alexa gratefully accepted the small plate of canapés Milena offered. She knew her stomach wouldn't hold anything down, but at least nibbling at the food would give her enough time to develop an A-grade poker face.

Because she was going to need it to get through the rest of the night with her heart intact.

CHAPTER NINE

RAFE WATCHED ALEXA join his sister at the table, a slight frown pleating his brow. He would swear there was something up with her, but she wouldn't catch his eye so that he could be sure.

He'd taken her away this week on the spur of the moment and he'd enjoyed himself more than he'd thought possible. Being a loner, he usually couldn't wait to leave whoever he was with to get back to his own company, but that urge didn't seem to arise with Alexa.

He knew he liked her more than was wise, but he didn't seem to have any control over that. Looking at her, with her midnight-black hair catching the glints of the down lights and her perfect lips tilted into a smile, he wondered, not for the first time, at his total lack of control around this woman. Like asking her to stay an extra week because he didn't want her to leave.

She'd burrowed under his skin and although he was still waiting for the novelty factor to wear off, it wasn't happening. If anything, the more time he spent with her, the more he wanted to, which had never happened to him before.

Pleasure was pleasure but this... Being with her went beyond that and he'd be kidding himself if he tried to convince himself otherwise. He liked her both in and out of the bedroom. He liked her curiosity about the world, her dedication to her country, her loyalty to her people. He liked the way she teased him and challenged him and he loved that she shared his sense of adventure, and that she wanted to make the world a better place for everyone. Even him.

He'd been wrong to call her a doormat; she was far from a doormat. She was loyal and honourable and dedicated. They were all qualities he admired and tried to adhere to himself. He just wished her dedication was focused his way, rather than Berenia.

But then, if it was, what would he do with it? It wasn't as if he was looking for a permanent arrangement. They'd married with the express intention that it would end. She wanted it to end. And so did he.

Didn't he?

Well, of course he did. Alexa was as constrained by her royal duties as his brother was, giving her little choice as to how to live her life.

For a man committed to living his life with as few encumbrances as possible that would never work.

'You still thinking of ending things with Alexa in six months' time?'

Rafe gave his brother a blank stare. Jag had always had the uncanny knack of knowing what he was thinking. The fact that he'd been staring at Alexa for a full five minutes might have also given him away. 'Of course.'

'Okay.'

Jag joined him in watching Alexa chatting with the other women who had joined her and their sister at the table, sipping his glass of red.

'Okay? That's it?' He cut his brother a brooding glance. 'You're not even going to try and tell me I'm wrong? Not going to try and give me some brotherly advice?'

A smile threatened to break out on Jag's face. 'Would you like me to give you some brotherly advice?'

'No.' Rafe didn't need advice. Especially about his love life. And since when did he think of sleeping with a woman as his 'love life'?

'You sure?' Jag asked. 'You look a little torn.'

Did he? Well, hell. 'I'm not torn. Alexa is...she's great. But she's not looking for anything long-term and nor am I. You know that.'

'I know some things are bigger than we are,' Jag answered enigmatically. 'But the Rebel Prince and the future Queen of Berenia? It would never work, would it?'

'No, it wouldn't.' Rafe's expression turned grim. 'You know I can't toe the royal line if I don't agree with it.'

'That's always been one of your great strengths, Rafa. You speak your mind. Alexa would no doubt appreciate having someone like that in her corner when she starts her reign.'

'Father didn't.'

'No. But he was an ass.'

Rafe gave a short bark of laughter. 'Not to put too fine a point on it.'

Jag grinned, and suddenly it was as if they were teenagers again and racing each other across the sand in dune buggies.

'Remember that day in—'

'The mountains? Yeah. I beat you to the top that day.'

Jag scoffed. 'We'll call it even. But I definitely won the—'

'You wish,' Rafe cut in on a laugh. 'I've always been better than you at fencing.'

'Dream on, lover boy. I'll give you a rematch any time you're game. But I was talking about the yacht race around the sound.'

'A close call, I admit. But again, lucky.'

Jag laughed at the outrageous call. He'd always been the better yachtsman, while Rafe had excelled at dune racing.

He'd been wrong to dread tonight, Rafe realised with a jolt of clarity. Wrong to put so much distance between him and Jag over his guilty conscience because he had missed his brother. Missed his easy companionship.

'Listen, Jag…' he let out a slow breath '… I need to apologise for walking away all those years ago when you became King. I should have stayed to help with the transition.'

Jag gave him a look. 'There's nothing to apologise for. I wanted you to go. You'd lived under Father's iron rule for far too long. Staying would have stifled you even more.'

'Still—'

'It's okay, Rafa. We're—'

Whatever Jag had been about to say was cut off when his eyes turned as hard as stone. Seconds later he was striding across the room to where Regan leant against the back of a chair, one hand cradling her belly.

Noticing nothing out of place, Rafe followed, wondering at the tense set of his brother's shoulders.

'Goddamn it, Regan, I knew we shouldn't have come here tonight,' Jag said, steel lining every word, his hard gaze riveted to his wife.

'Don't swear,' Regan admonished. 'I got the all-clear to fly this weekend, remember?'

Sick with dread that his brother's seemingly solid relationship had gone the way of his parents', Rafe was about to step between them, as he had done with his parents many times during his youth, when Regan let out a low moan. 'How was I to know that my waters would break tonight?'

Her waters had broken?

Comprehension dawned on Rafe in a brutal rush.

'If something happens to you,' Jag ground out, his voice ragged with emotion, 'I'll never forgive myself.'

'Nothing will happen. I'm in labour. I'm not dying.'

'A month early!'

'Babies come early all the time. It's—' Her breath cut off as another contraction hit her. Jag swore and lifted her into his arms.

Acting purely on instinct, Rafe pulled his phone from his pocket, dialling the emergency services as his eyes searched for Alexa.

Before he'd located her, he felt her hand go into his, squeezing gently. 'What can I do?'

'What you are doing.' He brought her fingers to his lips, his worried eyes on his sister-in-law and brother. After organising emergency services he dialled another number, relieved when the call was answered on the first ring.

A ripple went through the room as the guests started to get wind of what was happening.

'The ambulance is two minutes away,' Rafe told his brother. 'And a friend of mine who is probably the best obstetrician in Britain will meet us at the emergency door of the hospital.'

'Thanks.' Jag swallowed hard, his eyes watering.

'She's going to be fine,' Rafe assured him. 'You focus on her. I'll take care of everything else.'

Two hours later, Rafe felt ragged as he waited for news, any news, that Regan was okay and the baby had been delivered safe and well. He'd never felt so helpless as he had at the sight of his powerful brother brought to his knees with worry.

This was why he wanted nothing to do with love. It churned you up inside and spat you out, battered, at the other end. It was such a stupid emotion. He had no idea why people actually sought this kind of thing out.

As if reading his thoughts, Alexa glanced at him from across the room. Two steps and she'd be in his arms and he'd feel one hundred times better, but he resisted the urge. He didn't want that. He didn't want to rely on someone else to make him happy.

But wasn't that already what had happened? All week he'd talked with her, laughed with her, held her in his arms and danced with her and that was exactly how he'd felt. Happy. Content. *Complete.*

Two of Chase's top security operatives stood to attention at the door of the waiting room, four more coordinating with Jag's special envoy outside the building and outside the delivery suite.

'I'm sure she's fine,' Alexa offered tentatively, a wary expression clouding her eyes. She was only trying to make him feel better so why wasn't he holding her? Comforting her? Taking comfort *from* her?

'Coffee.' Milena returned, bearing three steaming mugs. 'The café is closed at this time, so it's vending machine only, I'm afraid, but what can you do?'

'Alexa doesn't drink coffee at night,' he said absently.

'I will tonight,' she said, straightening to go to his sister. 'I think I'd drink anything right now. Thanks for thinking of it.'

'I needed to do something and since Sherlock here—' Milena gestured to the Chase security expert Rafe had asked to stay with her during the whole proceedings '—wouldn't let me go for a walk, or go find a decent café, that's it.'

The security operative's expression didn't change as he handed over a bag of snacks to Milena.

She took it begrudgingly. 'And snacks. Anyone want one?'

Remembering how much fun he'd had feeding Alexa chocolates they'd bought that day at the market, his eyes cut to hers. As if her mind had deviated down the same path, her eyes turned smoky.

Breathing hard, he deliberately turned to his sister before he pulled Alexa into an unlocked supply closet and rid himself of all this tension with something stronger than coffee.

When he glanced back, Alexa had her bottom lip between her teeth and was staring at the floor. Before he could go to her a nurse pushed through the glass door.

Rafe's heart rose to his mouth.

The nurse smiled. 'It's a girl,' she said. 'And mother and baby are both healthy and doing well.'

A noisy breath shuddered out of his lungs. His sister whooped with joy and Alexa had a hand on her heart.

'Can we see them?'

'Of course. Her Majesty asked for all of you to come through.'

Almost dazed at the notion that he was an uncle, Rafe followed his sister and wife into the delivery suite.

The room was quiet as they entered, Regan reclining in the bed while Jag held a small bundle wrapped in white. For a woman who had just given birth, Regan looked awfully good. Not that Rafe had ever seen a woman straight after giving birth before.

'Oh, my… She's adorable,' Milena cooed. 'Congratulations.'

Grinning from ear to ear, Jag handed the precious bundle to his sister.

'I'm so grateful, Rafe,' Regan said, her brown eyes tired but filled with joy. 'Your brother completely lost it in my hour of need. If you hadn't stepped up I probably would have given birth on the dessert trolley.'

Jag scoffed at the very idea and Rafe turned away from the loved-up couple—only to freeze when he saw Alexa.

At some point Milena had passed the newborn over to her and she had his niece cradled against her chest, an adoring expression on her face.

A tight fist wrapped around his heart and squeezed. For a moment he couldn't breathe. Her long hair had drifted over one shoulder, glossy and black, her face a mask of serenity. It was like the time he'd first set eyes on her, another bolt of lightning hitting him square between the eyes, followed quickly by the sure knowledge that he could look at this woman for the rest of his life and never grow tired of it.

'Do you want to hold her?'

Somehow, Alexa was in front of him. Rafe frowned. *For the rest of his life?*

He saw her eyes widen. 'You've gone pale. If you don't want to…'

'No.' He kept his gaze on the baby in her arms. 'I'll hold her.'

As if he was standing on the outside looking in, he took the baby and cradled her in his arms. She was so tiny. So dainty. This perfect little being that was both vulnerable and needy. Taking in the glow on both her parents' faces, he knew that she would always be loved. She'd never have cause to feel insecure or abandoned by those she needed the most.

What would it be like if this was his child? His and Alexa's?

Emotion, thick and unwelcome, clogged his throat. Those feelings he'd had for her earlier increased tenfold. Feelings he'd never had for a woman before. Previously, his life had always seemed so clear-cut. One thing had led on to another and he'd never questioned it. He'd just gone with it and cared little about the outcome. But he cared now, he realised. He cared very much.

Alexa had never felt more like running than she did right now. When she had passed the baby to Rafe all she'd thought about was how it would feel if that tiny angel belonged to both of them. The chilly expression on his face told her that he most definitely had not been thinking the same thing.

As a result the car ride back to the apartment had been quiet, as if they were both lost in their own thoughts. But it wasn't a happy quiet as it should have been after the safe arrival of a baby. It was fraught with unspoken emotions. It was as if all the closeness of the past week had fallen away as if it had never existed. And perhaps it hadn't outside her own imagination.

As soon as they arrived at the apartment Alexa didn't wait around to see what Rafe intended to do; instead she headed for the spare room she'd been allocated and pulled her suitcase out of the walk-in wardrobe.

'What are you doing?'

Heart thumping, Alexa turned and blinked at him. His eyes were unreadable as he took in her suitcase and the clothing in her hands.

'Packing.'

'It's nearly midnight.'

'I know.' She flashed him a bright smile. 'Your odd hours must have rubbed off on me.'

Intensely aware of him watching her, she kept her movements smooth and unruffled as she folded a shirt and placed it in the case.

'I thought you were staying an extra week.'

'I was but then I remembered that I have a number of

meetings booked in for Monday that I can't miss.' She knew she was rambling but she couldn't seem to take a breath deep enough to oxygenate her brain.

'Get your father to attend them.'

'I can't. I'm sorry. I didn't think it through enough when you asked me to stay earlier. How beautiful is your niece, though? I love the name, Jana. It really suits her.'

'Forget the baby,' he growled. 'And leave the damn clothes where they are.' His hands descended on her shoulders as he turned her to face him, his jaw tight. 'I need you, Alexa. I need to touch you. I need to make love to you.'

There was something in his eyes Alexa had never seen before. A depth of emotion she knew had come from experiencing anxiety about the unexpected birth of his niece. It had affected her too, making her want to find space so she could process everything. But she could no more deny Rafe than she could stop the cycles of the moon.

Gazing up at him, she let her eyes drift over the hard planes of his face. This was what happened, she reminded herself brokenly, when you opened yourself up to uncertainty. You got hurt.

Because she had to go. She had to return to Berenia and pick up the reins of her normal life. She had to get back to what she knew, not only because it was what they had agreed upon from the start, but because she would only be staying an extra week in the vain hope that Rafe's feelings for her would change.

And she wouldn't torture herself like that. Not a second time. And not with a man who already had too much of her heart, little did he know it.

'Stay.' He cupped her face in his hands.

Alexa's heart felt as if it had just cleaved in two at the look in his eyes, the anguish of her own emotions like a chokehold around her throat. She so desperately wanted to tell him how she felt, tell him that if he needed her she'd be his for ever, but fortunately he kissed her and she stopped thinking altogether. Stopped trying to make this into something that it wasn't and gave into the passion between them, winding her arms around his neck and holding him tight for the last time.

When he woke in the morning Rafe knew she was gone. There was an emptiness in the room, a silence in his apartment he hadn't felt since before she had arrived.

An icy feeling of disappointment entered his heart, followed by a hot rush of anger. Of course she had left like this. Stealing away in the middle of the night as if she'd never even been here. He'd known she'd wanted to go, and yet he'd asked her to stay anyway. No, *begged* her to stay. A futile exercise.

Thrusting back the covers, he pulled on his clothes and headed for the kitchen. She'd left a note. A pitiful piece of paper that thanked him for a wonderful week, asking him to call her if he needed her for anything.

As if he'd do that.

He might have had feelings for her last night, feelings that ran deeper than any he'd ever experienced before with any other woman, but that had only been because of the drama surrounding the birth of his niece. It had unlocked something inside him—some emotion that had made him think, for the barest second, that he was in fact in love with Alexa.

Thank God he hadn't told her that during the heat of their lovemaking during the night. Thank God he hadn't confused sex with emotion when that was all it had ever been.

Intense, yes. Controlling at times. But love…no. This wasn't love. This was white-hot fury that he'd allowed a woman to get under his skin and she'd walked out on him in the middle of the night.

Had she thought he couldn't handle seeing her leave? That he'd try and stop her?

He wouldn't have. Not a second time.

CHAPTER TEN

RAFE GLARED AT the pile of paperwork on his desk as if the fierceness of his stare might get it done without him having to actually do anything. The promise of spring had completely left London, and rain lashed the windows of his office as if some angry god were throwing spears from the sky.

Not that he cared. He wasn't planning to leave any time soon and when he did he'd just be going home to an empty apartment.

Still, the gloom of the exterior seemed to invade the office, casting a dim glow that not even the bright lights inside could drive away.

Another email pinged into his inbox just as Hannah knocked on his door. Knowing that his EA would be harder to ignore, he turned towards the door, his jaw clenching when instead of Hannah standing in his doorway it was Milena in a bright pink coat, her hair cut into an edgy long bob.

He'd successfully dodged his family prior to Jag flying Regan and his precious daughter, Princess Jana, home by explaining that he was coming down with something and hadn't wanted to infect the baby. Which had been true. He'd felt like death warmed up for the past eight days. But now his sister had caught up with him.

'I thought you had left for New York,' he said pleasantly, deciding that heading her off at the pass was his best game opener.

'I had some things to finish up in Oxford before I left.' She strolled closer and flopped down in the chair opposite his desk. 'Then Hannah staged an intervention so here I am.'

Rafe frowned. 'Hannah did what?'

'Staged an intervention.' Milena's eyes moved over his face with deliberate slowness. 'I have to confess I can see why she did. You look awful.'

'I haven't shaved for—' he couldn't remember '—a few days. That hardly constitutes awful.'

'You haven't slept for a few days either, if the circles beneath your eyes are anything to go by.'

'Forgot to moisturise.'

'Ha! What's up?' Her voice went soft, her gaze following suit. Rafe ground his teeth together.

'Work,' he intoned. 'Now, is there any other reason for your visit?'

'How's Alexa?'

She reached for the glass paperweight on his desk and started fiddling with it.

His eyes narrowed at her innocuous tone. 'Is this one of your trick questions?'

He hadn't spoken to Alexa since she'd walked out of his life and he couldn't be sure if Milena knew that or not.

'No, this is me trying to ease into the conversation without getting my head bitten off.' She gave a sigh. 'I know Alexa is back in Berenia. Jag told me.'

'Did he also tell you why?'

'He told me that your marriage wasn't all that it seemed, if that's what you mean.'

Rafe gave a harsh bark of laughter. 'Always the diplomat, our brother.' He ran a hand through his hair. 'Look, he's right. Alexa and I married for political reasons and, according to recent reports, it seems to be working. I'm considering it my good deed for Santara.'

'Sorry, I'm not buying it,' Milena said bluntly. 'I know you, Rafe. You didn't just marry her for political reasons. It was real. I was there. I saw you both say your vows to each other. I saw you kiss her at the altar.'

The last thing he wanted was to remember kissing Alexa and he turned back to his computer. 'It's done, Milena. In three thousand, four hundred and thirty-two hours we'll be divorced.'

'Oh, Rafe.'

Pushing out of his chair in frustration, Rafe glared at his sympathetic sister before stalking to the window. He angled himself against the window, wishing he was standing out there so that the icy blasts could numb the sudden pain in his chest.

'You really, really love her, don't you?' Milena prodded gently.

'If this is love you can have it,' he growled. 'Next time I accuse you of the same thing you can throw this back in my face.'

'I don't want to throw this back in your face. I want to help you fix it. But I think you're afraid.'

'Really?' He didn't try to keep the sneer from his voice. 'First Alexa, and now you. What exactly do you think I'm afraid of?'

'Feeling. Love.'

Rafe scoffed. 'Love doesn't exist.' Even if for a brief moment he had thought he'd felt it for Alexa. 'And if you go around thinking it does you'll experience a world of pain.'

'Like we did as kids? I was young when Mum left but I remember how upset you were. You punched a hole in the wall, remember? You broke two knuckles and had to have your hand bandaged for six weeks.'

'How do you know I punched the wall?'

'I saw you. And ever since then, it seems to me, you've closed your heart off to everyone around you. Including me and Jag.'

Rafe gave her a bleak look. 'I'm always there for you if you need me, you know that.'

'I do.' She touched his arm. 'But you won't let us be there for you when you need us.'

'That's because I don't need anyone.'

But the words rang hollow inside his heart. If he didn't need anyone why didn't he feel okay with Alexa leaving? Why did his life seem so colourless all of a sudden?

Rafe swore.

Milena smiled. 'I know love isn't a comfortable concept for you but she loves you too.'

'How would you know?'

'The same way I know you love her. It's the way you look at each other. Like the other person is the most perfect person in the world for you. Jag and Regan have the same thing going on, and I swear one day I want someone to look at me the way you two look at your wives.'

Fear made him want to snap at her and say it wasn't true but, unfortunately, what she said fitted. It explained the hard lump in his throat on the morning he'd woken to find Alexa gone, and the hollow feeling inside him every day since. It explained why for the first time in his adult life he didn't want to get out of bed in the morning and face the day.

Rafe let his head fall into his hands and acknowledged what he'd always known to be true. He loved his wife. He loved Alexa, and it wasn't going to go away.

He remembered noticing her at a formal function when

she had been a shy teenager on the verge of womanhood. Even then there had been something compelling about her that had held his attention. Something about her that had made him want to protect her.

But her loving him in return?

'I think you're forgetting that she left, Milena. If you love someone you don't walk out on them in the middle of the night.'

'Like our mother?' she asked softly. 'Alexa isn't our mother, Rafe. And who knows what would have happened if our father had gone after her? Maybe she would have come back and our life would have turned out very differently.'

'I don't know—'

'And you won't if you give up.'

Those words jolted something deep inside him. 'I don't give up.'

His sister's brow arched. 'So why haven't you asked her why she left instead of presuming that you already know the answer?'

Because he was petrified of stuffing things up and feeling like a fool. Because he was petrified of feeling even worse than he did now. If that was even possible.

'How did you get to be so smart?'

'Observing two thick-headed brothers my whole life.'

Rafe gave her a faint smile and palmed his keys. 'I owe you one,' he said, heading for the door.

'I know.' She grinned broadly. 'And I'll be sure to collect on it.'

Alexa flicked through the pages of notes Nasrin had printed out for her. She was up to page twenty of fifty so she really needed to get a wriggle on if she was going to at least know something of the details about the one hundred guests who would be attending tonight's trade dinner. Usually she would have done this already, but she couldn't seem to muster the enthusiasm for it right now.

She knew what was wrong. She'd been back in Berenia for just over a week and nothing felt right. Not that anyone would guess. She'd upped her game face and had been putting on a good front. Had been trying to convince herself that it was silly to feel bad about something that had only been temporary to begin with. Which was exactly what she'd said to Nasrin when she'd been confronted with her EA's crestfallen face.

'But I was sure it was going to work out,' Nasrin had moaned when she'd returned *sans* Rafe. 'The way you looked at each other at the wedding. *That* kiss.'

The way Alexa remembered it, Rafe had been horrified to see her walk down the aisle, and she'd been similarly placed—or rather displaced—so she had no idea what Nasrin was talking about.

It had taken half an hour of convincing, but finally Nasrin had gone quiet on the subject, or perhaps she'd gone quiet because she'd had no choice. Either way, Alexa had been relieved to not have to talk about Rafe.

Her father had naturally asked where her husband was and when he planned to move to Berenia, but Alexa had put him off too, turning the topic of the conversation to business to distract him, all the while knowing that she really needed to come clean about her marriage sooner rather than later.

And she would. She'd just needed another week or so to mourn in private before she closed the 'Rafe' chapter of her life. She supposed it had been cowardly to sneak out of his apartment while he'd been asleep, but at the time she hadn't cared. She'd just wanted it to be easy. And she'd left him a note. *Thanks for everything. Call if you need me.*

Of course he hadn't called; she hadn't expected that he would. And that was okay, because that was easier too.

'Are you ready, Your Highness?'

Alexa glanced at Nasrin and gave a silent groan. She was still on page twenty, the illness she'd been fighting since her return to Berenia making her feel dizzy at times. 'I haven't quite finished the notes you made. Is there anything in particular I should be aware of? Any topics of conversation I need to avoid?'

Nasrin rattled off a couple of things for her to consider but Alexa had to force herself to concentrate. Don't mention climate change to the Minister of the Russian Interior, and remember to congratulate the Ambassador of France on their latest election results, and absolutely steer clear of the Prince of Tongase because he would bend her ear back about export deals given half a chance.

Logging the details in her memory, Alexa gave her reflection a quick once-over. She'd opted for a simple navy blue sheath tonight and pinned her hair back into a tightly coiled bun.

Her image said that she meant business and she did. The time she'd spent with Rafe lazing around in bed or exploring the countryside was like a distant dream that had happened to someone else.

'The King and Queen of Santara sent a thank you card for Princess Jana's gift. They won't be attending tonight, but that was to be expected. The King hasn't left his wife's side since the birth.'

Alexa gave Nasrin a small smile. The last thing she wanted to hear about was how much the King of Santara cared about his Queen. 'And my father?'

'He's waiting for you in the south parlour. Are you sure you're up to this, Your Highness? You look a little pale.'

'I'm fine.'

She wasn't fine. She wanted to lie down in her bed and go to sleep. Maybe for one hundred years. Smiling at the irony of how her mind had turned to a fairy tale, she shook her head. She'd been awakened by her very own Prince Charming—literally—but he still hadn't wanted her in the end. He hadn't even attempted to contact her since she'd left. Not that she'd wanted him to. A clean break was much better.

Heading to the south parlour, she knocked quietly before entering and found her father leaning against the fireplace. His eyes scanned her and he scowled. 'You don't look well.'

Alexa grimaced. 'Thank you, Father. The same goes for you.' Her father had been fighting a head cold since she'd returned, probably what she was struggling with herself, and should have been in bed. 'I'm more than happy to attend tonight's dinner without you if you'd rather rest.'

'I can rest when I'm dead,' her father argued. 'And you should have support tonight. That husband of yours should be here.'

Alexa had been hoping he wouldn't bring up Rafe's absence again but…so be it.

She gave a faint smile at the memory of the last time Rafe had muttered those words. Sealing his fate in agreeing to marry her.

But she couldn't think about Rafe right now, not in that way; she'd probably start leaking tears all over the place and her father would guess how devastated she was. But maybe now was the time to mention the true nature of her relationship with Rafe. That way, her father wouldn't have a lot of time to grill her about it, and it would give him time to process the details before they met up next.

Taking the bull by the horns, Alexa perched on the chair opposite the fireplace. 'Before we head down the stairs there's something I need to tell you about Prince Rafaele and myself. And I want you to know from the outset that the whole idea was mine so any complaints or issues you have should be solely directed at me.'

To give him his due, her father listened patiently as she gave him the CliffsNotes version as to what had happened, leaving out the part where she had fallen hopelessly in love with her husband and how he didn't love her back. That he would never love her back. Her father didn't need to know everything.

But she told him the rest. She told him about her proposal, and Rafe turning her down; she told him how they had never meant to actually go through with the wedding, and the marriage bargain they'd worked out between them. She also told him that Rafe had turned out to be nothing like she'd expected, and that he was actually a decent, hard-working man who cared deeply about those he loved. 'And now I'm back,' she said, struggling to remain composed. 'And, as you can see, ready to resume my duties.'

'I see. So what happens now?' he asked, his frown revealing how unimpressed he was with her actions.

'Now we stay married for five more months, and then quietly go our separate ways.'

'You should have told me this earlier.'

'Would you have listened?'

Previously, Alexa would never have asked her father such an impertinent question, but he needed to know that she wasn't the same person she had been before she'd married Rafe. She'd grown up in Rafe's arms and she didn't want to go back to the way things had been before. With her ostensibly being a yes person to please her father.

'Perhaps not,' he conceded. 'But I'm listening now.' He straightened his cuffs. 'However, it is time we went down to the receiving line. Our guests will be arriving at any moment.

'Of course. But Father...' Alexa mulled over her next words. 'I know you don't feel that I'm able to do this job alone, but I'm going to prove you wrong. I will make a worthy Queen of Berenia in Sol's stead.'

Her father stopped and frowned at her. 'I've never thought you incapable of being anything but an incredible leader of our people. But this is a lonely job, Alexa. It will be harder for you to find a suitable spouse once you become Queen, and I don't want you to rule alone. It's too hard.'

Her father's lined face turned weary and Alexa's heart jumped in alarm. 'Father—'

'I'm fine. Just... I miss your mother. And never more so than when you are opposite me looking as beautiful as she once was.'

'But I never knew that was how you felt.'

A faint smile twisted her father's lips. 'Why do you think I never remarried? There was no one to replace her. And I didn't want that for you. Rightly or wrongly, I didn't want you or Sol to become so attached to anyone that losing them would make you feel this empty.'

'Hence the reason you changed our nannies and tutors so often,' she said, finally understanding the logic behind that decision.

'I wanted you both to become more resilient than I felt at the time. Stronger. But you were hurt by love anyway, and then we lost Sol. I felt like I had failed you both.'

'Father—'

'Let me finish.' He grimaced as if explaining such deeply emotional issues was akin to having his skin flayed from his body. 'I thought that if I could force you to make a practical match it would save you from unnecessary heartache in the future. I can see that I was gravely mistaken about that. But finding you a life match was never about your capability to do your job. I hope you believe that.'

Alexa's stomach clenched tight. 'I don't know what to say.'

'There is nothing to say. You should have a strong man by your side to support you. And I hoped that Prince Rafaele would be that man.'

So had she. Or at least she had come to think that way. But while he was a very strong and compassionate man, he wasn't *her* strong and compassionate man. He might never be anyone's, given his need for independence and freedom from obligation.

Which was all she knew. Obligation and duty. Would those dual requirements always have to take precedence over love?

A lump lodged in her throat, threatening to defeat her composure once more, and once more she pushed it back. 'Shall we go?'

'Yes. It is time.'

Three hours later Alexa knew that if she didn't sit down very soon she would likely fall down.

The head cold she'd been fighting made it hard to focus on the group currently discussing the merits of trade taxes and border control.

Offering to email one of their party some of the ideas her team had come up with on tax reform, Alexa made her excuses and was considering going to find a dark room to hole up in when her eyes snagged on a figure in black at the entrance to the ballroom.

Unable to believe that it was really Rafe, the hairs on the back of her neck rose when his eyes found her.

His expression was grim, his clothes as beautifully cut as they had been the night at the Children's Charity ball. But there was a wildness to him, and she realised that he hadn't shaved, giving him an even more dangerous edge than usual.

The guests he would have bowled over if they hadn't moved out of his way thought so too, their curious glances turning to wary alertness as they quickly moved out of his way.

Alexa only noticed them peripherally, her whole being focused entirely on Rafe.

He stopped directly in front of her, his frown darkening. 'Your hair is up.'

'Yes.' A wave of dizziness at having him standing in front of her made her instinctively reach out for him.

Rafe swore under his breath, taking hold of her elbow. 'And you're unwell.'

Shaking off her initial shock, Alexa cleared her throat, easing her arm out of his hold. 'Just a head cold. But you look…' Gorgeous. Commanding. And so desirable she wanted to throw herself into his arms and never let go. It seemed so unfair when she felt like death warmed up. 'Almost like your usual self.'

'I haven't been my usual self since we met, Princess,' he answered cryptically. 'That aside, I'm taking you out of here.'

Seriously rattled to have him here, Alexa shook her head. 'I can't leave yet. The speeches haven't happened.'

'Are you giving a speech?'

'No.'

'Then you're leaving.'

Alexa frowned. 'Rafe, you can't just turn up here and—'

'Prince Rafaele? So good of you to join us.'

Feeling a horrible sense of *déjà vu*, Alexa nearly groaned at the sound of her father's combative voice behind her, sure that he wouldn't back down now that he knew the truth of their marriage.

'You might not think that in a minute, Your Majesty,' Rafe answered. 'My wife is sick, and I'm taking her out of here.'

'Really?' King Ronan raised a brow. 'You've remembered that you have a wife, then?'

'I never forgot.' Rafe held her father's stare. 'Not even for a minute.'

Unable to decipher the silent code going on between the two men she was surprised to see her father nod his assent. 'Good. I told her she was not well. She needs to lie down.'

'I can make my own decisions,' Alexa said hotly, her voice low so as not to cause a scene.

'You can,' Rafe agreed. 'But we need to talk and I'd rather not do it in a room full of interested people.'

Suddenly aware that they were on the receiving end of about one hundred pairs of eyes, Alexa groaned. 'Okay, fine.'

Holding her head high, she started forward, her legs so shaky that she might have tripped over her skirts if Rafe hadn't caught her up in his arms without breaking stride.

'Put me down,' she urged. 'You're causing a scene.'

'Probably.' He gave her one of his devil-may-care grins. 'It is something I excel at, it seems.'

Alexa caught the surprised glance of the footman who scrambled to open a side door for them and just managed to resist burying her face against Rafe's neck.

'Which way are your rooms?' he asked gruffly.

'I'm not going to my room with you,' she said, knowing that if she did she really might throw herself at him. 'And I need you to put me down.'

Obliging her this time, he lowered her to the carpeted floor in one of the side rooms off the ballroom.

'Thank you.' She smoothed her hands down her dress, aware that she was in danger of placing meaning on his actions that probably didn't exist. 'What I need is to know what you're doing here. And why you look like you haven't had any sleep in a week.' Because this close, she could see that his eyes were not as bright as they usually were.

He grimaced. 'You and Milena should form a club. She thinks I look terrible as well.'

'I didn't say you looked terrible…but…why are you here, Rafe? What do you want?'

'Are you so desperate to get rid of me?' he asked softly.

No. She wasn't desperate to get rid of him. On the contrary she wanted him to stay. She wanted—

'Actually you have Milena to thank for my presence here tonight.'

'Oh.' A shaft of disappointment speared into her chest, bursting the little bubble of hope she'd been nursing that he'd come to Berenia for her. 'I'm not sure I understand. Does she need something from me?'

'No, Princess.' Rafe gave her a faint smile, his eyes so dark they were almost black. 'Milena doesn't want anything from you. She came to my office today and pointed out that I'm an idiot.'

'Rafe, I'm sure she didn't mean—'

'She did.' He took her face between his hands. 'Because she knows that I'm totally and utterly in love with you.'

Oh, God…

Alexa groaned softly. She knew Milena would have meant well, but she really wished the other woman hadn't interfered. 'I'm sorry she said that.' She shook her head, her hands trembling. 'She mentioned the same thing to me at Jag's party but I knew not to believe her. I knew—'

'You should have believed her.' Rafe placed a finger against her lips. 'Because she's right. I do love you.'

Alexa's eyes flew to his. 'How is that possible? At the

hospital, when I handed you Princess Jana, you looked at me as if you never wanted to see me again.'

'That was shock. When I saw you holding the baby all I could think about was how it would feel if Jana had been ours.'

'You did?' Her eyes turned watery because she felt so *emotional* hearing him say that. 'But you said you don't need love in your life.'

'I *didn't* want love in my life,' he corrected. 'Which is why I didn't go after you when you left. It was easier to let you go than to face how much I had come to need you. Especially since my mother left in the middle of the night and I woke the next morning to find her gone.'

'Oh, Rafe, I'm so sorry I reminded you of that. I didn't know what else to do. I was so afraid I'd blurt out how I felt and that you'd... It was cowardly.'

'I didn't exactly give you a lot of reasons to stay. I am now.' His hand smoothed over her jaw, tilting her face up to his. 'Tell me what you didn't want to blurt out last night.'

Alexa's smile was tremulous. 'That I love you, of course. That I think I've always loved you.'

Rafe crushed her lips beneath his, and for a moment all Alexa could do was cling to him. Then reality intruded with a thud.

'Rafe, wait...' Her voice shook and her knees threatened to give out as she eased back. 'This can't work. You know it can't. Your life is in London and I'm the future Queen, and unless I abdicate to my cousin I—'

'Abdicate?' Rafe took her face between his hands. 'Princess, nobody's abdicating. You're perfect for this role.'

'Then what are you suggesting? That we have a long-distance marriage?'

'Alexa, you're my wife. You're going to stay my wife,

and I'm going to be your husband and support you in any way that I can. In Berenia.'

'You'll move to Berenia?'

He gave her a wide smile. 'What can I say? I'm a glutton for punishment. But my life is no longer in London. It's wherever you are.'

'But your business, your clubs…'

'I can run my business from anywhere if I choose to but seriously, Alexa, you're not hearing me. If you want it, my life is with you and wherever you are.'

'If I want it?'

'Yes. Do you? Do you want to spend the rest of your life with me as much as I want to spend the rest of mine with you?'

'Yes.' Finally giving into the insane level of happiness welling up inside her, Alexa laughed. 'Yes, yes, yes.'

She let out a shriek as Rafe wrapped his arms around her and swung her into the air. 'Rafe, I love you so much it scares me.'

'Only because you haven't come to trust how I feel yet. But you will. I plan to tell you every day so that you'll never feel insecure about your self-worth ever again.'

'I can't quite believe this,' she said, holding him tight. 'You were supposed to be the most unsuitable man on the planet.'

Rafe eased back so that he could look down into her face. 'And now?'

'Now I never want to let you go.' Giddy with emotion, she reached up onto her toes to kiss him and then pulled back at the last minute. 'We shouldn't. You'll catch my cold.'

'Princess, I don't think you have a cold. Your nose isn't even red.'

'My nose doesn't have to be red to have a cold. But I

am sick. I feel dizzy sometimes and my stomach is unsettled a lot.'

'Have you seen a doctor?'

'No.'

'Then you should because I don't think you're ill. I think
you're pregnant.'

'No, I'm not. I…' Alexa's eyes widened incredulously;
her mind swung back to when her last period was due.
She was late but in her misery she hadn't even noticed.
'I can't be.'

'There were a couple of times I didn't put a condom
on right away.'

Alexa stared at him wide-eyed. 'Oh, God.' She clapped
her hand over her mouth. 'What will we do?'

Rafe gave her a half smile. 'We'll have a baby.'

'I mean, will you mind if it's true?'

'Absolutely not,' he said huskily. 'I need to catch up to
Jag, but…' His eyes grew wary. 'Do *you* want a baby?'

Knowing by the tense set of his shoulders that he was
no doubt remembering his own childhood, Alexa clasped
his face in her hands. 'If we have made a baby together
I'll be the happiest woman in the world. I love you. I want
to have your babies, and I intend to smother them in love
and attention for ever.'

Rafe gave her a slow grin. 'Then how about you take
me your room now, just in case I'm wrong. We can get to
work immediately.'

Alexa threw her arms around his neck. 'With pleasure.'

EPILOGUE

RAFE HADN'T BEEN WRONG. Exactly two hundred and seventy days after their wedding Zane and Tobias had been born. Now they were rambunctious one-year-olds.

'Milena, can you grab Jana and Zane before one or both of them climb into the fountain again?' Rafe asked, scooping his remaining twin up and tucking him under his arm in a football hold before he could think about joining his brother and cousin.

'On it!' Milena yelled, pretending to be a wicked witch as she ran after the two children, making them squeal with delight.

Seeing the fun his twin and older cousin were having, Tobias let rip a loud squeal of indignation.

'Looks like you have your hands full!' Jag laughed, burping one of his own newborn twins against his shoulder. 'Where's Alexa?'

'Grabbing a coffee with Nasrin while she checks in with her father. Okay, buddy.' Rafe swung Tobias to the ground and waited for his little legs to steady beneath him. 'Go pull some more of Aunty Milena's hair out. We don't like the colour right now anyway.'

Tobias let out a war whoop and took off as fast as his legs would carry him. Rafe gave a loud sigh of relief. 'This parenting gig is harder than tending to a room full of Berenians with a chip on their shoulder.'

'Well, he is half Berenian,' Jag observed, patting his daughter's back.

Rafe gave him a bemused glance. 'Lucky for you that they are. Thanks to me, everything has completely settled down between our nations now. The Berenians love me.'

'Yeah, right.' His brother grinned back. 'And, speaking of Berenia, how's the new business venture?'

'Great. The new university is so popular we have to build more student accommodation to cope with demand.'

'You don't miss the nightclub scene?'

Since moving to Berenia, Rafe had sold off most of his clubs, keeping a few that Hannah had stepped into running for him. He now worked on restoring old buildings and returning them to their former glory and loved it.

He'd also opened up to his sister and brother, forging a bond with them that was deeper than ever.

'Everything is great,' he said, and meaning it.

'And you wouldn't swap it, right?'

Knowing Jag shared his sentiments, Rafe shook his head. 'Not in a heartbeat.'

'Where are the twins?'

His wife's voice from behind had Rafe swinging around. 'Princess.' Immediately at ease with her by his side, Rafe drew her into his arms and kissed her. 'The twins are over by the fountain with Milena. How's your father?'

'Determined to reign until he's ninety.'

Rafe laughed, kissing her again. 'I'm okay with that. The more time I get you all to myself the happier I am.'

'You'll always have me to yourself,' she promised huskily.

Jag mumbled something about finding his own wife before heading inside, but Rafe only had eyes for Alexa.

Kissing her again, he felt her move against him and groaned softly against her lips. 'You know accepting your marriage proposal was the best bargain I ever made, don't you?'

'You didn't accept my proposal,' Alexa scoffed. 'My father forced you to marry me.'

'Did he?' Rafe gave her an enigmatic look he knew would drive her crazy.

'Yes.' She glared at him. 'He did, didn't he?'

Rafe's grin widened. 'Have you ever known me to do anything that I didn't want to do?'

'No.' Her green gaze narrowed menacingly. 'Are you saying you wanted to marry me back then?'

'Let's just say no other man was ever going to have you after the way you kissed me that night.'

'You mean the way you kissed me,' she huffed.

'Want to argue about it inside?' he asked suggestively.

Alexa glanced anxiously over at the twins. 'How long do you think we have before the boys need us again?'

Rafe grabbed her hand and tugged her towards the Summer Palace. 'Long enough for me to show you how much I love you.'

'Oh, good.' Alexa's grin made his heart catch. 'My favourite thing.'

* * * * *

CINDERELLA'S ROYAL SEDUCTION

DANI COLLINS

My long-suffering family always deserves a dedication for cheerleading me in this career I've chosen, but when it comes to the nuts and bolts of actually getting a book written there are two people I absolutely cannot do without.

First and foremost, my editor. I've been lucky enough to work with Laurie Johnson on and off in the seven years I've been published. Thank you for helping me turn so many pumpkins into carriages, this book very much included.

Second and no less important, my RMT, Loretta. Thank you for keeping the carpal tunnel and shoulder gremlins at bay, for being a fan of romance, and for recommending I visit Sparkling Hills in Vernon, the spa that inspired the one in this book.

PROLOGUE

JUST ONCE, CASSIOPEIA BRODEUR wished she could be given enough time to sit and think before having to react to whatever catastrophe her stepmother, Maude, had set in motion.

She really wished that when she'd been fifteen and thinking she was welcoming her stepsisters into her family, she hadn't told them her friends called her Sopi.

"Soapy?" Nanette and Fernanda spoke English as their fourth language, but they'd heard the pun and laughed hysterically.

Seven years later, all of Sopi's childhood friends, including the ones who'd given her the nickname when they'd been in grade school, had moved on to university and world travel, interesting jobs and serious relationships and *cities*.

While Sopi was still here in Lonely Lake, scrubbing up after her spoiled stepfamily and the guests of the hotel and spa that bore her name.

Why couldn't Maude and the girls shove off back to Europe and quit destroying what was left of her life? They certainly made no effort to hide their disdain for this "backwater village" in the remote wilderness of the Canadian Rockies.

Oh, right, they had run through all of Sopi's father's

money and had nowhere left to turn. Yet they seemed determined to drive this place into ruin, too.

"*All* the reservations?" Sopi repeated with disbelief. "You canceled *all* of March?"

"Yes."

"On purpose?"

"Sopi." Maude used her most hideously patronizing tone. "We can't have families with children running around when we're entertaining royalty, can we? And we'll need the rooms."

"Royalty?" Sopi asked with a choke of hysterical laughter. "Is that a figure of speech?" The odd aging pop star turned up—emphasis on *odd*—but real celebrities with real money went to Banff or Whistler for their spring skiing.

"Rhys Charlemaine is the prince of Verina."

"Never heard of him," Sopi said flatly, even though it rang a distant bell. She barely had time to keep up with weather reports and the latest safety regulations, though. She didn't follow gossip on fading royalty.

"Honestly, Sopi. Your lack of education." Maude shook her coiffed silver head in despair.

Was she referring to the education that hadn't been paid for because instead Sopi's father's money had been used to keep Nanette and Fernanda in boarding school in Switzerland? The girls' absence had turned out to be a blessing, so Sopi didn't complain much about it, but honestly.

"Why on earth would a prince come here?" Sopi asked.

"Because I've arranged a week of heli-skiing for him."

With what money?

Sopi wanted to scream or maybe cry. She glanced

longingly beyond the windows where February skies were an intense blue over blinding white slopes across the valley. Last season, she'd skied once on the small commercial hill on the far side of the lake. This year she hadn't had a single opportunity—too busy trying to keep the spa afloat.

"And as for the accommodation," Maude continued absently, "the girls will move from the penthouse so he can use it, but they'll stay on the top floor. His entourage will take the rest of the rooms there."

"His *entourage*? Please tell me this isn't *all* complimentary." Sopi knew it would be and felt sick. Sick. Maude never let her peek at the books, but Sopi wasn't blind or stupid. She knew they were in the red and bleeding more every day.

"Of course we won't charge him." Maude's scoffing tone chided her as Silly Sopi. "This is exceedingly good exposure for us. Everyone will want to come here, especially while he's in residence. I've arranged a decent chef. That's long overdue." Her pointed look blamed Sopi for not having made that happen sooner, and Sopi couldn't even imagine what it was going to cost. "You'll need to hire more staff for the treatments."

"Maude." Sopi tried one more time, even though this argument had never made an impact. "There is no one to hire."

The occasional adventurous cosmetician or massage therapist joined them for a season, but the isolation of Lonely Lake wasn't for everyone. Plus, Maude and her daughters were a special kind of hell to work for. Their incessant demands and tantrums over inconveniences like having to wait for deliveries of a desired shade of nail polish impacted the spa's ability to retain qualified employees.

"You always make things harder than they are," Maude sighed. "People will beg to work for gratuities if you tell them who will be staying here."

The spa's bread-and-butter clientele were retirees soaking their arthritis in the hot mineral pools at an affordable price. Sopi couldn't deny that a high-profile guest would fill rooms, but, "Seniors on fixed incomes aren't known for their generous tips. If this prince and his cronies—"

"*Cronies?*" Maude's head came up. "Sopi, he's *thirty*. Unmarried. And it's time he changed that." Maude had been fingering through a collection of fabric swatches. She held up a square of cranberry silk. "Would this clash with Nanette's hair, do you think?"

As was often the case when Sopi spoke with her stepmother, Sopi's brain was racing to catch up. Even as she tried to formulate arguments against whatever Maude was demanding, she knew the struggle was futile. Her stepmother had gained control of the spa when Sopi's father died and kept a firm grasp on it. Sopi didn't have the resources to fight her for it, and Maude would no doubt clean out what was left of the spa's available cash to repulse an attack. Sopi would be bankrupt whether she won or lost.

Sopi's only choice was to try to keep the place solvent until she had enough in her savings account to mount a proper legal challenge. Maybe it was a fool's dream, but it kept her going.

So she was always mentally planning how to mitigate or adapt to or accomplish whatever ridiculous thing Maude insisted had to happen while doing the math, trying to calculate when she would be able to put her foot down and hold her ground.

Today, amid that familiar scramble, Sopi's brain

crashed into Maude's end goal. Maude wanted to marry one of her daughters to a prince. To a man who lived in a kingdom—or was it a principality? Who cared? It was far, far away.

If one left, they all would.

A tentative ray of hope gleamed like a beacon at the end of a long, dark tunnel, breaking a smile across Sopi's face.

"You know what, Maude? You're right. This sounds like a tremendous opportunity. I'll start prepping for it." Sopi's pulse pounded so hard, her ears rang.

"Thank you," Maude said in a beleaguered tone that echoed with, *It's about time.* "Leave moving the girls out of the penthouse until the last moment. They don't want to be inconvenienced any more than necessary."

Sopi nearly choked on her tongue, but she bit down on it instead. If she played her cards right, and if she threw her stepsisters in front of this Prince Charlemaine or whoever the heck he was, then maybe, just maybe, she could free herself of her stepfamily forever.

It was such an exciting prospect, she hummed cheerfully as she left Maude's office and headed upstairs to strip beds and clean toilets.

CHAPTER ONE

RHYS CHARLEMAINE WOKE before the sun was up. Before any of his staff began creeping into his suite with fresh coffee and headlines and messages that required responses.

He didn't ring for any of them. What privacy he had was precious. Plus, he had withstood enough bustle and fussing yesterday when he and his small army of assistants, bodyguards and companions had arrived. The owner of this place, Maude Brodeur, had insisted on personally welcoming him. She had hung around for nearly two hours, dropping names and reminiscing about her first husband, whom she had cast as a contemporary equal to Rhys's father—which he wasn't. He had been a distant cousin to a British earl and largely unknown.

Blue blood was blue blood, however, and she had clearly been using the association to frame her pretty, well-educated daughters as suitable for a man next in line to a throne. Her daughters had perched quietly while she rattled on, but there'd been an opportunistic light in their eyes.

Rhys sighed. If he had a euro for every woman who wanted to search his pockets for a wedding ring, he would have more money than all the world's tech billionaires combined.

Instead, he had a decent fortune built on shrewd investments, some of it in tech, but much of it in real estate development. Half of it belonged to his brother, Henrik. Rhys handled their private interests while Henrik looked after the throne's finances. They each had their lane, but they drove them side by side, always protecting the other's flank. Rhys might be the spare, a prince to his brother the king, but they were a solid unit.

Even so, he and Henrik didn't always agree. This detour to a tiny off-grid village in Canada had had his brother lifting his brows with skepticism. "Sounds too good to be true," had been Henrik's assessment.

Rhys's antennae were up, as well. On the surface, the property in a valley reminiscent of Verina's surrounding Alps appeared ripe for exploitation, especially with its hot-spring aquifer. That alone made it a unique energy opportunity. The remote location would be a challenge, of course, but there was a modest ski hill across the lake. It drew locals and guests of this hotel, but could also be picked up for a song and further developed.

Maude was claiming she wanted to keep the sale of the spa quiet for "personal reasons," pretending she didn't need the money. Normally, Rhys would steer clear of someone attempting to pull the wool over his eyes. He had his own reason for accepting her invitation, however, and it had nothing to do with whether or not this place was a sound investment.

Rhys shifted his pensive gaze across the frozen lake, searching for answers that couldn't be solved with money and power. He needed a miracle, something he didn't believe in. He was a man of action who made his own destiny, but the only action available to him at the moment was a path littered with disloyalty to his brother, if not the crown.

He supposed he should be thankful the doctors had finally discovered the reason Henrik and his wife, Elise, were failing to conceive. They'd caught Henrik's testicular cancer early enough that treatment had a reasonable chance of success. With luck, Rhys would not assume the throne. Not soon, at any rate, but Henrik would almost certainly be sterile.

That meant the task of producing future progeny to inherit the throne had fallen into Rhys's lap.

Which meant he needed a wife.

He tried not to dwell on how treasonous that felt. Henrik had worked tirelessly to regain their rightful place in Verina. Doing so had nearly cost him the woman he loved. The royalists who had supported their return from exile had expected Henrik to marry an aristocrat, not a diplomat's daughter. Somehow, Henrik had overcome their objections only to come up against the inability to make an heir.

Henrik and Elise deserved children. They would be excellent parents. Given everything Henrik had gone through, the throne ought to go to his child, not Rhys's.

None of this felt right to him.

A blue glow came on below his window, dragging Rhys out of his brooding. The lights in the free-form mineral bath illuminated the mist rising off the placid water, beckoning him.

His security detail had reported that the guest register was swollen with female names, many of them bearing titles or related to one. He wasn't surprised his intention to ski here had been leaked to the press, drawing the usual suspects. He had counted on Maude being canny enough to see the value in a full house. It made the place look successful and ensured she would still have a nice influx of cash even if he turned down her offer to purchase. She might even have thought a bevy of beautiful naked women would sway him to buy.

It wouldn't, but he appreciated the expediency of having a curated selection of eligible women brought to one place for his consideration.

He had no choice but to marry and was down to his last moments of bachelorhood. He decided to make the most of them. He dropped the pajama pants he'd slipped on when he rose and left them on the floor, mostly to reassure his staff that he hadn't been kidnapped. He'd learned to pick up after himself during his years in exile with his brother. He was a passable cook and could trim his own beard, not that he did those things for himself anymore.

He was a prince again, one who had believed his primary function was to ensure his family's economic viability while his brother ruled their country and provided heirs. His responsibilities were expanding, though, and the one duty he would happily perform—taking his brother's place while he battled his illness—was not open to him.

Heart heavy, he shrugged on his monogrammed robe, stepped into his custom-sewn slippers, searched out the all-access card Maude had given him, then took the elevator to the treatment level.

Sopi was so tired, she thought she was hallucinating when the man appeared across the mist rising off the pool. The spa area wasn't yet open, and the locks were on a timer. The only means of entry was the use of a staff card, and she was the employee on shift. The man's robe wasn't hotel issue, either, but that wasn't too unusual. Frequent guests often brought their own robes so it was easier to track where they'd left them.

Even so, she'd never seen anyone show up in anything like that gorgeous crimson with gold trim and embroidered initials.

As she squinted her tired eyes at the man's stern profile and closely trimmed beard, she recognized—

Oh God. He was completely naked under that robe!

She should have looked away but didn't. *Couldn't*.

Through the steam rising off the pool, she watched him unbelt and open his robe, drop it off his shoulders to catch on his bent arms. The muscled globes of his bare butt appeared as he turned and slid free of the robe, draping it over the glass half wall that formed the rail around the pool. He was sculpted like an Olympic swimmer with broad shoulders, narrow hips and muscular thighs.

He pivoted back to face her across the pool, utterly, completely, gloriously naked. A shadow of hair accented the intriguing contours that sectioned his chest and abdomen, streaking out to dark nipples and arrowing down his eight-pack abs to—

He dived into the water, shallow and knife sharp, barely making a ripple.

She pushed her face into the stack of towels she held, no longer breathing as she tried to suppress her shock and abject mortification. She fought to push back a rising blush of hot embarrassment and something she didn't even recognize.

Because she had not only seen their special guest, the prince of Verina, in a private moment. She'd seen the crown jewels.

And of *course* she was standing on the far side of the pool where the spare caddy of clean towels was tucked beneath an overhang, next to the bar that operated in the summer months.

To escape, she would have to circle the deck, walk over the little bridge that separated the main pool from the portion that jutted out from the cliff and move past the robe he'd thrown over the rail near the glass doors into the building.

There was a small splash of water breaking as he surfaced near her feet.

"Good morning." His voice was surprised and carried the gravel of early morning.

Oh *God*. She made herself lift her face and briefly—very briefly—glanced his way.

Okay. Only his head and shoulders were visible. That ought to have made breathing possible, but dear Lord, he was good-looking. His cheekbones were carved marble above his sleek beard. Was he deliberately using the short, dark stubble to accentuate how beautiful his mouth was? Because it framed lips that managed to be both well defined and masculine, swirling wicked thoughts into her mind just looking at them. His hair was slicked back, his eyes laser blue and lazily curious.

"En français?" he tried.

"What? I mean, pardon? I mean, no. I speak English. Good morning," she managed *very* belatedly and clumsily.

At least he didn't know who she was. She had put on her one decent dress last night, planning to form part of the greeting party with Maude and her stepsisters. A last-minute mix-up with a delivery had had her changing into jeans and boots to drive two hours each way so she could fetch high-grade coffee beans and other groceries that Maude had ordered specifically for the prince's menu.

"I'm restocking towels." Not staring or tongue-tied or anything. She hurried to shove the stack into the caddy, snatching one back. "I'll leave this one with your robe. Our…um… European hour is actually…um…ten o'clock. At *night*."

"Euro…? Oh." The corner of his mouth dug in on one side. "Am I supposed to wear a swimsuit?"

"Most of our guests do." All of them. "Aside from the few who prefer to sauna au naturel. At *night*," she repeated.

"The sun hasn't come up. Technically, it's still night." He lifted a dark winged brow at the gleam of bright steel along the seam where pearly peaks met charcoal sky.

"Point taken." She drummed her fingers against her thigh, debated a moment, then decided to tease him right back. "But technically the pool isn't open yet. You're breaking our rules either way."

"What's the penalty? Because I don't expect any-one here packed a bikini top. Only a few will bother with bottoms. We don't wear them at the health spas at home. I expect that's where your 'European hour' label came from."

Pressed against the wall of the pool, he looked ex-actly like every other guest who might fold his arms against the edge and gaze at the view or strike up a friendly conversation with passing staff.

Except she knew he was naked, and his banter was flipping her heart and fanning the nervous excitement in her stomach. She hugged the single towel to her mid-dle, trying to still those butterflies.

"At least I understand why Maude didn't want chil-dren running around this week. Apparently, we're host-ing a nudist convention."

He smiled, the light in his eyes so warm she curled her toes in her sandals, unable to stem the shy smile that pulled at her own lips.

"You Americans are so adorably prudish."

Oh no, he didn't. She narrowed her eyes. "And you French are so—oh, I'm sorry. Are you not French?" She batted her lashes as his good humor blanked to affront.

Since Maude's announcement that he was coming here, she'd taken the time to learn that Verina was a small kingdom in the Alps between Switzerland, Germany and France. Verinians spoke all of those countries' languages and, having overcome an uprising twenty years ago that had had their neighbors sniffing and circling, trying to extend their borders to encompass Verina for the next fifteen years, were fiercely patriotic to the flag they still flew.

"I find people from *North* America to have very conservative views about sex and nudity," he clarified.

She nodded her forgiveness of his faux pas and explained, "We're not that prudish in Canada. We keep our clothes on because we're cold." She pointed at the lazy drift of tiny flakes hitting the steam off the pool and dissolving. Strangely, she wasn't feeling the chill nearly as much as she usually would, standing out here in the predawn frost. Heat radiated from her middle. Her joints were melting and growing loose.

"You must be in this pool often, though. You've never swum naked in it?"

"Never." She couldn't recall when she had last had a chance to swim at all. She vacuumed and scoured and restocked and never enjoyed the luxury she provided to everyone else.

If I can just get Maude and the girls out of here was her mantra. If she could take control of the books and balance them, quit financing trips and clothing for women who brought no value to the spa, only drama, she could relax instead of burning out.

"It's very freeing. You should try it."

"I'm sure it is." He had no idea of the constraints she was under, though.

"No time like the present."

As she met his gaze with a rueful smile, certain he was mocking her for her modesty, something in his gaze made her heart judder to a stop in her chest then kick into a different rhythm.

He was looking at her with consideration, as though he'd suddenly noticed something about her that had snagged one hundred percent of his attention. As though he was serious about wanting her to strip naked and jump in the pool with him.

More insistent tugs and pulls accosted her midsection. A flush of sensual heat streaked up from her tense stomach, warming her chest and throat and cheeks. Her breasts grew heavy and tight.

She *never* reacted to men—not like this, all receptive and intrigued. Her last date had been in high school and ended with a wet kiss that hadn't affected her nearly as strongly as this man's steady gaze. The dating pool in Lonely Lake was very small unless she wanted to get together with guests, and she didn't do that because they didn't stick around.

That's what this is, she realized, clunking back from a brief, floaty fantasy of a prince taking an interest in a nobody like her. This wasn't *real* flirty banter. He wasn't genuinely interested in her. He was only inviting her to join him in the way male guests occasionally did because she was *here*, not because he found her particularly attractive. How could he? She looked especially hellish this morning. She was frazzled and exhausted, no makeup, clothes rumpled as though she'd slept in them. Joke was on him. She *hadn't* slept.

Maybe this wasn't even happening. Maybe she would wake after being dragged from the igloo room and defrosted from a hypothermia-induced delirium.

"I'm sure you'll have plenty of company soon enough," she said in a strangled voice. She nodded upward at the windows lighting behind curtains as guests began to stir. "I'll check the saunas. They're banked at night, but I'll make sure they're up to temperature for you."

As the owner, Sopi could have asked that he wear a towel around the resort, but she didn't want to introduce herself. She was too embarrassed at thinking, even for a second, that he might genuinely be interested in her.

Besides, if he climbed out to shake her hand, buck naked, she would die.

Rhys watched her walk away with a surprising clench of dismay, even though he knew better than to flirt with the help.

He hadn't even realized anyone had been on the pool deck until he'd surfaced after swimming the length underwater. But there she was, face buried in a stack of towels like an ostrich, her dark hair gathered into a fraying knot, her uniform mostly shapeless except where it clung lovingly to a really nice ass.

Arrogant as he innately was, he didn't expect servants to turn their face to the wall as his father had once told him his great-grandmother had demanded of palace staff.

This young woman had obviously recognized him. Nearly every woman of any age reacted to him—which he made a habit of ignoring. His reputation as a playboy was greatly exaggerated. Affairs complicated an already complex life. When he did entangle himself, he stuck with a long-term arrangement with a sophisticated partner, one who had a busy life herself. He kept ties loose until the woman in question began to suggest marriage would improve their relationship, invariably claiming it would "give us more time together" or "draw us closer"—two assumptions he knew would prove false.

Sometimes they brought up a desire for children, and he had had good reasons for putting that off, too. Until recently.

But until very recently, Rhys hadn't believed he'd have to marry at all. Staying single had been his greatest luxury and one of the few genuine freedoms available to him. Occasionally, he had thought a wife might be the best way to stave off the fortune hunters who constantly stalked him, but marriage and family were yet more responsibilities on top of an already heavy mantle. He had thought to indefinitely postpone both.

Besides, he didn't deserve the sort of happily-ever-after his brother was striving for.

A shrieking giggle from a balcony above had him glancing up to see a pair of women in negligees exhibiting all the excitement of children spotting a monkey at the zoo. Their bare legs and cleavage flashed as they posed against the rail and waved.

And so it starts, he thought tiredly.

He looked for the young woman who had seemed so charmingly real, planning to ask her to lock out the masses for another thirty minutes.

He couldn't see her, and his irritation ratcheted up several notches. It had little to do with the looming interruption of his peaceful swim. She was gone, and he was uncomfortable with how annoyed that made him. He hadn't even asked her name.

She worked here, he reminded himself. He would see her again, but the knowledge did nothing to ease his impatience.

He shouldn't *want* to see her again. He wouldn't be able to approach her when he did. A guest coming on to an employee was a hard limit. There was an entire hotel brimming with beautiful, available, *appropriate* women if he wanted to get laid.

His nether regions weren't twitching for the silk-draped knockouts hurrying to throw on robes and rush down here, though. He was recollecting a face clean of makeup and eyes like melted chocolate framed in thick lashes. She'd had a tiny beauty spot below one corner of her mouth and what had looked like a man's wedding band on a thin chain in the hollow of her throat. Whose? A father, he imagined. She was too young to be a widow.

She could be married, though. She was very pretty, neither voluptuous nor catwalk slender, but pert with small, firm breasts, narrow shoulders and that valentine of a derriere. He had wondered how tall she would be if he stood beside her. He might get a crick in his neck when he leaned down to taste her pillowy lips—

No.

With a muttered curse, he caught his breath and dived to the bottom of the pool, using the pressure and exertion to work out his animal urges.

It didn't work. She stayed on his mind all day.

Sopi remained emotionally wired until she heard the prince had left the building. She watched the helicopter veer across the valley, climb above the tree line and wheel to the far side of a peak.

Deflated and depleted, she slipped away to her cabin

for a nap. Of the half dozen tiny A-frame guest cottages, this one was farthest from the main building. At some point, probably when the stove conked out, it had become a storage unit for spare mattresses and mini refrigerators. Sopi kept one plugged in for her own use, and the heat still worked, so it was quite livable.

The tiny loft above the storage area was hardly on a par with the rest of the accommodation at Cassiopeia's, though. Even the employees had proper flats in the staff lodge tucked into the trees. That building was boxy and utilitarian, but they each had their own bedroom, bathroom and kitchenette. It was well tended and cozy.

Until her father had died very suddenly when she was fifteen, Sopi had lived in the manager's suite across from the kitchen. Somehow that had been given to the manager Maude had hired to run the spa that first year. Maude had taken over the suite when she came back to run things herself, except her version of managing was to delegate everything to Sopi.

Sopi had meanwhile bounced through guest and staff units as they became available. Eventually, she had wound up on the fringe of the property while Maude's daughters had appropriated the top suite when they returned to complain about having to live here instead of gadding about Europe.

Sopi didn't love tramping through the snow in the dark, but she did love having her own space. She had managed to warm it up with a few cherished items of her mother's—a blue velvet reading chair and a faded silk area rug. Her bed, purchased from the buy-and-sell ads, was a child's bunk bed with a desk beneath. Cartoon princesses adorned it, but they inspired her to dream, so she hadn't painted over them.

A long time ago, a guest had started the silly rumor that the owner of this hotel was descended from royalty. He had thought Sopi's mother had been the daughter of an ousted king or something.

Sopi's mother had already been gone by that point. Her father had only chuckled and shaken his head. It was a nice legend that might bring curiosity seekers to the spa, he'd said, but nothing more.

Sopi sighed and climbed into her bed without eating. The stacked milk crates that formed her pantry were empty. She hadn't had time to buy a box of cereal or replenish the instant soup she kept on hand to make with the kettle that was her most reliable friend.

Her head hit the pillow, and she plunged into a sleep so deep she wouldn't have heard a bomb go off.

Yet when the distant rat-a-tat of helicopter blades began to sound in the distance, her eyes snapped open.

Dang. She'd been dreaming something sexy about hot pool waters sliding silkily across her skin while a pair of blue eyes—

Ugh. She was so pathetic.

And wide-awake now that a mixture of self-contempt and guilt had hold of her. She glanced at her phone. It was full of text messages from staff. Some made her laugh. They all got on really well, but it was work, too. She had a quick shower, dressed and hurried back.

After putting out three proverbial fires, she was in the mani-pedi salon listening to a nail technician complain about an order of decals shaped like high-heeled shoes.

"They were supposed to be more bedazzled, but instead they're this plain black, and when you put clear polish on them, they curl up and fall off."

Sopi frowned and took the polish and decals to a

bench at the back of the salon. All the mani-pedi chairs were full of buzzing women hoping to meet the prince later.

From the time she was twelve, Sopi had apprenticed in all the treatments under a multitude of formally trained staff. She didn't have any certificates on the wall, but she could pinch-hit with nearly any service from foiled streaks to Swedish massage. If there'd been a chair free, she would have pitched in to help with the roster of guests begging for polish, but she had too much to do elsewhere anyway.

At least she'd taken the time last week to give her own toenails a fresh, if unremarkable, coat of pale pink polish. She stuck the decals of high-heeled shoes on each of her big toes and shellacked them in place with clear polish. She bedazzled one with a couple of glinting sequins to see if that would help hold it in place and make it look prettier.

She was curled over, blowing on her toes, distantly listening to a pair of women speculate on what time the prince would appear for dinner and whether he would invite anyone to join his table, when she picked up a call that had her frowning and hurrying barefoot down the hall to the massage therapy rooms.

Karl, their beefy Norwegian masseur, wasn't on the schedule this week, but Sopi spotted him about to enter a closed door.

"Karl!" she whispered. They strongly discouraged any conversation above a whisper in the spa area to ensure the guests enjoyed a relaxing stay. "It's your wife." She offered her phone.

Face blanking with panicked excitement, Karl took the phone and spoke rapidly in Norwegian.

"I have to go," he said, ending the call and trying

to pocket Sopi's phone. "The midwife is on her way. It's time."

"Finally! Hurry home, then." Sopi couldn't help grinning as she stole back her phone. "I hope everything goes well."

"Thank you." He started away, turned back, clearly in a flummoxed state of mind. "My phone is still in there. He's on the table!"

"Karl." Sopi took his arm and spoke calmly and firmly. "Don't worry about your client. I'll cover your massage. Get your phone and go home to your wife."

He nodded, knocked gently and led Sopi into the room.

"Sir, I'm very sorry," he said as he entered. "My wife has gone into labor, but I'm leaving you in good hands. Literally. Ah, there it is." Karl retrieved his phone from the small shelf above the essential oils. He turned to Sopi. "And she did text me, but I missed it because I silence it out of habit when I'm consulting with a client. The prince felt a twist in his lower back while skiing. He wants to be sure it doesn't turn into anything serious."

Sopi nodded dumbly, throat jammed as she avoided staring at the muscled back on the massage table, a sheet draped loosely across his hips and legs.

"Thank you," Karl said to her as he hurried from the room.

Sopi drew a breath and choked on a speck of spit. She turned her cough into a cleared throat, managing to croak, "I apologize for the switch. Karl was on call this week. I don't think he would have come in for anyone else but you."

The prince's shoulders tensed as though the sound of her voice surprised him.

She moved to tug the sheet over his exposed foot and

straightened the rest of it as she moved up the far side of the table. When she started to tuck the edge of the sheet under the band of his underwear, she realized he wasn't wearing any. Big hairy surprise. How was this her life?

CHAPTER TWO

"I'M NOT FORMALLY trained, but I've apprenticed under all of our registered therapists. I have over four hundred hours of treatments."

It was her. She had a touch as light as her footsteps moving quietly around the table. The room held a vague scent of citrus and sage, but he detected a scent beneath it. The sharp bite of nail polish and something more subtle, like sun-warmed peaches.

"Is your injury serious enough I should arrange a doctor or physiotherapist to come in? I don't want to exacerbate anything."

"You can't hurt me." He nearly laughed at the idea, but there was already an uncomfortable compression in his groin that might become a serious ache if he didn't keep a firm grip on his straying thoughts. "I typically ask for a man because women usually aren't aggressive enough. It's only a small twinge. I should have warmed up properly with my swim this morning, but the pool became too busy for laps." Too busy, period. He'd left when the first women arrived and had had to swim up a stream of crestfallen faces on his way to the elevator.

She set a hand on the back of his calf and squeezed, then moved it down to his ankle and squeezed again. It was a silent communication to let him know where she was, but it was surprisingly firm. Confident.

"I'll use our unscented oil. If there's significant inflammation, I can add geranium or yarrow."

He almost suggested she could dress him like a salad, but bit it back. He didn't usually have to filter himself quite so carefully when he was alone with a woman. He was the one naked and facedown, pretty much at her mercy, but an urge to pursue gripped him. He had to be careful.

"Whatever you think is best."

"How was the snow?" She was on his left side.

"Good." Amazing, actually. The sun had come out and the powder had been chest deep, but he barely recalled it now as he heard the click of a cap and the quiet friction of her palms rubbing together. He discovered he was holding his breath with anticipation.

Her fingertips settled in his middle back, light as a leaf coming to rest on the ground. Slowly, she applied pressure until she was leaning into him, prompting him to exhale until there was nothing left in his lungs.

As he drew in his next breath, the warmth in her hands stayed firm, penetrating his skin. She began to move in sweeping strokes, spreading the oil before her touch slowed and grew more exploratory.

Rhys had a massage at least once a month. He was as athletic as possible given his busy life of travel and meetings. He worked out regularly and ran marathons on treadmills, but he had a knack for storing tension in his shoulders and neck.

She found it, squeezing his trapezius muscle on either side, not working it, but acknowledging it. It wasn't supposed to be erotic, but he found her greeting of that tension both teasing and soothing. A comforting warning that she would be back.

It fostered a sense of connection that he instinctively knew would make for both heaven and hell. He probably should have called this massage off right here and now, but the temptation to feel her hands on him was too strong. Even though he doubted he'd be able to relax when—

He grunted with shock as she set her thumb into a spot next to his spine and sent a white-hot blade between his ribs.

"Sorry." Her touch lifted away. "Trigger point. I'll come back to it."

"No." It was as if she'd found something in him no one else had ever discovered. "Do it again."

"I just felt all this tightness here." Her hand got into the crook of his neck and shoulder while she pressed into the trigger point again with the point of—

"Is that your *elbow*?"

"Too hard?" She lifted away.

"No."

The pressure came back, the pain intense for the space of three breaths before it faded into a release of tingles like fairy dust, so profound he groaned in relief.

"There we go," she murmured, hands sweeping to soothe before she moved to the other side.

For the next ten minutes, she worked his shoulders, alternately persecuting and appeasing before she moved into his lower back. She even nudged aside the sheet to get her elbows into the tops of his glutes. It was another pressure point, hurting like hell before the cords in his lower back relaxed and his muscles turned to pudding.

He had never considered himself kinky, but this was bordering on erotic. The whole time he was blinded by intense sensations, he was equally aware of the sensual brush of her breast against his hip and what might have been the tickle of her hair falling against his spine. When he lifted his hips slightly, trying to give himself room to grow, she straightened away and drew the sheet up over his tailbone.

"I'll try going after that area with reflexology." She uncovered his feet. "Tell me if this pressure is too much?"

Her thumbs dug against his instep. He nearly levitated, but the endorphin rush was worth it. By the time she'd gone up his calves and into his hamstrings, he was hers. He'd never been in such a state of sublime arousal. She could have tied him to the bed and shown him a riding crop and he'd have begged, "Yes, please."

She worked his arms, and it took everything in him to keep them lax rather than flexing to drag her close. He ached to touch her as intimately as she was touching him, but he had to stay motionless and let her drive him mad.

This was torture. Genuine torture.

"Would you like to turn ov—"

"No," he growled. He was fully hard. If she looked him in the eye, she would know how badly he wanted to drag her atop him and see how much abuse this table could take.

A surprised pause. "I'll finish with your neck and scalp, then?"

"Yes."

She moved to stand above his head. All he could see through the face cradle was her bare feet.

Each of her big toes wore a silhouette of a woman's shoe against a background of pink. The plain one was peeling up. The other was bedecked with jewels and winked at him as she curled her toes and set gentle fingertips against the back of his neck.

"If I've been too rough—"

"You haven't." He closed his eyes in pleasure-pain. "This is the best massage of my life. I have to cut it short before it turns into something else."

He thought he heard a small *"Eep."* He definitely heard her swallow.

"Stay mean," he growled.

Her laugh was garbled and semihysterical, but she obeyed. She did cruel things to his trapezius muscles, turning snarling pit bulls into docile golden retrievers.

The final act was a merciless grip of all four fingertips of both hands into the muscles at the base of his skull. She held him in a dull headache for what felt like ten minutes before the pain evaporated into a sensation of sunshine dawning after a long, harsh winter.

She speared her fingers into his hair and erased his memory of pain, leaving the tranquil buzz he'd only previously experienced postcoitally.

"Take your time rising and dressing." Her voice sounded throaty and laden with desire, causing a fresh rush of heat into his groin. "Drink some water."

He couldn't move. Wait. He picked up his head, but the door was already closing behind her.

He felt drugged as he sat up, peeved that he hadn't asked her name. Probably for the best. He looked down at his lap, as ready for sex as he'd ever been.

If she could put him through his paces with a massage, what would sex with her be like?

The strong tug between his thighs told him thoughts like that were unhelpful.

As he pulled on his robe, he resented the hell out of his position. Curse tradition and snobbery and an illness that had put the future on his doorstep. Ten years ago, he could have had an affair with a spa worker and no one would have known or cared.

Once he'd moved back into the palace, he'd had to become more circumspect in his choices, but he still could have managed a fling with someone whose connections were less prestigious than his own. There would have been blowback, but an affair wasn't marriage.

That's what Rhys had to court now, though. Any relationship he started would have to be taken to the finish line. Was he really going to go against the grain with a pool-girl masseuse? Refuse to do his duty to his brother and the crown in favor of appeasing his libido?

He cursed, annoyed. One dinner was all he was after, before he made the rounds through the more expected choices of potential brides. Was that so much to ask? One evening to get to know her before he was forced to settle?

It was a selfish rationalization he shouldn't even contemplate.

He poured a cup of water from the cistern and threw it back like a shot of scotch. As he kicked into his sandals by the door, he almost mistook the speck on the tiles for a spider, but no.

He bent and touched his fingertip to it, picking up the silhouette of a woman's shoe, just like the one that had been coming off her toe. Huh.

Pinching it between his finger and thumb, he tucked it deep into the pocket of his robe, considering.

Flushed and confused, Sopi hurried to get as far away from the prince as possible, all the way to the other end of the building, where the service entrance to the kitchen was located. She stood on the back stoop in the cold dusk, trying to bring herself back under control.

She had provided a lot of massages, usually to women, but many to men, and had never once felt so affected by the experience. It hadn't been lascivious, either. It had been...elemental. She'd never become so entranced by a deep and genuine yearning to ease and soothe and heal. Yet touching him had been stimulating, too, keeping her in a state of alert readiness. Like petting a giant cat.

Or a man in peak condition who appealed to her on a primitive level.

She could have stroked her hands over him for hours, like a sculptor lovingly sanding her creation to a fine polish. In those last seconds before she'd asked him to roll over, she had felt a strong urge to splay herself atop him. Blanket him with her body while soaking in his essence.

Truthfully, she'd been lost in her world at that point and had been shocked back to reality when he declined to turn faceup.

I have to cut it short before it turns into something else.

She'd been stunned. Embarrassed that she'd aroused him, but shaken and inflamed by the idea. All the banked sexual energy she'd been suppressing as she administered the massage had suddenly engulfed her in a rush of carnal hunger.

If he hadn't told her to "stay mean," she didn't know what she might have done, but she'd found the concrete knots at the base of his skull. *Heavy is the crown*, she'd thought, wondering what his life was like back in Verina.

She would never know.

A sudden shiver had her realizing she had cooled past comfortable. She went inside, where the kitchen staff was scrambling to prepare for the dinner rush.

Without being asked, she slipped into the change room and put on her prep cook garb, then spent an hour peeling potatoes and scrubbing pots.

She was at her sweaty, sticky worst when she headed back to her cabin for a shower. The sound of squabbling as she approached through the trees almost had her turning back.

"Sopi!" Fernanda said when she spotted her. "Where have you been? I've been texting you."

"Oh?" Sopi pretended to scan her phone.

"She blocks us, you stooge," Nanette said pithily.

"Only when I'm working," Sopi said sweetly as she slid between the two towering beauties to unlock her door. "The paying guests are my priority, seeing as they support us." Hint, hint.

"Well, this has to do with the prince, so you ought to have been paying attention." As she entered uninvited, Fernanda wrinkled her nose at the clutter.

"She wants to make a fool of herself and wants you to help," Nanette informed Sopi with an eye roll.

"Why are you here?" Fernanda charged. *"The same reason."*

"To shower with me?" Sopi asked facetiously. "I don't usually entertain there."

"Shocker," Nanette muttered with an examination of her nails.

Always a joy spending time with family. Sopi bit back a sigh.

"The dining room could use you both to hostess this evening," Sopi said, mainly to Nanette. She never lifted a finger unless Maude pressed her. "We have a full house. Tables will turn over three or four times at least."

"Unavailable. Sorry," Nanette said with a saccharine smile.

"Not even for the chance to seat the prince?"

"He's not eating downstairs," Fernanda jumped in to say. "That's why I'm here. Women are lined up out the door at the salon to get one of these." Fernanda handed Sopi a sheet of toe decals.

Sopi frowned. "They're defective. I was in the salon earlier. They fall off."

"Yes, I know that. That's why *you* have to put it on. To make sure it stays."

Sopi shook her head, almost thinking there was a compliment in there, but definitely a backhanded one.

"If you're not going to help in the dining room, I have to shower and hurry back. Stick it on yourself. It's not rocket science."

"Forget the dining room," Fernanda said with a stamp of her foot. "No one will even show up there. The prince is dining privately. With a woman who has one of these stuck to her toe."

"What?" When she had pushed her feet into her closed-toe kitchen clogs, Sopi had noticed that she'd lost her plain shoe decal during the massage. She had only managed to keep the bedazzled one. She removed her snow boots now but self-consciously kept her socks on.

Nanette straightened from leaning against the decommissioned stove, wiping her hands across her backside as she did. "It seems the prince met someone who interests him, but he doesn't know her name. His assistant put the word out that this woman only has one shoe." She flipped her hair. "Apparently, she knows who she is, and he wants her to come to his suite this evening if she would like to dine with him."

"He—that's silly," Sopi said, hyperaware of the hot blush that flooded into her cheeks. It was a tremendous long shot that he could be talking about her. "Fernanda, he's going to know right away whether you're the woman he is trying to meet. If you don't already have a decal, you're not her."

"Well, his bodyguard doesn't know that, does he? If I can get in to see him, the prince can decide if I'm the right woman or not."

Sopi opened her mouth but couldn't find words. Fernanda wasn't the brightest candle on the cake and tended to be very self-involved. She came across as selfish, but she wasn't mean, just firmly stuck between thoughtless and clueless.

"I tried to tell her." Nanette grew more alert, like a jackal that scented something on the air. She was definitely the brains in the family, calculating and sharp.

"Yet here you are. Wanting the *same thing*," Fernanda hissed at her sister. "So it's not such a stupid idea, is it?"

"Wait." Sopi held up a hand. "Did you say there's some sort of run on at the salon?"

"Yes! Everyone is trying to get one. The girls tried to tell me to come back later, but there's no time. Can you just…" Fernanda unzipped her knee-high spiked-heel boot and dragged off her sock. "Hurry." She wiggled her toes. "I need to dress."

"Fernanda—" Sopi looked to Nanette for backup, but Nanette was also removing her ankle-high snakeskin boot. "I don't even have polish—oh."

Fernanda had absconded with a handful of bottles from the salon. Nanette had brought a tiny tube of fast acting superadhesive. She handed that over with a pointed look. *She* wouldn't lose her decal, come hell or high water.

"You're going to parade to his suite with everyone

else, all wearing one shoe so he can see you have a decal on your toe?" Sopi asked with bemusement.

"I'll wear proper open-toed evening shoes, won't I? Honestly, Sopi." Fernanda rolled her eyes.

Right. Sopi was the one being ridiculous.

Since it was the fastest way to get these two women to leave her private space, Sopi sat on the stairs to her loft. She motioned for Fernanda to set her foot beside her thigh.

"I put a pair of these on earlier," Sopi mused as she very carefully placed the shoe on Fernanda's toe. "I guess I should dress up and come with you. Maybe it's me he's looking for." It was a deliberate effort to provoke a reaction, so she shouldn't have been stung by Fernanda's dismissive snort.

"Oh, right. Have you even spoken to him for one second?"

"I have, actually." Sopi was always annoyed when these two put on that tone that disparaged her as a backwoods hick who lacked their refinement.

"What did you talk about?" Nanette asked, gaze narrowed.

"Nothing much." She shook the bottle of polish. "He didn't even ask my name." It was another dig.

She swiped the brush across the decal, varnishing the shoe into place. When she looked up, Fernanda was scowling with suspicion.

"Have you given any thought to how you'll walk back with wet polish on your toe?" Sopi asked.

"That's why I brought the glue," Nanette said, nudging her sister aside and eyeing Sopi shrewdly. "What would you wear?" she asked.

"Hmm?" Sopi glanced up from trying to break the seal on the glue nozzle.

"To dine with the prince."

"Oh." She hadn't given one iota of thought to actually doing it, but she'd come this far into needling them. She let bravado take her a few more steps. "I have some things of my mother's. There's a vintage Chanel I've always wanted an excuse to wear."

"How am I only hearing about this now? Show me." Nanette sounded genuinely impressed, but maybe Sopi was that desperate to finally take her by surprise.

She finished gluing the shoe to Nanette's toe, then trotted up the stairs to her loft.

In the chest beneath the window, she kept a handful of keepsakes—her parents' wedding album, the Christmas ornaments that hadn't broken over the years and her audition tape to a televised singing contest that might have been her big break if her father hadn't passed away the week she was supposed to appear.

Moving all of that aside, she drew out a zipped fabric box that also stored her summer wear. She dumped her clothes onto the floor and drew out the tissue-wrapped dress.

Sopi bit her lip as she noticed the moths had been into it. Voraciously.

Nanette arrived at the top of the stairs and said, "Oh my *God*. I thought *I* lived in a hovel."

"Don't you *dare*," Sopi said, voice sharpened by the strike of painful knowledge that she had lost a prized possession. This rag only proved she was nowhere near the prince's league. "You live here for *free*. Who do you think *pays* for that?"

"You just said it. It's free. No one is making you live like this. You're the one who plays the martyr all the time. 'Oh, woe. If you don't play hostess, I have to.'"

"'Oh, woe,'" Sopi shot back. "'I can't put a sticker on my own toe.'"

"Exactly," Nanette said with a hair flip and a complete absence of apology. "Set standards for yourself and refuse to compromise them." Her scathing glance dismissed Sopi's handful of possessions and the dress that was definitely not living up to her claims.

Such a cow. If Sopi was the cretin they thought, she would push Nanette down the stairs, taking out Fernanda, who had come up behind her to make a face of amused disgust as she looked around. God, she hated both of them.

"Oh, Sopi, no," Fernanda said when she saw the dress. Her tone held the depth of sympathy one saved for muddy dogs found starving in ditches. "You have to store vintage pieces properly. Otherwise they fall apart when you wear them. Everyone knows that. What a shame."

"Clearly your standards aren't being met here," Sopi said through her teeth. "Kindly leave my hovel and never come back."

"Does this mean you won't do my hair?"

"Seriously, Fernanda?" Sopi glared.

"You don't have to be so sensitive! I don't understand why she treats us like this," Fernanda complained as the two women went down the stairs.

They left, and Sopi hurried to lock the door so they couldn't return. Then she went into the shower and wept over old dresses and lost parents and foolish fantasies about unattainable men.

When she turned off the water, she stared at the bedazzled shoe on her one toe. Stupid. She picked it off so her nail was an ugly, chipped mess, and she left it that way as a reminder to stay grounded.

Then she wished even harder that the prince would marry one of her stepsisters and get them all out of her life for good.

"Say that again," Rhys growled at his assistant.

Gerard shifted uncomfortably. "I did as you asked. I put the word out that you were trying to locate the woman with the little shoe on her toe."

"You said I had met her already? That I knew who I was looking for?"

"Perhaps I wasn't clear on that?" His assistant's shoulders hunched up to his ears. "It seemed self-explanatory, but…" He trailed off, miserable.

"And now there's…how many women in the hall?"

"Fifty? Sixty?"

"All with one shoe on her toe."

"I'm afraid so, sir." Gerard swallowed.

"What am I supposed to do? Walk the line as though inspecting the troops, looking for her among them?" He'd been trying to be discreet. Rather than make it clear he was looking for someone on staff, he had thought he would get word to her through the grapevine. She could then quietly appear in his room if she was interested.

"How did they even get up here in the elevator?"

"The one shoe, sir. The bodyguards—"

Rhys pinched the bridge of his nose. "Suggestions on how to get rid of them?"

"Perhaps if you simply ate in the dining room? Mingled? Gave them a chance to say hello?"

Rhys had no appetite. "That never works. It only encourages them to approach me later." But he had to find himself a wife, and what was he going to do? Put a staff member in the unnerving position of having to walk a gauntlet to reach him for a single date that would go nowhere?

If she was out there and wanted to see him, she would already have knocked on his door. No, she was either too self-conscious or wasn't interested.

What a galling thought. Deep down, however, he knew it was for the best.

It still infuriated him.

"Fine," he growled. "Tell them I'll dine downstairs after all."

When the news came that the prince would in fact need a table, Sopi experienced a rush of panic. She definitely, positively didn't want to see him. After brooding for a solid hour, she had decided that what he must have meant when he cut short her massage was that he thought *she* was turning it into something it wasn't.

Unsurprisingly, her stepsisters both appeared within minutes of the announcement, eager to marshal rivals to terrible tables and have an excuse to brush past the prince's table while he ate. He would sit with the handful of upper-crust bachelors who had accompanied him onto the slopes and were providing further red meat for the marriage-minded women hungry for a good match.

Sopi gladly relinquished the reservation desk and slipped into the laundry room to help fold sheets and towels.

With nearly every guest now rubbing elbows in the dining room, the rest of the building was quiet. She stuck with her friends in housekeeping, joking and exchanging light gossip about the guests as they restocked the linen cupboards and performed the turn-down service in the top-floor rooms.

She did the prince's room herself and, as she plumped

the pillow, noticed the tiny black shoe on the night table. It sat atop one of the burgundy portfolios Maude liked to use for special event meetings. She would make a note from a bride or other VIP guest, then snap it shut and hand it off to Sopi with instructions to make things happen.

Sopi's pulse tripped at the sight of the tiny shoe, but a bodyguard stood by observing her, so she closed the drapes, set wrapped chocolates on the pillow and left.

Eventually, the guests retired from the dining room to hit the hot pools. Most of them were drunk and she resigned herself to a lot of cleanup later but helped the kitchen recover first.

While she was there, Maude pulled her aside with another list of to-dos. By the time they were done, it was time to close the pool and saunas. As Sopi marshaled the stragglers out, fully eight people tried to bribe her into calling them if the prince showed up after hours.

She bundled the last naked nymph into a robe and onto an elevator, then switched everything to service. That locked off the treatment level to all but the staff cards. She sighed in relief, facing miles to go before she slept, but the closing chores were ones she almost enjoyed. She could do them at her own pace and no one ever interrupted her.

Humming, she wheeled the mop from the closet and got started.

Midnight and Rhys was wide-awake, standing at the window, wired.

Wondering.

Swearing at himself. At his brother. At life.

For two hours, he'd been surrounded by beautiful, eligible, well-bred women, none of whom had been the one he wanted to see. It wasn't like him to be so fixated. He didn't like it. He'd seen the dark side of humans who became obsessed.

The darkest night of his life replayed uninvited. His well-practiced ability to block it didn't work this time, and his head filled with the shouts and crashing and what he'd thought had been fireworks inside the palace.

He'd been ten, old enough to take in the full horror of being invaded by soldiers in military garb and the gravity of their holding his parents at gunpoint below. He'd been too young to make a difference, though. In fact, he'd made things worse. He had screamed and rushed to the top of the stairs, where Henrik was being held off by a soldier.

If he had halted beside Henrik, his parents might still be alive. He had gone for the soldier's gun, though, and the soldier had crashed him in the face with the butt of his rifle, splitting his cheek and knocking him onto his ass.

Rhys had heard his mother scream. She had started to race up the stairs to him. A soldier below grabbed her arm and yanked her back. His father intervened, and the tension below erupted into four shots that left his parents crumpled on the floor.

Rhys could still feel the unnatural strength in Henrik as he'd gripped the shoulders of Rhys's pajamas and dragged him backward, behind the half wall of the upper gallery. Rhys had been limp with shock, gaze held by the cold stare of the soldier who had shot his parents so remorselessly.

He would never forget the ugly lack of humanity in that pair of eyes. He would forever carry the weight of guilt that if he hadn't given in to his own impulses, his parents might be alive today.

Distantly, he'd been aware of Henrik stammering out pleas. Promises they would never come back if they were allowed to leave. He'd somehow got Rhys onto his feet and pulled him down the service stairs and out of the palace.

Shock had set in and Rhys didn't recall much of the days after that, but guilt remained a heavy cloak on him. Guilt and loss and failure. He was grateful to Henrik for getting them out, but a day never went by where he didn't feel sick for escaping. For surviving when his parents had died because of his rash actions.

A day never went by when he didn't feel their loss as though pieces had been carved out of his heart. His chest throbbed even more acutely with apprehension over Henrik's diagnosis.

Why Henrik? It should be him staring into the muzzle of a life-threatening diagnosis, not his brother. If he lost Henrik—

He couldn't let himself think it.

This was why he hadn't wanted to marry and have children. This agonizing fear and inability to control the future were intolerable.

He swore under his breath.

If grim introspection was the only mood he could conjure, he needed a serious distraction. He walked across to the folio Maude had given him, the one he had said he wanted to review when he had made his abrupt exit from the dining room earlier this evening.

Maude's eldest daughter, a lithe beauty, had fallen into step alongside him as he departed, offering an excuse about fetching something from her room. Her purpose had been obvious, though. She had deliberately created the impression she was the one he'd been seeking as his dinner companion. In the elevator, she had set her pretty silver shoe next to his, not quite nudging, but definitely inviting him to notice her toe.

This constant circling was exhausting. In the space of a day, he'd come around from thinking he *should* marry to impatience for task completion. Maude's eldest was exactly what was expected of the royal family— well-bred, smoothly sophisticated and picture-perfect beautiful. She struck him as the possessive type, too. Overtures from other women would no longer be a problem. She would make damned sure of it.

"Please allow me to arrange a more peaceful dining experience for you tomorrow," she had offered with the silky sweetness of a white chocolate mousse. "We often close the solarium for honeymoon couples."

Honeymoon was a deliberate choice of word, he was sure. *So* exhausting.

"I'll let you know." He had cut away to his own room, not the least bit compelled to spend another minute with her, let alone a lifetime.

As he flipped open the folio, interest in purchasing this property nonexistent, the tiny black shoe fluttered to the carpet. All the darkness in him folded in on itself, becoming a burst of light with a single focus. *Her.*

He tried to shake it off. He had no business obsessing over anyone, let alone the least suitable woman here. How did he even have the energy to experience a rush of masculine interest? He ought to be physically exhausted from his day of skiing, but he couldn't shake this buzz of sexual hunger. This sense of something being unfinished.

Maybe he could work it out in the pool.

He stripped where he stood and pulled on his robe. This time he had the sense to bring one of his bodyguards and ordered him to stand at the door to ensure he wouldn't be stalked.

The lights were dimmed in the change room, the mirror and taps polished, the floor dry. The music and water feature were both turned off, along with the jets in the tub. It was blessedly silent as he walked past the still water of the indoor pool and hot tub. Through the fogged windows, he saw steam rising off the mineral pool in gentle wafts against the black sky.

Just as he was about to walk outside and dive in, however, he heard a noise down the short hallway that led to the sauna area. A woman was singing.

The scent of eucalyptus carried with her voice on the humid air. A bucket of cleaning supplies stood outside a door to a steam room. The sound of spraying water cut off, and he clearly heard her crooning a modern ballad that reverberated beautifully off the tiled walls.

He stood transfixed as *she* emerged to drop a long-handled scrubbing brush into the bucket. Her hair was in a messy ball atop her head, but tendrils stuck to her damp neck. She wore light cotton pants and a baggy smock, both heavily soaked at the cuffs. Without looking his way, she quit singing and sighed. She picked up the bucket and carried it down the hall and around a corner where an authorized-personnel-only sign hung.

What was she doing cleaning the sauna at midnight? She was a goddess who possessed a healing touch and a siren's voice, not a scullery maid.

He crossed his arms, scowling as he listened to a door open and close. He waited for her to reappear.

And waited.

Had she locked herself in a utility closet? He followed to the end of the hall, where he found two doors. One opened to a closet that was empty of all but fresh linens and cleaning supplies. Her bucket sat on the floor inside it.

The other door read Emergency Exit Only. Door Locks Automatically.

It hadn't set off an alarm when she went through, so he pushed it open. The night was clear, the air bracing. A narrow footpath had been stamped into the snow. He glimpsed a maintenance building in the trees.

Don't, his rational head warned.

He felt for his key card, tried it against the mechanism on the outside and saw it turn green. He stepped into the cold and let the door lock behind him.

CHAPTER THREE

To hell with it. That was what Sopi had been thinking the whole time she'd been scrubbing the saunas. She felt grimy and sweaty and resentful and *entitled to enjoy herself.*

Not in the treated waters of the hot pool, though. No, she was going to the source, the original spring that had been formed by long-ago explorers, possibly ancestors of the nearest First Nations tribe. No one knew exactly who had dammed the hot water trickling out of the mossy ground, forming a small bathing pool on a bluff in the woods, but through the 1800s and into the early 1900s the small swimming hole had been used by hunters and snowshoers who heard about it through word of mouth.

Eventually, an enterprising railway baron had built the first rustic hotel here. He had brought in a crew to dig a proper pool by hand, and that hole had eventually become what was the indoor pool today. He had lined it and filled it with snow that he melted and heated by piping water from this tiny hot spring. Since this natural, rocky pool was impossible to clean, the hotel wasn't allowed to let guests use it. It was kept as a heat source and a point of interest. In the summer, the gate next to the pump house was left unlocked so guests could picnic on the bench nearby, enjoying the view of the lake and the soothing trickle of the water.

Tonight, Sopi's were the only footsteps as she veered off the path to the maintenance shed and wound through the trees. The snow wasn't too deep under the laden evergreens, but she was only wearing sandals. By the time she emerged and shoved at the gate to open it against the accumulation of snow, her feet were frozen and aching.

She waded through the knee-high snow the final few yards. As she reached the edge of the pool, she kicked off her sandals and stepped into the hot water. It hurt like mad, but was a relief, too.

She hadn't been to the pool in a long time. Not since she had come out here to cry after getting the news her father had passed from a sudden heart attack. This had always been her sad place, and that moment had been one of her saddest. Since it wasn't something she liked to revisit, she didn't come here often.

She had forgotten how peaceful it was, though. The height of the trees hid it from hotel windows. The only reminders of civilization were the fence and gate and the distant hum of the pump house. She turned her back on those man-made things and faced the lake. The slope fell away, allowing a clear view of its sparkling, snow-blanketed surface.

The longer she stood here, the better she felt. The waters truly were capable of healing, she decided with a sigh of reclaimed calm. She started to pull her top up over her head but froze when she heard the crunch of footsteps.

Really? She almost screamed in frustration. Who? *Why?* She twisted to glare at—

"Oh."

"You're not supposed to swim alone." The prince's

breath fogged against the frosty air. He wore his robe and rattled the gate to open it farther before he took long strides through the snow in his slippers. As he came closer, she was able to read his frown of dismay in the moonlight reflecting as a faint blue glow off the surrounding snow. He abandoned his slippers next to her sandals and stepped into the water, hissing at the bite of heat.

She looked back the way he'd come, expecting at least a few bodyguards and one or two of his cohorts, if not a full harem of adoring women.

"Are you lost? What are you doing here?" she asked him.

"What are *you* doing here?"

"You inspired me," she admitted truthfully, although Nanette's pithy talk of refusing to compromise had also lit a fire of rebellion in her.

"To try skinny-dipping? This is hotter than the pool."

"It is. Too hot in the summer, which is the only time this area is open to the public." She nodded at the sign obscured by a buildup of frozen condensation. "No swimming allowed."

"Ah. I've inspired you to break rules." His mouth barely twitched, but he sounded pleased. "Live dangerously."

"Not really. I happen to know it's tested regularly and is always found to be potable." The fence kept wildlife out, so risk of contamination was next to zero.

"That takes some of the thrill out of it, doesn't it?"

His words made her think of her stepsisters' disparagement of her. Their contempt had gone far deeper than a scoff over a moth-eaten dress. They knew she wasn't any match for a man in his position. *Sopi* knew it. She was standing here prickly with self-consciousness, aware that she was still covered in sweat from laboring in the spa. Definitely not anywhere near his exalted level.

The water beckoned, but she murmured, "It was a dumb impulse. We should go back."

He dragged his gaze from the frozen lake, eyes glittering in the moonlight, but his expression was inscrutable. "I wanted you to join me."

"Here?" She shook her head. Part of her was tempted. Where was the harm in a nude swim with a stranger? And where had such a reckless thought come from, she wondered with a suppressed choke of laughter. But he was the first man to make her consider such rash behavior. Everything about this was a rarity for her.

"For dinner," he clarified. "Did you...get that memo?"

The air that came into her lungs seemed to crystallize to powdered ice. "I didn't imagine for a minute you were looking for me. Besides, every woman here got a decal—"

"I know that," he cut in, sounding aggravated. "Now."

She bit back a smile. "You could have sent me a proper message."

"I didn't know your name. My assistant asked the booking clerk, but Karl was listed as my masseur. Who *are* you?"

She hesitated. Tell him everything? Would he care?

"I know this is inappropriate," he growled into the silence that she let stretch out with her indecision. "That's why I didn't want to make overt inquiries."

Inappropriate? It hadn't been, not really, until he used that word. Now she reeled, astonished that he was making this private conversation into more than she would have let herself believe it to be.

"If I'm out of line, say so. We'll go back right now."

"I don't know what this is," she admitted, hugging herself against the cold, because the hot water on her feet wasn't enough to keep her warm when she was outside at midnight before spring had properly taken hold. "My father bought this hotel for my mother. She named it after me. Cassiopeia. My friends call me Sopi."

"Cassiopeia." He seemed to taste the syllables, which made her shiver in a different way. "Maude is your mother?" He sounded surprised. Skeptical.

"Stepmother. She took control of the spa after my father died. I wasn't old enough to do it myself and… Well, I'd like to challenge her now, but lawyers cost money and… It's a long, boring story." She doubted he would believe the spa ought to belong to her anyway, not when she stood here all sweaty and gross. "I'm really cold. Can we—" She looked for her sandals.

"Yes. Let's warm up." He skimmed off his robe, tossing it to hook on the fence before he made his way farther into the pool. Naked, of course, carefully choosing his footing on the slippery rocks.

She looked to the sky, begging for guidance from higher powers.

"It's deeper than I expected," he said with satisfaction. He sank down as he found one of the rocky ledges that had been set in place for seating. "What are you doing? You said you wanted to try this."

"Alone."

"I'll turn my head." His tone rang with *prude*.

She was wearing a bra and underwear, basically a bikini. She knew that was a rationalization to stay here and swim with a man who intrigued her, but she also liked the idea of proving she *could* interest a prince, even if she was the only one who would ever know it.

Could she?

With an internal tsk, she decided to—for once—do something for herself. She stepped out of the water long enough to drop her drawstring pants and throw off her top.

She gingerly made her way into the pool, one eye on his profile to ensure he wasn't witnessing her clumsy entry. She winced at sharp edges pressing into her soles, bent to steady herself with a hand on a submerged boulder and let out a sigh as she sank to her shoulders and heat penetrated to her bones.

The pool was about four feet deep and maybe six feet wide. The prince had found one of the best perches facing the lake. She bumped her foot into his and he looked at her.

"Cheater," he accused as he noticed her bra strap.

She ducked under, unable to resist the lure of baptizing herself even though her hair would freeze into its tangled bun. Her long, strenuous day began to rinse away as she did it again. She came up with another sigh of sheer luxury.

"I didn't bring a towel. This is literally the dumbest idea I've ever had, but I don't regret it one bit."

"I would be a gentleman and offer you my robe, but then I'd have to streak like a bald yeti across the snow to get back inside."

"I'm pretty sure I saw one of those this morning."

His teeth flashed white. "Have you always lived here? You're Canadian?"

"I am. My mother was Swedish, I think. I don't have much information on her. She was an only child, and my father was funny about her family. Didn't like to talk about them. I don't think my grandparents approved of him."

"Why not?"

"Snobs, maybe? He sold two-way pagers and the early mobile phones into the European markets. Not very sexy at the time, but it was lucrative. That's how he paid for this." She nodded toward the hotel hidden by the spiky trees. "Then Silicon Valley crashed the party. His heart trouble started when my mother passed, and financial worries made it worse."

Sopi didn't know what kind of means Maude had pretended she had, but based on what Sopi had learned since, she believed Maude had misrepresented herself and worked on her father's desire for Sopi to have a mother with the goal of taking over his bank account and assets.

"It's a strange purchase for someone in that industry, especially since you don't have cell service beyond the hotel."

"My mother was struggling as a new mom in a new country. Dad traveled a lot, and she didn't have anyone to rely on. She wasn't working and felt very isolated. She loved her spa visits, though. She came here on one of them, talked to the owner who was thinking of selling. My father bought it for her."

"Romantic."

"Not really. It was worse for wear, and she had a lot of challenges with its remote location. She knew what she wanted, though, and made it happen. It was quite successful until she passed a few years later."

"What happened?"

"A bad flu that turned into pneumonia. Can we not talk about that? I was quite young, but it still makes me sad."

"I understand," he said gravely.

She recalled a bleak line in the history of Verina stating his parents had been killed in an uprising, forcing him and his brother to live in neighboring countries for fifteen years. For the first time, she wondered if the platitude he'd just used was actually true. Maybe he really did understand the hollow ache inside her.

He had braced his elbows on nearby rocks above the surface and tipped his head back to look up at the clear sky.

She took stock of where she was, soaking with a prince in the wilderness, the only sound a distant hum and a closer trickle of water seeping from the seams in the rocks and off a worn ledge into their bath.

"There you are." He tilted his head. "The trees were in the way. Cassiopeia."

Hardly anyone used her whole name, not when they addressed her. She'd begun to think *Cassiopeia* only applied to things that weren't really hers.

"A queen, if memory serves." It was hard to read his expression with the shadows and his beard.

She almost mentioned the silly rumor about her mother being descended from royalty but thought he might think she was trying to elevate herself to his stratosphere.

"A vain one who gets tied to a chair for eternity," she said instead. "Maybe I am vain." She didn't look for the W in the sky, having searched it out nearly every starry night since childhood. "My tiny mind was blown when I learned on the first day of school that not everyone had their own constellation."

He snorted. "I don't."

"Because you're a star on earth."

"Don't," he said flatly. The steam seemed to gust off the water so there was no mist between them, only clear, dry air that stung her cheeks and nose. "Don't put distance between us."

She swallowed her surprise, but a lump lodged in her chest, one that her voice had to strain to speak around. "There is a continent and an ocean between us." Among other things. His mountain of society and stature, her vast desert of education and life experience.

"Rhys," he said, laying down a gauntlet. "If you're going to reject me, use my name so I'm clear that you mean me." It was such an outrageously arrogant statement she wanted to laugh, yet he drew her in as his equal by offering the familiarity. Such an enigmatic man.

"I thought I was pointing out the obvious," she said quietly.

"You're the least obvious person I've ever met. Any other woman would be naked and straddled across me by now, whether I wanted her here or not. You wouldn't even come to dinner with me. Why not?"

Cowardice.

"I didn't think you were serious," she repeated. "Where would this even go? That's not opportunism talking. I don't have affairs with rich, powerful men. You tell me what happens. How long does it last? What happens when it's over?"

His eyes were obsidian, his jaw gleaming like wet iron. With a muttered curse in what sounded like German, he turned his glower toward the frozen lake below.

He didn't tell her she was wrong.

Sopi felt for another of the worn rocks that provided a rough seat and settled onto it. "Do you want the truth?"

"Always," he bit out.

"Maude wants you to marry Nanette. I thought if I

facilitated that, I could get rid of all three of them and finally have my home to myself."

A pulse of astounded silence, then he barked out a humorless laugh. He snapped his head around to glare at her. "I'll marry if and whom *I* desire. It won't be either of them. I promise you that right now."

She kissed goodbye her pipe dream of being free of her stepfamily, which left her to contemplate whether she should allow herself to get closer to this compelling man who, for the moment, at least, was not that far away.

"I don't know what happens, Sopi. I wish I did," he said cryptically.

At the sound of her nickname on his lips, she found herself trying out the sound of his. "Rhys." It caught with tugging sensations in her chest and across her shoulders.

He looked at her.

Everything altered. The air shimmered and the earth stood still. Her scalp prickled and her breasts grew tight and heavy.

"That does not sound like a rejection, *süsse*." His voice melted her bones. He extended a long arm across the surface of the water, palm up in invitation.

She hadn't consciously meant to turn this into anything, but her hand went into his. She floated across the short space between them, drawn by his firm grip to set her hand against his neck. The top of her foot hit a rock, and she reacted with a jerk of her knee, knocking it into his.

He made a noise of concern and gathered her into his lap. His hand cupped her knee and he soothed her kneecap with his thumb. "Tell me," he murmured. "Do you feel the same when I touch you?"

"The same as what?"

The hand behind her back ran up to cradle her neck. With the lightest squeeze, he had her shuddering and turning her torso into his.

"Like that," he growled, lips coming close enough to nibble at her chin. "The way you made me feel on the table today."

Streaks of light and heat seemed to shoot through her at the graze of his whiskers and the mere touch of his mouth on her skin. She cupped his wet beard and searched for his lips with her own, not really knowing what she was doing, only knowing she needed the press of his mouth to her own.

They both moaned as their lips parted and slid and found the right fit. Forever, she thought. She wanted the forceful play of his mouth to consume hers forever. Then his tongue touched her inner lip, delved, and the taste of him shot lightning through her again, spearing a jolt of pleasure straight between her thighs.

She jerked away to catch her breath, stunned, but went straight back after his mouth, pressing the back of his head to encourage him to ravage her.

He growled and they kissed with more fervor, wildly, deeply, a sound rumbling in his chest like a predatory animal. His arms flexed around her, drawing her tighter into his lap and twisting her chest to rub against his.

Her bra shifted as they slithered against one another, abrading and annoying her as it kept her from feeling him with all her skin. She tried to scrabble behind herself with one hand and release it, but his confident fingers met hers and easily unclasped it. She drew back to pull her arms free and he threw it into the snow.

As she pressed herself into him, their mouths crashed together again. His hand swirled a rush of water across her ribs right before his palm flattened against her skin, stroked and shifted, teasing at her waist and shoulder blade and back to her rib cage until she couldn't stand it. She twisted, offering her breast, and finally he claimed the swell in a firm clasp. He shaped and caressed and made her forget everything but the feel of him fondling her so blatantly.

She realized a keening noise was coming from her lips and tried to bite it back, but he caught her nipple in a light pinch and once again she had to break from their kiss to catch her breath—the sensation was so sharp.

"Too much?" He bowed his head over hers as she buried her face in his neck, as though shielding her from something. "You're killing me."

She realized that wasn't just her own heart slamming unsteadily against her rib cage. His was, too. And that hard shape against her hip was him, fully aroused.

She stilled, shocked and stunned and wickedly curious.

"I don't have a condom," he muttered. "This is definitely the best and worst idea you've ever had." He found her ear and flicked his tongue along the rim, making her shudder. "Are you on anything? Should we take this upstairs?"

Dazzled, it took her a moment to realize what he was asking. "I'm not on anything. I don't do this. I've never done it."

"I'm not a guest. You're not an employee. Not right now. That's not what this is. It's two people who can't keep their hands off each other." He cursed and shifted her, but the sound he made was more a groan of suffering. He sucked on her lobe so hard she nearly came out of her skin. Then he applied his teeth, just short of pain, holding her in a tingling state between fear and trust.

If she pulled away, it would hurt, but she didn't want to go anywhere. She petted her fingers across his wet beard, soothing the beast who held her in his tense jaws. Her pulse throbbed in her throat and low in that secretive place between her clamped thighs.

"I mean I've *never* done this," she admitted in a quavering voice. "Made love. With anyone."

His arms nearly squashed her breathless, and a strangled noise came out of him.

"Are you serious?" He took hold of her wet, knotted hair, holding her so her nose was nearly touching his. His eyes were depthless black orbs, threatening to pull her into another universe. Her heart galloped so hard, she thought her chest would explode.

"Who would I sleep with? No one has ever made me feel like this."

"How?" His hand tightened in her hair, pulling her head back to expose her throat. He licked along the artery, and her nipples contracted to such tight points, they felt pierced. She pinched her thighs together.

"Like I'm on fire," she gasped. "Like I need your hands all over me to put it out."

His ragged laugh rang with satisfaction. This time when he claimed her breast, she arched into his touch. He caught her nipple in the crook of two fingers and applied tender pressure until she set her open teeth against his neck.

His caress was so delicious, she found herself sucking the skin of his neck against her teeth before she realized what she was doing and pulled back.

"Mark me, *süsse*." He gentled his touch and circled his thumb around her turgid, stimulated nipple, soothing. "Don't be scared. I won't hurt you. But I do want this." His arms hardened as he lifted her.

Her shoulders and chest came out of the water. As the cold hit her and tightened her nipples even more, he closed his mouth over one. The sudden shifts in temperature and his hard pull sent a jolt of electricity through her. She squeaked and clenched her hand in his hair.

He made a noise of sympathy and drew back to blow and lick circles around her nipple, making her sob under a fresh onslaught of blinding sensation.

She didn't know what to do. Wires of tension pulled in her abdomen and lower. It was more than she could take, but she was greedy, too. She folded her arms around the back of his head and he captured her nipple again, sucking more gently this time, while she moaned in abject pleasure, head falling back so her hair was in the water.

When he finally let her sink back down into his lap, she was trembling and panting. He was so hard against her hip, she thought he must be in pain. Perhaps he was. He was breathing in deliberately measured breaths, and his thighs opened wider to cradle her more deeply against him.

"Do you want me to…" She didn't know what to do. What to offer. But she knew she was dying to touch him.

"I want you to let me do this." His hand slid to catch against the elastic of her underpants. He paused, the fabric pulled far enough from her hip the first ripple of hot water began to caress her bare skin.

Breathless with anticipation, she nodded.

He drew her panties down. The small shift bounced her naked backside against his thighs. Her stomach wobbled at the light abrasion of his leg hair against the sensitive cheeks of her bottom. He pulled the cotton off her ankles and flicked it over his shoulder, joining her bra somewhere in the snow.

"And how does this feel, *süsse*?" His fingertips trailed across her outer thigh to her hip while she absorbed the eddies of hot water moving freely against her most intimate places.

She could hardly breathe. She thought about his touch trailing into those places and shifted restlessly, her nose finding its way into the wet whiskers under his jaw.

"I don't know what to do," she confessed with embarrassment. "I've never touched a man."

"Then by all means, find out what you've been missing." His teeth flashed in a brief smile, but he chucked her chin. "And come here. I want to kiss you again."

She pressed her mouth to his, joyously returning to this wondrous place where she could flagrantly gorge herself on the taste and feel of his lips and tongue and the beard that was rough and silky and utterly compelling.

Shyly, one arm firmly encircling his neck, she let her other hand drift to caress across his shoulder. Those tendons were tight and straining, but not in the way they'd been this afternoon. His pectoral muscles were taut, too, flexing beneath her touch as she dipped her hand below the surface.

Was that his nipple? She scraped her thumb across it, and he made a low sound of pleasure in his throat, one she couldn't help teasing out of him a second time before she shifted to make space for her hand to trail between them, down to the fierce shape pressing so insistently against her hip.

As she closed her fist on the girth of him, his fingers bit into her waist where he anchored her on his thighs. His teeth took hold of her bottom lip, and she felt the rumble of his pleasured groan vibrate in his chest.

How utterly fascinating. She moved her hand, learning the shape of him, discovering what made him hiss or release sounds of delicate agony.

"Am I hurting you?" she broke their kiss to ask.

"No." He stole brief, hungry kisses. "Squeeze tighter."

She looked down at where the dark water obscured her view of him. "I feel cheated."

"So do I." He nuzzled under her chin. Beneath the water, he skimmed his hand along the back of her thigh, but stopped where her leg sat pressed to the top of his.

She tucked her chin and kissed him, squeezed him more boldly and allowed her legs to relax.

His flesh pulsed in her fist and he tilted her, rolling her into a more aggressive kiss that flipped her heart on its edge. Her inner muscles clenched in anticipation, but his fingertips only teased behind her thighs, the barest touch skimming lightly across the fine hairs that protected her folds.

She sobbed with denial. Opened her legs more. Tried to tell him wordlessly what she wanted. He made a low sound of satisfaction and his touch moved to the front of her thighs, stroked inward and upward, until she was the one biting his lip, aching with expectancy.

When his hand finally, firmly covered her, her stomach fluttered and she groaned into his mouth. He seemed to brand her with his intimate touch, claiming her so thoroughly, she had to break their kiss and exchange breathless pants with him.

"If we do this right, we'll do it together," he said in a voice like smoke and velvet. "Yes?"

"Yes," she breathed. Then opened her mouth in a silent scream because he lifted all but one finger from her and gently worked his wicked touch against her.

"Keep stroking me, *süsse*," he urged in a whisper.

"I like it. It feels like this." He found the most sensitive place on her body and pressed without mercy, two fingertips now slowly circling to draw her into a place of mindless pleasure.

She shook, groaning with abandon into his naked shoulder, not realizing she had tightened her hold on him until he gave an abbreviated thrust into her grip and made a ragged noise against her ear.

"Like that, yes." His breath hissed with concentrated pleasure. "We're going to kill each other." He rocked his touch, unhurried as he stoked the fire within her. "I couldn't be happier than to die right here, tonight. Like this."

It was the most singular experience of her life, to communicate completely with touch. To caress him and sense his pleasure as acutely as she experienced her own.

He became her entire world. Nothing mattered in these concentrated seconds except his touch passing across her bundle of nerves, his pulse against her palm, the wall of his iron-hard body shifting with light friction against her skin.

Tension coiled in her abdomen. Through her whole body. She licked his skin and kissed him with abandon, trying to make him understand how exquisite he was making her feel. How he was torturing her beyond what she thought she could stand, yet she never wanted him to stop.

In a subtle move, he hitched her a fraction higher and his touch probed. Her inner muscles tightened at the intrusion of his finger. She shivered despite being so hot she thought she would incinerate. He bit tenderly at her lips with his own, teasing kisses of reassurance as the pressure of his palm rocked where she needed it most.

She saw stars. Gripped him tightly in her fist and matched the rhythm of his thrusts with a lift of her hips against his firm hand. The crisis rose. She tasted copper and thought she might have bitten his lip. She wasn't sure, but he didn't complain. He only kept up the wild caresses that carried them both over a waterfall so they plunged freely off a cliff into the mist.

CHAPTER FOUR

RHYS VAGUELY WONDERED if there was an aphrodisiac in these waters, because he had never climaxed so hard in his life. Despite aching from the force of it, he wanted nothing but to pull Sopi astride him and sink into the satin depths he'd claimed with his touch.

He gently cradled her trembling body against his unsteady heart, trying to find his breath. Trying to find a shred of sense, because all-night lovemaking had a place—and it wasn't a primordial pond in the frozen wilderness.

With a virgin disguised as a woodland nymph.

He didn't disbelieve her about her inexperience, but he was incredulous that such a passionate woman hadn't found someone to share her sensuality with.

No one has ever made me feel like this.

Him, either, and that shook him. He wasn't entitled to this sort of high. His deepest instincts began to war, one side warning him that he couldn't have this. The other, greedier side wanted to mate and mate some more. Grind himself against her until they were nothing but dust.

She posed a very serious danger, this curious, unassuming goddess of a woman.

He rose abruptly, making her gasp at the shock of cold air on her wet skin.

He twisted to ease her back under the warmth of the water, seating her on the flat ledge he'd vacated.

She blinked in surprise, mouth pouted and shiny from their endless kisses, all but her collarbone hidden from his insatiable gaze.

"I'll fetch you a towel and a robe." He waded out of the water, welcoming the bracing slap of winter frost that cleared his head so he could think.

"You don't have to," she said in a small voice behind him.

"I want to," he insisted, pushing his wet arms into his robe and belting it tightly. "Two minutes."

Sopi was reeling from what she'd done with the prince. Her whole body tingled with lassitude, the kind that made her want to groan in luxury at how deliciously sated she felt. She couldn't think of any other experience that had left her so dreamily satisfied.

His abrupt departure caused her a pinch of distress, though. The longer she sat here, the more she began to feel self-conscious about her lack of inhibition. About waiting here like a harem girl for the sheik to return.

When she heard his footsteps crunching through the trees, she sat a little straighter, mouth trembling into a shy smile of greeting.

It wasn't him. It was one of his bodyguards. The clean towel and robe he carried glowed like an armload of snow as he approached.

Throat locked, eyes burning in mounting horror, Sopi watched him look indecisively between the soggy pants and shirt she'd left atop her shoes and the snow-covered bench nearby.

"The prince offers his regrets that he couldn't bring these himself. He said he will speak to you in the morning. Um… Here?" He shook out the items and hung them on the fence, then stepped through the gate and stood with his back to her.

"What are you doing?" she asked, appalled when he stayed there.

"I'm to escort you safely indoors."

Her embarrassment turned to outrage. "I'm fine. *Go.*"

"With respect, I have my orders. Take your time."

She stewed with impotent fury as she realized her choices were to argue while she boiled or end this as quickly as possible. Why was the practical choice always to give in?

And why hadn't Rhys come back himself? Had she turned him off? Had he finished with her already? Was he mad that she hadn't put out with *actual* sex?

Growing more and more horrified by what she'd done, she waded out and shook the robe open, struggling into it without bothering to dry herself. When she scooped up her clothes, she glanced at the thick snow on the far side of the pool and decided to find her underwear in the morning, when it was light.

Moments later, she stomped through the trees toward her cabin, surprising the bodyguard into saying, "Ma'am?" He hurried to follow her new direction.

She ignored him, aware of him trailing her, but she didn't even look at him as she got to her door, unlocked it, then closed it in his face, locking it again from the inside.

With hot, dry eyes and wet, tangled hair, she fell into bed.

Rhys had returned to the deserted spa in time to hear Nanette trying to pull rank on his bodyguard.

"I'm the owner. I can go anywhere I want," she insisted.

"Your mother claims to own it," Rhys had said flatly, moving forward to prevent her from realizing he was coming from the hallway to the building's exit, not the men's room.

Nanette faltered, frosty expression morphed into welcome.

"That's what I mean, of course. My mother is the owner. Your Highness," she added with a sweet smile especially for him. "When I saw your man standing guard, I wanted to be sure you had everything you need."

"Everything but privacy."

Her smile stiffened, and she looked past him. He waited for her gaze to come back and held it with his most unapologetically imperious glare.

She sniffed and said, "I'll leave you to it, then."

"Do." He waited until she was out of earshot before he muttered his instructions to his bodyguard to take a robe and towels to Sopi, aware Nanette would stake out his floor to see whom he brought back to his room.

Rhys rarely took action without considering the consequences. If he did, he would currently be wondering if a deflowered virgin was incubating a royal baby. He'd had the presence of mind to stay this side of sane with Sopi, thankfully, but he wouldn't expose her as his lover to the likes of Nanette until such time as he'd weighed the ramifications for both of them. What little she'd told him about her relationship with Maude meant there could be consequences for her.

She had also left him with the impression that she was the rightful owner of this property, if not legally, at least morally. Her father had bought it for her mother,

who had lovingly restored it, but Maude was the one
trying to unload it in a private sale under the radar.

That had his mind churning as he took the elevator
back to his floor, passing Nanette in a chair in an alcove,
hair twisted around one finger, an open book in her lap.

"Good night," she said as he passed, shoe dangling
from her toe.

He nodded curtly, entered his room and went directly to the window on the north wall. He thought he
might have seen a flash of movement in the trees but
wasn't sure.

Annoyed, he went back to the folio Maude had given
him.

Lawyers cost money, Sopi had said.

They did but, as it happened, he had an abundance
of both.

Sopi's morning went from bad to worse very quickly.

She woke with the worst type of hangover—the
sober kind that piled nausea on remorse with none of
the blurry celebration of alcohol to dampen her memory or give her an excuse for behaving so wantonly. She
didn't even regret the sex part. She had wanted that,
but she felt very much like she'd fallen for a line from
a playboy who set up conquests like bottles on a log,
simply so he could shoot them down.

At least no one would know, she told herself. Then
her walk of shame past the pump house turned up fruit-
less. One of the hotel's maintenance men must have
checked the gate and gathered her bra and underwear.
She could only pray her things would be thrown away
rather than turned in to Lost and Found.

By the time she was heading into the back door of
the hotel and passing Maude's office, her phone was

exploding with the usual work-related texts. Sopi had her head down, reading complaints about late deliveries and equipment needing repair, and didn't see Maude waiting for her until her stepmother's haranguing voice said, "Sopi."

Hiding her wince, Sopi detoured into Maude's office. "Good morning."

"Two of Fernanda's friends are arriving in Jasper in an hour. They don't want to wait for the shuttle. Can you collect them?"

"Fernanda can't do it?" Wasn't that the obvious solution?

"She's tied up."

Doing what? Sopi didn't ask. She was too relieved to have an excuse to disappear for three hours. Plus, the drive was always pretty. Minutes later, she was admiring the golden gleam of snow off the craggy peaks above her and caught the stub tail of a lynx as it slunk into the trees.

Maude's information on the women's flight was completely wrong, of course. Sopi wound up with time to kill, so she engaged in retail therapy while she was in the bigger center. Then she sat in the airport addressing as many texts and emails as she could.

When the chartered flight finally arrived, there were a dozen women, too many for Sopi's SUV, *and* they'd already arranged for a private shuttle.

Annoyed, but completely unsurprised—this was classic Fernanda—Sopi drove home alone.

Rhys had grown up on the sort of palace intrigue that had resulted in the murder of his parents. The infantile game Maude was playing, trying to sell this property without telling the person it would affect most gravely, was nothing more than a mosquito-like annoyance to him.

Things took a turn into adult parlor games when Rhys decided to play along while he turned the tables. He kept hearing Sopi ask, *How long does it last? What happens when it's over?*

They had barely even started and couldn't really continue, not properly. That infuriated him, but after their intimacy last night, he couldn't ignore the way Maude was going behind Sopi's back. He was convinced Maude would pursue the sale with someone else if he declined, so he decided to go through with it. He had Gerard call Maude first thing and tell her to expect the prince's counteroffer later today.

Rhys then sent his bodyguard to fetch Sopi. He wanted to come clean about his purchase and include her in the negotiations. Maybe they could work out some other arrangement while they were at it. He knew it was next to impossible, though, and that put him on edge.

When his bodyguard returned with Cassiopeia's neatly bagged delicates and the news that she had driven away in a company vehicle, he nearly snapped.

This was the only time they had!

He was in a brooding, foul mood when Gerard knocked and entered carrying his trusty tablet. "I relayed the stepdaughter's details to the palace for the due-diligence investigation, sir. You'll want to see this. The palace investigators dug fairly deeply into the Brodeur background—"

"And Maude is on the run from the law?" he surmised facetiously. "Shocking."

"Um, no, sir. Maude and her daughters don't seem to have a criminal record of any kind. But Cassiopeia's mother is a Basile-Munier."

Rhys snapped his head around. "But they died out."

Nevertheless, his blood leaped as he took the tablet and scrolled through the report. It included an image of a birth certificate and a short article by a historian who had visited this spa some years ago. The man had been trying to prove the owner was the surviving child of a prince who had disappeared from public life after an assassination attempt. That prince and his wife had had a daughter late in life. She'd eloped against her father's wishes.

A marriage certificate and a title search on this property all seemed to indicate Sopi's mother was that same woman.

"Is this real?"

"A DNA test would confirm it, although I'm not sure where we'd get a sample. Miss Brodeur seems to be the only surviving member. But if you scroll to the photo at the bottom, it would seem, um, like mother like daughter. And granddaughter."

Rhys stared at a scan of a dated color photograph of two women who both had Sopi's cheekbones and chin, rich brown hair and gleaming dark eyes.

The room was absolutely still and silent, but he felt as though a gust of wind hit him. Went through him. Nearly knocked him on his ass.

This was too easy. Too perfect. This wasn't how life worked. Not how it should do in any case, not for him.

At the same time, a roaring thrill went through him. He could have her. He *would* have her. His agile brain quickly found the rationale for it. A commoner would have been a fight, but a royal would be accepted without question. Even better, she was a lost princess whose story would pull the spotlight from Henrik. His brother dropping out of public life while he sought treatment would barely be noticed by anyone.

"Forget driving down the price of the spa. I want a swift sale, immediate possession and binding terms."

The checkers game he'd been playing with Maude was flung into the air. This was now grand master chess with a side hand of high-stakes poker.

Within the hour, Gerard had the contract finalized. Maude agreed that the transfer of ownership would remain confidential until such time as Rhys saw fit to announce it. Rhys informed her he would retain all staff but no longer needed a marketing VP or brand ambassadress. The people holding those positions—Nanette and Fernanda—would have to vacate their suite by the end of the week.

"Your late husband purchased this property for his wife?" Rhys asked as he and Maude set their electronic signatures to the final deal. He was curious whether Maude knew of Sopi's royal blood.

"I understood she had an inheritance of some kind enabling her to renovate it. We rarely spoke about our previous marriages, to be honest. I'm just delighted to finally have this albatross off my hands. I run it as a folly, but it's more work than it's worth."

As Gerard double-checked and pronounced everything settled, Rhys said to Maude, "Would you and your family dine with me this evening?"

"Oh, Nanette and Fernanda would love that."

No mention of Sopi, her considerable contribution to the business or how this sale would impact her.

Maude's complete disregard for her stepdaughter incensed Rhys, making his delight in outsmarting her grow exponentially until a bellow of triumph was nearly bursting from his chest.

It was a warning sign that he felt far too strongly about this. About *Sopi*. If he felt anything, it ought to be the comfortable satisfaction that he had uncovered an opportunity that benefited his brother and was moving strategically to seize it before anyone else could.

Even when he had the spa sewn up, however, Rhys's powerful sense of urgency didn't ease. He tried to pace it off, aware that Sopi would be furious with him, but his deal with Maude was the least of the shocks she would receive tonight.

When Sopi returned and confronted Maude over the wasted day, her stepmother frowned and said, "Oh, you know how Fernanda gets distracted when she's excited. She and Nanette have been invited to dine with the prince tonight. That must be why she mixed things up."

It was a prevarication if not an outright lie. Sopi was dying to say, *Oh, really? Because last night, when I was with the prince, he told me he wasn't interested in either of them.*

But she didn't want to reveal she'd been with the prince. She hadn't felt sordid when it happened, but after brooding on it all day, she was convinced she'd behaved like those women he'd spoken of so disparagingly. The ones who straddled him whether he wanted them to or not.

She went about her afternoon checking in with staff and pitching in as necessary. When a handsome young man approached her as she was covering the booking desk, she smiled in greeting, caught off guard when he used her full name, not the *Sopi* on her name tag.

"Cassiopeia Brodeur?"

"Yes." This was more the type of man she ought to aim for, she thought absently. He was polite and well dressed, but his attitude didn't scream wealth and privilege. He returned her smile, but with polite reserve. He didn't move the needle on her body temperature one millimeter, which was delightfully unthreatening if a little disappointing.

"Please call me Sopi. How can I help you?"

"I'm the prince's assistant, Gerard. This is for you." The small envelope he offered was imprinted with the royal crest.

Her heart tripped, and she ducked the envelope below the edge of the desk to hide how her hands began to tremble.

"Thank you," she said in a strangled voice, cheeks scorching. She wanted to glance around guiltily but held his stare and her smile even though it began to feel forced.

"He asked if I could also take your number?" He offered his telephone with a contact already started in her name.

She balked. Rhys had gotten her naked last night, then fobbed her off on his bodyguard when he was finished with her. She wasn't up for a do-over, if that's what this was about.

"Perhaps if you read his message," Gerard suggested, correctly interpreting her mutinous expression.

She withdrew the card, which was a single sheet, not even folded. It was some kind of high-grade linen stock in ivory with raw edges, also embossed with his crest.

His fine-tipped pen had dug in deep and left small trails, as though he'd rushed to write his brief message, barely lifting the pen. Or had written it in anger.

Where the hell did you go today?
Dinner.
No excuses.

Splotch went the ink on the final dot.

She bit her lip and slid the card back into the envelope, glanced at Gerard.

"Seven p.m. in the dining room with the rest of your family? I'll tell him you're confirmed?"

The rest of her family? *Yech.*

He must have read her reaction. "If there are any impediments, please bring them to my attention so I may iron them away."

She resisted asking him to squash her family flat.

"I'll be there," she said, not sure if she was telling the truth. At least she'd bought a new dress today, still stinging over the incident with her stepsisters. The new one wasn't designer or flashy by their standards, but it had come from an upscale boutique and cost more than Sopi's weekly earnings. She had planned to return it on her next trip to Jasper.

"Excellent. And would you be so kind…?" He offered his phone again.

She hesitated, then gave him her number. He tried it, smiling when a ping sounded in her pocket. "Please let me know if I can assist you in any way."

Perhaps he could offer her some strategies on facing the prince after last night?

For the rest of the afternoon, every time she tried to think up a reason to cry off the dinner invitation, she touched the card in her pocket and could hear Rhys's deep voice warning, "No excuses." Why did she find his profanity-laced impatience so reassuring? It brought a secretive smile to her lips every time she thought of it.

At five fifty-five, Maude called her. "Sopi. We have a disaster in the kitchen. You'll have to run out or breakfast won't happen tomorrow morning."

Here was her excuse to skip dinner, but a devilish part of her refused to seize it.

"We're expected to dine with the prince this evening, aren't we?" she asked with a full pound of smugness. "I had a note from him, personally inviting me. I don't want to be rude."

A pause that was loud enough to *thunk*. Maude might have swallowed. "I assumed you would decline. You tend to set yourself apart from us."

Oh, was it was *her* who did that?

Actually, maybe she did. She had never forgiven Maude for keeping her father in Europe or for spending all his money. Still, Sopi pulled the phone from her ear and scowled at the screen. Maude was sounding particularly petty about a simple dinner invitation. Was she that embarrassed of her unrefined stepdaughter?

"Well, tonight I'll join you," Sopi said cheerfully. "Since it's not often I get a chance to dine with royalty." She hung up and stuck her tongue out at the phone.

Then she suffered a churning stomach for the next hour as she showered and dressed. Her hair, which she never bothered to cut because she always wore it up, was ridiculously long, falling to her waist. At least it had a hint of wave, but it tickled her lower back, where her new dress had a circular cutout.

The dress was a sleeveless knit with a high collar, but it made her look fuller in the chest than she was, which balanced hips that were a shade wider than her stepsisters' fashion magazines told her they ought to be.

She wasn't much for makeup, but her cheeks were pale with nerves. She gave them a swipe of blusher and painted her lips with a pink gloss. She hadn't thought about new shoes when she'd been shopping today so she had only the plain black pumps she wore when she played hostess in the dining room.

As she went onto tiptoe in the bathroom, trying to see her bottom half in the mirror, the butterflies in her stomach turned to slithering snakes. She was kidding herself. Not only would she not measure up to Nanette and Fernanda, she would look downright foolish in everyone's eyes, trying so hard to impress.

Just as she started to kick off her shoes, however, Gerard texted that the prince was sending an escort for her.

Sopi choked on her tongue, texted back that it was unnecessary and decided to do what she'd been doing for years now—brave things out for one more day.

She had put up with Maude's proprietary orders and her stepsisters' snobbery because the alternative was to cede the territory to them and wind up with nothing. Cassiopeia's was her home. She would fight for it to the bitter end.

Which came sooner than she'd expected.

What happens when it's over?

It would never be over. Rhys had found the woman he would marry. The knowledge should have afforded him nothing beyond a contented sense of completion. He didn't like the gnawing sense in him that he needed to leap and snatch and hold on tight. Gerard had assured him Sopi had promised to join them for dinner, but she had become so important to him in the last few hours, Rhys feared that if she wasn't in the dining room when he got there, he might well devolve into shedding blood.

He stalked from the elevator across the short bridge that overlooked the foyer below to the dining room reservation desk. He was as combat ready as any of his ancestral knights, vibrating with a drive to claim.

The babble inside the dining room went silent as he appeared. Everyone rose with a muted shuffle of chairs. A small pocket of women stood to the side of the reception desk. One of them was backed into a corner behind a potted palm.

The tension in their small group hit him like a battering ram, but the sight of Sopi's drawn cheeks and bravely lifted chin reached out to claw into his chest.

"Ladies," he greeted.

Sopi stiffened and skimmed her gaze to a distant corner, refusing to make eye contact.

"Your Highness," the rest murmured.

So. They'd told her about the sale. And she was taking it badly.

Rhys kept an impassive expression on his face, but he wanted to catch her by the chin and force her thick lashes up, so she looked directly into his eyes. He wanted to ask how she dared let these women take advantage of her. Didn't she realize who she *was*?

No. She didn't. Steps had been taken to bury it too deeply.

He had thought to make a dramatic announcement here in the dining room, but as he read the angry hurt in her, he realized he couldn't spring it on her like that. She would hate and blame him a little longer, but he could withstand it.

Any guilt Rhys might have experienced for his underhanded actions in buying the spa dried up, however. It was past time Sopi learned the truth about her mother and herself. He couldn't wait for the transformation.

Maude's younger daughter demanded his attention by stepping forward and offering a curtsy with a breathy, nervous giggle.

"Your Highness, some of my friends have just arrived." She waved at a long table with a half dozen women down either side, all looking his way with anticipation. A few empty seats had been saved in the middle. "We wondered if you might enjoy a more lively evening? They're anxious for a chance to meet you."

"Another time." He glanced impatiently at Maude.

"Of course," Maude said smoothly. "We have a quiet table reserved at the back. Sopi?"

"This way." Sopi didn't smile, and her voice was cold and pointed as an icicle aimed at the middle of his chest. She led the way through the staring crowd.

Ingrained protocol nearly had him offering an arm to escort Maude and her eldest daughter, but he shunned them at the last second, moving ahead of them, all his attention on the sensual swish of loose hair across the top of a stunning, heart-shaped ass that swayed provocatively as she wound her way between the tables.

Dear God, that *hair*. How dare she hide such a thing from him? It was an instant fetish he would need a thousand nights to indulge.

It was a good thing the place was filled with mostly women, because if he caught any man, even one of his lethally trained bodyguards, checking her out, he would duel to the death.

He gritted his teeth, trying to suppress this unwelcome surge of possessiveness. Where was it coming from? It was more than his innate preference to act on his decisions the minute he made them. It was positively primeval. It was an aspect of that wildness he knew lurked in any human, and he didn't like it. He

only hoped it would ease up once he knew she was his.
It had to. Otherwise they were doomed.

He was given the position at the head of the table,
Maude on his right, Nanette on his left. Sopi sat on
Maude's right and glared at Fernanda, who shrugged
across at her in a silent, *Don't blame me*.

"I want to thank you for your hospitality," Rhys said
as their champagne arrived and was poured. "I'll be
leaving tomorrow."

"You won't stay the week?" Maude murmured, but
she was drowned out by Fernanda's, "Us, too, in a few
days. Finally!" Fernanda raised her glass.

Sopi choked strongly enough they all lowered their
glasses. Her eyes glimmered as she shot hard looks at
each of them.

"You suck. You all suck," she croaked.

There was a collective gasp from tables nearby.
Maude said a sharp, "Sopi! Consider who you're speaking to."

Rhys said nothing, pleased to see she possessed a
spine after all. She would need one.

"*All* of you." She rose and glared directly at him with
betrayed hurt sharp as the edge of a knife.

Her hand jerked, but before she could fling the contents of her wine at him, Rhys's bodyguard caught her
wrist.

"Stand down," Rhys barked at him, also rising.

Sopi shrugged away from the bodyguard's hold and
stepped away from the table. She threw her glass to the
floor in a shattering statement.

"Go to hell. Every single one of you." She stalked
out.

"*Someone* doesn't know which side her bread is but-
tered on," Nanette said into her champagne.

"True," Rhys bit out, sending Nanette a dark glower that made her blanch. He set his hands on the table to lean over the three women. "Those who betray others to get what they want should expect the same treatment. Skip the meal and start packing. Be gone by midnight."

"What—"

He ignored the women's cries of shock as he straightened and sent a curt nod to Gerard. His assistant would ensure the staff were notified that Maude and her daughters no longer gave the orders and, in fact, were no longer residents of the hotel.

As the buzz of gossip and speculation spread like wildfire through the room, Rhys jerked his head at his bodyguard to lead the way to Sopi's cabin.

How stupid could she get? She had genuinely thought her worst humiliation was allowing a man with more experience to talk her out of her clothes and take a few liberties with her person. She had thought letting down her physical guard where his sexual intentions were concerned had been the careless act, but no. Last night's dalliance had been some kind of misdirection so she would be blindly ignorant of what Maude was really doing.

What *he* was doing. Of course he wasn't interested in her. He had toyed with her the way some executives spun fidget spinners while brokering a deal.

The pressure in her chest threatened to crack her breastbone, but Sopi refused to scream or cry or release any of the aching sobs branding her throat.

Fine, she'd been thinking for the last twenty minutes, after Fernanda had spilled the beans that Maude had definitely meant to be delivered a few days from now, no doubt after ordering Sopi to load their damned lug-

gage for them. Maude had hissed in warning and Nanette had said, "For God's sake, Fernie. Mummy told
you it's confidential."

"What?" Fernanda had had the gall to cast it as a
good thing. "She'll be happy. Mummy sold it all to the
prince. We'll all be out of your hair by next weekend.
You should be happy, Sopi."

Sopi had been utterly speechless, standing there in
shock as the prince arrived and everyone stared. She
had moved on autopilot, only feeling reality hit her as
they reached the table. Instead of holding a chair for
their guest the way she would as a hostess, the prince's
assistant, Gerard, had moved behind her and held her
chair.

It had been so unexpected, it had knocked her out
of her stasis and into a plummeting realization that everything had changed. The one dream she had clung to
was gone. The only home she had ever known would
never be hers.

The nascent fantasy she had had that a prince—a
damned royal *prince*—might see something in her beyond a penniless chambermaid had burst like a bubble, leaving her coated in a residue of disillusion and
humiliation.

Slamming into her cabin, she kicked off her shoes.
Hard. So that one dented a cardboard box and the other
went flying toward the bathroom door.

She wrenched at the dress she'd bought with him
in mind. It was meant to be pulled on gently to retain
the shape and prevent snags in the delicate knit. She
dragged roughly at it. Tried to tear it because she hated
it. She yanked it off and dropped it where she stood and
wiped her feet on it. She was panting and shaking, still

trying to catch her breath after her sprint through the snow-laden trees, filled with an endless supply of *hate*.

With a final twist of her foot, she flicked it to the side and shoved at a stack of boxes, freshly delivered this afternoon and left for her to move to a more convenient location. Everything was always left to her to do, and she was *sick* of it. She shoved the stack even harder, so it fell with a tumble.

The crash wasn't nearly as satisfying as she had hoped, especially when it was followed by a loud stomp of a heavy foot leaping onto her stoop. The door flung open to let in a burst of cold air that swirled like a demon around her nearly naked body.

Him. The instrument of her ruin.

"Bastard," she muttered and turned away to take her narrow stairs two at a time.

Below her, she heard the door click closed. She glanced down from the loft and gripped the rail with humiliated rage as she watched him take in the clutter and the mess of boxes. He picked up her dress and gave it a light shake.

"Come right in," she said scathingly. "Act like you own the place."

He lifted his gaze, and she instantly felt naked. Not just physically, which she mostly was, but as though she was utterly transparent. As if he could see through her sarcasm to those puerile fantasies she'd spun in her head. It was so agonizing to be seen this way, she had to hold back a sob and turn away. She yanked out a drawer in her dresser, digging for jeans and a pullover. The stairs creaked as she stuck her legs into her jeans.

He appeared in the loft and flicked his gaze in harsh judgment of her used furniture and what she had always thought of as a cozy living space. As her turtleneck nearly choked her, and she yanked at her hair enough that it had some slack outside her collar, she saw the loft through his eyes and was mortified to realize it wasn't humble. It was shabby.

Angry that he was seeing it and forcing *her* to see it, she said, "I was being facetious. What I really meant was get lost."

What she really meant were two words she had never said to anyone, no matter how badly Nanette had ever baited her, but she was feeling them this evening. She really was.

He draped her dress over the footboard of her bed. "We'll continue this discussion in my room."

"Gosh, I would love to accommodate you, Your Highness, but I have to pack and find a place to live. Because if you think I'm going to work for you, you need to see a psychiatrist about your loose grasp on reality."

"My people will pack for you. Socks," he said, nodding at her bare feet.

"I'm not going anywhere with you."

"*Süsse*, I will carry you out of here kicking and screaming if I have to. We are not talking here."

"There is nothing wrong with the way I live." Everything was wrong with it, but she would die on the hill of defending what was left of her home after the way he had treated her. "This is what a person has to do when they're kicked around by people who have more power than they do."

"I know that!" he shouted, then seemed to pull himself together with a flex of his shoulders and a clench of his jaw. "It reminds me of the way my brother and I lived when we were in exile. I hate it. I won't stay here, but you and I will talk. Am I carrying you?"

Shaken by that completely unexpected admission,

she only hesitated long enough for one brow to go up in a warning that he was dead serious.

She swallowed and told herself she was only cooperating because this was too small a space for the explosive emotions still detonating inside her and radiating off him. She found a balled-up pair of socks and sat on the top stair to put them on with her boots, aware of him looming over her the whole time.

"I don't know what we could possibly have to say to one another," she muttered.

"You will be surprised," he promised in a dark vow. He followed her down the stairs and out the door.

His bodyguard flanked them as they crossed to the hotel and blocked anyone from joining their elevator.

Sopi refused to make eye contact with the wide stares that came at them from every level of the foyer.

"I forgot my phone," she murmured as she realized her hands and pockets were empty.

"It will be retrieved." He let her into his suite himself, waiting while the bodyguard moved through in a swift check of all the rooms. Rhys stationed the man outside his door with, "Only Gerard, and only if the place is burning to the ground."

"Yes, sir."

Rhys let out the sort of breath that expelled hours of tested patience.

Sopi hugged herself and moved to the window where she noted he had quite the view of naked women frolicking in the pool below.

"I was in here last week," Sopi murmured. "Packing Nanette's and Fernanda's things to move them down the hall so you could have this suite. Except that's not what I was doing, was I? You've all been cooking this for ages, and I just did the heavy lifting so they could be on their way faster."

"If they're still here in three hours, I'll set them on the stoop myself."

Taken aback, she realized that whatever fury she was nursing, he had plenty of his own. "If you're so angry with them, why—"

He held up a hand to stop her, pausing in removing his suit jacket before finishing his shrug. He threw his jacket over the back of a chair and loosened his tie on the way to retrieving stapled documents from a stack on the desk.

He dropped one set onto the coffee table. "That's a copy of the offer Maude accepted today." *Slap.* "That's the transfer of Cassiopeia's into your name."

CHAPTER FIVE

"WHAT?" STUNNED, SOPI stepped forward in shocked excitement, unable to believe it. She pulled up as she realized such a thing would have to come with conditions. Her excitement drained away. "Why?" she asked with dread, fearing she already knew.

His beard darkened where he bit the inside of his cheek. His irises glowed extra blue and laser sharp as he branded patterns on her skin with his gaze. "Last night, you asked me where this was going."

"It's not going anywhere. You made that perfectly clear when you didn't come back to the pool afterward." Her heart hammered in her chest.

"Nanette was loitering in the spa. I was protecting you by sending my bodyguard."

"Sure you were," she choked. "That's also what you're doing here, I guess?" She waved at the paperwork.

"I am," he said in a voice so gritty it left her feeling abraded all over. "Nanette knew I was with someone last night. I could have revealed you, but I wasn't ready to. I wanted time to consider exactly how I would answer your question."

"And this is your answer?" She was growing more appalled by the second. How did he manage to hurt her so easily? So *deeply*? Despite last night's intimacy, they were still virtual strangers. He shouldn't be able to impact her like this. "You went behind my back to cut a deal to buy my *home*?"

"I wanted to talk to you about it." Her temper didn't faze him. He stood as an indifferent presence, unrepentant and untouched. "You weren't here. From now on, you're not allowed to be angry with me for actions I take if you don't show up to hear my side of it before I take them."

"Wow. Sure," she agreed, laying on the sarcasm with a trowel. "I will be sure to never be angry with you in future when I *never see you again*."

"Dial back the histrionics. We have a lot to cover, and you don't want to peak too early."

Her blood boiled. She shot her arms down straight at her sides, hands in tight, impotent fists.

"I have a right to be angry, Rhys! You bought property stolen from *me*." She jabbed at her chest. "Now you want to gift it to me like you're doing me a favor—" Her voice caught, but she forced out the rest, each word like powdered glass in the back of her throat. "But I expect you want favors in return, don't you? Virginity is quite the precious commodity these days, isn't it? You make me sick!"

She turned to wrench at the door latch, but he was on top of her, surrounding her and catching her hand in a firm but strangely gentle grip as he caged her. His deep, velvety voice growled into her hair, causing tickles against her ear that made goose bumps rise on her nape.

"It's a wedding gift."

"To who!" She tried to shove her elbow into his gut.

"You." He spun her and pinned her to the door. "Now

settle down before my bodyguard bursts in here and I have to kill him for trying to touch you again."

"You really have lost half the cards from your deck. I'm not marrying you." She pressed her forearms against his chest, forcing space between them, so astounded she didn't have the sense to be intimidated. "We've known each other two *days*. Why would you even suggest such a thing?"

"Because the gradual approach is not open to me." His jaw clenched as he studied her flushed, angry expression.

She didn't want to be aware of his heat and weight pressing into her, but she was. She really didn't want to *like* it. She turned her face to the side, resisting and rejecting.

"You were going to come to my room last night. Weren't you?" His voice was smoke and mirrors, casting a spell she had to work to resist.

"If you had come back to the pool and asked me yourself, I probably would have, yes." She lifted her chin but winced internally as she admitted it, hating herself for that, too. "Were you planning to propose if I had?" she scoffed.

He backed off a fraction. "I wasn't thinking much beyond how badly I wanted you in my bed."

"That's a no, then." She gave him a firm nudge, but he was immovable.

"Everything changed while you were playing hide-and-seek this morning."

"I was doing my *job*." Her voice faded into a discouraged sob that rang in her chest as she realized she no longer had one of those.

He sighed and gave a comforting brush of his thumb against her jaw. "Maude was determined to sell the spa,

Sopi. Someone else would have bought this property if I hadn't. Be happy it was me."

"You people need to quit telling me how to feel about this." A burning ache of blame stayed hot in her throat.

"Don't lump me in with your stepfamily," he warned, not even flinching. He only grazed her cheekbone with his fingertips as he tucked a wisp of hair behind her ear. His voice changed. Gentled. "And hear what I'm saying. Your life would have toppled regardless. Whether you're happy about it or not, I'm offering you a cushion. A velvet one. With gold tassels."

His words, edged in irony, held a quiet finality that shook her to the core. Her world *was* shattered. All she had known had been upended and was sliding beyond her reach.

Her heart began to tremble and she pushed harder on his chest, freshly angry, but scared now, too. "Let me go."

He waited a beat, then stepped back and dropped his hands to his sides, watchful.

She hugged herself, moving into the room to put space between them so she could think, but she remained too anxious and confused to make sense of any of this. Marriage? Really?

"I've always thought that if I were to marry, it would be to someone I love. Someone I *trust*. I'm not going to marry to get a *thing*. Especially not to get something that should already be mine."

"I wanted you to be here while I negotiated with Maude." He sounded brisk but tired as he moved to the bar and poured two glasses from a bottle of whiskey that was already open. "If it were up to me, I would have hired the lawyers you needed to fight Maude, taken a partnership in the business in exchange, but there was no time. Plus, all of my business dealings are scrutinized. I can't foot the bill on a stranger's legal fight—or gift a hotel to a woman with whom I am having an affair—without causing a lot of questions to be asked. Buying this property as a present for my future wife, however…"

She shook her head, unable to take in that he really meant that.

Nevertheless, a distant part of her was processing that *she* would finally be the boss here. All her friends would have secure jobs. That was as important for the village as for the spa. She grew dizzy with excitement at the prospect.

But why her?

"Is this like a green-card thing or something?" she managed to ask. "Would it be a fake marriage?"

He snorted as he came across with the glasses. "Not at all."

"You're genuinely asking me to marry you. And if I do, you'll give me this hotel and spa, all the property and rights to the aquifer. Everything," she clarified.

"If you'll live in Verina with me and do what must be done to have my children, yes," he said with a dark smile.

She was still shaking her head at the outrageous proposition but found herself pressing her free hand to her middle, trying to still the flutters of wicked anticipation that teased her with imaginings of how those babies would get made.

She veered her mind from such thoughts.

"Why? I mean, why *me*?" She lifted her gaze to his, catching a flash of sensual memories reflected in the hot blue of his irises.

"I've already told you. I want you in my bed."

"And that's it? Your fly has spoken? That's the sum total of your motivation?"

His eyes narrowed, becoming flinty and enigmatic. "There are other reasons. I'll share them with you, but they can't leave this room."

That took her aback. "What if I don't want to carry your secrets?"

"You're going to carry my name and my children. Of course you'll keep my secrets. Would you like to tell me yours?" He regarded her over the rim of his glass as he sipped, as though waiting for her to tip her hand in some way.

She shrugged her confusion. "I'm not exactly mysterious," she dismissed. "The most interesting thing that's ever happened to me is happening right now. You realize how eccentric this sounds?"

"Eccentric or not, it's a good offer. You should accept it before I change my mind."

She snorted. "You're quite ruthless, aren't you?" She spoke conversationally but knew it as truth in her bones.

"I do what has to be done to get the results I want. You understand that sort of pragmatism, even if you've pointed your own efforts in dead-end directions. I look forward to seeing what you accomplish when you go after genuinely important goals."

"This is my *home*. It's important to *me*."

"Then claim it."

A choke of laughter came out of her. "Just like that? Accept your proposal and—" She glanced at the paperwork. "I'm not going to agree to anything before I've actually reviewed that offer."

"Due diligence is always a sensible action," he said with an ironic curl of his lip. He waved his glass toward the table, inviting her to sit and read.

Gingerly, she lowered onto the sofa and set aside her whiskey.

Rhys kept his back to her, gaze fixed across the valley as he continued to sip his drink, saying nothing as she flipped pages.

His behavior was the sort of thing a dominant wolf would do to indicate how little the antics of the lesser pack affected him, but she was glad not to have his unsettling attention aimed directly at her as she compared the two contracts. Aside from the exchange of money on Maude's—and the fact that hers finalized on her wedding day—they were essentially the same.

"I want possession on our engagement. *If* I decide to accept your proposal," she bluffed, fully expecting him to tell her to go to hell.

"Done. On condition we begin the making of our children on the day our engagement is announced." He turned, and his eyes were lit with the knowledge his agreement had taken her aback. "We'll keep the conception part as a handshake agreement. No need to write that down in black-and-white."

He brought her a pen. His hand was steady as he offered it. Hers trembled as she hesitantly took it.

"Are you completely serious?" she asked.

"Make the change. Sign it. I'll explain why I want you to marry me. You'll accept my proposal, and Cassiopeia's will be yours."

Inexplicable tears came into her eyes. This was too much. Too fast.

"What if we get engaged and I back out?"

"I expect you to go into this with good faith, Sopi. I will."

And he expected her to sleep with him. Get started

on making his babies. She might not have the option of backing out on their marriage if that happened.

She wanted to sleep with him. That was the unnerving part. Not for Cassiopeia's or a wedding ring or babies. For the experience. To be able to touch him and feel…

She swallowed, hearing him say her life would have changed regardless. He was right about that. Which made her stupid to turn this down. It was probably the best outcome she could anticipate. Her alternative was to let him have Cassiopeia's while she tried to sue Maude for a slice of the purchase price. Good luck with that. Maude was headed out of the country. Sopi would most likely lose any settlement she won to lawyer fees anyway.

She told herself she was only signing as a matter of hearing him out, not really committing to changing her entire life.

Shakily, she made the change and set her signature to the page, feeling so overwhelmed her head swam as she rose to bring the pages and pen to him.

He set the contract on an end table and inked his name next to hers, handing it back to her for her inspection.

She moved away from the intensity of his gaze, trying not to think about the full severity of what she was edging toward. She returned the document to the coffee table and picked up her drink, took a bracing sip of scorching whiskey.

"The floor is yours, Rhys." The alcohol left a rasp in her voice. "Tell me what sort of husband I'll get for the price of a spa."

"No more sarcasm," he said flatly and threw back the last of his drink, then went to pour another. "I offer more than a damned spa in exchange for marriage. You'll have security of every kind. Wealth and power and a type of fame that can be tiresome but has its uses. It can be very effective when used for altruistic acts. I thought that might interest you." He cannily noted the way she swung to face him.

"Why would you think that? You don't know me." She demurred, forcing her gaze elsewhere while she took another nervous sip.

"I know more about you than you do," he said with a cryptic sort of confidence that made her feel as though the floor shifted beneath her. "You want this place because it's your home, not to develop it. You care about your employees and work alongside them because they're your friends. You never ask them to do a task you wouldn't do yourself. In fact, you look after complete strangers better than you look after yourself."

"I'm just trying to keep the place running." She shrugged off his compliment.

"You're self-effacing and self-sacrificing. You'll need that."

"Being nice doesn't mean I'm ready to have children." If she was quick to help others, it came from being bounced into friends' homes when her father had traveled, which had happened frequently. She had learned to pitch in to fit in and be welcomed.

When her father had remarried, she had thought he would finally stay home and they would live more as a family. Maude had had expensive tastes, however, and his business had been declining, forcing him to travel even more. What Sopi had really learned from the humbling experience of losing everything was the importance of ensuring she could offer support and attention to her children before making any.

"If I could give you more time to absorb all of this, I would, but time is a luxury I no longer have. My brother has testicular cancer. It was discovered when he and his wife failed to conceive."

"Oh." She swayed, knocked back by the news but wanting to move toward him, to offer some sort of comfort. "I'm so sorry."

He was steely and still, his frozen demeanor holding her off. She stayed where she was.

"What…?" She didn't know what to ask, how to respond.

"They're pursuing treatment options right now. Obviously, we hope he will survive, but even if he does, he will almost certainly be sterile. I'm next in line, therefore I need an heir. And a spare. Turns out they have their uses," he stated with grim humor.

He sipped, and she copied the motion, stunned to her toes.

"Are you aware of Verina's history?" he asked. "Support for my brother has never been higher, but we still have a handful of detractors looking for a foothold. We can't afford any show of weakness. I have to take action to secure the throne before any of this comes to light."

As whiskey slid down her throat like a rusty nail, she glanced at the contract she'd signed.

"I see the urgency, but I still don't understand why me? I mean…" She had to clear her throat to speak, not wanting to state baldly that he might become king. She certainly didn't want to picture herself at his side if he did. "You're, um, saying your son or daughter is likely to rule Verina. There are thousands of blue bloods to choose from as a mother for those children. There are a hundred in this *building* right now." She waved at the walls.

"True. And I came here expecting to find my bride among those women." He tilted the last of the liquid in his glass. "I'm expected to marry someone with that sort of pedigree." He was eyeing her in that penetrating way again. "Henrik's wife, Elise, is the daughter of a diplomat, schooled much as all the women here." He waved at the walls. "But her father lacks a title, and it was a long, hard-won fight for Henrik to be allowed to marry her."

"Then—" That made her a poor choice, didn't it? She suddenly felt as though the floor was falling away, leaving her grappling with such profound disappointment, she realized that she *liked* the idea of marrying him.

"I don't personally care about bloodlines. If I must marry, I want a woman who will be honest with me and show some integrity, rather than tie myself to someone like your stepsisters. I would much prefer to share my bed with someone I want to share my bed with," he added pointedly.

The hot coals in the pit of her belly seemed to glow bright red, as if he'd blown on them, sending heat through her limbs and up into her cheeks and deep into the notch between her thighs. Her scalp itched and her breasts felt tight.

"I don't even have your sister-in-law's education," she said. "I'm as common as clover. You really want to fight that hard for sex?"

He didn't laugh or reassure her that yes, he wanted her *that much*. Instead, his expression turned even more grave.

"You're not a commoner." He spoke with matter-of-fact solemnity. "Your mother was the daughter of Prince Rendor Basile-Munier. He tried to retake his principality of Rielstek when the USSR fell apart. There was an attempt on his life, and he fled to Sweden, where he lived out his days."

He spoke so confidently a jolt went through her. It evaporated into a pained sense of setback. Of stinging anguish that this marriage really wouldn't happen.

"Someone has been embellishing." Regret sat as an acrid taste in the back of her throat. "Did you overhear a local gossiping? I've never heard names and details like that, but it's pure nonsense."

He cocked his head. "Why do you believe that?"

"Because I would know if my mother was a princess! Instead, I know when and how that rumor got started. A guest claimed to be writing a history of some kind. He asked my father if my mother had been a princess. My father said that, like most writers, the guy had a screw loose. Mom would have told him if she was secretly royal. Even though it wasn't true, I was young enough to be taken by the idea. I told some staff, and it turned into a joke. It's a sort of urban legend, something employees repeat to prank the tourists. It's not true, Rhys."

"Yes, it is," he stated. "That historian was an extremely well-regarded academic. I studied from his textbooks myself. Unfortunately, he passed on before this particular work was published. That's why our staff had to dig to find it and why your heritage isn't common knowledge."

"No." She shook her head, growing agitated. "My mother would have told me. My father would have known."

"Not if her father had actively tried to bury their identity, worried for their safety."

"No, Rhys."

"The property in Sweden is still in your family's name. The caretakers live rent-free. They had no incentive to reach out, but they have provided some documentation to our palace investigators. Our team is looking for a means of DNA testing, but they're quite satisfied with the evidence they have so far—especially once they compared photos from your social media pages to your grandmother."

He took out his phone and showed her a photo of a woman in a tiara and a sash. She could have been Sopi dressed in costume.

Sopi dropped her glass, having completely forgotten she was still holding it.

Thankfully, it only held half an ounce of liquid and didn't break. She scrambled to retrieve it and shakily set the glass next to the contract she had signed. *The one agreeing to their terms of engagement.*

She shoved her butt onto the sofa cushions and set her face in her hands, concentrating on drawing a breath while the whole world spun in the wrong direction, pulling her apart.

"I didn't think you were aware," he commented drily.

"This can't be true, Rhys. Does Maude know?"

"I didn't tell her. If I gave a single damn about her, I would look forward to her reaction when she realizes I'm making you my wife and that any future regard you bestow upon her will be strictly on your terms."

Sopi was convulsively shaking her head. "I can't marry you. You can't really expect me to move to Europe with you? Turn into a princess overnight?"

"I've just explained that's what you already *are*." There was no pity in his voice. "I'm exactly the sort of husband you were meant to have."

"But you can't *want* me! I—"

"I damned well do." He sat on the chair to her left, only one hip resting there so he was crowded into her space. His knee brushed hers, and he forced her hands down so she had to lift her gaze to his. "I've explained what's at stake for me and my country. Hell yes, I want to engage myself to a lost princess. We'll be the feel-good media storm of the year."

"You expect me to tell people?" It was another blow she hadn't seen coming. She was going to have a bruise on her forearm where she kept pinching herself, trying to wake up.

"Of course I do. You're ideal."

"No, I'm not!" She waved at the bargain jeans and top she wore.

"You will be."

"You're not listening to me!"

"I've heard every word. You're shocked by ancestry that has been hidden from you. You're already home-sick because this place is your connection to your parents. You're afraid to become my wife because it feels bigger than you ever expected to be."

"I'm afraid of *you*." She realized she was trembling. "How can I trust you when you're forcing all these things onto me?"

"I'm only giving you what you're supposed to have. Do you want to tear that up?" He pointed at the contract they'd signed.

No, but she didn't want to accept that she had no say over anything, not even who she *was*.

He drew a long breath that tried to neutralize the charged energy between them. "I'm just the messenger, Sopi."

"You're proposing to be my *husband*. Maybe you're fine with marrying a stranger, but I'm not." She was a stranger to herself, and it was so disconcerting her brain was splitting in two.

"We're not strangers," he scolded in that tone that crept past her defenses like wisps of drug-laced smoke, filling her with lassitude.

"Sure, you know everything about *me*." She was trying really hard not to become hysterical. "All I know about you is that you swim naked and get whatever you want!"

He let that wash over him, then snorted as if he found something in it funny. He drew a breath and rose, nodding in a way that suggested he was conceding a point.

He pulled out his phone, said, "Gerard. We'd like the dinner we missed. When do you expect Francine? Good. Send her up. I want Sopi to meet her."

"Who?" Sopi asked as he ended the call.

"The new manager of Cassiopeia's until such time as you make changes."

"This is happening too fast, Rhys."

"I know." Now, he almost sounded as if he pitied her. He stepped closer and cradled her jaw, giving her cheekbone a light caress with his thumb. His hand felt a lot warmer than her face.

Despite being wary of trusting him, she rested in that reassuring palm. She wanted to throw herself into his arms. He was the only solid thing in a crumbling universe.

Murmured voices outside the door had him releasing her to invite a middle-aged woman to enter. She had a sleek blond bob and an elegant figure in a crisp suit. If she was jet-lagged, she didn't show it a bit. Her handshake was firm, her smile friendly. Her English held an accent similar to Rhys's, somewhere between French and German.

"Francine will be your proxy once our paperwork

is finalized and you take possession," Rhys said with a nod to their contract.

"I'll take the first week to observe, then communicate my recommendations." Francine mentioned her credentials, which were stellar. "I've taken possession of the office and all the equipment. I thought to also start an audit, if you agree?"

Sopi glanced at Rhys. "I can't afford her." Maybe after a year of penny-pinching, but not when Maude had just drained the coffers dry.

"You can," Rhys assured her. "Once the press release about us goes out, this place will thrive. Go ahead with the audit," he instructed Francine.

Sopi's chest felt compressed. Agreeing to hire Francine felt like an acceptance of marriage and all the rest.

"Francine will ensure future profits will continue to support her well-deserved but exorbitant salary. Even if you were going to be here, I would recommend you move forward with her as your manager."

I will be here, Sopi wanted to argue. She couldn't hold his unwavering gaze, though. Her eyes were growing too hot and damp.

"We'll come back in a few months," he offered in a gentle coax, as though trying to soften a blow. "The ski hill has accepted my offer to purchase, but they want to finish the season. When I come back to finalize that, you can check in here."

It was a thin lifeline, but she grasped it. "You promise?"

"I do."

She gave Francine a timid nod, pretty sure it was the equivalent of pushing the button that would blow up her bridge back to her old life. Even though it was already on fire.

Francine smiled and departed, revealing the room service trolley had arrived. The bodyguard wheeled it in before returning to his station outside the door.

More out of habit than anything, Sopi began transferring the dishes to the small dining table.

Rhys was right there to help. She stepped back, startled to find him so close. "I can do it."

"So can I. I've waited tables."

"When?"

"When I had to." His mouth pursed and his movements slowed as he took care with the setting of their cutlery. "I've been through this sort of transition, Sopi. Both directions. I wasn't given time to pack a bag or hire staff or worry about anyone beyond myself and my brother."

He spoke in a distant tone, as though consciously removing himself from painful memories.

"Online it says you were ten when the revolution happened. I don't understand how anyone could break into a home and commit violence against innocent people."

"Power is an aphrodisiac. The justification was that my father did nothing for Verina. It wasn't until he was gone that people realized the difference between a leader who serves his country and autocrats who take from it."

She couldn't tear her eyes from his grim face.

"I'm so sorry. How did you cope? Where did you go?" He hadn't had any velvet cushions to land on.

"There's a small lake on our border with France. Some of the servants were escaping in a rowboat and took us across with them. We were taken into a protective custody by French authorities, but several governments squabbled over us through those early years, all eager to wage war on our behalf. The real goal was to take possession of Verina, not that we understood it at the time. We only wanted our parents. Our own beds."

"Are you saying you were political hostages?" She was appalled.

"Pawns. Well-treated orphans on whose behalf they claimed to operate. Eventually, a Swiss diplomat who had been a close friend of our father's was able to take us in. He saw to our education with a focus on politics so we understood what was happening to us and Verina. We quickly realized the only help we should accept from any government was the basic human right to move freely. Henrik was sixteen, I was fourteen when we finally moved out on our own."

"That's when you lived…"

"Poorly. Yes," he said shortly. "It was a frustrating time, some of it typical adolescent rage, but we were realizing how badly we'd been used. That the people who should have helped us were operating from their own motives. The greater loss was hitting us, as well. We were mature enough to see the damage that had been done to all of Verina. The path forward to repair not just our own lives, but those of people who we were meant to protect and lead, was daunting. I honestly don't know how Henrik faced being the one. We were eating out of dented cans, barely making the grade at school because we were working any spare moment we had just to pay rent on a moldy apartment. He proved himself to be worthy of the role, though, showing the necessary leadership, making the hard decisions."

"But you were there, supporting him. That had to be important, too."

"To some extent, I had to become what we both hated. A gambler and a hustler, playing politics and digging at social cracks. Eventually, protesters in Verina forced a proper election. When the legitimate government was reinstated, we returned. Then we had to find our feet as royals all over again in a very different environment."

"Are there still detractors? Are you in danger?"

"No worse than any other dignitary. In fact, we're quite popular, having lived as the common man. We're seen as an inspiration. Plus, we brought prosperity back to Verina. Henrik's resumption of the throne after the conflict makes him an emblem of our country's resilience. We have to work hard every day to maintain stability and goodwill, though."

That stability was under threat by his brother's illness. Rhys had so much to carry—dark memories and concern for his brother and responsibilities to live up to. She searched his face, wondering how *he* managed.

"I didn't tell you all of that to downplay what you're going through. I'm saying I can be your guide as you move from being a hidden royal into the spotlight. I've done it. I know the pitfalls and how to navigate them."

"Why can't I just stay here and be…me?"

"Is that really what you want?" His frown of disapproval struck particularly deep. "After learning all that is available to you, all that is yours *by right*, you want to continue scrubbing floors? Is that who you are, Sopi? A coward?"

CHAPTER SIX

"COWARD!" SOPI REPEATED stiffly, flinching and looking away, then lifting her lashes to throw a scold at him. "I'd think you were above name-calling."

Rhys took it as a good sign that she wasn't curled on the sofa weeping, but on her feet, consistently pushing back while taking most of this on the chin.

"Peer pressure, *süsse*," he mocked lightly.

"Not funny."

"It infuriates me that your grandfather was unable to retake what ought to be yours," he admitted with anger he would always struggle to suppress. "I've been there. I want you to fight for what belongs to you."

"You do see the irony in that statement, I hope?"

"I refuse to apologize for buying this property. It was cheaper and more expedient than hiring lawyers. Less public, too." He drew out a chair for her. "Maude will get her comeuppance in other ways. Sit. Eat. Digest," he suggested drily.

"I don't—" She cut herself off and grumbled, "I'm not hungry."

"So we'll get to know one another and you'll begin to trust me."

After a brief hesitation, she gave a shaky sigh of defeat and sank into her chair.

Rhys stayed behind her, his attention caught by the loop of hair that had been teasing him ever since she had dragged this turtleneck over her head in her squalid little cabin.

He gathered the mass in his fist and gently tugged. She stiffened, then leaned forward so he could work the tresses from inside her shirt. When every last strand was free, he combed his fingers through it, pleased when she shivered in reaction.

"You'll speak to me before you ever think of trimming this," he ordered.

"Even what I do with my hair is up to you now?" Her voice quavered.

The fractures in her composure were showing after all. He wound her hair in a rope around his fist and set a light kiss on her crown.

"That was the teasing demand of a lover, *süsse*. Don't take it so much to heart."

"We're not lovers."

Everything in him wanted to contradict her. Prove to her in the most basic way that the chemistry between them meant that their engaging in a physical relationship was as inevitable as their marriage.

But he heard the tremor of fear that underlay her bravado. Her remark about being unable to trust him had been a slap in the face. He was doing what he could to buffer her from the sharp edges of her new reality, but she was still being knocked around by it.

"We're not the sort of lovers I want to be. The kind I hope we will be very soon." He released her hair so it fell down the front of her shoulder and over the swell of her breast, then set his hands on her shoulders, noting the tension in her, much like an animal ready to bolt. "I'm not going to force you, though. You can relax."

Her shoulders softened slightly, and he thought he glimpsed a pout of consternation on her lips when he released her and moved to take his chair across from her. Mixed feelings? That was progress, at least.

"I do need an heir, though," he reminded her, glancing at the wine in the bucket. The bottle was open and ready to pour. He drew it out and gathered the moisture with the towel.

She choked on a humorless laugh, one that said she had given up. When he glanced back at her, she was staring at him through eyes that glimmered with tears.

"It will be okay, Sopi. I promise you." He poured lightly since she'd already had whiskey.

"What would it even look like? Marrying you?" She gulped before they'd toasted. "Besides the fast track to making babies."

"The wedding or the marriage?" He held his glass for the clink of hers. "Both will brim with protocol and adherence to tradition, I'm afraid, but we'll carve a personal life out of it. Henrik and Elise manage to." He set aside the dish covers, releasing an aroma of sage and roasted apple as he revealed slices of elk with risotto and creamed spinach.

"Would we divorce if it didn't work out?"

"I never undertake anything with a mind-set that I'll fail. Short of a catastrophic betrayal, let's agree we'll make every effort to work out our disagreements. But divorce is legal in Verina, if it comes to that."

"And the baby?" she asked as she picked up her cutlery.

"Babies. Plural, if we might be so blessed. What about them?"

"*Would* you see them as a blessing? Or are children merely something you're ticking off a list? Like 'wife.'" Her gaze was admonishing, but that wasn't why he flinched.

Losing his parents had been the most painful experience of his life. The mere thought of losing Henrik was sending fractures of agony through him. Children were sheer emotional peril, something he would have avoided forever if he could.

"I've always been ambivalent about having children," he prevaricated. "I've met enough in my travels to know they can be moody little brats, but they can also be quick to offer unconditional love to a complete stranger."

"They're like tiny humans that way," Sopi said drily.

"Indeed."

She had relaxed a little. Humor had returned the sparkle to her eyes.

He was tempted to take her hand, make a move, but forced himself to sit back and give her space to relax.

"I was leaving the raising of progeny to Henrik. Aside from not being particularly anxious to marry and not wanting to overshadow him by having children before he did, he was always a more paternal man than I saw myself to be. Maybe that was my impression because he was my older brother and made all the decisions for us in those early years when we lived on our own. He very much wanted children with his wife. Elise wants a family very badly. This has been a terrible blow for both of them. I'm torn up taking this action," he admitted heavily. "It feels like a betrayal to them both."

"Will that affect how you feel toward your children?"

"No," he dismissed with confidence. "I don't know what sort of father I'll make, but I would try to emulate my own. He was caring. Busy and firm and he set very high standards, but he was encouraging and capable of humor and affection. I miss both of my parents every day."

"Me, too. My father worked away a lot, but when he was home, we were always laughing and he was proud of any ribbon or test score I brought home. He talked about me running Cassiopeia's as though it was a given, never saying anything like, *When you marry*, or suggesting I needed a man to look after me."

"Did he never want to bring you with him?"

"He offered to send me to school in Europe. I had my friends here. I think we both thought there would be time later to connect." She twirled her glass, mouth pulling to the side. "There wasn't."

"No," he agreed pensively. Time, that bastard, loomed like a vulture over everyone. "How do *you* feel about children?"

"I guess I pictured myself with a family eventually. I always wanted a brother or sister, so I've always known if I had children, I would have at least two or three. It bothers me that my parents aren't alive to be grandparents, but I miss *having* family." Her mouth tried to smile, but the corners kept pushing down.

That was, perhaps, the thing that terrified him most about his brother's diagnosis. What family would he have if Henrik wasn't here?

He had to reach out then, offering his hand with his palm up, but it wasn't a pass. It was comfort and a desire for it in return. Recognition of affinity.

"I think we've found something I can give you that you truly want, Sopi. I will take care of your children very well. I promise you."

"I believe you, but what about—" She looked at his hand, her own still clinging to her cutlery, knuckles white. "Do you think... Please don't laugh, but I always thought I would be in love when I got married."

Ah, love, that priceless gift that could exact too much.

"I've never been in love. I can't claim to be capable of it." Like every other intense emotion, he was wary of it. "I believe we will come to care for each other, though."

"I don't know if that's enough." She set down her knife and fork. "I'm really scared, Rhys."

"I know."

"But I don't want to be a coward."

"Being afraid doesn't make you a coward. Giving in to fear does. Bravery is pushing forward despite the cold sweat."

"Peer pressure again?"

"You *are* my equal." If not a mirror image, at least a complementary piece that promised a greater sense of wholeness. He hadn't expected to find such a thing, ever.

In fact, it unnerved him to some extent, niggling at his conscience. He reminded himself this marriage was for Henrik and the crown, not himself.

"Trust me," he cajoled. "And I'll prove you're my equal. *You* will."

She bit her lip. Her hand hovered over his so he felt the heat off her palm radiating against his own. He made himself be patient, not reaching to take despite his craving to grasp and squeeze.

Very slowly, the weight of her soft palm settled against his.

He closed his hand in a possessive grip, experiencing a leap of something in his blood. Conquest? Or something even more profound and basic, like finally coming up for air when he thought he was drowning?

He breathed through it and brought her hand to his mouth, setting a light kiss on fingers that went lax with surprise.

"Welcome to your new life, Princess."

Rhys sent her to bed alone, which left her feeling ambivalent. She tossed and turned, waking unrested to the discovery this hadn't been a dream. They ate a light breakfast and she was given a memo to sign advising the staff that she was the new owner, that Francine was the manager and they should proceed with business as usual.

Then she was given a copy of the press release. It announced her as the recently discovered Basile-Munier princess, stateless but newly engaged to Prince Rhys Charlemaine of Verina. She would take up residence in the palace of Verina with her fiancé immediately.

"Leave your phone with Gerard. He'll field all those messages," Rhys said as her dated smartphone began percolating like a boiling-over pot. He frowned at her clammy, nerveless fingers and warmed her hand in a reassuring grip. "A new one will be waiting for you in Verina."

And then what? She almost wanted to say, *Shouldn't we go do that thing now?* They had a handshake agreement, didn't they?

Rhys seemed intent on getting to Verina first. Aside from the bellman, who kept his eyebrows in his hairline as he loaded their luggage into the helicopter, Sopi saw none of the staff or her friends. She gave the bellman a weak smile and a wave before all that she knew fell away below her.

She had never flown before but knew right away that the jet they boarded out of Jasper was not the av-

erage commercial experience. Rhys waved her into an
ivory-colored leather recliner against a window and
took the one next to her. They were served fresh coffee in bone-china cups that rested on a polished ma-
hogany table that unfolded from a concealed cupboard.
A large-screen television was muted but ran the news
with market numbers tracking across the bottom of the
screen. Rhys handed her the remote and invited her to
watch anything she liked.

Rhys's assistants and bodyguards remained in the
cabin at the front of the plane, in seats that faced the gal-
ley and were closed off from this more luxurious area.

That was when Sopi began to see how different her
life would be. Ironically, she felt shut out of the place
where she belonged, rather than ushered into a higher
sphere.

Through the flight, Rhys talked in a dozen languages to a multitude of people. Gerard came back several times to request her approval on things she had no
business approving. When they stopped in New York to
refuel, a stylist came aboard with half a dozen outfits.

By the time she landed in Verina, she no longer recognized herself. She wore a sheath with a forget-me-not
print that had been altered to fit her perfectly. A pair of
low-heeled sandals finished the sweetheart look.

When Sopi rejoined Rhys from the stateroom, hair
and makeup elegantly disguising how pale she was, he
glanced up, did a double take, then clicked off his phone
and set it aside.

"You look lovely."

"Thank you," she said shyly. "I feel like an actress
in a costume." Playing the part of a woman who said,
"Gosh!" and fell out of trees while rescuing kittens.

"The trick is to own the role. If you believe it, everyone will."

"Are you acting?" she asked, unsurprised when his mouth twitched and he said a decisive, "No."

She hadn't thought so. They began their descent, and her stomach knotted so tightly she could hardly breathe.

"Don't be nervous," Rhys said, reaching across when she wrung her hands in her lap while they drove from the airport. "They're surprised by how quickly this is happening, but pleased. Elise is very down-to-earth. You'll like her."

Meeting a king and queen was the least of her nerves. She was *engaged*. She had taken possession of Cassiopeia's. That meant she had to follow through on the rest of her agreement with Rhys. What if she was bad at sex? What if he lost interest after the first time? What if she didn't get pregnant? She had so many what-ifs floating in her head, she couldn't articulate them.

They were shown directly into the formal receiving parlor for the king and queen. The sun was coming up, piercing through a stained-glass window to cast prisms of light around the couple who had risen early to greet them.

Henrik was in his early thirties, a clean-shaven version of Rhys. His innate vitality belied any hint of illness. His wife, Elise, was a delicate blonde with a warm smile.

"Why don't I show you around the palace," Elise said after a few minutes of innocuous conversation about Canada. "I'll help you get your bearings, then leave you in your room to rest."

Sopi shot a look at Rhys. He gave a small nod to indicate she should go with Elise, but her ears were already burning, certain she was being removed so he could speak freely about her to his brother.

"I'm not the storyteller our butler is. Do ask Thomas to take you around when you have a free hour. He conducts the tours when we open the palace and gardens for public viewing in the summer," Elise said.

The main floor of the palace consisted of a grand ballroom, the throne room, a cavernous dining hall and a veranda that overlooked gardens and the lakeshore. Elise pointed to a green door. "Panic ensues if we go below, so try not to."

But that's where I belong, Sopi wanted to protest. Once again, she experienced the sensation of being shut out of her own life. Her real one.

She clasped her sweaty palms together, lips pinned closed while she mentally searched for the words to tell Rhys he'd made a huge mistake. That *she* had.

Elise took her up a wide flight of stairs, where she waved negligently toward one wing. "Our residence. Your room is next to Rhys's." She waved in another direction, where maids were scurrying to move boxes stacked in the hall into a room with open double doors. "Still unpacking. Best to stay out of their way a little longer."

"Unpacking?" It was the first time Sopi had spoken. Her voice cracked. "I only brought one suitcase." Rhys had said the rest of her things from the cabin would follow shortly.

"Rhys said you needed a wardrobe. Those are from my usual designers. My assistant arranged it. The stylist will help you source more."

Sopi felt sick. This was exactly the laissez-faire attitude her stepsisters had taken, buying clothes on someone else's tab that they might never even wear. Sopi couldn't—wouldn't—become like them.

She looked back the way they'd come, pretty sure she could find her way to where Rhys was still meeting with his brother.

"Come. I want to show you my favorite place. I think you'll like it." Elise led her through a door and up a set of spiral stairs that climbed a tower. When they stepped outside, they stood on a wall that overlooked the lake.

The view was breathtaking. A light breeze picked up Sopi's hair and caressed her skin, soothing her ragged nerves.

In a way, it even looked like home with the lake and the surrounding mountain peaks. Verina was a small country, but it packed exquisite scenery into every square inch. As they slowly paced to the far end, the quaintest of villages came into view, one with stone bridges and red roofs and the tall spire of a church. Beyond it, the grassy hills were dotted by patches of snow and grazing goats.

"This is where Henrik proposed to me the day he was allowed back into Verina. He brought me straight up here before showing me anything else. He said he wanted a good memory to replace the one he'd left with. Do you know how they left?"

"I read about it. It's tragic." Her heart still ached for Rhys.

"It is," Elise agreed. A poignant smile touched her lips as she gazed across the valley. "They lived with us for a while."

"Your father is the diplomat who helped them?"

"Rhys told you that?" She studied Sopi openly.

"He was trying to bolster me, explaining that he

hadn't always lived like this. I wasn't born into this sort of life. It's very…overwhelming."

"It can be." Elise nodded thoughtfully. "Did he also tell you why he's rushing you?"

Sopi bit her lip, nodded. "I'm really sorry about Henrik."

She half expected Elise to be angry that Rhys had revealed their private heartache, but Elise only looked anguished and maybe a little relieved not to have to relay the details herself. Her worried gaze switched to the distance.

"They're very close in their own way," Elise said, adding in wry warning, "It can be annoying. They grouse at each other over insignificant things, refusing to talk it out properly. Men." She rolled her eyes. Sobered. "They're fiercely protective of one another, though. It's amazing. To a point. Henrik is worried about him." Now her face was nothing but hollow shadows. The cords in her neck stood out with stress.

"Henrik doesn't think I'm good enough for Rhys." Sopi clasped her suddenly aching stomach. "It's okay. I don't think so, either."

"That's not what I'm saying at all." Elise caught her arm, her grip strong. Urgent. "I'm asking you for a favor. I want Henrik to be confident that Rhys can handle all he faces, otherwise Henrik will step in and try to carry some of his burden. I know that Rhys is taking on a lot. He'll have to cover Henrik's duties to the throne, arrange a wedding. Then he'll have a wife and the making and rearing of children. It's so much to ask of you both. *I know that.* But this is the man I love. He's all I have."

She wouldn't even have Henrik's child. That grief was a dark knowledge lurking in the backs of Elise's eyes. Her anguish twisted up Sopi's conscience so she instantly wanted to ease her mind any way she could.

"Henrik is opting for a very aggressive treatment. It will give him his best chance at surviving, but he needs to give all his focus to getting through it."

"Of course," Sopi murmured. This poor woman had enough on her plate without Sopi whining about having won an ancestral lottery and not knowing how to handle it. "Of course, I'll do whatever I can. I understand the stakes, perhaps not as intimately as you do, but I know how important it is that this marriage take place and—" result in babies "—work. I know Rhys and I have to project the best possible image."

"Thank you." Elise drifted her eyes closed with relief and gratitude. "I wasn't sure if… But Rhys is a very good judge of character. I should have known he wouldn't attach himself to someone who would put her interests ahead of others."

You're self-sacrificing. You'll need that.

She smiled weakly, wondering if the reason she was ideal was less about her blue blood and more about her willingness to shelve her own needs in favor of others'. She was realizing she had done that to her own detriment in the past, but how could she switch gears now? As it turned out, this king and queen weren't a pair of demigods demanding to be served. They were a couple in love who faced a heart-wrenching situation. Sopi genuinely wanted to do anything she could to ease their suffering.

Even if it meant sleeping with a man she barely knew.

Sopi's liquid-eyed glance as she followed Elise from the room stayed with Rhys as his brother remarked, "You're moving very quickly. I expected you to bring her here for further discussion, not drop it into the press as you left the tarmac."

They had stayed on their feet after the women left, both given to pacing during heavy discussions.

"You disapprove of her?" Rhys's hackles went up.

"I don't know yet," Henrik stated with characteristic frankness. "You have to marry, Rhys. That's a fact, but I expected you to explore your options. How could you know within two days that she's the right one?"

"Look at who she is."

"Oh, on the surface, she's perfect. I heartily agree the spectacle of her background works to my advantage. I'm talking about a more personal connection, though. Wouldn't you rather marry someone you care about? *Love?*"

"Not a requirement for me," Rhys rejected bluntly. "I believe Sopi and I will have a very comfortable arrangement in the long run."

"Comfortable," Henrik scoffed. "That's your aspiration for a life partner?"

"I don't wish to be moved by greater forces," he said truthfully, still uncomfortable with the compulsion that had drawn him toward Sopi in the first place.

"You don't want a marriage like mine?" Henrik folded his arms, frowning.

"No one will ever have a marriage like yours." Rhys smiled with sincere fondness for his sister-in-law. "Elise is one of a kind." If there was such a thing as soul mates, Henrik had found his. Because of that, Rhys was as concerned for Elise as he was for his brother. "How is she coping, now you have more information?"

Henrik let out a weighty sigh. "Exactly as she always does. Brave and stubborn and deaf to anything but the outcome she is striving for." Henrik was wry, yet his voice grew unutterably heavy. "I hate myself for doing this to her."

"It's not your fault."

"I still question everything I've ever done." Henrik poured himself fresh coffee, then ignored the cup. Squeezed the back of his neck.

Rhys knew the feeling. Was Henrik's diagnosis a rebalancing of scales for some action Rhys had or hadn't taken? He desperately wanted to believe there was some way he could take control of what was happening and change it.

"I should have convinced her to move on years ago," Henrik said. "If she was married to someone else, she would have the children she wanted by now."

"She doesn't want another man's children." The doctor had floated the idea of using Rhys's sperm, but none of them had been comfortable with that proposal.

No, Henrik had declared. If Rhys's heir would inherit the throne, his brother ought to be married to the mother of his child.

"If Elise was capable of loving another man, that would've happened by now," Rhys said. "I don't know why she's so enamored. You're not as charming as you think you are," he chided. "But she loves you blindly and unfailingly."

Henrik sent him a look of reproof at the insult but nodded agreement. "It's true. I'm luckier than I have a right to be. Happier, too. That's why I want this for you." He turned on the head of a pin, switching from humbled husband to imperious monarch and domineering older brother in the space of a breath. "This life is hard enough. The wrong partner could drain you dry. You want someone by your side who strengthens you. You won't find that with a stranger, Rhys."

Henrik's words caused an unsettled sensation in Rhys's chest. The flip side of caring that deeply was a carrying of the other's pain—*in sickness and in health* went the vow, didn't it? Rhys didn't want the sort of agony his brother and sister-in-law were currently going through, but he couldn't voice that apprehension.

"Sopi is more than meets the eye," he said instead.

"She's up to *everything* that might be asked of her?" Henrik was obliquely referring to taking the title of queen, should it become necessary. "If Elise didn't love me the way she does, she would have left this life a long time ago. Do you realize that, given your plan for a quick engagement and marriage, you're going to have to play the star-crossed lovers who couldn't wait? Is she up for *that*?"

Rhys had realized that. There wouldn't be any announcements about Henrik's condition until Rhys was married with a baby on the way. Typically, a royal wedding would take a year of planning. His and Sopi's would happen a couple of months from now. Six weeks, if they could manage it. Their engagement party would be organized as soon as possible.

"Love at first sight," Rhys declared with an unconcerned smile. "Sopi and I will sell it. Don't worry about any of this. Concentrate on getting through the treatment. For all our sakes. I want my brother, and I want my king."

Henrik grumbled an agreement, and they turned to other things.

CHAPTER SEVEN

SOPI NAPPED AND woke disoriented, desperately needing reassurance. Rhys was tied up with the king, though. When she did hear from him, it was a message from Gerard requesting she dress for a hastily organized, informal dinner to meet Verina's prime minister and a handful of other dignitaries.

Informal it might be, but Sopi was put in a full-length off-the-shoulder velvet gown. It was such a dark shade of indigo it was nearly black. Subtle ruching ensured the otherwise straight fall of sumptuous fabric accentuated her curves, and a slit at the back allowed her to walk. Dozens of shoes had been delivered, and she stepped into a silver pair with mirror-finish heels before moving toward the lounge between her room and Rhys's.

Nervously, she knocked, then entered when she heard him call, "Come in."

He was nursing a drink but lowered his glass as he took in her appearance. Her heart soared at the sight of him in a white jacket with satin lapels and a black bow tie. His beard was freshly trimmed, his demeanor so quietly powerful, he seemed to reach out and grab her from across the room while remaining untouchable himself. Unattainable.

"You look stunning." His voice was as smooth and

rich as the satin-lined gown that caressed her skin as she moved.

"Thank you." Her hair had been wound onto her head in a crown, and she self-consciously touched the amethyst pendant at her throat. "These are beautiful." The weight of the matching earrings told her they hung in her lobes, but she still wanted to clasp them to ensure she hadn't lost them. They were one more extravagance she wasn't comfortable accepting. "Can we talk about...all of this?"

"After dinner? Our guests will arrive any minute. We should be downstairs to greet them." He set aside his drink and came across to offer his arm. "You don't have to knock," he said as he led her from the room. "This is your home. By the time we're married, we'll have taken over this entire wing."

About that, she longed to say, but they were approaching the top of the stairs, where Henrik and Elise had just arrived.

Sopi subtly squeezed Rhys's sleeve as she practiced the deferential nod she'd been taught by the protocol coach. They followed the couple down to the formal receiving room.

They spent the next few hours dining and making small talk with people who acted pleased to meet her, but Sopi wasn't so naive she didn't know she was more a curiosity than anything else.

Through it all, Rhys remained a watchful presence, within touching distance yet rarely touching her. Sopi was intensely relieved when the evening concluded and they retreated to their lounge.

"Be honest," she demanded as he closed the door. "How bad was that?"

"I thought it went well."

"Really? Because every time I looked at you, you were... I don't know. Displeased?" Distant. Aside from offering his arm, he'd been completely hands-off when she had been longing for a sign of approval or affection. Acceptance.

"I would have stepped in if you were floundering. I thought you handled yourself beautifully." He poured fresh drinks.

"Then why are you so..." She studied his guarded expression as he brought her a nightcap. "Tense," she decided. "Like you're trying not to yell at me or something."

His brows went up. His mouth twitched, and some of the stiffness in his expression eased to amusement.

"It's not that type of tension, Sopi. My mind has been elsewhere most of the night." His gaze slid to the door to his bedroom.

Her scalp prickled. All she could say was a faint, "Oh."

He sipped. His gaze was full of laughter at both of them, causing pulls of attraction in her middle.

"I'm really nervous," she admitted into her glass. "Maybe once it's over with, I'll relax."

"Over with." His humor disappeared in a flash of something more feral. "You're not anticipating our love-making?"

"I don't know what to expect, do I?"

His expression softened slightly. "I told you I won't force you. If you have misgivings, let's address them."

She opened her mouth, but nothing came out. All she could see was the obvious love between Elise and Henrik. They weren't heavy with pet names or physical affection, but their smiles at each other were very natural. They glanced at each other frequently and seemed to read each other's thoughts. It spoke of a truly special link—the kind Sopi would have wanted for herself if she'd known such a connection was possible.

"Sopi?" Rhys prompted.

She crossed her arms, not wanting him to think her juvenile with her romantic longings.

"Every time I want to complain about what's happening to me, I think of what your brother and Elise are going through. Then I feel petty. But I always thought my stepsisters were petty, presuming that the world would simply provide all they needed. Dresses and jewelry and fancy dinners." She fiddled with her pendant. It wasn't the whole of her reservations, but it was a big part of them.

"You're not like them," he assured her. "You won't become like them."

"You'll stage an intervention if I show signs?"

"The minute you deliberately flash your cleavage to get a man to break out his wallet, I will draw you aside for a lecture, I promise you." A dangerous, smoky edge imbued his tone.

"Now you sound possessive." And there was no reason she should find that titillating.

"I am," he stated without apology. "It's another reason I want to address any concerns you have. Once you're in my bed, I will be highly resistant to your leaving it."

Until the deed was done? That thought made her melancholy. She realized her feet were protesting the heels and sat to remove them.

"Everything is so *big*, Rhys. I'm twenty-two. I should have room to make mistakes at this age. Date the wrong man and get a little drunk in public." She had barely touched her wine at dinner, terrified of becoming clumsy or loose tongued. "No one this young should get married to anyone."

"She said with wisdom beyond her years." He shrugged out of his jacket and loosened his tie. "This *is* a lot of pressure, Sopi. I'm not going to tell you you're wrong to feel it and struggle with it. The fact that you're aware of the downside of your new position, not blinded by the shine, tells me you're smart enough and strong enough to handle what you face."

"Every time I try to tell you I'm wrong for this, you tell me I'm right," she grumbled. "I'm afraid you only want to marry the person I'm supposed to become, not the person I *am*."

"They're the same person."

"No, they're not!"

"They are," he insisted. "Listen, if you want me to tell you where you're failing, I will. You're limiting yourself," he stated bluntly. "Think bigger. Let yourself grow."

"I can't!"

"Why not?"

"I don't know!"

She hung her head in her hands, embarrassed that she was acting so childish, yelling like a toddler. She didn't even know where her reluctance to reach higher stemmed from. Maybe that stupid audition tape?

She lifted her face, frowned with self-deprecation as she realized that probably was it.

"When I was fifteen, I made a tape for a singing show," she admitted. "It was a lark with a friend. We weren't serious, but I made it to the top ten, and the organizers wanted to fly me to Toronto."

"That doesn't surprise me." His expression cleared at

the switch of topic. "I heard you in the sauna the other night. You have a lovely voice."

Had it only been some thirty-six or forty-eight hours ago that they had kissed and groped each other in the hot pool?

She shrugged off the compliment, mumbling, "Thanks, but it felt like a fluke. It was exciting, though. I started thinking bigger." She gave him a doleful look.

"You wanted to sing? Professionally?" She saw the wheels turning in his head, trying to assimilate this information with the path they were on. "What happened?"

"My father died. I had to bow out, and I was too sad to try again. I think I felt safer staying home. Staying small." She hadn't put that together until now, but she saw how illogical it was to let that experience hold her back. "Maybe I'm still feeling that way."

"I completely understand how losing a parent stunts your growth." He came to sit across from her. "I don't judge you for it. But you have essentially been running Cassiopeia's. And you were doing it without any real support. That's no small task." His expression grew introspective as he studied her. "I'm not surprised those promoters saw something in you. You possess initiative and determination and star quality. One way or another, you were destined for greatness, Sopi."

She shook her head, dismissing that.

He didn't argue, which left her hearing his voice echo in her head. Somehow that held even more impact.

She thought of the sense of expectation she had felt from Elise earlier. From everyone, starting with the maid who had asked what time she should wake her, to the text from Gerard confirming her schedule for tomorrow.

People wanted things from her—they always had. In fact, she had to wonder if Maude had begun putting everything on her plate because Sopi had stepped in to take the lead every time her stepmother had attempted to.

Ugh. Maybe Rhys was right and she had been putting all her efforts into micromanaging in a misguided effort to take the control she instinctively desired.

She scowled at him, starting to think maybe he did know her better than she knew herself.

"Did you always believe you would get back here after you were exiled?" she asked.

"I did," he said with simple honesty. "I had to. I couldn't…" He squinted as though looking into the past. "I couldn't accept that my parents' lives had been lost for no reason. That's why I was angry when we lived so poorly. I couldn't believe that our parents had given their lives so we could live like that, barely surviving. Intellectually, I know life can be cruel and not every wrong is righted, but I had to believe the wrong against us would be corrected. It was the only way I could get through my grief."

She nodded thoughtfully. "I accept that this has to happen. I do. I want to stop fighting it, but I think I'm mourning my old life. Do you ever pine for that simpler time?"

"Occasionally," he admitted. "I miss the pleasure of listening to a live band while pouring beer behind a bar, not filtering every word through the lens of political impact. You're the first person to make me feel like that man again, if you want the truth. As though the veneer is unnecessary. I don't have to be anyone but myself. I can swim naked," he summed up with an ironic smile.

But you're you, she wanted to say. His air of confidence and control wasn't a veneer. It was an innate part of him. She didn't have anything like it.

Rather than protest, however, she basked in the quiet knowledge that she offered him something no one else did. What would he give her, though?

A sudden hollow sensation in her heart made her smile wobble. She longed for the things every human yearned for: passion and emotional bonds and intimacy.

"What if the sex is awful?" she asked with tentative anxiety.

The corner of his mouth dug in. "The sex will be fantastic. You'll have to trust me on that. Until I prove it," he added slyly.

Her inner muscles clenched in a most telling way, causing heat to flood through her. She didn't ask about the rest, but surely if they were talking like this, and shared their bodies, the rest would manifest?

"Okay," she murmured.

He cocked his head, arrested, gaze locking onto her while his whole body seemed to gather like a predator about to pounce. "You want to go to bed? Right now?"

"I'm starting to realize I'll be scared either way, so yes. I think so."

"You're scared of me?" His head went back and his narrowed gaze flashed with something she couldn't identify.

"I'm terrified of all of this," she said with a wave of her hand. "Who you are. How you live. How you expect *me* to live. But I'm realizing that I can't let fear hold me back. I have to confront it."

He swore and looked to the ceiling. Started to speak. Took another moment to find words.

"I don't want to say no to you, Sopi. I want you in

my bed *right now*. But not as some sort of bravery challenge. I want you to *want* to be there. With *me*."

"I do!"

"Do you?" he challenged. "Who do you want to sleep with? The prince or the man?"

"The man. The warm body. The hands that erase all the frightened thoughts from my head," she admitted baldly.

After a long moment of consideration, he stood and held out one of those hands, palm up with invitation. "I can do that."

She set her hand in his. Felt the squeeze in her chest when he closed his grip over her fingers and drew her to her feet.

"I have to know that this much is real, at least," she whispered.

"It's very real." He skimmed a light caress around the shell of her ear and set her dangling earring to quivering. "I want the touch that empties my mind, too. I want that like water and air."

His touch tickled beneath her jaw, inviting her to lift her mouth in offering. She loved the feel of his silken whiskers as she petted along his jaw, drawing him down.

His kiss was gentle—too gentle. She pressed into her toes, wanting the conflagration to consume her.

He was too strong and easily flexed his muscles to draw back from her. One heavy hand on her hip kept her from closing the distance. He teased her by rubbing his lips lightly against hers, and his breath wafted hotly over her mouth as he spoke.

"This is our first time, *süsse*. I'm not going to race you to the finish line." He slowly eased his mouth over hers again, taking his time as he deepened the kiss.

He didn't have to crush her mouth to inflame her, she realized as she melted under his lazy, thorough veneration of her mouth. She grew lethargic, curling her arms around his neck while she leaned her weight into him, wallowing in the sheer freedom to kiss him the way she'd been dying to since their skinny-dip.

When she had her fingers speared into his hair and his embrace was the only thing holding her up, he lifted his head.

"The world outside our bedroom is always going to be a difficult place, Sopi. Even the world inside a bedroom can be complicated. My hope is that ours will be a retreat from the chaos. Out there—" He nodded at the door to the hall. "I need the princess who is willing to play a supporting role. That's convenient, but it's not why I want you. In here…" He drew her to the door of his room. "I want *you*. Just you."

Her heart stumbled as she crossed the threshold into the lamp-lit room.

"I always knew that sex would be a step I couldn't take back. I think that's why I held back from taking it." It was another aspect of her fear of reaching too high.

"That's why I don't want to rush you." He stood behind her and found a pin in her hair, gently extracting it. "If you want to slow down or stop, tell me. If I don't have your trust with your body, I don't have your trust at all." His mouth nuzzled against the nape of her neck, and he inhaled, making her shiver in delight.

"I'm worried you'll think I'm silly or dumb."

"We frolicked like otters in a pond. We're past silly and dumb."

She had to chuckle at that, but when she lifted her hands to help with the pins, he growled a noise of protest.

"Let me do it. There was a comic book in my youth,

one with a Valkyrie whose long hair was always hiding the most intriguing curves and shadows on her figure. I have latent fantasies I'm looking forward to indulging."

"Good thing my fantasies run to comic book nerds, I guess."

He barked out a laugh of enjoyment and slipped his arm across her collarbone, hugging her into his shaking frame. "I've been called worse."

She was smiling, hands on the muscled forearm that held her so firmly, cheek tilted into his strong shoulder. A whimsical, wistful happiness filled her. A sense of possibility.

"This is really why I'm here, Rhys," she confided softly. "I don't think I could have lived with wondering where this might have gone."

He turned her in his arms. His face was solemn as he plucked the last two pins that held her hair. He unwound the long braid and surprised her by looping it behind his own neck, leaving the tail against the front of his opposite shoulder.

"Me, either," he admitted gravely, making her stomach lift and dip.

This time when he kissed her, it wasn't slow and tender and gentle. It was hot. Thorough. Carnal. His beard scoured her chin, and his arms squeezed her breath from her lungs. She grabbed the tail of her own hair where it hung against his shoulder and pulled, tying them together while an aching noise throbbed in her throat.

If she thought to be the aggressor, she had sorely overestimated Rhys's willingness to submit. He cupped her head and ravaged her mouth, raking his lips possessively across hers, delving to taste and not stopping until she was trembling.

When he broke away, they were both panting, and he

wore a satisfied look as he admired her through half-lidded eyes.

"My only regret about the other night is that I didn't get to see you. Not properly." He turned her and flipped her unraveling braid to the front of her shoulder as he unzipped her. Slowly. Inch by inch, cool air swirled into pockets of heat. Sensitive goose bumps rose on her skin.

"Rhys." Each of her heartbeats thudded in a slow pound of anticipation that made her sway under the impact.

"I've been thinking constantly about it. The smoothness of your skin." He parted her dress at her spine, fingertips tickling into the small of her back.

She arched in pleasure, spears of heat thrown like lightning bolts into her loins by his hot, proprietary touch.

"How you were so shy, then not." He found the clasp on her strapless bra and released it. As it loosened, his caress traced where it had sat, moving forward until he took her breasts in his hot palms. "How your nipples felt against my tongue."

They hardened so quickly, they stung. His thumbs passed over them, strumming such a fierce pleasure through her, she squirmed, pushing her backside into his hips. She immediately felt how hard he was and wriggled a little more enticingly.

"And that," he said in a voice growing guttural. "How you give as good as you get. You made me lose my mind. I didn't behave that wildly as a teenager." He held her nipples in a pinch that hovered on the precipice of pain, keeping her very still as her pulse seemed to ring in each of those points, bouncing off the hard palms that cupped her.

"Losing control like that scares the hell out of me."

He scraped his teeth against her nape and thrust into the cheeks of her butt. "I still want to go there with you again."

She covered his hands, unsure if she wanted to stop him or urge him to be more aggressive. He held her in an erotic vise, but all she did was turn her head so he could kiss her. He did, stimulating her until she ached with yearning. She dragged one of his hands down to cup where she was growing damp and distraught with need.

His strong hand stayed there as she rocked, teasing them both until she was shaking with desire.

"You're so close, *süsse*." He nipped at her ear. "What do you need?"

"I don't know," she sobbed. "You."

He growled and released her, turning her and brushing the open dress down. When he nudged her backward, she thought he was helping her step out of the puddled velvet, but he took her farther, until she felt the edge of the mattress against the backs of her legs and sat.

She only wore her panties and found herself knotting her fists in the duvet as she gazed up at him uncertainly.

"Trust me?" he asked.

"I do." She nodded, even though her heart pounded with nerves.

He smiled darkly and pressed her shoulder so she let herself fall onto her back.

"This is what it means to be mine. All of you." He leaned over her to drop a kiss on her chin, her breastbone, little presses of silken beard and soft lips all the way down her middle. Lace abraded her thighs as he stole her underwear while trailing kisses from her navel to her hip bone.

He held her gaze very boldly as he parted her knees and dropped to the floor at the side of the bed. His effortless strength pulled her toward him. Her thighs went onto his shoulders, and she gasped as he stropped his beard on each of her inner thighs, making her shiver with anticipation.

He blew softly on her fine, damp curls, and she trembled again until the damp heat of his mouth settled with ownership against the most intimate part of her. With a small cry, she reflexively tried to close her legs against the intensity of sensation. She had known what sex was, but she hadn't known it was surrender. Not like this. She would belong to him completely after this. She already did, because she struggled to absorb the onslaught of sensation, but she didn't fight it.

He was in no hurry, taking his time building her tension until she ached all over. She hadn't known that arousal had this ability to consume. She could hardly breathe. Her blood was fire in her veins. Each moment was a drawn-out agony of spearing pleasure that coiled her tighter, and then a pulse beat of eternity waiting for it to happen again.

She lost her ability to speak or form conscious thought. She couldn't process how wickedly good this felt as he swept her with starkly intimate caresses. Arching, writhing, she let the crisis overwhelm her, too greedy for it. Too ready. In moments, she was mindlessly saying his name and shuddering under the force of a shattering orgasm.

A beautiful, floaty feeling came on the heels of it. She didn't have the strength to pick up her head but ran her fingers into his silky hair, trying to convey how lovely he had made her feel.

He didn't stop. He switched from soothing to a fresh,

deliberate assault that sent a spear of acute desire twisting through her.

"What are you doing?" she gasped, shocked that she could go from satisfaction to craving in seconds.

"Do it again," he commanded and went back to pleasuring her mercilessly.

"I can't."

His touch penetrated, and the sensations redoubled. She didn't think she could handle it. He tossed her into a place of intense excitement, but her hand in his hair urged him to continue, and suddenly she was soaring again, higher, abandoning any restraint as she released jagged cries of ecstasy.

He soothed her again, letting her catch her breath, but he didn't let her sink into satisfaction. He teased. Made her say his name again so the pleading of it echoed in the room.

He shifted his kisses to her inner thighs, and she could have wept with loss. Her thighs were still twitching, her skin damp and her heart unsteady.

He rose to set his fists on either side of her hips and tracked his gaze avidly over her naked, trembling form. His face was angular and fierce, his smile savage. "We both needed that."

"Do I...do that to you now?"

"Do you want to?" He pushed to stand straight and yanked a hand down his front to tear his shirt open. "Next time," he decided just as brutishly. "The thought of your mouth—" He squeezed himself through his trousers and hissed his breath through his teeth before he dragged at his clothes to remove them. "Still with me, *süsse*?"

"Yes." She swallowed, mesmerized by the way the lamplight gilded his skin to pale bronze. She had only caught a glimpse of him at the side of the pool. Now, staring at him unabashedly, when he was so close she could touch and he was naked and fully aroused, he made her weak.

He started to reach toward the nightstand, caught himself in his fist again, and his breath hissed through his teeth. "My first time, too, *süsse*. Naked. I don't know if I'm going to hang on long enough."

He came down alongside her, his hand sweeping from her hip to her waist to her rib cage while his mouth pressed against her shoulder.

She felt dazed, not having given thought to what this really was. She flashed her gaze up to his, fearful that this was all simply an act of procreation for him, not the starkly profound union it was for her.

He was watching her, maybe tracking the myriad emotions accosting her. Nerves and desire and something new and sweet were moving through her, feelings she didn't know how to interpret, but that made her feel incredibly vulnerable.

His eyes were glittering with feral lights of excitement, but there was a surprising gentleness in him as he caressed her now. He picked up what was left of the braid in her hair and turned his wrist to wrap it around his hand. When his grip was tucked close to her neck and she couldn't move her head, he kissed her. The light restraint held her captive for his teasing, barely there kisses. Heat flowed into her loins, and she crooked her knee and rolled her hips into his.

He broke their kiss to glance at her knee. "The way you respond will be my undoing." He released her hair and trailed his hand down to claim her mound. His touch delved into slippery heat, making her jolt.

"Too sensitive?" He eased away so he was only cupping her.

"Not enough," she complained, rolling fully into him and taking hold of the taut shape of him. "I've never felt so greedy in my life," she admitted. "I want to know how it will feel, Rhys. I want you inside me."

She found herself on her back, the agile strength of him caging her. It was intimidating, yet she didn't feel unsafe. Not physically. Everything that made her feel secure in life had long spiraled beyond her control, but here, trapped by him, she was safer than she'd ever been.

He shifted atop her, using his strong thighs to push her legs apart. She felt the shape of him, the heat and hardness against her unprotected flesh. He nipped her chin and cupped her breast, then bent his head to take her nipple into the hot cavern of his mouth.

She groaned with abandon, twisting and scraping her hands across his shoulders. "Rhys, I can't take this."

He lifted his head, shifted and guided himself against her. She felt the pressure. The forging stretch of him pushing into her. She gasped. This was way more intimate than she had expected.

He paused. "Let me see your eyes."

His were nearly black, atavistic. And yet he smiled. A wicked, satisfied smile. Perhaps even conspiratorial, as though he saw something similar in the windows to her soul that was alive in him.

In that second, she had no defenses against him at all. Not physically or emotionally. She felt intensely vulnerable as he pressed, stretching and filling her until they were locked together. Her knees reflexively bent to hug his hips, somehow making him sink even more flush against her, settling deep within her.

She hadn't realized that sex was so raw. So deliberate. It struck her that she had met him mere days ago, but it was a startling moment of alignment. Of sharing an experience.

"Hurt?" he murmured.

She barely heard and barely comprehended. She was lost to the magnitude of the moment. She couldn't keep her eyes open as waves of emotion washed over her. There was a sweet sense of achievement and the stinging discomfort of uncertainty. But there was also a tender yearning that closed her limbs around him, needing the reassurance of his hot body tight against hers.

"When you're ready," he said against her ear. He kissed across her jaw and temple, the pressure light and frustratingly elusive.

Before she consciously knew what she wanted or what she was signaling, her body shifted restlessly beneath his. Her inner muscles clenched, and the golden light from the lamp seemed to fill her. Possibility arrived within her, stoking a slippery heat in her loins, filling her with renewed hunger and yearning.

"Yes," he hissed. "Exactly like that." He licked into the delicate hollow beneath her ear. As he withdrew, everything in her clenched to hold on to him.

He cupped the side of her neck so she felt the pressure of his strong palm against her throbbing artery. She didn't know which was hotter, his skin or hers.

He returned, flooding her with such a wave of pleasurable sensations, she groaned. The arousal that had been banked while she adjusted to this new act spun through her, catching at her with its tendrils, dragging her back into the sharp tumble of acute desire.

He thrust again, and she felt the strain in his back against her palms as she roamed her touch, urging him on. He kept the pace slow, giving her time to adjust, but her body knew what it wanted. The next time he returned, her hips tilted in greeting. Her thighs clenched on his hips, fighting his next withdrawal, making him hiss in a combination of pleasured excitement and disciplined exertion.

She slid her hands to his lower back and lower still, digging her fingernails into his buttocks to drive him into her with more power.

He began to move faster, setting her afire. Their skin dampened with perspiration. They kissed and kissed again, catching at each other's lips while groaning in an earthly mingle of noises. Her reactions were pure instinct. She arched and pressed her tongue into his mouth, locked her calf across his backside and made noises of agony.

With each thrust she lost a little more of herself, but she threw herself willingly into their erotic struggle. Their fight to reach completion together. Her climax approached, and he grew more ardent, as if he sensed it. Her entire world narrowed to the destination they sought, and suddenly it was there, vast and full of endless possibility.

For one heartbeat, she thought the way he stiffened meant he was in paradise without her. Then a profound, crashing wave engulfed her. After that, she didn't know which of them trembled or shook, which pulsed or contracted, only that they were in this maelstrom together. Thrown and tossed, battered and exalted. Both equally, utterly, gloriously destroyed.

CHAPTER EIGHT

As Rhys dragged free of her, the final caressing stroke on his sensitized skin was pure, velvety bliss that jangled against his nerve endings. He landed on his damp back, the blankets tangled beneath him, and listened to Sopi take a full breath and release it as a hum of supreme satisfaction.

He lay motionless, a castaway barely alive on a remote island beach. The storm had left him weak and boneless, fighting to catch his breath.

Beside him, Sopi was still panting. Her damp arm was against his. Somehow their hands found each other, and their fingers entwined in a silent reassurance that they had made it through to live another day.

Warning signals crept through the fog of his recovery, though. He had somehow managed to keep enough wits about him to be gentle and ensure her pleasure, but he had been completely abandoned to their lovemaking. Lost to a pleasure that was even more exquisite and profound than he'd anticipated. Addictive, even.

It was the novelty of being naked without protection, he assured himself, even as his hand tightened on hers, wanting to draw her deeper into his protective sphere. He closed his eyes and fought the sense of a rising force within him that wanted to somehow bind her to him.

He should have realized her effect on him was dangerously intense when he'd tracked her like a damned arctic wolf following the scent of his mate into the snow. With the clarity of hindsight, he saw how he'd leaped on the convenience of her royal blood so he could have this—her naked body beside his own.

Now they'd embarked on the making of a child. The reality of that hit him like a meteor from space, crashing emotions over him—responsibility, concern, pride, excitement and a fear of the unknown. Terror of the uncontrollable.

He threw his free arm across his eyes, hand knotting into a fist as he tried to stave off the maelstrom of conflict. If he reacted this powerfully to the mere possibility of making a child, how would he cope if they'd actually made one?

He had put himself in an impossible position, he realized, and there was no way to change it now.

"Thank you," Sopi murmured, stirring beside him. She rolled and bent her knee so her soft thigh settled on his. Her head turned into his shoulder, and her damp lips pressed against his skin.

His nerve endings leaped and the spent flesh between his thighs pulsed with a fresh rush of heat. The compulsion to gather her up and roll atop her and consume her all over again was nearly more than he could withstand.

This was impossible.

Intolerable.

But he couldn't push her away, dewy virgin that she was. He might hate himself for giving in to his desire for her, but he would hate himself even more if he hurt her.

He lifted his arm from between them and opened his legs so her knee fell between his own, cuddling her into his side.

"*How* was a woman with that much passion still a virgin?" he asked in a voice graveled by satisfaction.

"I was saving it all for you, obviously." Her fingertips drew a lazy circle across his abdomen.

His heart gave a rolling pound of thrill at the thought. He was too rational and forward-thinking to put virginity on a pedestal, but there was something deeply satisfying in the sense of promise in her words.

He was in so much trouble.

"Was it…okay for you?" she asked tentatively.

He groaned and caught her teasing hand. "It was exquisite. You are." He brought her hand to his mouth so he could lightly bite her fingers. "But you should probably go to sleep before I start thinking we should double-check whether it was really that incredible."

She hummed a sensual noise of amusement and moved against him restlessly, drying his throat. "How can I sleep if there's any question in our minds?"

He was still at war with his elemental self, but the primitive won again. He promised himself he would withhold more of himself this time and pulled her atop him.

Her hair spilled around him, and he was lost.

Sopi wasn't so inexperienced that she believed falling in love two weeks into a relationship was a realistic expectation. Even so, she was quite sure she was on her way. Rhys was such a remarkable man!

The more she learned of Verina's history and how hard he had struggled to return to their homeland, the more she admired him for all he had accomplished. He was earnest in his support of his charities and keen to develop green initiatives. He had a dry wit and a sharp intelligence, and he genuinely cared what happened to his country and the world.

When they were in public, he gave her room to find her way while remaining a steady presence, always backing her up when she was unsure. In private, he offered romantic gestures like touching a rose to her chin or putting a ring on her finger while they stood on the palace wall overlooking the lake.

And then there were the nights, the magnificent nights when they couldn't seem to quench their insatiable passion for each other.

How could she not fall for a man who did all those things to her and for her and...

She counted the days again, heart tripping over itself and tripping up her brain.

She was only a day late, nothing to get excited about. A lot had happened lately. She was handling the move to Verina and her new title and all the public attention fairly well, but this was a huge deal. It could easily be throwing off her cycle. She was often late when she was stressed. She certainly didn't feel any different. No nausea or sore breasts, which she knew from friends were very typical signs.

Even so, her hand went to her abdomen and her eyes closed over emotive tears. She bit her smile, trying to keep the beams of happiness from bursting out of her like balls of sunlight.

This had to be love she was experiencing. Why else would she be this elated at the idea of being pregnant? Obviously, love for her child was taking root in her, but a baby was pure wishful thinking at this point. No, this was more. This was a certainty that she wanted Rhys's baby.

Because she loved him.

She waited a few more days before she said anything to him, not wanting to get his hopes up. They were dressing for their official engagement ball in Paris. It seemed a bit overkill when they were marrying in a month, but the party covered the fact that Henrik had come to a Paris clinic for surgery.

When their maids and valets and assistants left them alone, she clutched her hands before her and watched Rhys check his bow tie in the mirror. He turned and tracked a gaze rich with admiration over every inch of her.

"You're stunning."

"I'm late."

He flicked his glance to the clock. "Fashionably. We're the guests of honor. It's expected," he dismissed.

"No, I mean…" She nearly ruined her lipstick, biting back her smile at the way he'd misinterpreted her.

He actually swayed backward as comprehension struck. "Late," he repeated blankly. "Are you…sure?"

He wasn't smiling, and her own smile faltered.

"I'm sure I'm late. I'm not sure of…anything else. Sometimes I'm off if I have a lot going on in my life." She hitched a shoulder, reminding herself that she didn't want to mislead him, but she had rather hoped for more excitement. "I'll…um…make a doctor's appointment when we get back to Verina, but I thought you'd want to know."

She started to move forward into his arms. In the last days, they'd become quite comfortable in offering affection when they were alone, but something in his demeanor made her falter.

"Are you…not pleased?"

"No, of course I am," he assured her. "But if it hasn't been confirmed…"

She nodded, cheeks feeling skinned. In her mind, this conversation was supposed to swirl with excitement and laughter. Her tentative words of love had been on the tip of her tongue. Now her emotions were crashing into each other like a ten-car pileup.

"I don't mean to be lukewarm." He caught her by the elbows and brushed his lips against her cheek. "This is exactly what we want, but Elise had a lot of disappointments. Let's wait to be sure before we celebrate."

Was that really what was going on? She searched his expression, but he avoided her gaze, moving to open the door. He offered his arm again.

"We should go. I want Henrik to be able to leave the party as soon as possible if he needs to."

Rhys kept his emotions firmly locked down, fearful of letting one out lest they all spill. There was a part of him wanting to scream with pride and excitement, but no. It wasn't even confirmed yet, and a thousand things could still go wrong. There could be medical implications for Sopi. Why had he not thought of that before they'd had unprotected sex? How irresponsible of him.

Then there was the guilt, wider and darker and deeper than any of those other emotions, especially when he looked into his brother's eyes and accepted Henrik's congratulatory handshake on his official engagement.

Henrik's words had been a public expression of his approval that Sopi was joining their family, but Rhys felt like a traitor, holding the secret of his potential heir in the shadows of his heart.

Now Henrik was beside him in a more informal capacity.

"You're right," Henrik said, watching Sopi. "She's more than she seems. You chose well."

Rhys couldn't argue. Sopi was fully embracing the woman she had been meant to become. She wore an elegant, one-shouldered gown in champagne silk with sparkling beadwork scrolling around her waist. Her hair was in a knot and adorned with sparkling pins. If Rhys stared at it too long, he began thinking of the silky feel of it slithering across his stomach and thighs—a distraction he couldn't afford.

He dragged his attention from where Elise was introducing Sopi to a founder of a charity and met his brother's shrewdly assessing gaze.

Henrik had stood to toast them and had been the first to cut in when Rhys had started the dancing with Sopi. Henrik had since danced with his wife and made the rounds to speak with guests, but he was pale. Rhys thought he should call it a night.

"You're both quite convincing," Henrik said.

"In what way?"

"That you're in love."

"That's the point," Rhys said, grimly aware that the infatuation he was displaying wasn't nearly as manufactured as he had planned it to be. When he wasn't fantasizing about having sex with Sopi, he was telling Gerard to check in with her, to ensure she didn't need him. Or he was trolling social media, ensuring no one was saying anything that might impact her growing self-confidence.

Meanwhile, she was taking on palace duties and public appearances like a pro, earning goodwill wherever she went. The one time she had prevailed on him for his opinion, she had just received Francine's report on Cassiopeia's. She had wanted him to confirm her instincts, worried she was too invested to be objective. She wasn't.

In every way, she was rising to the challenge of her station. He couldn't be prouder. Now she was likely fulfilling their most important duty, and he didn't know how to handle how vulnerable it made him feel. How guilty.

"Elise is convinced Sopi's in love with you," Henrik commented.

Rhys yanked his attention back to his brother. When their gazes clashed again, his brother's held rebuke.

"I can't control how she feels." And there, too, he was at war with himself. In every way, he wanted to pull her in, hold her tight, but there was that clear-thinking part of him that saw the peril in it.

"Do you return those feelings?"

"Read my diary and find out." They had long ago perfected their ability to speak about private subjects in public and express annoyance with each other without it being readable on their faces. "Why would you ask me something like that? Here?"

"At your engagement party?"

"I don't interfere in your relationship with Elise. Kindly show me the same consideration."

Henrik laughed outright. "We're not counting the three years you badgered me to propose to her?"

"You were miserable. I was concerned about mankind as a whole."

"I was giving her a choice. I didn't know what my future would look like. Would I regain the throne and make her a queen? Lose all those investment gambles we were taking and force her to live in a shack? I didn't know if they would *accept* her. I loved her too much to start our life together on a string of false promises."

"I haven't made any false promises to Sopi."

"Haven't you? As I said, you're very convincing. If you're not *actually* in love…"

Rhys muttered a curse under his breath. "I care about her. Of course I do."

"She more than cares, Rhys. She's putting her heart into this. Into *you*."

He knew that. If she was carrying his child, she was so deeply invested, he couldn't quantify it.

And even though Sopi wasn't a needy person, she did have needs. He had promised to be her anchor and foundation and sounding board, which he was. He couldn't take many steps back from that, but he refused to take further emotional ones forward.

The resulting conflict was both a sense of walls closing in and a rack of tension, pulling him toward a breaking point.

"I would prefer you focus on yourself and your own wife," Rhys said. "I'll worry about Sopi."

"I have never understood your desire to close yourself off this way. What is the worst that could happen, Rhys? Elise is my source of strength. Let Sopi become that for you."

His brother could die. That was the worst that could happen. And the helplessness he felt at the prospect of that was more than he could bear. How was Sopi supposed to help him through such a thing? He wouldn't put that sort of burden on her.

No, he had to maintain what was left of his reserve for all their sakes.

Sopi somehow kept a smile on her face, but she kept looking to Rhys, anxious that his reaction to her possible pregnancy had been so tepid.

He was locked in a discussion with Henrik. Elise

was right. The two were very close. Sopi was both envious and jealous, having always wished for a sibling, especially one she could confide in the way the men seemed to confide in each other.

She was also a teensy bit threatened by their closeness. Elise had found her place in that dynamic a long time ago. She knew how to pry her way between them and where her marriage took precedence over the fealty between the brothers, but Sopi came up against it like a force field.

Until this evening, she had thought that was the source of this distance she sensed between them. An inequality of sorts. Tonight, she had seen the true problem. She might be in love, but Rhys wasn't.

Which turned her engagement party into a nightmare.

The chatty woman monopolizing her finally took a breath. Sopi was able to say, "Will you excuse me? I need to visit the powder room."

On her way down the hall, she veered onto a balcony for a moment to herself. Her arrival interrupted a couple who broke apart with a stammer and a blush before hurrying away. Their clinch had been tame, but their deep embarrassment meant it had been a very private moment. That left Sopi agonizing for a similar emotional connection with Rhys.

Oh, irony, you devil. Initially, she had balked at marrying him, worried this fairy-tale world she'd risen to would be more than she could handle. Now she wanted the whole package. The declaration of love and the happily-ever-after.

It would come with time, she tried telling herself, trying not to cry. Other things were settling into place. Her friendship with Elise was growing by the day, and even she and Henrik shared a laugh now and again. The job of being a princess wasn't proving too onerous. She looked forward to being a mother.

No, this was old-fashioned bridal nerves, maybe even hormonal changes making her feel like she needed more from Rhys.

As she blinked to clear the blurred vision of the Eiffel Tower, a sixth sense made the hairs stand up on the back of her neck. The door clicked behind her and there was a scuffed footstep.

"Well, well, well."

The voice might as well have been a knife blade tracing down her spine. Sopi's back went tense and rail straight. She fought the urge to clench her fists as a hot-cold flush of angry dread washed over her.

She knew instantly who the voice belonged to and stole a brief second to erase any traces of despondency from her expression. In the busy days since she had left Canada, she had only fleetingly thought of her stepmother and stepsisters. Francine had mentioned their names in relation to some unpaid invoices, but otherwise, Sopi had not missed any of them one bit.

With a fresh layer of composure in place, she turned and faced Nanette.

Her stepsister wore a striking black gown that plunged down the front to her belly button. The frothy chiffon skirt had a slit to the top of her thigh. She wore gold evening shoes peppered in bling and her bloodred lipstick matched her nails. Her lips parted in a malevolent smile as she approached with the slink of a stalking cat. Or a slithering snake.

"Fancy meeting you here."

"I didn't know you were invited," Sopi said. If she had, she might have taken steps to change that. She wasn't feeling hostile or vengeful toward her stepfamily, but neither was she eager to speak to any of them again.

"I'm insulted you didn't make a point of inviting us. I had to come as a plus one. But I suppose you can't be expected to grasp the finer points of etiquette, given your rustic upbringing."

Sopi had precious seconds to weigh her options. Making a scene was not one of them, but she couldn't allow Nanette to intimidate her. The little bit of confidence she had developed in recent weeks had already been battered by the knowledge Rhys wasn't falling in love with her the way she was falling for him. But her self-worth was too hard-won for her to let this confrontation knock her flat. Rhys would be disappointed in her if she let Nanette get the better of her, and she would be disappointed in herself.

Which left her taking a similar approach to her old one. She kept the peace by grasping at patience and speaking politely while trying to project the sophistication she was desperately trying to develop.

"It's lovely to see you again either way," she lied. "Where are you making your home now?"

Nanette laughed, but it was the patronizing chuckle of a superior amused by the antics of a lesser creature. "Full marks for *that*."

Sopi didn't let herself be drawn into whatever crass reaction Nanette was trying to provoke. "Your mother and sister are well?" she persevered.

"Oh, we're really doing this? Yes, Mummy leased us a bleak little walk-up in Vienna because she had to take what she could get on short notice. Fernanda and I would prefer to be here in Paris. You might have mentioned the royal bloodline." She narrowed her eyes with malevolence.

"I'm surprised your mother never unearthed it. She's always found my family to be so enriching." Okay, now she was descending to Nanette's level. She glanced to the glass doorway back to the hallway, noting the shift of one of the bodyguards against the glass. She signaled that she was fine and he should let her handle this.

"Well, look who finally grew a pair," Nanette said after a beat of astonishment.

Sopi realized her hands had closed into fists and consciously loosened them. She and Nanette both wore heels, but the other woman was taller. Sopi had to lift her chin to look down her nose at her.

"Someone told me once that I should set standards for myself and not drop below them," Sopi said with a meaningless smile. "This conversation is one of those things plummeting past acceptable. Excuse me."

"Oh, is acknowledging your stepsister beneath you? Now that you have a title and a presumably concussed fiancé?"

"Of course not," Sopi lied, even though alarm streaked through her veins. "You've taken *so many* pains over the years to tell me that you're far too well-bred to behave in a crass manner."

"It's not crass to pay back a double cross," Nanette shot back. "It's survival."

"You're accusing *me* of a double cross?" Sopi choked on a ball of outrage. "You sold my home behind my back!"

"Is that what happened? Because this whole thing feels like a setup. How did you even know him?"

"I didn't."

"You must have," Nanette snapped, growing genuinely angry. "How did he even find out who you were?

Is it even real? I can't believe he actually wants you, title or not. Do you have money? Does he need it?"

"That's enough." A hot flush of temper stung her cheeks. "Stop before this turns ugly."

"Ugly is throwing people out into the snow at *midnight*."

"I didn't ask that you be treated that way." Was she sorry? Probably not as much as she should be.

"You took control of the hotel that night. Of course that order came from *you*, you hideous bitch."

Don't engage, Sopi told herself. Through the windows, she saw another shift of light, but she was determined to handle this herself.

"I didn't order it," she insisted, but she was piqued enough to bite back. "The timing of your departure was always your choice, Nanette. You could have left long ago. Months. *Years*, in fact."

"Oh, does the student think she's becoming the master?" Nanette asked with a hoot of astonishment. "Allow me to demonstrate how much you still have to learn, Sopi. Start compensating me for the insults you've delivered or I will go straight back into that ballroom and tell everyone you're a janitor with a side hustle that looks like brothel work. No one believes you're in *love*," she dismissed scathingly. "You obviously compromised him in some way and now you're blackmailing him."

"*Who* is resorting to blackmail?"

Nanette tilted her head and smiled with false charm. "Make it worth my while to keep my mouth shut or I will."

Sopi moved closer, driven by old anger and new hurt and feelings that were so fresh and raw, she hadn't processed them, but she damned sure wasn't going to be walked on by this harridan ever again. And she wouldn't let Nanette harm Rhys to get at her, either.

"Think about what you're doing, Nanette," she warned in a voice that originated in a grim place behind her heart. She had to tilt back her head and her body was quivering in reaction, but a frightening thrust of power emboldened her. "Look at who I am now. You do *not* want to start a war with me."

"I know exactly who you are. You're a joke, Sopi."

"My name is Cassiopeia." She leaned in. "But *you* can call me Your Highness."

Nanette struck like a viper with a slap that snapped Sopi's head to the side. She was so stunned, she stumbled back a few steps, hardly able to make sense of the fact that she'd been struck, let alone retaliate.

The door behind her crashed open. There was a blur of movement as Rhys took hold of Nanette and thrust her toward a bodyguard.

"Get her out of here. Have her arrested for assault."

"What? You can't do that to me!" Nanette's screech of protest and furious struggle halted when the bodyguard mentioned handcuffs. With one hate-filled glare, she let the burly man escort her from the balcony.

"Are you hurt?" Rhys positioned himself to block any view of her from the windows.

"I think so." She ran her tongue in the space between her teeth and cheek and tasted copper. Beneath her testing fingers, her jaw was scorching hot.

She was shaking, though, and stepped closer to him, expecting him to pull her into his arms.

He only shifted to settle one tense arm around her. "We should get ice on that. Let's go upstairs."

"What are people going to think if we leave? Did anyone see?"

"I'll issue a statement. Don't worry about it."

He looked so incensed, her stomach flipped with apprehension. He moved to hold the door for her.

Thankfully, the balcony was right off the hallway to the elevators and powder room. They only had to cross to where one of his bodyguards was already waiting with an open car. A handful of people glanced and murmured with speculation, but within seconds they were silently traveling up to their suite.

"I'm really sorry," she whispered, heart thudding at his granite profile. "I didn't mean for anything like this to happen. I didn't even know she was here."

He looked to the guard. "Find out who brought her. Blackball him."

The man nodded and touched his ear to repeat the instruction to someone else.

"Rhys." She set a hand on his arm. He was like iron. Marble. The sort of rough diamonds that came out of the earth flawed and hard and only good for drilling into rock. "I don't think whoever brought her is to blame."

"He lied to get her past security. If I'd seen her name on the list, I would have had them turned away."

They arrived in their suite, and he barked at her assistant to get an ice pack.

Wide-eyed, the young woman complied, hurrying back with a compress wrapped in a hand towel. "Should I call a doctor?"

"I'm fine," Sopi insisted.

"Write down these names." Rhys recited Sopi's stepfamily. "I want alerts on all of them. Reports. Where they live, who they're seeing. Financials. Any pressure points. Tell Gerard I want my lawyer and PR on the phone as quickly as possible."

"Yes, sir." She hurried away, leaving them alone.

"I don't think she came here planning to hit me. I provoked her," Sopi admitted miserably. "I should have walked away instead of letting her get under my skin. It was my first chance to push back after all these years and I…" She'd been upset over *him* and his reaction to her news. She had taken it out on Nanette. "I told her to call me…" She cringed. "Your Highness."

"She should. It's who you are," he asserted coldly.

She shook her head. "No, I was stooping to her level. This is my fault—"

"The hell it is." She had never seen him so hard-hearted. "Has she hit you before? You should have told me."

"No! Never. I didn't imagine she was capable of it. That's why I waved off the bodyguard. But I really don't think she'll do anything like it again. You're over-reacting."

"I am *not*," he hurled at her. "This sort of thing gets quashed at the larva stage." He pointed at the floor. "Otherwise it grows into a goddamned siege."

Oh. She started to understand what was driving his pitiless rage. She sank onto the sofa and lowered the ice from her face. "Can we please talk this out?" she asked tentatively.

"There's nothing to talk out. I'm doing what has to be done. We won't go downstairs again. You can undress, have a bath, make yourself comfortable, but keep that ice on your face." His gaze bounced off the spot that was probably hued red by the ice. "I shouldn't have left you alone. I thought you were going to the ladies' room." He flinched with self-recrimination before his expression hardened. "It won't happen again."

"Rhys, this isn't your fault."

Something in the way he gathered himself told her

he was traveling inward to a place that wasn't reachable. Not right now anyway. Not by her.

"A bath sounds nice," she murmured, wanting some time alone herself. "Call me if you need me."

Sopi woke hours later and realized Rhys hadn't come to bed.

Puzzled, she went in search and found him in the guest room.

"I didn't want to disturb you," he said when she hovered in the door. "You should get your rest."

"It's nothing, Rhys. I'm totally fine." A faint red mark, but nothing a sweep of makeup wouldn't hide. She crossed to lift the covers and join him.

He caught them, stopping her. "What are you doing?"

"I want to sleep with you." She released the blankets and crossed her arms to catch up her nightgown, smoothly skimming it up and over her head. She dropped it to the floor and stood nude in the moonlight.

"I'm not at my best, Sopi."

She had noticed, and she didn't know how to change that except to get close to him physically.

She lowered to sit on the bed, hip aligned to his, and began unraveling the hair she had braided before she went to bed. She did it slowly, in the sort of tease he usually enjoyed.

"I'm not in the mood to play." He spoke through his teeth, catching at her hands to stop her. "I'm too wound up."

"Then you need to relax." She shifted to brace her hands on his shoulders, leaning over him. "Want a massage?" That always turned into lovemaking, but that's where she was aiming. She desperately needed to reconnect with him and assure herself they were still okay.

Was this about her possibly being pregnant? About Nanette? Or was it something deeper? Something she had done?

She didn't land the kiss she went seeking. In one lithe movement, he had her on her back and loomed over her.

"You shouldn't be in here, Sopi. I don't have a good grip on myself."

"You sound like a werewolf. I'm not *afraid* of you," she said with a small laugh, petting his beard but catching enough to give a gentle tug. "You would never hurt me. I know that." She slid her hand to the back of his head, inviting him to kiss her.

"No, but—" His fingers dug into her shoulders, and his neck muscles bunched in refusal. He really did need a massage. He was gripped by something rigid and painful and clearly needed release.

She lifted her head to press her mouth to his.

With an animalistic groan, he pressed her flat beneath him and raked his lips across her own.

It wasn't the gentle seduction she was used to. It was raw need. A quest to drag her into some dark place he already occupied. As she moved with greeting beneath him, trying to settle into a more comfortable position, she could feel through the blankets that he was already aroused. He hardened his arms around her, keeping her in place as he scraped his teeth down her neck. His mouth opened in damp suction against her skin before his hand took possession of her breast, plumping it for plundering.

When he sucked, pleasure streaked like golden lightning from her nipple to her loins. They normally built up to this sort of intensity. His boldness threw her into an electrical storm, but she gloried in the wildness of it. This wasn't the civilized man she knew, but she recognized him in a far more primitive way. Her mate.

She grasped at his straining shoulders and back, encouraging him to keep ravaging her. She grew a little rough herself, catching a fist in his hair and dragging him up to kiss her. She stabbed her tongue into his mouth.

He didn't let her become the aggressor. He cupped her jaw and took her mouth with blatant eroticism until she was limp beneath him, pulsing all over with anticipation.

Then, with a noise like a wounded animal, he yanked the blankets from between them. One of his strong arms hooked under her leg, hiking it high so she was utterly helpless as he guided his turgid shape against her wet folds, moving easily in the gathered moisture, stoking the ache and strumming chords of pleasure through her.

"Stop me," he commanded, the crest of his sex demanding access.

She shook her head, too caught up in her own craven need. "Do it," she urged.

With a guttural sound, he thrust, driving easily into her slippery depths. As he came flush against her, he gave an extra pulse of his hips to ensure he was firmly seated inside her.

She had never experienced anything so earthy before. So primeval. He smothered her with a kiss, and when she bent her free knee, he gathered that one on his other arm and knelt to brace above her, pinning her with her legs open as he withdrew and thrust, watching her.

She was surrounded by him. Claimed by him and willing to be whatever he needed in this moment. She lost herself in the pools of his blue eyes as he undulated with power and purpose. She wanted to lift to kiss him, but her hair was pinned under her back, holding her head against the mattress. The restraint added an erotic twist to their coupling. She couldn't move except to caress damp skin stretched taut over hard muscles and sinew and bones.

And she couldn't escape the pleasure he relentlessly wound tight inside her. She grew sweaty and so acutely aroused, she couldn't stand it.

"Rhys," she sobbed.

He shifted, tucked his hands beneath her cheeks to tilt her hips. The new angle meant fresh nerve endings took his next thrust. Lust surged in her. Something pure and sharp and splendid.

He dropped his head to taste her lips, and she licked between his own with utter abandon, submerged in a hot pool of lava, thick and melting and incendiary.

She urged him to keep going, never let this stop, but she couldn't withstand this intensity. Just when she thought she would burst into flames, the world exploded around her.

He plunged deep and stayed there, pulsing hard within her as she twisted in the throes of her own unbearable pleasure, both of them groaning in carnal ecstasy.

Drained, Rhys realized he was crushing Sopi and forced his still twitching muscles to shift him off her.

He had known he was at his worst when he had finished making statements and recalibrating their security. He'd taken a cold shower to cool his temper, but he'd still been too edgy to sleep. He had wanted sex, but Sopi had been asleep, and he had known his mood wasn't gentle. He'd made himself come to this other bed and had been lying here aching with arousal, seriously reconsidering whether they should marry after all, given the way he was reacting.

When he'd heard her moving through the suite, the beast in him had nearly howled for her.

And she had arrived as though in answer, stripped naked and offered herself.

Such a fight he'd put up, too. He'd taken her with all the finesse of a rutting boar. What if she was pregnant?

With his gut aching, he asked with dread, "Did I hurt you?"

"Of course not," she chided, rolling toward him.

"I was rough." He didn't let her touch him, not trusting himself to stay off her. He sat up on the side of the bed.

"Rhys." She came up behind him, knees bracketing his hips. She wrapped her arms around his shoulders so her breasts pressed into his back. Her scent was all around him, almost impossible to resist in its inducement to turn and take her in his arms, especially when she said, "We've been vigorous before. It was exciting."

It had been a snap of something inside him.

He had been lying here berating himself for hesitating at the door to the balcony. He had wanted to give Sopi the chance to assert herself with her stepsister, but the sudden flash of Nanette's swiping hand had nearly turned him homicidal. It had been all he could do to stay this side of civilized and leave Nanette to the authorities.

His feelings for Sopi were becoming way more than he could handle. He couldn't let her go, though. What if she was already pregnant?

She nipped at his shoulder and rubbed her lips to soothe, fanning all his basest instincts. "I would have told you if you were hurting me. Honestly? I liked that you let go for once. You made me feel sexy and desired. Needed." Her voice held a throb. She was a bright woman. She knew he was holding back from her emotionally.

Much as he hated himself for hurting her, he stood to confront her, trying to cement the barriers in place for both of them.

"My losing control isn't a good thing, Sopi."

Even in the dim light he saw the flash of injury in her expression. He heard it in her voice.

"It wasn't *bad*," she argued, but he heard her quaver of uncertainty. "It means we're at a place in our relationship where we can get a little wild and still have full trust. You wanted me to trust you, and I do."

"You might be pregnant!" He paced away, hand going into his hair and giving a yank of frustration.

"For heaven's sake, you weren't *violent*. We just got to the good part a lot faster than usual."

"I was still crude as hell."

"It was uninhibited. Passionate. It was lovemaking at its finest. Literally *love*making. For me, at least," she added with a hesitant lilt in her tone.

"Don't," he commanded, naked and cold in the shaft of blue light from the window. "Don't fall in love with me, Sopi."

"Why not?" she cried in a flash of angry pain that left a mark on his heart.

"Because I can't fall in love with you." And he couldn't stay here and watch her eyes fill with tears like that. "You can sleep here. I'll go to the other bed."

He left before he couldn't.

CHAPTER NINE

SOPI MOVED THROUGH the next minutes and hours and days in a type of shell shock. Rhys didn't love her, didn't want to love her and refused to talk about it.

She made a doctor's appointment for later in the week, now equally as anxious as she was excited by the idea of being pregnant. She distracted herself by staying on top of things at the palace and making appearances with Rhys and having a fitting for her wedding dress—which should have been one of the happiest things she'd ever done, but it was all she could do to hold back sobs of wretchedness.

In public, she and Rhys continued to play the part of devoted lovers, but they were sleeping apart and barely speaking except in stilted bursts. A few times she caught a look of deep regret on his face, but she always looked away and shored up her own defenses, too hurt by his rejection to bear his remorse over breaking her heart.

She should probably regret all of this. A pregnancy would tie her to a man who didn't love her, but the truth was, she *deeply* wanted to be pregnant. Maybe it wasn't the best circumstances, but since leaving Canada, she'd been feeling very rootless. She needed family. She knew that now. A baby would give her the deep connection to another human being that Rhys was so reluctant to provide.

Which was why she was so devastated to get her period while she was dressing for her doctor's appointment.

Reeling in anguish, she tried to dismiss the maid who entered. "Can you leave me alone, please?" she said, trying to stifle the rush of tears.

"Yes, but the prince said when you're ready, he's in the lounge…" She curtsied and hurried away.

Rhys had arranged to take her to the appointment himself. She allowed herself one silent scream into a wet facecloth, then blew her nose and repaired her makeup.

Bracing herself, she walked into the lounge. Found a distant smile for Gerard.

"Will you please cancel my appointment and give us the room?" she asked him.

"Of course." He sent a brief glance of surprise between her and Rhys's arrested expression, then made himself scarce.

Rhys was headed to a meeting after the appointment. He wore a suit and tie. It fitted him as beautifully as every other piece of clothing he owned, but she thought he looked gaunt.

For the first time in days, his shields seemed to thin as he searched her expression. "What's wrong?"

Besides everything? She didn't know how they had gone from so great to so terrible in less than a week, but telling him she might be pregnant seemed to have been the instigator. Was she supposed to be happy that was no longer an issue?

"I'm not pregnant," she announced through a tight throat.

A flash of something that might have been agony

streaked across his features, and he rocked on his heels, nudged off his keel for the first time since the night of their engagement party.

He quickly schooled his expression into something more cautious. "A miscarriage?"

"I told you I might just be late," she said defensively. "It happens when I'm stressed." But even as she dismissed it as no real loss, her heart hit rock bottom. She waited in vain for a hug and some expression of sorrow that came anywhere near to the devastation wrapping itself around her.

She heard him draw breath to say something, but he seemed to change his mind at the last second. She heard it anyway.

Next time.

Her cramping middle knotted even more. She stood paralyzed by torment as the full scope of what she'd done began to hit her. She had agreed to marry him. To sleep with him until she had his babies. Plural. And she would do that while knowing he would never love her. Then she would have to make a life with him and their children.

While he wore a look of such regret, she felt sick.

Her eyes brimmed until she couldn't see him through her curtain of misery.

"We can try again, but not tonight," she choked. "There's no point. I'll tell you when I'm..." Fertile? Receptive? "Able."

"Sopi," he said to her back, but she closed her door. Shut him out as neatly as he'd been shutting her out.

He leaned his hands on the back of the sofa and breathed through the fiery agony that gripped him. This was why he didn't want to fall in love with her. The baby hadn't even been real yet. He hadn't allowed himself to believe she was pregnant, trying to wait until the doctor had confirmed it before he let himself get attached to the idea of being a father, yet he was as devastated as if she'd been months along and he'd already felt the damned thing move.

In his helplessness, he had searched desperately for words that might wipe that anguished expression from her face, knowing a platitude about trying again wouldn't cut it.

She'd heard it anyway and shut him down. *I'll tell you when I'm able.*

He ran his hand down his face, aching to make love to her again. Not to conceive, but to feel her. Hold her and smell her hair and say nonsense things across the pillow.

Henrik was wrong. He hadn't chosen well. He had chosen selfishly. Yes, she ticked all the boxes. A thousand women could have done that. He had allowed his baser instincts to guide him, though. He had given in to the primeval part of himself, manipulated her into their engagement only to cause her all this pain.

He went through the motions of his day, and when he returned to the palace, he ate alone, brooding, trying to see how they could forge a way forward.

He woke to the disturbing news that his brother and Elise were returning within the hour from Paris and wanted to see him the moment they arrived.

Throat dry and appetite nonexistent, he nearly fell over when Sopi hurried into the breakfast room, an anxious look on her face. She wore a jacket with a straight skirt since she was due at a school later today. Her hair was in a rope-twist ponytail, her makeup light.

"Why are they coming back in the middle of his treatment?" she asked, voice thick with apprehension.

"I don't know." He didn't like any of the possible answers.

Whatever she read in his expression had her crossing to him and pushing her cool hand into his stiff one.

"I won't stay if they don't want me there, but I'll come to their room with you."

He should have said it was unnecessary. He was a big boy, but it was all he could do not to crush her slender fingers. He kept her hand in his until word came that his brother had arrived. Then he drew Sopi with him down the gallery to the monarch's wing.

His throat was full of gravel, his chest nothing but broken glass. Thank God for Sopi, because she found a warm smile for her soon-to-be in-laws as they were shown into the private parlor where Henrik was seated. He looked gray. Elise stood beside him, clasping his hand. They were both beaming.

"Oh," Sopi breathed in relief. "We thought you were staying in Paris for the entire course of your treatment. Is everything going well?"

"As well as can be expected," Henrik said with a dismissive flick of his hand. "I toss more than I eat, but the doctors aren't too concerned. I have a three-day break now, and we missed sleeping in our own bed. Plus, we had news we couldn't wait to share." He looked up at his wife.

Elise was blinking tearful eyes at him.

"We're pregnant," Henrik said.

The announcement hit Rhys like a shock wave. Distantly, he heard Sopi's breath rush out as though she'd been punched. He recovered first, probably because he was used to staying on his feet through life's groin kicks. He wanted to hold on to Sopi's hand, somehow protect her from what she must be feeling, but she pulled her hand free of his.

He was genuinely happy for the pair, though. They'd waited so long for this.

"That's amazing." He moved to kiss Elise's cheeks. "No one deserves such good news more. Congratulations." He shook his brother's hand, unable to hide his astonishment.

"We're as shocked as you are," Elise said as she accepted the shaky embrace Sopi offered.

Only Rhys detected how pale Sopi was and how unsteady her smile was.

"We had completely given up trying after my diagnosis," Henrik said. "But we had a last hurrah before my surgery." He winked.

"Henrik!" Elise nudged his shoulder, blushing and laughing. "That's untoward."

"It's a miracle." He caught her hand again and kissed it. "We won't be making any formal announcements, but we wanted you both to know. I've put a lot on your shoulders lately and we have discovered how counterproductive that sort of pressure can be. Better to...how shall I say? Celebrate what you have rather than pin your heart to an uncertain future."

"But never give up hope, either," Elise hurried to add.

"No, you never do, do you?" Henrik said to her with an emotive look at his wife. "How did I ever get so lucky?"

"We'll leave you to rest," Rhys said mechanically as all the implications of this news began to penetrate his skull.

Sopi walked in a daze back to their wing, unaware whether Rhys had offered his arm or not. She was too encased in throes of envy. She was genuinely pleased for them, of course, especially now she'd had a taste of how disappointing it was to fail to conceive. Even so, she had to press the tremble of anguish from her lips.

"That opens up fresh possibilities, doesn't it?" Rhys asked as he closed the door to their lounge in what sounded like an ominous click.

She spun around, gasping for the breath he had knocked out of her even before she knew where he was going with that cryptic statement. She only knew it was bad.

"Like *what*?" she asked.

His hand was in a fist against his thigh. "We don't have to marry now."

It took her a few moments to find words—her ears were ringing so badly.

"Was it always about *having* to and never about *wanting* to?" she managed to ask.

"Yes." He was utterly still, his profile carved from granite. "If I had to marry, I thought it should be you." He swallowed loud enough for her to hear it. "But I'm realizing how self-serving that was. I didn't recognize how many pitfalls there were for you. This is your chance to walk away before any real damage is done."

Her heart being in tatters notwithstanding?

"You're going to put that on me?" she asked, pressing her hand between her breasts. "I can walk away if *I* want to?" What happened to committing in good faith?

"No," he stated flatly. "I'm going to tell you to go. You'll be better off," he had the nerve to proclaim.

"How does that compute?" she asked, voice husked by gall.

He closed his eyes as though suffering something

unbearable. "You don't want to marry me, Sopi. You never did."

"No, *you* don't want to marry *me*," she flung at him. "*I love you.* I would want to marry you if you wanted me, but you *don't.* Is it because I didn't—"

"Don't finish that sentence," he cut in sharply, speaking through his teeth. A muscle pulsed in his jaw. "But that's part of why I'm doing this. It's one thing for a couple to want children and discover they can't make it happen. This damned title puts far too much demand on you to perform. I can't put that on you. Not when I saw how much it hurt you when…" He lifted a helpless hand.

She didn't tell him she could live with that sort of pressure if he loved her. He didn't contradict her on not wanting to marry her, though—which was probably the cruelest thing anyone had ever done to her.

He broke the charged silence by drawing in a deep breath. "I'll make arrangements for you to travel back to Canada."

"Don't bother," she said flatly, no longer the doormat who allowed lesser people than him to walk all over her. "Thanks to you, I have resources of my own." A house in Sweden, for instance.

"I know it doesn't seem like I'm thinking of you, but I am," he said gravely.

"No, you're not!" She really ought to be grateful to him for all he'd done, but she was too angry. "You're doing this because you like *pain*. I don't understand why you feel a need to punish yourself, but fine. I'll lean into it and be the point of agony you need. You're welcome."

CHAPTER TEN

THE FINAL FLIP of Sopi's magnificent hair as she had walked out on him might as well have been a bullwhip that continued to flay him over the ensuing days.

It stung especially deep when he informed his brother and Elise that she was gone. They both stared at him with exasperation and bewilderment.

"But I liked her," Elise protested in an injured tone. "What if the next woman you choose isn't…her?"

Rhys hadn't thought that far ahead. Now the remark was salt in a wound, rubbing and rubbing. Henrik might have an heir on the way, but more children were next to impossible for them. Rhys would still have to marry and make a few spares.

The idea of lying with anyone but Sopi made him sick.

He buried himself in work, trying not to think of her, trying not to let Sopi's absence cause more work to fall on Elise. As for Henrik, Rhys had to stay ahead of him or he would stubbornly refuse to rest.

"You're starting to look sicker than I am. Walk with me," Henrik commanded one morning. He was home again for the weekend, and spring sunshine was breaking through the breakfast room window.

They were no sooner on the path along the lakeshore,

a refreshing breeze skating across the lake, when Henrik said, "What do you plan to do about Sopi?"

"Nothing. We called it off."

"Why? And don't give me your fabrications about things not working out. You didn't have to convince me she was right for you. I saw it with my own eyes, only for you to turn around and tell me you were mistaken. You're never wrong," Henrik said drily. "In fact, I don't think you were acting. I think you genuinely love her."

He loved her so much he couldn't breathe for missing her. She had only been in his bed a few short weeks and he reached for her in the dark every night. When he heard a footstep in the lounge, his heart leaped in anticipation. When Elise had a light spell of morning sickness, he wondered how Sopi would have coped.

He wondered if she would have children with someone else and wondered how he would make his own when he only wanted one woman in this world.

They had arrived on the end of the floating wharf, rebuilt three years ago, but in the same spot where they had climbed aboard a rowboat with the servants two decades ago.

"I do love her." A weight came off his chest as he admitted it out loud for the first time.

"Then go get her, you idiot."

He wanted to. He was barely surviving exactly the sort of loss he had feared when he pushed her away, but cowardice wasn't the only thing that had driven him that day.

"I haven't been coping well with your diagnosis, Henrik. I keep thinking it should be me going through this, not you."

"Don't," Henrik growled.

"*I* was the one who tried to attack the guard." His voice had roots in the horror of *that night*.

"You were a child," Henrik said quietly. "Terrified and reacting in the moment. You can't blame yourself for actions taken by monsters. It took Elise a long time to convince me that my responsibility was for the future of Verina, not its past. Yours, too. We can strive to maintain peace and ensure Verina prospers, Rhys. We can't undo what has already happened."

"I still think… I cost us *them*. Cost *you*. My actions pushed you into all of this long before you were old enough to handle it. You deserve to be happy, Henrik. You've fought so hard for everything. The crown, Elise, a baby. Now you're fighting for your life. I couldn't stomach the fact that everything you have had to struggle so hard for had just fallen into my lap. A woman I love who has a title?" He laughed drily. "For a few days, we thought she was pregnant, and I was so…" He looked into the sun to try to burn back the wetness in his eyes. "I couldn't accept how happy I was. How easily all of that happiness had come to me."

"So you pushed her away to punish yourself? What happens if you have to take the throne? Will you marry someone you hate just so you can feel truly miserable?"

"I don't want to think of it, Henrik." His heart was being crushed in a thorny vise. "I don't want the throne. I want my brother, alive and well."

"Well, today is your lucky day. I'm here. And I'm going to be a good brother and tell you that I want you to be happy. Not pinheaded." He frowned with impatience. "Don't you dare martyr yourself and expect me to praise you for it. Yes, love demands sacrifice. More often, it gives us the strength to crawl through hell and come out the other side. How do you think I got through those early years? How do you think I got out of this palace that night? *You.* I would have died here if I hadn't been so determined to get you out alive."

Rhys's heart lurched, and he swallowed, but the lump in his throat remained. "I felt like a responsibility back then. A weight." That was why he'd worked so hard to ensure they got ahead. "I've always wanted to make up for that somehow."

"And that's what Sopi is? Your payment?" He snorted at the twisted logic. "This will come as a shock, Rhys, but you are not a god. You cannot influence the outcome of what I face. All this hurt you're causing yourself and Sopi achieves nothing."

He was starting to realize that.

"But maybe you're right to let her go. Let her find someone who will love her the way she deserves to be loved."

Rhys snapped his brother a glower.

"Oh, did that sting?" Henrik taunted. "Good."

"You're lucky I'm in a hurry or I'd push you into the lake," Rhys muttered.

He took out his phone as he strode into the palace, dialing for Gerard—who had a standing order to stay in touch with Sopi in case she needed anything.

Or, as the case was right now, Rhys needed *her*.

The caretaker of the Basile-Munier "cottage" was actually a penny-pinching widower who welcomed Sopi with a warm hug. He lived with his daughter in the village and came up daily to garden and check on the place.

The house was, in reality, a mansion of two stories with turrets on either end. It faced the azure water of a fjord and had a cobbled driveway surrounded by natural forest. The cream-colored siding, green tin roof and gingerbread rickrack made it look like a white cake with spearmint frosting. Sopi adored it, especially after she filled the half-barrel tubs with geraniums and discovered the path down the slope to the village.

She had meant to stay only a few days to lick her wounds, but she was thinking of lingering until the midsummer festival. The baristas in the village had told her the sun would set behind the mountains, but only for an hour. Most people stayed up to watch it set and rise, enjoying dancing and food, drinking and song for a solid twenty-four hours.

Hopefully there would be some forgetting among all that.

Sighing wistfully, she climbed past the abandoned house with the sod roof, always inspired by the resilience it symbolized. People had lived there once. They had dug into the hillside and hibernated through the long winters, probably with a half dozen children underfoot.

People survived the most amazing things. She could survive this heartbreak.

Ah. There was a different wildflower. She bent to pluck it. The barista had told her one of the festival traditions was for young women to pick a bouquet of seven different flowers. If she put them under her pillow, her future husband would appear in a dream.

Sopi had a daisy and some clover and what looked like a buttercup. She didn't know the name of anything else she'd found. There was a cluster of delicate pink things with serrated petals and what she thought was thistle, so she had wrapped a tissue around the stem. Now these little crimson things were dangling off a drooping stem like bleeding hearts.

How apropos. Oh. And forget-me-nots, she noted wryly, stooping to pluck a few. That made seven and a rather sorry-looking bouquet, but desperate times.

Adjusting her shopping bag on her shoulder and her sun hat on her head, she finished the steep ascent to the small lawn and the patio where she ate every evening until the mosquitos chased her inside.

"Oh." She halted and the tissue-wrapped bouquet dropped to the grass. Yearning coiled around her, squeezing the air from her lungs.

Rhys sat in one chair and had his feet propped on another. Watchful.

"What are you doing here?" she asked, bracing herself.

"The house was locked. Your cell service is terrible. I've been trying to guess your Wi-Fi." He set aside his phone.

She almost told him it was MoreFishInTheSea, but admitted, "It's one of those nonsensical things with dashes and mixed caps."

She set her bag on the table to dig for her keys and hide her anxiety at him showing up out of the blue like this. "How are Henrik and Elise?"

"Fine."

He wasn't bringing bad news, then. That was good, she supposed, but her tension remained, wondering why he was here. She unlocked the back door, and he came into the kitchen with her.

"This is beautiful." He moved across the open space to the lounge, where the big picture windows looked onto the sloping lawn, the village below and the sparkling fjord winding around a bend in the distance.

"Thank you. I'm having trouble leaving." She loved it rather desperately, maybe for the connection to her mother that it was. She moved to put away her handful of groceries, then poured two lemonades. "I can see why my mother wanted Cassiopeia's. It must have made her feel at home."

He nodded and glanced at the view again, hiding his thoughts.

She set her hat on a stool, then brought the glasses over.

"Thank you," he murmured absently, swinging his gaze back to her as he took the glass. Whatever preoccupying thoughts had been in his face creased into a scowl. "Damn it, Sopi, it's been *nine days*."

"Oh." She touched the hair cropped to chin length. "The salon in the village does that thing where they donate hair to kids with cancer." And she'd been *mad*.

She turned to look at the view. Sipped. Felt him blistering her profile with his hot stare. Goodness, that was satisfying, even though her heart was still raw.

"See, if you were still my lover, I might have consulted you," she dared to taunt. "But you aren't. Would you like to sit outside?" she asked politely. "There's usually a nice breeze."

"The irony is, Sopi," he said through gritted teeth, "I love you most when you're digging in your heels and standing up for yourself. I'm going to hold a grudge about this for a long time. Probably until it grows back, but I love you for doing whatever the hell you want."

She wanted to say something pithy, but her vision blurred. She frowned at the smeared vision of green and blue beyond the windows. Bit a lip that began to tremble.

"What am I supposed to say to that, Rhys?" Her voice was barely a wisp.

"You could say you'll marry me."

"You'll forgive me if I don't leap on that offer *again*." She moved to set aside her glass before she dropped it.

"Tell me to go to hell, then. I deserve it." His glass also went onto a side table. He cupped her face and made her look at him. "You were right. I thought I needed to suffer. I have."

"Why?"

"Because I didn't know how to be happy. Not like that. Not without feeling guilty for it. I was so disappointed that you weren't pregnant, Sopi. So crushed. I don't know how I'll function if we have trouble conceiving. There, I've admitted it. I'm not impervious. I hurt and fear and damn well need you beside me or I can't bear the uncertainties of life."

Each husky word took strips off her heart.

"And I didn't want a baby because I needed an heir. I wanted a baby with *you*. The one that would make us into a little family of our own. But I couldn't accept that desire in me without feeling I was stealing something from Henrik. From people who don't have *this*."

He didn't have to tell her what *this* was. She felt it as a sparkling force field around them. One that made her feel as though she floated four feet above the ground.

"And now?" she asked in a thready whisper, eyes dampening.

"Now I know that living without you is more punishment than people are meant to withstand."

"It felt like you were punishing me. That you didn't want me to be happy. That no one does."

"I know." His expression was agonized, but he gave a little tug to the tendril of hair dangling against her jaw. "But this tells me that you will go after your own happiness somehow, someway. And I hope that means you'll take another chance that I can give you the happiness you deserve."

Her mouth trembled as she wavered.

"This time you know exactly what you're getting," he coaxed. "You know you're my equal. That I want *you*. Because *I love you*."

Her tears brimmed. "I love you, too. A *lot*."

"Thank God," he breathed and caught her as she threw herself into his arms.

Their first kiss was hard, but tender. Apology and reunion, but it slid quickly toward passion until they were practically consuming one another.

He let out a growl and scooped up to cradle her against his chest. "Where's the bedroom?"

She pointed at the stairs.

"Hell, no. I'll save my strength for more important things." He set her on the sofa and joined her, covering her laughter with a kiss.

EPILOGUE

Cassiopeia's Spa and Retreat,
Canada, six years later

RHYS WAS IN his robe, waiting for his wife, but he quickly discovered she had left their suite. His bodyguard said something about ice cream, and Rhys went down to the darkened dining room and through to the kitchen that had been closed for the night.

"*Süsse*, I thought you were changing?" He didn't mention the pool or they would have company for sure.

"I went to say good-night and was reminded of a promise I'd made." She wore her evening gown and the anniversary diamonds Rhys had given her before they had come away on this business vacation, but she dug the ice cream scoop into the bucket herself, handing cones to each of their three children.

"Will you take a picture of me, Daddy? I want to show Reggie," their eldest, Sarah, asked. She was third in line for the throne after Rhys and her cousin, Reginald. Fortunately, none of them were worrying about taking Henrik's position anytime soon. He'd been pronounced fully in remission last month.

Even so, the early years of a family drawn close by health challenges had made Sarah and Reggie almost like twins. They were close in age, temperament and intelligence and missed each other terribly if they were away from each other more than a day or two. Rhys found it endearing and hoped they never grew out of it.

"It's bubberscutch," Robbie said, getting some on his nose with his first lick. He grinned, always their entertainer.

Rhys wiped the ice cream away with his fingertip, chuckling and dropping an affectionate kiss on his son's messy hair.

"Maybe you could share one with Marcus?" Sopi suggested as their baby held out a hand and said, "Pea?"

Rhys took fifteen-month-old Marcus from the nanny. He'd been a surprise, and there'd never been a more welcome one. Rhys loved all his children so much, he thought he would burst.

And then there was his wife. Sopi made cones for the nannies, then one for herself before she returned the bucket to the freezer and dropped the scoop into the dish pit.

"You've come a long way, Princess," he teased as she rejoined them.

"Right?" She chuckled. "I didn't want to call the chef back just for this." Her tongue swirled along the edge of her cone.

He had plans for that tongue. First, however, they had to get their children back into their room and their beds, if not actually asleep.

"We'll all go swimming *in the morning*," Rhys promised a short while later when they had everyone abed.

He quickly whisked his wife down to the treatment level.

"I was going to put on a bathing suit," she protested.

"Why? You won't be wearing anything for long." He

collected a spare robe and towels—he learned from his mistakes—and they slipped out the door into the falling snow.

Snickering like conspirators, they made their way through the dark to the private hot pool that was more than a source of healing, magical waters. It was a return to the place where they'd fallen in love. They quickly stripped naked and immersed themselves in its warm embrace.

* * * * *

CHOSEN AS THE SHEIKH'S ROYAL BRIDE

JENNIE LUCAS

For Susan Mallery, Christine Rimmer, and Teresa Southwick, in gratitude for an amazing weekend full of laughter, food, wine, and brainstorming.

I couldn't have written this book without you.

CHAPTER ONE

"You can't be serious!"

Omar bin Saab al-Maktoun, King of Samarqara, replied coldly to his vizier, "Always."

"But—a bride market?" The vizier's thin face looked shocked beneath the brilliant light from the throne room's high windows. "It hasn't been done in Samarqara in a hundred years!"

"Then it is past time," Omar replied grimly.

The other man shook his head. "I never thought you, of all people, would yearn for the old ways."

Rising abruptly from his throne, Omar went to the window and looked out at his gleaming city. He'd done much to modernize Samarqara since he'd inherited the kingdom fifteen years ago. Gleaming steel and glass skyscrapers now lined the edge of the sea, beside older buildings of brick and clay. "Not all my subjects are pleased by my changes."

"So you'd sell your private happiness to appease a few hardliners?" His adviser looked at him blankly. "Why not just marry the al-Abayyi girl, like everyone expects?"

"Half of my nobles expect it. The other half would revolt. They say Hassan al-Abayyi is powerful enough without his daughter becoming queen."

"They'd get over it. Laila al-Abayyi is your best choice. Beautiful. Dutiful." Ignoring Omar's glower, he added, "Marrying her could finally mend the tragedy between your families—"

"No," Omar said flatly. He'd spent his whole reign trying to forget what had happened fifteen years before. He wasn't going to marry Laila al-Abayyi and be forced to remember every day. Shoulders tight, he said, "Samarqara needs a queen. The kingdom needs an heir. A bride market is the most efficient way."

"Efficient? It's cold as hell. Don't do this," Khalid pleaded. "Wait and think it over."

"I'm thirty-six. I'm the last of my line. I've waited too long already."

"You'd truly be willing to marry a stranger?" he said incredulously. "When you know, by the laws of Samarqara, once she has your child, you can never divorce her?"

"I am well acquainted with our laws," Omar said tightly.

"Omar," his vizier said softly, using his first name by the rights of their childhood friendship, "if you marry a stranger, you could be sentencing yourself to a lifetime of misery. And for what?"

But Omar had no intention of sharing his feelings, even to his most trusted adviser. No man was willing to lay his deepest weakness bare. A king even less. "I've given my reasons."

Khalid narrowed his eyes. "What if all the kingdom united, and begged you to marry Laila al-Abayyi? Then you would do it?"

"Of course," Omar said, secure in the knowledge that it would never happen. Half of his nobles were Hassan al-Abayyi's minions, while the other half violently opposed the man and insisted Omar must choose a bride from a competing Samarqari family. "All that matters is my people."

"Yes," his vizier said, tilting his head thoughtfully. "So for them, you'd risk everything on an old barbaric tradition."

Omar's jaw tightened. "A thousand times and more, rather than risk Samarqara falling back into war."

"But—"

"Enough. I've made my decision. Find twenty women who are brilliant and beautiful enough to be my queen. First make sure they are all willing to be my bride." Omar strode out of his throne room in a whirl of robes, calling back coldly, "And do it now."

Why had she been stupid enough to agree to this?

Beth Farraday looked right and left nervously inside the ballroom of the elegant Paris mansion—*hôtel particulier*, they'd called it, a private eighteenth-century palace with a private garden, worth a hundred million euros, in the seventh arrondissement, owned by Sheikh Omar bin Saab al-Maktoun, the King of Samarqara. Beth knew those details because she'd spent the last twenty minutes talking to the waitstaff. They were the people Beth felt most comfortable talking to here.

Gripping her crystal flute, she nervously gulped down a sip of expensive champagne.

She didn't belong with these glamorous women in cocktail dresses, all the would-be brides who'd been assembled here from around the world. Like a modern-day harem, she thought dimly, from which this unknown sheikh king would choose his queen.

The other nineteen women were so incredibly beautiful that they wouldn't have needed to lift a finger to get attention. Yet they'd all achieved amazing things. So far, Beth had met a Nobel Prize–winner, a Pulitzer Prize–winner, an Academy Award–winner. The youngest female senator ever to represent the state of California. A famous artist from Japan. A tech entrepreneur from Germany. A professional gymnast from Brazil.

And then there was Beth. The nobody.

She *so* didn't belong here, and she knew it.

She'd known it even before she'd taken the first-class commercial flight from Houston yesterday, and gotten on the private jet awaiting her in New York, where she'd met the other women traveling from North and South America. She'd known it from the moment her brainiac twin sister had asked her to take her place in this dog and pony show.

"Please, Beth," her sister had begged on the phone two days before. "You have to do it."

"Pretend to be you? Are you crazy?"

"I'd go myself, but I just barely saw the invitation." Beth wasn't surprised. She knew Edith had a habit of letting mail pile up, sometimes for weeks. "You know I can't leave my lab. I'm on the edge of a breakthrough!"

"You always think that!"

"You're much better at schmoozing anyway," her sister wheedled. "You know I'm no good with people. Not like you."

"And I'm totally princess material," Beth replied ironically, as she'd paused in pushing a broom around the thrift shop where she worked.

"All you have to do is show up at this event in Paris, and they'll give me a million dollars. Just think what this could mean to my research—"

"You always think you can make me do anything, just by telling me you're saving kids with cancer."

"Can't I?"

Beth paused.

"Yes," she'd sighed.

Which was why Beth was in Paris now. Wearing a red dress that was far too tight, because she was the only potential bride who didn't fit sample size. She didn't fit in, full stop. After being driven in a limo, like all the other women, from their luxury hotel on the avenue Montaigne to this over-the-top mansion, she'd spent the last few hours in this airless, hot ballroom, watching beautiful, accomplished women go up one by one to speak to a dark-eyed man in sheikh's robes, sitting in tyrannical splendor on the dais.

Except Beth. The sheikh's handlers seemed bewildered by what to do with her. They'd apparently already decided that she wasn't remotely their boss's type. With that, she fervently agreed.

She looked up at the scowling man sitting in his throne on the dais. She watched as he imperiously motioned these amazing women forward, one by one, with an arrogant movement of his finger. And to Beth's shock, the women obeyed, not with glares but with blushing smiles!

Why would they put up with that? Bewildered, Beth finished off her champagne. These other women were huge successes! Geniuses! She'd even recognized Sia Lane—the most famous movie star in the world!

Beth knew why she herself was here. To help her sister help those kids, and perhaps selfishly see a bit of Paris in the process. But the other women's reasons mystified her. They were all so accomplished, beautiful and well known—they couldn't need the money, could they?

And the king himself was no great shakes. Beth tilted her head, considering him from a distance. He was too skinny to be handsome. And he was rude. In West Texas, where she was from, any host worth his salt would have welcomed every guest from the moment they'd walked through his door. King or not, the man should at least have common manners.

Putting her empty flute on a passing silver tray, Beth shook her head. And what kind of man would send out for twenty women like pizza, to be delivered to him in Paris so he could choose his bride?

Even if Omar al-Maktoun was some super rich, super important ruler of a tiny Middle Eastern country she'd never heard of, he must be a serious jerk. Lucky for her, she wasn't his type. A lump lifted to her throat.

Lucky for her, she was apparently no one's type.

There was a reason why, at twenty-six, Beth was still a virgin.

Memories ambushed her without warning, punching through her with all the pain still lingering in her body, waiting to pounce at any moment of weakness. *I'm sorry, Beth. You're just too...ordinary.*

Remembering Wyatt's words, she suddenly felt like she was suffocating, gasping for breath in the too-tight cocktail dress. Blindly turning from the stuffy ballroom, she fled out the side door, where, like a miracle, she found a dark, moonlit garden in the courtyard.

Closing her eyes, she took a deep breath of the cool air, pushing away the memory of the man who'd broken her heart. She didn't need to be loved, she told herself desperately. She was helping her sister, earning money for important research. She was lucky. She'd gotten to see a bit of Paris this afternoon. The Eiffel Tower. The Arc de Triomphe. She'd sat for an hour at a sidewalk café and had a croissant and a tiny overpriced coffee, and watched the world pass by.

That was the problem. Beth wiped her eyes hard in the dark courtyard garden. Sometimes she felt, unlike her super busy sister, that all she did was watch the world pass by. Even here, in this fairy-tale Parisian mansion, surrounded by famous, glamorous people, that was all she was doing. She wasn't part of their world. Instead, she was hiding alone in the private garden.

Not entirely alone. She saw a dark shadow move amid the bare, early spring trees. A man. What was he doing out here?

She couldn't see his face, but she saw the hard, powerful grace of his stride and the tightness of his shoulders in his well-cut suit. By the hard edge of his jaw, Beth presumed he was angry. Or possibly miserable. It was hard to tell.

She wouldn't have to think about her own problems if

she could help someone else with theirs. Going toward him, she said in halting, jumbled high school French, *"Excusez-moi, monsieur, est-ce que je peux vous aider—?"*

The man turned, and she gasped.

No wonder she hadn't seen him at first amid the shadows. He was black-haired, black-eyed, in a black suit. And his eyes were the blackest of all.

"What are you doing here?" His voice was a low growl, in an accent she couldn't quite place, slightly American, slightly something else.

The stranger was so handsome she lost her voice. She wished she hadn't come over. She didn't know how to talk to a man like this.

It's not his fault he's handsome, she told herself. She took a deep breath, and tried to smile. "I'm sorry. You just looked sad. I wondered if I could help at all."

His expression became so cold, it was like ice. "Who are you?"

Beth wondered if she'd offended him. Men could be so touchy, as prickly as a cactus on the outside, even when they were all sweet beneath. At least that was her experience with her male friends, all of whom called Beth a "pal."

"My name is—" She caught herself just in time. She coughed. "Edith Farraday. *Doctor* Edith Farraday," she emphasized, trying to give him a superior, Edith-like look.

His sensual lips curved. "Ah. The child prodigy, the cancer researcher from Houston."

"Yes," she said, surprised. "You must work for the sheikh?"

That seemed to amuse him.

"Every day," he said grimly. "Why aren't you in the ballroom?"

"I got bored. And it was hot."

His gaze lowered to her red gown, which was far too small for her. Involuntarily, she blushed. She yanked up the neckline, which barely covered her generous breasts. "Yes, I know the dress doesn't fit. They didn't have anything in my size."

He frowned. "They were supposed to have every size."

Beth rolled her eyes. "Every size from zero to four. It was either this or my hoodie and jeans, and those were wet. It rained this afternoon when I was walking around the city."

He looked surprised. "You didn't rest in the hotel today like the others?"

"What, beauty sleep, so I'd look extra pretty when meeting the sheikh tonight?" She snorted. "I already know I'm not his type. And this was my only chance to see Paris. I'll be sent home tomorrow."

"How do you know?"

"Because his handlers don't know what to do with me. Plus, I've waited in that ballroom for hours, and the man still hasn't done me the great honor of crooking his mighty finger in my direction."

The man frowned. "He was rude?"

"It's fine, really," Beth said brightly. "The king's not my type, either."

The handsome stranger looked nonplussed. "How do you know? You obviously haven't done any research on him."

Beth frowned. How did the man know that? Did it show? "You got me," she admitted. "I know I should have looked him up on the internet, read up on his likes and dislikes and whatnot, but I only found out about this two days ago, and I was just too busy working before the plane left yesterday..."

He seemed shocked. "Too busy?"

"Frantic." She'd had to rush to set up the thrift shop's spring sale before her boss had grudgingly agreed to let her take her first vacation days in a year. Beth coughed. "At the lab, I mean. Super busy at the lab."

"I imagine. It's important work you're doing." The man

waited, obviously expecting her to continue. But beneath the intensity of his gaze, all her carefully memorized explanations of Edith's highly technical research fled from her mind.

"Yeah. Uh. Cancer is bad."

He stared at her like she was an idiot. "Yes. I know."

"Right," she said, feeling incredibly stupid but relieved he hadn't pushed her further. She changed the subject. "So you work for the king? What are you doing out here? Why aren't you in the ballroom?"

His dark eyes glinted.

"Because I don't want to be." It struck her as the obvious answer—and yet no answer at all. A cold breeze, a vestige of the last throaty gasp of winter, blew against her bare arms and chest. Looking at him, she shivered. But not from cold.

The man towered over her, his dark suit fitting perfectly over his broad shoulders and powerful, muscular body. She'd never been so attracted to anyone like this. She felt shivery inside, overwhelmed just from being close to him. He was taller than her, bigger in every way. She felt power emanating off his body in waves. But even more dangerous than his powerful body were his eyes.

Black pools reflecting scattered bits of light, they lured her, pulled her down like a dark sea, treacherous and deep, threatening to drown her.

Beth forced herself to look away. "Well," she said unsteadily, "I should probably go inside. And wait for the king to crook his finger at me." She sighed. "It's what I'm getting paid for, after all."

"Paid?"

She looked back in surprise. "Yes. Each of the women gets a million dollars, just for showing up. And an extra million for each additional day they're invited to remain." Her lips lifted.

"Just the chance to be Queen of Samarqara should be enough," he said irritably. "A bribe shouldn't be necessary."

"Yeah, right," Beth scoffed. "I'm not sure why all these incredibly accomplished women are here, but I'm guessing the money might be a part of it." She frowned, thinking of her own sister. "After all, even if you're famous and really good at your job, you might still need money."

"And you?" Opalescent, dappled moonlight caressed the edge of his dark brows and slash of high cheekbones. "Is that the reason you're here?"

"Of course," she whispered. She'd never had a man like this pay attention to her. What was she saying? She'd never *met* a man like this before, never, not in her whole life. He was straight out of a fairy tale, straight out of a sexy dream.

Every time this stranger looked at her, every time he spoke, her heartbeat grew faster. He was just a foot away now, and she was starting to hyperventilate. With each rapid breath, her full breasts pressed up against the overly tight sweetheart bodice of her red strapless cocktail dress. They were threatening to pop out entirely. Especially as he drew closer in the shadowy Parisian garden.

"So you're only here for money," he said flatly.

"Cancer research is expensive." Her voice trembled a little in spite of her best efforts.

"I imagine so." He stopped, looking down at her. "But I never imagined the women would be paid just to come here."

"You didn't?" Beth exhaled. He obviously wasn't close to the sheikh, then. She was relieved. At least he wouldn't tell his boss what an idiot Dr. Edith Farraday had looked like in the garden, trembling and panting over a few careless words from a stranger. The real Edith would be horrified. Or—she paused suddenly—maybe she shouldn't make assumptions.

"Who are you to the king?" she said hesitantly. "An attaché? A bodyguard?"

He shook his head, staring down at her incredulously. "Do you really not know?"

"Oh, are you some kind of cousin? Someone famous? I'm sorry. I told you, I've been busy. I was so tired I fell asleep on the plane. And today, I've been walking around Paris…"

She was babbling, and she knew it. The man lifted a dark eyebrow, his towering, powerful body now just inches from her own. In the play of moonlight and shadow, his hard, handsome face held hers, as if she were a mystery he was trying to solve.

Beth, a mystery? She was an open book!

Except she couldn't be, not this time. Whoever this man was, she couldn't let him find out her secret: that she wasn't Dr. Edith Farraday.

Until this moment, it had all just seemed like a favor, a chance to help sick kids, and see a bit of Paris. But the king was paying all that money for a reason. To meet Dr. Edith Farraday, not some ordinary shop girl from Houston.

And to her horror, she suddenly realized there was a legal name for what she and Edith were doing: fraud.

Nervously, Beth yanked up the stupid neckline of the red silk gown. She was in danger of falling out of it, especially as the man drew closer and her breaths became hoarse. No wonder he kept glancing down at her, then sharply looking away.

She felt ashamed, cheap and out of place. She wished she'd never come here, and was safely back at home wearing her usual baggy outfits she got for almost nothing at the thrift shop. No man ever looked at her in those for long.

"I should go," she choked out. But as she turned to go back inside the ballroom, the man's voice was husky in the shadows behind her.

"So what do you think of them?"

She turned. "Who?"

"The other women."

Beth frowned. "Why?"

"I'm curious about the opinion of someone who, as you say, doesn't have a chance with the king. If you don't, then who does?"

She narrowed her eyes. "Do you promise you won't tell the sheikh?"

"Why would you care if I did?"

"I wouldn't want to hurt anyone's chances."

He put his hand to his heart in a strangely old-fashioned gesture. "I promise I won't repeat it to anyone."

She believed him.

Reluctantly, she said, "The movie star is his obvious choice. She's the most famous beauty on earth right now."

"You're talking about Sia Lane?"

"Yeah. It's true she's incredibly beautiful. And charming." She paused. "She's also just plain mean. She harassed the flight attendants for hours on the private jet from New York, just because they didn't have the sparkling water she wanted. Then when we arrived at the hotel this morning, and the porter nearly dropped her designer suitcase, she threatened to destroy his whole family if she saw a single scratch. She's the kind of person who would kick a dog." She tilted her head. "Unless, of course, she believed the dog might be helpful to her career."

He snorted. "Go on."

Guilt made her pause. "I shouldn't have said that." She shook her head. "I'm sure she's a lovely person. Perhaps I just caught her on a bad day."

His dark eyes gave nothing away. "If she's the worst choice, who's the best?"

"Laila al-Abayyi," she said instantly. The man looked oddly pained, but she continued eagerly, "Everyone loves her. She's, like, Mother Teresa or something. And she's from Samarqara, so she knows the language and culture—"

"Who else?" he cut her off.

Confused at his sharp reaction, Beth frowned. "Bere Akinwande is beautiful and kind and smart. She'd make a fantastic queen. And there are others. Though to be honest, I don't know why any of these women would want to marry the king."

"Why?" he demanded.

"Oh, I don't know, because he's the kind of man who set up something like this to find a wife?" She rolled her eyes. "Seriously. This whole thing is just one camera short of a reality show."

"It is not easy for a man in his position to find a worthy partner," he said stiffly. He tilted his head. "Any more, I imagine, than it is easy for a lauded scientist such as yourself to take time from your important work to waste on the painful process of finding a husband the old-fashioned way."

Beth stared at him, disgruntled, then sighed as her shoulders relaxed. "You're right. Who am I to judge? At least he's paying us for our time. We're not paying *him*. I should thank him," she said cheerfully. "And I will, if I ever get the chance."

A voice came behind her.

"Dr. Farraday? What are you doing out here? You're needed in the ballroom."

One of the handlers was standing in the open doorway to the ballroom, impatiently motioning her inside. Then his eyes widened as he saw the stranger behind her. Glancing back, she saw the handsome stranger give a small shake of his head.

"Forgive me, Dr. Farraday," the handler's voice changed strangely, "but if you'd be so kind as to return to the ballroom, we'd be very grateful."

"Well, well. It seems I finally get to meet His Highness." Beth gave the handsome stranger a crooked grin. "Wish me luck."

Reaching out, he touched her bare shoulder. He looked into her eyes. His voice was deep and low, and made her shiver. "Good luck."

Beth's knees went weak. Trying to act cool, she pulled away and said good-naturedly, "It doesn't take luck to fail. I fail at everything. I'm a pro at it."

The man frowned, puzzled. And she remembered too late: Beth had failed. Edith hadn't.

"I mean—never mind. Bye." Turning, she quickly followed the handler out of the garden.

But as she went back into the hot, crowded ballroom, and saw the sheikh sitting on the dais, she wasn't nervous anymore. She wasn't thinking about the powerful king who'd moved heaven and earth to bring together the most accomplished women in the world, merely to choose a potential bride.

Instead, Beth couldn't stop picturing the handsome stranger who'd nearly brought her to her knees with a single touch, in the moonlit shadows of a chilly Parisian garden.

In the garden, Omar stared after her, still in shock.

Was it possible that he'd just had an entire conversation with Dr. Edith Farraday without her realizing who he was?

No, surely. She had to know.

But if this was a come-on, at least it had novelty value. No woman had ever pretended not to know him before.

He'd arrogantly assumed that every woman who'd agreed to come to the *palais* tonight wished to marry him. Was it possible one didn't even know his identity? That she'd actually had so little interest in him that she hadn't bothered to read newspapers, gossip magazines, or just look him up online? It seemed incredible.

But his instincts told him that Dr. Edith Farraday hadn't been pretending. She truly had no idea who Omar was.

Just as he himself hadn't known that Khalid was paying the twenty women to come to Paris. It made sense—as the potential brides his vizier had selected were all so famous and successful—that they could hardly be expected to toss their busy schedules aside, merely for the chance to become Omar's queen. But still… It might have bruised a lesser man's ego, to realize that the chance of marrying him hadn't been enough to make women fly here from the Americas, Asia, Africa and Europe.

Which was why Khalid hadn't told him the details, obviously. He'd told his vizier to arrange it, and arrange it the man had. It was Khalid sitting in the ballroom of his Paris mansion right now, meeting each woman personally. His friend was the one who'd winnow the twenty down to the ten whom Omar would meet personally tomorrow.

Khalid was the one who'd created the criteria for choosing the twenty potential brides, and arranged for them to be brought to Paris. When Omar had first seen the list that morning, he'd been surprised to discover how career-driven and ambitious the women were. But then, hadn't he himself insisted the women must be brilliant to be his queen? Surely the woman he chose would be willing to give up her career, no matter how illustrious. What greater fate could any woman aspire to than becoming Queen of Samarqara?

There had just been one name on the list that had immediately displeased him.

"Why did you invite Laila al-Abayyi?" he'd demanded that morning. "I told you I cannot marry her."

"No," his old friend said cheerfully. "You told me you'd only marry her if all our nobles agreed she should be queen."

"Which they will not."

"The future is unknowable," Khalid said.

"Not this," Omar replied sourly. "I'm surprised she'd even agree. How can it not be humiliating for her to compete?"

His vizier had smiled, his dark eyes glinting strangely. "Like you, sire, Miss al-Abayyi puts Samarqara's needs above her own. Her father was so insulted by your bride market plan that he was threatening to cause trouble. Then Laila announced that she approved of your plan, and that she, too, appreciates the old traditions. That calmed her father down. She accepted my invitation for diplomatic purposes, purely for the good of the nation."

For the good of the nation, plus a million dollars, it seemed.

A million dollars *per day*.

Omar set his jaw. So be it. He'd avoided marriage for long enough. He was thirty-six years old, and if he died, there was no one to inherit the throne. His only family left was Khalid, a distant cousin who wasn't even an al-Maktoun, but an al-Bayn. Omar needed an heir. He couldn't risk a return to the violent civil war that had nearly destroyed Samarqara during his grandfather's time.

Nor could he risk a love match. He'd never be such a fool again.

No. He was older now, wiser. Marriage was for dynastic reasons only. And in the month since he'd ordered Khalid to arrange the bride market, he'd successfully avoided thinking about it. It wasn't difficult. Omar was always busy with affairs of state.

But tonight, after finishing a diplomatic meeting in the embassy, when he'd returned to the residence, he'd found himself on edge, knowing the women were there. The process had begun.

As king, Omar would only nominally make the final decision. According to the traditions of the bride market, his council would advise him of the woman they felt best suited to be his queen.

But she wouldn't just be Omar's queen. She'd also be his wife. The mother of his children. The woman in his bed and at his side. Forever.

If you marry a stranger, you could be sentencing your-self to a lifetime of misery.

Grimly, Omar pushed Khalid's warning away. The bride market had already begun, and in any event, his vizier and council could hardly choose worse for him than he'd once tried to choose for himself.

But still…

Tense and restless as he waited for the women to finish the interviews in the ballroom, he'd paced his private quarters. He'd known he couldn't meet the brides. Not yet. It wasn't protocol. But he'd found himself unable to either stay or go. So he'd gone outside in the dark, shadowy courtyard garden, trying not to think of either the future or the past.

Then he'd been interrupted by a beautiful, sensual, surprising woman. He'd been violently drawn to her, first by her incredible body, lush and ridiculously curvy in that tight dress. Then he'd been drawn by her frank, artless words. For a moment, he'd been distracted, even amused, as well as attracted.

Until even she had said that Laila, the half sister of his deceased long-ago fiancée, should be his bride.

Was there no escaping the past?

Looking up at the moonlight now, Omar felt a new chill. He'd thought the bride market would make it easier to have a clean break. Instead, tonight he was haunted more than ever by the memories of his first attempt at acquiring a bride, some fifteen years before. What a disaster that had been.

No, not a disaster. A tragedy.

One that must never happen again.

A low curse escaped him. Setting his jaw, he followed Dr. Edith Farraday back inside the ballroom. Standing quietly against the wall so he wouldn't be noticed, he watched her from a distance, as she spoke earnestly to the vizier on the dais. Feeling his gaze, she glanced back, and their eyes met.

Then her gaze narrowed.

If she hadn't known who Omar was in the garden, she must know it now. Her look was genuinely angry—even accusing.

A hot spark went through him as Omar looked slowly over her curvy figure in that tight dress.

His relationships of the last few years—shallow, sexual and short-lived—had been mostly with ambitious, cold, wickedly skinny blondes with a cruel wit. The opposite of black-eyed Ferida al-Abayyi, the fiancée he'd lost.

Dr. Farraday was different from all of them. She was neither a cool blonde nor a sensual, sloe-eyed brunette. Her long, lustrous hair was somewhere between dishwater blond and light brown. She had a dusting of freckles over her snub nose. Her heart-shaped face was rosy, her lips full and pink, and her eyes—it was too far to see the color, but they were glaring at him now in a way he felt all the way to his groin.

But if her face was innocently wholesome, her body was the opposite. She was a bombshell. That dress should have been illegal, he thought. Clinging to her curvaceous body, the silk whispered breathlessly that, at any moment, it might fall apart at the seams, and leave her incredible body naked and ripe for his taking. In that dress, Dr. Farraday could rule any man.

Or maybe it was just him. Looking at her in the brighter lights of the ballroom, all he could think about was taking her straight to his bed. Her skin, when he'd briefly touched her shoulder, had been even softer than silk. He could only imagine what the rest of her would feel like, naked against his own.

He took a deep, hoarse breath.

Omar could not seduce her, or any other woman here. The bride market was not about casual, easy seduction. In spite of Dr. Farraday's remark about reality shows, it was a serious tradition, not an episode of *The Bachelor*.

The only way he would have the luscious Dr. Farraday in his bed would be after marriage. And she had far more to recommend her than just mind-blowing sex appeal. Her résumé had stood out from the other nineteen, because she was a research scientist specializing in the same childhood leukemia that had killed Omar's older brother, long ago.

But if he hadn't read that, he'd have had no idea that the woman had graduated from Harvard at nineteen with both an MD and a PhD in biochemistry. At twenty-six, she already led a team in Houston, doing bleeding-edge research. Edith Farraday rarely left the lab, he'd heard.

Someone like that should have been daunting, cold, formidable. But Dr. Edith Farraday didn't act like her résumé. She was so different in person, Omar thought, that she almost seemed an entirely different woman.

She was warm, kind, self-effacingly funny. Even though she was different from his usual type, he was overwhelmingly attracted to her. Or maybe it was *because* she was so different.

Omar blinked when he heard the whispers in the ballroom suddenly explode, as a low rumble of shocked noise swirled around him. He'd been recognized by the other women in the ballroom. Without a word, he turned and disappeared back into the garden, and then to his private quarters in the residence.

But at the end of the evening, he stood alone in the upstairs salon, watching through the window as, below him, all twenty of the would-be brides climbed into limousines waiting to take them back to the luxurious, five-star Campania Hotel on the avenue Montaigne.

"The things I do for you, Your Highness." His vizier's

voice came behind him. "Are you ready yet to just be sensible and marry the al-Abayyi girl?"

Not dignifying that question with a response, Omar turned. "You've made your decision which ten will be sent home?"

"It wasn't easy." Khalid paused. "Except for the last one. I barely spoke ten words to her before I knew she wasn't your type."

He was speaking of Dr. Edith Farraday, Omar realized, and said irritably, "I don't have a type. Why does everyone think I have a type?"

"Because you do."

Omar replied, annoyed, "And Dr. Edith Farraday isn't it?"

"Beautiful girl, but a little too common for you, I thought. She's put on weight since her last published photographs, too. Her dress looked outrageously tight." Khalid blinked. "Am I wrong?"

Omar stared back out the window. He watched as Dr. Farraday got into the last limo. She looked back up wistfully at the mansion, as if she knew that she'd never come back, as if trying to remember everything.

It doesn't take luck to fail, she'd said. *I fail at everything. I'm a pro at it.*

What a strange comment for a world-famous genius to make, he thought. Because she hadn't yet found a cure for biphenotypic acute leukemia, all her accomplishments meant nothing?

But she would understand, as few could, how it felt to be single-minded in pursuit of one's duty—for her, curing cancer, for him, the responsibility of leading a nation.

Common, Khalid had called her. And he was right. Edith Farraday didn't have the imperious edge, the formality, the arrogance of a queen. She was unorthodox, a little undignified, and yet…

And yet…

Omar wanted her. Suddenly, and beyond reason.

No. A pulse of danger went through him. Any of the other women would be a safer choice, even Laila al-Abayyi. Because he could not, dare not allow emotion into this choice. Never again. The cost of loving, of wanting, was too high—it brought destruction, not just on him but upon innocent people.

In spite of knowing this, though, Omar gripped the edge of the translucent curtain as he watched the limo drive out past the gate. Dr. Farraday had warmed him in the garden. Warmed?

The image passed through his mind of her voluptuous figure, her full breasts pushing up against the ruched silk, fighting a battle for modesty and losing. Her eyes sparkling in furious indignation as she'd glared at him across the ballroom, unconsciously licking her full, pink lips—

A rush of heat went through him, straight to his groin. He nearly groaned aloud.

But he could not seduce her. He could not even kiss her. Not unless and until he formally proclaimed her his bride on the steps of his royal palace in Samarqara.

And he could never choose Dr. Farraday as queen. Khalid was right. She was too open, too honest, too sexy. Not at all appropriate. So he should send her away. At once, if not sooner.

"Sire?" his vizier asked. "Shall I send the Farraday woman home?"

But as Omar turned, all he could think about was how seeing her in the cold, dark garden had been like seeing the bright, warm sun after a long-dead winter. And he heard himself growl, "One more night."

CHAPTER TWO

SO THAT WAS THAT.

The next morning, when Beth heard the hard knock at the door, she lifted her backpack to her shoulder and looked at her luxurious hotel suite one last time.

In the soft morning light, the suite looked magical, like a princess's bedchamber, with a fireplace and four-poster bed, a wrought-iron balcony edged with pink flowers, and a white marble bathroom bigger than her whole studio apartment back home. She'd taken pictures to show her friends back at the thrift shop.

Outside, the morning sun was soft over Paris. Beneath the Eiffel Tower, white neoclassical buildings glowed as pink as frosted cupcakes. She saw birds flying over the avenue Montaigne, soaring over the fresh blue sky.

Beth looked at her hoodie and jeans, which had been freshly cleaned and pressed by the hotel staff overnight. Unlike the other brides, she'd traveled light, with only a backpack, which was now stuffed with her neatly folded silk cocktail dress from last night. The king's staff had made it clear they didn't want it, and she knew someone at the thrift shop certainly would.

She took a deep breath. She was glad to be returning home. She didn't belong here, in this glamorous world.

Her place was in her Houston neighborhood, in her studio walk-up apartment near the community college, where she'd been taking part-time classes until her heartbreak over Wyatt made her drop out. Since then, her part-time job at the thrift shop had become full-time, and she biked to work each morning, rain or shine, because she couldn't afford car insurance, much less a car. She sometimes worked extra jobs to make ends meet, and in her spare time, she volunteered at the local soup kitchen, the food pantry and the senior center. That was the life she knew.

But Beth wanted to remember this Paris adventure, down to the last moment. Because she knew it would never happen again.

After her shock last night, realizing she'd been talking to the actual king the whole time in the garden, she'd expected to be awake all night, agonizing about what an idiot she'd been. Instead, she'd slept like a log, wrapped in soft cotton sheets that had a thread count higher than her paycheck. After a long, hot shower that morning in the palatial bathroom, she'd eaten breakfast in bed, brought by room service, with toasted baguettes called *tartines* slathered with butter and marmalade, and fresh, flaky chocolate croissants that melted literally like butter in her mouth, and drunk fresh-squeezed orange juice and strong coffee with fresh cream.

But her time as a princess was over. When her phone buzzed an hour before, she hadn't even bothered to check the message. She already knew what it would say: she was being sent home.

Now, the knock. She hesitated, staring at the door. Once she answered it, she knew she'd find a servant waiting to escort her to the minibus that would take her back to the airport, along with the rest of the rejected ten. How could it be otherwise, when after criticizing a famous movie star, Beth had actually insulted the king as well—right to his handsome, sensual face?

Beth flinched, remembering how stupid she'd felt when she'd finally spoken to the man on the throne, only to discover it was just a regular chair, and the man was just a vizier and that only the ten women to make the next cut would have the honor of actually meeting the king in person.

"But where is he now?" she'd asked as a creeping suspicion built inside her.

The vizier replied with a disapproving stare, "His Highness is busy with affairs of state."

And then, like a flash, Beth had known.

Why aren't you in the ballroom?

Because I don't want to be.

Who else but the king could choose whether he wished to attend such a gala in his own residence? Who else could be so arrogant, wear such a well-cut suit and be able to lounge in the residence's garden at his leisure? She remembered the handler's shocked look, and the handsome stranger's small shake of the head.

You must work for the sheikh? she'd asked. Amused, he'd replied, *Every day.*

As she stood beside the vizier in the ballroom, her horrible suspicion built to certainty. Then she'd felt someone's gaze behind her. Turning, she'd seen the handsome stranger himself now beside the door, watching her across the ballroom with cool, inscrutable eyes. And she'd remembered her own embarrassing words. *I don't know why any of these women would want to marry the king... This whole thing is just one camera short of a reality show.*

At any time, the king could have revealed himself and stopped her. Instead, he'd just let her carry on making a fool of herself. Angry and humiliated, Beth had glared at him for a moment in the ballroom. Then she'd turned away, cheeks burning. When her interview with the vizier was finally over, the king was nowhere in sight.

She told herself she was relieved she'd never see him again. Just being near him had done crazy things to her. She shivered, her cheeks even now flooding with color at the memory.

He should have had the common decency to tell her who he was, straightaway. The man had no manners whatsoever. And if she ever saw him again—

The knock pounded again on her door, even harder and louder. Gripping the straps of her backpack, Beth answered the door with a sigh. "All right, I'm coming—"

Standing in the doorway, she saw King Omar himself, dressed from head to toe in regal sheikh's robes.

Her jaw dropped as she took an involuntary step back. His black eyes pierced her. His powerful body seemed to fill every inch of the doorway as he looked down at her grimly.

"So. You know who I am."

It was a statement, not a question. Trembling, she nodded. All her earlier ideas of pointing out his bad manners flew straight out the window. Her knees were trembling, and all she could think was that he'd discovered she wasn't Edith. Why else would the king himself come to see her, rather than just having his servants escort her onto the Minibus of Shame?

"Why are you here?" she whispered through dry lips.

"I have good news and bad news, Dr. Farraday." His husky voice was faintly mocking. "The good news is— you're coming with me."

Where? To jail? "Then what's the bad news?" she blurted out.

"I'm afraid word has gotten out." He paused, and fear rushed through her body, until he continued smoothly, "Paparazzi have surrounded this hotel. I'm here to escort you and the others out the back." He motioned to a servant hovering behind him in the hotel hallway. "Saad will get your luggage."

She indicated the backpack on her shoulder. "This is all I have. This, and the clothes on my back."

The king's dark eyes flickered over her. "I will send for more clothes for you."

Beth shook her head in confusion. "It's not necessary—"

"Isn't it?" His gaze lingered over her oversize gray hoodie and baggy jeans as she stood in the hotel suite. She suddenly wished she had something nicer to wear. But that didn't make sense. If he hadn't learned her real identity, which it seemed he hadn't, what did she care what the king thought of her as he took her to the airport?

And yet, somehow, she did care. Remembering how his darkly intense eyes had traced down her bare throat last night to her overflowing breasts, she blushed. Last night, it had felt like she'd wandered into a romantic dream, with the two of them alone in a moonlit Parisian garden.

Dream? No. He'd made a fool of her.

The third man to do that, she thought, and her heart lifted to her throat. "I don't understand," she said stiltedly. "The good news is that you're taking me to the airport personally?"

"No." His dark eyebrows lowered. "Back to the mansion."

Beth frowned, bewildered. "All twenty of us are going back?"

"Only the ten who are staying another night."

Beth stared at him.

"I made it to the top ten?" she whispered. It was so unexpected she hugged the thought close to her chest.

The sheikh frowned at her. "You are not pleased?"

Beth's feelings were so mixed up she hardly knew how she felt. "Um…are you sure it's not a mistake?"

He snorted, then tilted his head, considering her. "You are different."

A flutter went through her heart. "I am?"

"Yes." Their eyes locked, and his gaze electrified her

body, from her fingertips to her toes and everywhere between. "So will you come?"

No. She had to say no. She'd gotten the million dollars for Edith. Only a fool would press her luck—

"Of course," she blurted out.

A slow-rising smile lifted his sensual lips. "This way, if you please, Dr. Farraday."

Dr. Farraday. As Beth walked with him down the hotel hallway, his servant following behind, her heart fell back to her canvas sneakers.

Remembering how angry she'd been at him for not disclosing his identity in the garden, she felt ashamed. Talk about the pot calling the kettle black.

And if he found out—*when* he found out—

Oh, this was getting dangerously complicated. She'd never imagined he'd choose her to stay another night, not in a million years!

But one more day would mean another million for Edith's research. Then tomorrow, she'd go home for sure. Surely she could fake it for another twenty-four hours. No one the wiser, and no one hurt.

But as she left the Paris hotel, going out into the bright sunlight where the limos waited, Beth barely noticed the paparazzi with their lifted cameras and shouted questions, and the bodyguards holding them back. Looking up at the handsome, powerful billionaire king beside her, she felt equal parts intoxicated—and afraid.

For the first time since she could remember, she'd been chosen for something. The king didn't think Beth was *ordinary.* He thought she was different. That she was special.

The thought warmed her all over. Until she remembered he hadn't chosen Beth.

He'd chosen Edith.

* * *

"You collected the Farraday woman from her hotel suite? Yourself?"

Khalid's voice was shocked.

"I had no choice. She wouldn't answer the phone." Standing in the grand salon back at his Paris residence, Omar looked out irritably at the hordes of paparazzi now clustered outside the tall wrought-iron gates. Someone had tipped off the press about the bride market. Who? He wondered grimly. One of his scorned would-be brides? Or perhaps one of the ten he'd kept?

Perhaps Sia Lane, the movie star Dr. Farraday had called "downright mean," had decided to hedge her bets with a little more publicity?

Whoever'd done it, the story had exploded instantly. It was too juicy for the media to treat it otherwise, with the famous playboy king of a small Middle Eastern kingdom bringing women from around the globe to choose a queen. The story was making news everywhere.

It's one camera short of a reality show, Dr. Farraday had said. She was right.

Dr. Edith Farraday. Just thinking of her warmed Omar. She'd looked shocked in the hotel suite two hours before, as if she'd never expected to be chosen.

Perhaps he'd been wrong to choose her. But how could he send away the one woman who was different—the one who made his body come alive? He'd told himself that all his initial concern was overcautious. So he was attracted to her. What of it?

Attraction wasn't love, or the kind of mind-blowing lust that caused civilizations to crumble.

He just wanted her. And there was some mystery in her that he couldn't quite understand. Her lovely expression, frank and honest, had a way of changing, becoming guarded. As if she were hiding something from him. But what?

Today, he'd find out.

Then he'd send her home tomorrow.

"You shouldn't have escorted her yourself. It's not how it's supposed to be done," Khalid continued, obviously disgruntled. "If you escort one lady from her hotel suite, you must do the same for the rest. Otherwise it gives the appearance of favoritism."

Omar dropped the curtain abruptly and turned to face the other man. "Dr. Farraday *is* my favorite," he said bluntly.

His vizier's expression soured. "But surely, she isn't as beautiful or elegant as—"

"Say Laila al-Abayyi's name, and I'm sending you straight back to Samarqara."

The other man paused, and his mouth snapped shut. Then he ventured, "Dr. Farraday does not seem to have the same polish as the others. Perhaps she has spent too much time in her lab. The brief time I interviewed her, she was far too artless and frank in her speech. The council would not approve of her obvious lack of diplomacy."

Thinking of Dr. Farraday's casual, accidental insults to him in the garden, Omar was forced to agree. He said shortly, "She amuses me. Nothing more."

"Ah." His vizier's face looked relieved.

"I collected Dr. Farraday from her suite because it was expedient. And I did not escort her to her room here."

Although heaven knew he'd wanted to.

That morning, the other nine women had all rushed from their hotel rooms immediately after the phone call informing them they'd made the top ten. They'd clustered together, filling up the first limousine. Leaving Omar alone with the luscious Dr. Farraday in the second limo.

Sitting beside her on the drive from the hotel back to his Paris mansion, he'd been aware of her, so aware. It had taken all his willpower to make polite conversation with her, when his mind had been on something else altogether. He'd wanted to pull up the privacy screen to block out the view of the driver and bodyguard in front, so he could push her against the soft calfskin leather of the wide back seat, pull off that ridiculously baggy sweatshirt and discover the delights of the amazing curves she'd flaunted last night.

"Very well, sire..." his vizier said haltingly. "Of course you must enjoy your amusements in the midst of a serious business. So long as you consider your actual choice wisely. It took some trouble to bring these women to Paris."

"Some money, you mean," Omar said coldly. "I heard about the payments."

"You are displeased with my method?" Khalid shook his head. "It's nothing to your fortune. A mere rounding error."

He glowered. "That isn't the point."

"Then what is?" His friend looked stubborn. "A bride price is part of the tradition, you know that. Isn't it better for the payment to go to the brides themselves, rather than the antiquated custom of paying their fathers?"

Omar could hardly argue with that. "Of course," he bit out. "But still..."

"Still?"

He could hardly explain that it had hurt his pride. His friend would say, with some cause, that it was well deserved. He growled, "I never gave you authorization."

"You just told me to arrange it. And made it quite clear you didn't wish to be bothered with the details."

Another thing Omar could not argue with. He scowled.

Khalid's eyebrows rose. "And surely you approve of the results. All these women are beautiful and brilliant. Just as you commanded."

"Yes," he was forced to concede. Based on their pictures and resumes alone, they were more accomplished than he'd ever imagined. "Assuming they are willing to give up those brilliant careers to be Queen of Samarqara."

"And why would they not?" Khalid replied indignantly. "Being Samarqara's Queen is surely the greatest honor any woman could imagine."

Omar hesitated. He'd assumed the same thing himself, and yet suddenly he was not so sure.

He himself had been forced to leave college at twenty-one and ascend the throne, casting all personal ambitions aside after his father had died. But he'd known that would be his fate from the day his older brother had died. As the only heir of a country that could still remember the horrors of civil war, Omar had always known he must put his country's needs above his own. Any man of honor would have done the same.

And so it was with this marriage. After the awful tragedy with Ferida, he'd put marriage off indefinitely. Until, in New York on a recent diplomatic visit, he'd seen an elderly couple walking down Fifth Avenue. They hadn't been special, or rich, or beautiful. But they'd held hands tenderly as they walked together. The man had gazed down lovingly at his wife, and she at him. And Omar had felt a sharp pain in his throat.

He did not expect that kind of devotion. Why would he? His own parents' marriage had been a disaster. Selfishly trying to find love only brought pain, or worse—death.

Coming home, Omar had ordered his vizier to begin the preparations for the bride market. He wanted this marriage finished. Done. Before he ever let himself again be tempted by something so destructive as a foolish dream.

He would take a bride who felt the same. A woman who'd put others first, as Omar did. Who would see the sacrifice not just as a burden, but an honor.

At least most of the time.

"One of the ten women would see it as a greater honor

than the rest," his vizier said slowly. "She has no other career than to be a dutiful daughter and the pride of her people. She already speaks our language, knows our customs—"

Omar cut him off with a glare. Setting his jaw, he said with some restraint, "Bring the ten in now."

His vizier's jaw tightened, and he looked as if he were biting back words. Then he bowed and went to open the door to the grand salon. Outside, in the elegant hallway, ten women were waiting.

Eight of them, he'd meet for the first time. The ninth, he was trying to avoid. The tenth, he could hardly stop thinking about. He'd speak with Dr. Farraday last. She would be his dessert. His whipped cream. His cherry on—

Realizing he was starting to get aroused, he stopped the thought cold.

Because his vizier was right. As much as he desired Edith Farraday, she seemed an unlikely queen. Aside from her lack of tact, it was almost impossible that she'd be willing to give up her life as a research scientist. It was obviously her obsession, in spite of her strange reluctance to talk about it. And Laila was a nonstarter.

So he needed to seriously consider the other eight. Any one of them could be an appropriate queen, one the council would approve of, and if he were lucky, one he could admire and respect. So, for the rest of the afternoon and evening, he'd meet with each woman privately, for as long or short a time as he deemed appropriate.

But the plans for today had been that he'd get to know his ten potential brides by touring the sights of Paris with each of them separately. That would be more difficult with paparazzi outside the gate, holding up their cameras as reporters yelled obnoxious questions. Anywhere they tried to go, the paparazzi would follow.

But at least it would not last long. Tomorrow morning, he'd send five more women home. The remaining five, the true contenders, would return with him to Samarqara to meet the council in preparation for the main event: the bride market itself.

Now, standing beside the banquet table, Omar watched as the ten women entered the grand salon of his Paris mansion.

Nine women looked like carbon copies, though all in different shades and colors—classically beautiful, slender, elegant, tall and perfectly dressed in sleek designer outfits.

Then there was the last one, shorter than the rest, and rounder. Her cheeks were pink, her eyes bright, her light brown hair wavy and wild. Against his will, his eyes traced over her. Her curves were invisible beneath the baggy hoodie and jeans. But his body stirred, becoming instantly hard.

Why her?

Omar couldn't answer the question, even to himself.

As the women entered the grand salon one by one, he stood near the end of the banquet table in his full sheikh's robes, making eye contact with each one, giving each a welcoming nod, as he did during any other diplomatic endeavor. The women each smiled, or preened, or nodded back coolly, in their turn.

And in spite of his best efforts to be open-minded, he found himself unimpressed, in spite of all their obvious charms. He was bored by them, beauty, success and all.

Except for the woman who came in last, looking pink-cheeked and miserable, hanging in the back of the salon. The one who wouldn't meet his eyes.

Dr. Edith Farraday. And again he felt it, along with his powerful attraction—that mystery he couldn't solve. As Khalid had pointed out, Omar had already made it clear by his attentions that she was his favorite. So why did she hang back, behind the rest? Why did her hazel eyes look haunted and guilty, as if she'd committed some crime?

He didn't like ambiguity. He wanted her mystery solved. Now. Tonight.

And in a perfect world, he would have solved the mystery with them both naked in bed.

"Welcome," his vizier said formally, spreading his arms wide in his robes. "I will be presenting each of you in turn to His Highness, the King of Samarqara. Please—" he indicated the tables full of drinks and lavish food "—until your name is called, please feel free to mingle and relax."

Omar sat down at the chair at the end of the table. Standing beside him, Khalid motioned to the first woman.

"Miss Sia Lane."

The beautiful blonde came forward and gave a slightly ironic nod, then at his motioned invitation, sat down in the chair beside him. His vizier said gravely, "Sire, Miss Lane is a very well-known actress from Los Angeles, California."

"Pleased to meet you, Your Highness," she said.

"And you, Miss Lane." It wasn't surprising that his vizier had chosen her to make the cut. She was the world's most famous beauty, and her chilly glamour reminded him of many of his past mistresses. On paper, Sia Lane would make an excellent bride, a prestigious new member to join any royal family, as when Grace Kelly had become Princess of Monaco or Meghan Markle became Duchess of Sussex.

But when Omar reached out to shake Sia Lane's hand, her skin felt cold and dry. He felt nothing, in spite of her beauty. He dropped her hand.

"Welcome," he said gravely. "Thank you for coming to meet me."

"My pleasure," the blonde murmured, fluttering her eyelashes at him, arrogantly sure of her own appeal. He recalled Dr. Farraday's tart assessment: *She's the kind of person who would kick a dog, unless, of course, she believed the dog might be helpful to her career.*

Taking his wry smile for praise, the movie star tilted

her chin in a practiced move he'd seen in her films. They spoke briefly, then he dismissed her with a polite nod. She seemed almost surprised, as if she'd expected to be proclaimed his queen, here and now.

Khalid called the next woman forward. "Dr. Bere Akinwande."

"Your Highness," she said politely, with a short bow. Speaking with her as she sat beside him, he thought Dr. Edith Farraday's character assessment was correct once again. She seemed an excellent choice to be his queen—a doctor, she spoke six languages, and had been nominated for a Nobel prize. She spoke earnestly of the work she was doing, the difference it could make in the world, and thanked him twice for the "donation" he'd given her. She did not try to flirt. She'd clearly come for the money, but then—he thought again of Dr. Farraday's important research—could he blame her for that?

Dr. Bere Akinwande was accomplished, intelligent and pretty, but when he shook her hand, again, he felt nothing.

"Laila al-Abayyi," his vizier intoned, his voice solemn.

Omar repressed his feelings as he was formally introduced to the young Samarqari heiress. Looking in her lovely face, he saw the same black eyes, the same dark beauty, the same masses of long, shiny dark hair that he remembered seeing in her half sister Ferida, fifteen years ago. Ferida, whom he'd arrogantly demanded as his bride, before it had all ended in death and sand—

Dropping her hand, he said shortly, "Goodbye."

"Goodbye?" Laila said, looking bewildered at being cut off when she'd been in the middle of shyly praising the improvements of his rule.

"You may return to your room. I will not meet with you later."

"You—you won't?"

"I thank you for your intercessions with your father. But any further contact between us would be unwelcome."

Laila turned pale. "Oh. I—I see…" With a hurt glance toward the vizier, the brunette fled the salon.

"Sire," his vizier said in a low voice for his ears alone, "that was unconscionable—"

"She should not be here." Omar's jaw was hard as stone as he turned on him. "Do you understand? I will not marry her. Ever."

His vizier's eyes narrowed, then he gave an unsteady nod. Turning, he called the next potential bride's name.

Omar was glad of the chance to calm the rapid, sickening beat of his heart, as he offered the same polite courtesy to the next woman, then the next, expressing gratitude for their visit to Paris. They always thanked him in return, smiling, their eyes lingering appreciatively over his face and body. So far, so good.

But after that, he started to feel like a bank manager, not a king. The entrepreneur from Germany, tossing her hair, explained in detail that she was seeking investors for her tech start-up. The gymnast from Brazil, smiling flirtatiously, told him of her desire to build an expensive new training facility in São Paulo. The senator from California, her gaze falling to his mouth, wished to discuss favorable trade negotiations for her state's dairy farmers. And so on.

Many of the women had clearly come to Paris to pursue their career goals, as Dr. Farraday had. Only a few of them seemed blindly ready to toss their important careers away for a Cinderella fantasy that had little to do with the rigors of actual leadership.

He wasn't sure which was worse.

But he was always aware of the one woman in the background, standing by the wall, hovering in the corners, moving in the shadows. One woman who, in spite of her obvious determination to be invisible, shone out for him like no other.

Finally, his vizier's voice said grudgingly, "And finally, sire, Dr. Edith Farraday. A well-known cancer researcher from Houston, Texas."

Watching her as she came forward, Omar could have sworn that she flinched at the sound of her own name. Why? Was she so unwilling to meet with him?

Her earlier words came floating back: *I don't know why any of these women would want to marry the sheikh.*

Was it possible that, even though he was so attracted to her, she wasn't attracted to him at all?

No, surely not. Women always fell at his feet. He was the King of Samarqara, billionaire, absolute ruler of a wealthy kingdom.

But then, was Dr. Edith Farraday, child prodigy, high-minded scientist, the sort of person to be impressed by money and power? For all he knew, she had a boyfriend back home. An ordinary but perfectly satisfying man who was content to let her be the superstar, while he cooked her dinners and rubbed her feet. She might find that sort of man much more appealing to her lifestyle than some playboy king who, until this very moment, had been unable and unwilling to commit to anything beyond his own rule.

It was a discomfiting thought.

"Oh. Hello again," Edith said uneasily, her eyes darting to the right and left, as if she felt guilty. Guilty?

Was there a boyfriend?

The question set him on edge.

"It's a pleasure to finally be properly introduced," Omar said gravely. He looked over her outfit, the exact same hoodie and jeans that she'd worn when he'd knocked on her hotel room door that morning, and tilted his head curiously. "Did the new wardrobe I had sent to your room not meet with your approval?"

"The clothes are beautiful, thank you," she said, her eyes guarded.

"And yet you are not wearing them."

"They really weren't necessary. I'm only going to be here one more day."

"And a night," he pointed out.

She looked away evasively. "I suppose. But I knew if I wore them, your people couldn't return them to the store. So I didn't touch them."

Omar stared at her incredulously. "You're worried about the cost?"

She actually blushed. "I suppose it's silly but... I don't like taking advantage of people..."

Then her voice abruptly cut off. Her cheeks turned from pink to bright red.

He frowned, puzzled by her reaction. "You're not taking advantage. You're my guest. I want you to be comfortable."

"Oh, I am," she said in a strangled voice. She tried to smile, but her face was stiff and awkward.

"Is there some reason you wish to rush back to Houston?" He watched her. "A boyfriend back home?"

Her eyes flashed wide. "What?" she said quickly. "No!"

Omar relaxed. "So you miss your work at the lab, then."

"Oh. Yes. Of course I do." She paused, then blurted, "I'd hoped to see more of Paris today. But I was just told that we won't be allowed to leave the mansion this afternoon?"

"An unfortunate circumstance, with all the paparazzi outside the gate."

She bit her lip. "I know I'm being silly, it's just... I didn't get a chance to see the Louvre yet, or climb the Eiffel Tower. The line for tickets was too long. I was hoping..." Squaring her shoulders, she shook her head. "Ah, well, it doesn't matter."

"The Louvre? You like art?"

"I wanted to see the *Mona Lisa*. Who doesn't?"

"You've never seen it?" It seemed strange she'd never been to Paris before. He was sure the other women had visited many times, for school trips or family vacations, or, as in the case of Laila al-Abayyi, because their families owned lavish penthouses with a view of the Seine.

Dr. Farraday was indeed very busy in the lab, it seemed. Totally and utterly dedicated to her cause since she was a teenager.

Not a bad quality for a queen, an important part of him argued. Sadly it was the part of him that wanted her in his bed.

But Dr. Farraday had a quiet beauty, in a way that perhaps a man wouldn't notice right away, especially in those baggy jeans and hoodie, with her hair pulled up in a ponytail. She wasn't even wearing makeup.

As accustomed as Omar was to women constantly trying to get his attention, it was strange indeed to meet a woman who seemed determined to evade it. In fact, if he hadn't seen her in that tight red dress yesterday, he might have easily overlooked her even now.

Surely not. Was he so shallow as that?

When she didn't sit down beside him, Omar rose abruptly to his feet. "Thank you for coming to Paris to meet me, Dr. Farraday."

"No problem." She gave him a crooked smile. "Thanks for the two million for cancer research."

He couldn't look away from her smile, or the way her eyes suddenly sparkled beneath the chandeliers. "You must tell me about your latest scientific breakthroughs."

The smile on her face dropped away. Why? Because he'd reminded her of the important cancer research she was neglecting to be here? She gave an awkward laugh. "I, uh, don't like to talk about it. Most people find the details very dull."

"Try me. I'm not a scientist, but I do keep up on developments in the search for the cure for biphenotypic acute leukemia."

Her voice was a croak. "You do?"

Omar gave a short nod. "Perhaps later, while discussing your research, we could also discuss an additional donation from my country's charitable fund."

There. The perfect bait to make any scientist talk.

And yet she still didn't.

"Uh—maybe later," she managed. She glanced around the salon, then leaned forward to whisper, "Why did you really want me to stay in Paris? For an insider's opinion on your potential brides? Or just for comic relief?"

"Maybe I like your company," he said. "I enjoyed talking to you in the garden."

"You should have told me who you were..." Then she shook her head. "Never mind. It doesn't matter."

"No, you're right," he said softly. "I should have told you. I was just surprised. I'm not accustomed to people not recognizing me."

"That's funny. I'm used to being invisible. To everyone." As their eyes locked, her face looked strangely vulnerable. "Why did you choose me?"

She didn't know how beautiful she was, he realized. How could any woman as beautiful, incredible and important as Dr. Edith Farraday have such a low opinion of her own value?

She hadn't known who Omar was when they'd met in the garden last night. That had seemed strange enough. But it seemed Dr. Farraday didn't know who *she* was, either. Or how truly amazing she was.

Even now, with his vizier and servants and the other would-be brides watching their every move, all Omar could think about was how much he liked her. Perhaps she could be taught diplomacy, and she'd give up her lab and—

He stopped the thought cold. His body was willing to argue anything that would allow him to seduce her.

"I wanted you to stay because I'm curious," he said.

Her expression became guarded. "Curious? About what?"

"About you," he said honestly, even as he told himself he couldn't have her. She was too consumed by her important work. She would make a poor queen, if forced to quit her research, and she'd be desperately unhappy. She was absolutely forbidden to him. He was sending her home tomorrow.

And that, of course, made him want her even more. He ground his teeth.

"Sire." His vizier appeared at his elbow. "It is time for your first date."

"Yes." With an inward sigh, Omar gave Dr. Farraday a brief, respectful bow. "Until later."

She gave a brief smile. "Of course. Good luck."

She was wishing him luck? On his dates with other women?

"You truly are a mystery." The last low word hung between them, intimately, like a promise. He held out his hand.

She hesitated, then took it.

As their palms touched, Omar felt an electric shock against his skin, passing through muscle and blood and bone. When he enfolded her smaller hand in his own, his whole body came alive.

He dropped her hand. And the question echoed through his heart like a curse: Why her? Why did his body react to the one woman he already knew he could not make his queen? The universe had a strange sense of humor.

No, not strange, Omar thought grimly as he watched Dr. Farraday depart the salon. His jaw was tight. *Vengeful.*

Beth waited in her room all afternoon, but the king didn't come. She read books, paced around her elegant room, left frantic messages for her sister in Houston. She ate lunch brought to her room on a silver tray. She changed into one of the new dresses he'd had sent to her, nervously watching the hours tick by.

But he never came.

Good, Beth tried to tell herself. She glanced at the gilded antique clock on the fireplace mantel. Ten o'clock at night. Obviously, his other dates had gone well. Perhaps he'd already chosen one of the other nine as his bride.

She told herself she was relieved. She couldn't continue this farce for much longer. It was horrifying, exhausting, even terrifying, to pretend to be someone she was not.

Beth shuddered, remembering the moment the king had casually mentioned that he "kept up on developments" in biphenotypic acute leukemia!

Her cheeks burned. All they needed was one in-depth scientific conversation and he'd realize that Beth knew nothing at all about it. She'd tried to memorize the scientific jargon, honestly she had. But her brain just blocked it out.

Even in elementary school, Edith had been the genius, not her. So Beth had simply stopped trying. Let her twin sister be the one to excel in academics. She would be good at something else.

The trouble was, at twenty-six, Beth was still trying to figure out what that something else was. She was starting to suspect it might be nothing.

She should be glad that Omar had forgotten about her. Beth would be able to go home in triumph, knowing Edith now had two million for research. And she didn't even need to feel guilty about coming here under false pretenses, as long as the king chose a better bride than Beth. Which was basically any of the other nine women—except Sia Lane.

For some reason she couldn't fathom, she felt protective of the king. It was ridiculous. Handsome, powerful and rich, he was the last person on earth who needed Beth's protection. And yet something about his gentle nature suggested a kind heart, beneath all the arrogance and ferocity. Some dark past, Beth thought. As if he'd been hurt before.

And she already knew he deserved better than that cold-hearted, beautiful, two-faced movie star as his wife.

She paced over the white fluffy rug on the pale gray floor. The bedroom she'd been assigned in his royal residence was even more luxurious than the hotel suite on the avenue Montaigne. Glamorous and sleek, with Art Deco flourishes, the pretty, feminine room was silver and white except for the brilliant splashes of pink and red provided by the flowers in the silver vase on the vanity table.

Beth stopped. If she could only be sure he would choose a wife who would love him, someone obviously worthy, like Laila al-Abayyi! Then she could leave tomorrow with a clear conscience, if not a joyful heart.

Seeing herself in the full-length mirror, she caught her breath. All the time she'd spent getting ready tonight for a so-called date had made her look...different. She wasn't wearing her usual baggy clothes. Nor was she packed like a sausage into a too-tight gown.

The clothes he'd arranged to be sent to her room were— perfect.

Beth didn't have an easy body to fit. She was petite, and unlike her totally skinny, size two sister—Edith often forgot to eat in the lab whereas Beth had never seen a slice of cake she didn't like. Beth's waist was small, but she was cursed with big breasts and big hips. The modern, straight-shaped styles just looked like oversize sacks on her.

But now, staring at the new gown that was fitted to her shape, Beth came closer to the mirror, staring at herself in amazement. The dress was a deep sapphire, in soft silk. She'd brushed out her frizzy light brown waves and made her hair glossy and straight, hanging to the middle of her back. She'd experimented with the boxes of brand-new makeup in the en suite bathroom. She'd put on eyeliner, mascara, lipstick. It was the first time she'd worn makeup in a year, since the night her boyfriend announced he was breaking up with her for a girl who was, in his description, "more interesting."

Wyatt's harsh breakup had been the second time a boy-friend had told Beth she wasn't desirable. Against such evidence, she'd decided that, in addition to not being good at school, she apparently wasn't good at relationships, either. At least not romantic ones. So rather than risk being hurt again, for the last year, she'd just opted out.

Now, Beth looked at herself. Her hazel eyes glittered dangerously, lined in black. Her lips looked glamorous, full and red. Her hips thrust forward, forced by the angle of her designer stiletto heels.

There was a brief hard knock at the door.

"Wait," Beth said, whirling around.

But too late. The door pushed open, and Omar stood in the doorway, dressed in his regal sheikh's robes that made him look almost too sexy to believe he was even real. His black eyes widened as he stared at her, standing in the dress in front of the mirror.

Her cheeks burned with indignation. "You should have waited a minute before you flung open the door like that. You might have walked in to find me naked!"

Her voice faltered as his dark eyes narrowed at her words. He wasn't touching her. He was on the other side of the bedroom. So why did she feel such a blast of heat from his gaze? Why did waves of awareness—hunger—suddenly wash through her like an earthquake?

"You are right," Omar said in a low voice, his gaze slowly tracing over her. "You look...."

For a moment, beneath his hot gaze, Beth couldn't breathe. When he didn't finish the sentence, she managed with a crooked smile, "Weird, right? I look weird?"

His voice was low. "You look beautiful."

With an intake of breath, she met his gaze. "I do?"

He came forward. His black eyes reflected the moonlight from the window as he looked down at her, his tall, powerful body just inches from hers.

"More than beautiful." Reaching out, he cupped her cheek and said huskily, "You look tempting beyond belief."

As she felt his touch against her skin, all rational thought disappeared from her brain. His gaze fell to her lips, and a pulse of electricity went through her body. Her knees went weak.

He turned away. Reaching into the large wardrobe, he selected a new, faux fur coat, and wrapped it around her bare shoulders in an old-fashioned, almost courtly gesture.

"Are we going somewhere?" she breathed, still dizzy at his nearness.

Silently, he nodded.

"I thought you were doing all your interviews—dates—whatever you call them," she stammered, "here at the mansion."

"You're my last date. I'm taking you out." He held out his arm. "Shall we?"

Nervously, she put her hand around his arm. She could feel the warmth of his body through his sleeve. Feel his strength and power. Blood rushed through her veins as her heart pounded. She swallowed, lifting her gaze to his.

"Where are we going?"

Looking her over slowly in a way that made her melt inside, he glanced at her stiletto heels then gave her a low, sensual smile. "You'll see."

CHAPTER THREE

INTERVIEWING POTENTIAL BRIDES had been even less enjoyable than he'd imagined. For Omar, it had been a long day.

For the sake of the bride market, he had cleared his schedule of all diplomatic and governmental meetings today. He'd done it reluctantly, because there was never enough time for affairs of state, whether he was negotiating new trade treaties, building new business alliances or dealing with rival factions amongst his nobles.

Ruling was serious business. Unlike most billionaire bachelors, Omar didn't take holidays. He didn't *do* vacations. For fifteen years, since he'd inherited the throne, he'd been keenly aware of his duty. His people needed everything he could give. He could hardly risk their prosperity or security while he selfishly relaxed on a beach, or slept in, or went out partying at night.

He'd sworn he'd never be like his father, who'd been self-indulgent and weak, allowing Samarqara to fall into poverty and disarray and ignoring his sickly Samarqari-American wife to enjoy one mistress after another, abrogating his royal responsibilities to the powerful oligarchs, especially Hassan al-Abayyi.

But it had taken Ferida's death for Omar to realize he must never be like his grandfather, either. Yes, the man had been strong, mercilessly destroying all his enemies to maintain his grip on power, hold Samarqara together and end the civil war. But the cost of his single-minded ruthlessness had been too great. It had burned everything it touched.

A good ruler had to balance between strength and compassion. A treacherous tightrope to walk. Which was why Omar could never rest. Why he had no honorable choice but to sacrifice his own needs for those of others.

And that included marriage.

But an equal sacrifice would be demanded of his queen. Any potential bride must understand this, and realize that beneath the glitter and glamour of crowns and palaces, the royal family were, at their hearts, just servants, working to improve the lives of the Samarqari people.

The women he'd brought to Paris were all incredibly intelligent and ambitious. He'd been sure they would intuitively understand what would be expected of them.

But with a few possible exceptions—Dr. Edith Farraday, Dr. Bere Akinwande and, regrettably, Laila al-Abayyi— they hadn't. They seemed to think of Omar as a bank offering limitless investment money, or a glamorous, romantic prize to be won, rather than a potential partner in personal sacrifice.

Omar had thought the bride market would make finding a wife and queen efficient, if not easy. Simply put, he was looking for the best—a brilliant, beautiful woman with dignity, strength, integrity. A woman he could be proud to call his own, a queen who would serve the people well, a loving mother for his future children.

That was the theory, anyway.

In practice, he felt like he'd wasted an entire day, making small talk with women he couldn't remotely imagine spending a honeymoon with, let alone a lifetime.

And the one he lusted for, he could not have.

By the end of the evening, Omar had almost felt tempted to put marriage off a few more years. But even that option was lost, because thanks to the paparazzi, the whole world had now heard of his bride market. The international mockery of it was already high. If, on top of everything, it also proved a failure, leaving him still a bachelor at the end of it, both Samarqara and its king would be a laughingstock.

No. Omar had started this path. He had to finish it. In the end, if he, with the advice of his council, made the correct choice, his new queen would be admired and adored by his people. His unorthodox choice of using the bride market would no longer be a cause for mockery, but respect.

Somehow.

But first...

Omar glanced at Dr. Farraday, now sitting beside him in the backseat of the luxury SUV. His driver in the front, sitting beside the bodyguard, had managed to escape the paparazzi with skillful driving and death-defying turns down dark alleyways. Omar and Dr. Farraday—Edith—had already enjoyed a brief private, after-hours tour of the Louvre. He'd seen her beautiful face light up when she'd seen the famous *Mona Lisa*. He'd enjoyed watching her. Very much.

Now, as they drove back through the dark streets of Paris, it was very late. The privacy screen was up in the SUV, and the two of them were alone.

For better. Or for worse.

He glanced down at her, so impossibly desirable in her diaphanous silk sapphire gown that fit perfectly against her hourglass figure, lingering against her wide hips, her tiny waist, her deliciously full breasts. She was petite, feminine, perfect. He caught the scent of vanilla and strawberries in her light brown hair, falling sleekly down her shoulders, over the sensuous faux fur of her jacket.

Their thighs were just inches apart on the soft, supple leather of the car seat. His whole body was aware of her every movement. Her every breath. It was all he could do not to turn to her, push her back against the seat and crush her body with his own, plundering those sweet red lips in a hungry kiss.

Omar's body felt taut just thinking of it. He forced himself to look out at the passing lights of Paris. He knew Dr. Edith Farraday was too tactless and forthright to be his queen, if she even were willing to give up her career to be a full-time diplomat, wife and mother, which he doubted. He would not dishonor her—or himself—by betraying the laws of tradition, and giving in to his desire.

No, he'd done that once before, when he was too young and arrogant to know better, and it had ended one life and changed others forever, including his own. Never, ever again would he try to take what he did not earn.

"Where are we going now? Back to the mansion?"

Her voice trembled. She met his gaze nervously, before her long dark lashes trembled shyly against her rosy cheeks.

He smiled. "You mentioned the Eiffel Tower."

She blinked. "You remembered?"

"How could I not?"

She looked down at her hands folded in her lap as she mumbled, "I'm not used to men paying attention."

His gaze traced the adorable smattering of freckles across her nose. "You spend too much time in the lab."

Her gaze flashed up at his in chagrin.

"Edith—"

"Beth," she whispered.

Omar frowned. "What?"

She lifted her gaze to his. "My friends call me Beth."

"Beth?"

"It's—it's a nickname."

There was something strange in her voice that he didn't understand, especially since her eyes shone at him with honesty. More mystery, he thought, and unwillingly leaned forward in the back seat of the SUV, searching her gaze in the moonlit Paris night. "As you wish. Beth."

She looked relieved, and then a wicked gleam came into

her eyes as she murmured, tilting her head, "And shall I call you Omar?"

He narrowed his eyes at the breach in protocol. As he was king, no one was ever allowed to use his first name, unless and until expressly invited. Had no one told her?

Then he saw her mischievous grin and realized she was teasing. She expected him to refuse. She was counting on it.

Humor. The one thing no other woman had tried today.

"Of course," he replied with equal innocence. "Omar."

He said that to shock her, and he succeeded. He smugly noted her wide eyes and parted lips. "I was kidding!"

"I am not."

"But, Your Highness, I couldn't possibly—"

"You will call me by my first name." He was distracted by the flick of her pink tongue against the corners of her red lips. He wanted to kiss those lips. Hungered for them. "Let me hear you say it again."

"I couldn't," Beth stammered in the silence, broken only by the hum of the SUV's engine and the traffic noise as they drove through Paris. She took a deep breath. "Look, Your Highness—"

"Omar," he corrected fiercely. The command he'd given her as a response to her joke suddenly was an absolute need. He wanted to hear his name on her sensual, delectable lips.

She licked those lips nervously.

"Omar," she whispered.

Her voice electrified his body. He went so hard, he nearly groaned aloud, just from hearing the two syllables of his given name on her mouth, on her lips and teeth and tongue and breath.

What was happening to him?

He'd never felt such attraction before. He clenched his jaw. He had to put a stop to this, regain control.

He should have his driver return to the residence. He should have his servants escort Beth to her room and put her on a plane back to America at once. Because Omar could not let himself feel this way. Not when he knew he could not choose her as his queen.

Or could he?

The thought infiltrated his soul like a whisper of wind through the wavy green grasses over the sand dunes of the southern Caspian shore.

Had he been hasty counting her out? Could Dr. Beth Farraday be his bride?

No, he told himself firmly. Lust was not enough. She would make a terrible queen. She was committed to her lab. Sacrificing her research would be out of the question. She was too outspoken. Too careless of the opinions of others. Too awkward in high society.

Too warm. Too sensual. Too joyful.

Why would a woman like that wish to be trapped in the gilded prison of a royal palace?

"I have a question," Beth said softly. She peeked at him out of the corner of her eye. "You don't have to answer if you think it's rude."

Curiosity pricked him. "Go on."

"Why are you doing this bride market stuff?" She shook her head, looking wistful. "You're good-looking, charming, rich, powerful. I mean, if someone like *you* has a hard time finding a partner, what hope is there for the rest of us?"

"I wasn't having a hard time," he corrected, stung. "I simply wished to honor my country's traditions, and be efficient in my choice of queen."

She snorted. "Efficient? You're spending millions!"

"Money means little to me. Not as much as quickly finding the right woman."

"But—why not just marry a Samarqari girl?"

Beth was probably thinking about Laila. His jaw tightened. "My grandfather did that. But when he elevated one noble Samarqari family over all the others, a quarrel turned into a civil war, which spread as all families were forced to pick sides." He set his jaw. "Half a million people died, including all my grandmother's family and nearly everyone in my own, except for my father, who was eight years old, tucked in a Swiss boarding school."

He watched as the color drained from her face. "I'm sorry. I didn't know the history."

"I'm sure." Omar allowed himself a smile. "It's something I admire about you."

She snorted. "My total ignorance?"

"Your single-minded devotion to your life's work." Looking at her, he said quietly, "My older brother died of biphenotypic acute leukemia when I was a child."

She turned pale. "I'm... I'm so sorry."

"I'm only telling you so you'll understand how much I respect what you're doing." Slowly, he reached out a hand and tucked a long tendril of her hair back from her face. "I admire you, Beth. So much."

He felt her shiver. Her eyes were wide and luminous in the moonlight.

He realized his hand was still tangled in her long hair. It felt soft, so soft. He wanted to move his fingers against her cheek. He wanted to stroke her full, swollen bottom lip with his thumbs. He wanted to kiss her deeply, and reach his hands beneath her fur coat to stroke every luscious curve of her body in the blue dress.

The SUV stopped. They'd arrived at the Eiffel Tower, overlooking the shadows and early spring greenery of the Champ de Mars. A moment later, the back door opened. His uniformed driver waited.

Omar got out of the SUV, then reached back for Beth. Just touching her hand made it difficult not to kiss her. For a moment, after the driver departed, the two of them stood on the dark, deserted sidewalk, their hands remaining entwined beneath the moonlight.

"Why have you never married before now?" she whispered.

The question made pain slice through his throat. He pushed the vicious memories away. "Because I did not wish to."

"That's no answer."

"Isn't it?" He thought of his mistresses in the past. Cool blondes with cold natures, quickly seduced, quickly forgotten.

Nothing like this. Nothing like her. A woman like Beth, so open, so direct, so obviously kind, would be a partner for life.

"You asked me why I did this, Beth," he said in a low voice. "Why did you?"

Her cheeks went pink, and she bit her full, red lower lip. She looked away. "I told you. For the money. And to see Paris."

Yes, she'd said that before. But, for some reason, this time her words bothered him.

What had he expected? That she'd suddenly confess that, busy and weighed down with the responsibility of her obligations, she'd secretly hungered for a real human connection—more than a temporary lover, a permanent partner? That she'd say she'd been disappointed too many times by romance, and had never completely gotten over a devastating tragedy of the past?

That she'd say, for the sake of her country, she'd decided to cast her fate to the winds and settle for whatever the universe offered her?

No. Beth Farraday was a scientist. She didn't believe in fate. Not the way that Omar did. But growing up as he had, as the leader of his nation, he'd seen too many coincidences, split-second turns of fortune that, like a flip of a coin, could have gone either way, not to believe in fate.

Like the fate that had made him king, when his older brother had died too young.

Like the fate that had caused Omar, fifteen years before, to choose a bride who already secretly loved another man, who'd taken her own life rather than be forced to become Omar's queen.

No. That last wasn't fate. It had been Omar's fault alone, for selfishly, blindly, putting his desires above all.

Beth's eyes cut through him. "What is it?"

He'd intended to interrogate her. Instead, he had the sudden discomfiting thought that she saw right through his outward mask to the pain beneath. He dropped her hand. "Come. I've made special arrangements for our visit."

As they walked beneath the base of the Eiffel Tower, she tilted her head back, her eyes dazzled by the lights illuminating the monument as well as the Paris night.

"I've never seen anything more beautiful," she whispered.

Omar looked at her joyful expression, at the way her hazel eyes danced. "I have."

It was such a small thing, bringing her here, and yet she seemed almost intoxicated by happiness. For a smile like that, he thought, he would have taken her to a thousand Eiffel Towers.

Strange that Beth Farraday wasn't impressed by the thought of becoming a queen, a billionaire's wife, the envy of half the world. But she was overjoyed by the thought of seeing a tourist attraction visited by millions of people every year.

"It's just too bad it's closed," she sighed.

"Not for us," he said.

"What do you mean?"

With his bodyguard following at a discreet distance, he led her to the private entrance, where he spoke quietly in French to a waiting guide. It had been arranged as a favor for the King of Samarqara, in the interest of international diplomacy.

Omar turned back to her. "Stairs or elevator?"

"Stairs."

"There's a lot of them," he warned.

"I'm not scared."

He smiled, liking her fearlessness. "This way."

They walked up the stairs to the first platform, and then the second. Even in high heels, she kept up with him. When they came out onto the viewing area, she gasped. She couldn't look away from the beauty of the city at their feet. And he found he couldn't look away from her.

"Thank you," she whispered, looking out at the sparkling lights of the French capital. He saw tears in her eyes. "I'll never forget you made this possible."

"You're giving me too much credit."

"You're wrong. I'll always remember this moment," she said fervently, and he found himself wishing that she was talking about him, not some iconic building made of steel.

Was it irony, or punishment, that he hadn't had that thought about any of the other nine potential brides?

No, not nine. Eight. He'd ignored Laila al-Abayyi's existence after their brief introduction in the salon. She was the only one he'd refused to meet with privately today.

For the other eight, Omar had dutifully knocked on their doors at the residence to escort them to the garden or salon or library for a private hour of discussion. Half had giggled and blushed, as if all their obvious sense had surrendered in face of the primordial Cinderella dream. The other half spoke to him as if they were at a job interview, giving well-planned business presentations about whatever company or cause they were hoping he might invest in, while also giving him subtle signals they might be interested in taking the discussion to bed.

None of them seemed interested at all in the political and

economic situation in Samarqara, and how they personally could influence the country. None bothered to interview Omar as a potential mate or lifetime partner. Did they not realize the seriousness of this choice?

No, he thought dimly. How could they?

But the last woman had truly shocked him, when she'd bluntly offered him a blow job in her bedroom to "seal the deal"—offering it with cold eyes, as if it were a simple transaction: one blow job equaled one royal crown!

Omar shuddered. Sia Lane might be the most famous movie star in the world, but she left him cold. He'd immediately refused, stating the simple truth that the tradition of the bride market did not allow him to even kiss any woman, until he'd chosen her formally as his bride.

Sia had shrugged. "Fine, follow protocol. But I'm the best. You'll choose me."

Perhaps he should, in spite of his distaste. It wouldn't be hard to convince the council to select an internationally famous movie star, who'd create huge publicity for Samarqara. And at least she wasn't Laila, the half sister of the woman whose life he'd unthinkingly destroyed.

When Omar closed his eyes, he could still imagine Ferida walking out into the desert to die.

"What are you thinking right now?"

Beth was looking at him. *Through* him. As if she saw everything, all the faults and weaknesses, which, as king, he fought so hard to hide and repress.

Of all the many reasons he couldn't choose to marry her, this was the strongest of all.

"That the night is growing cold." An icy wind blew against them on the platform, and he turned, holding out his arm. "Come. Dessert has been arranged."

As they were seated in the glamorous restaurant inside the Eiffel Tower, they were given the very best table. They were the only customers, as the restaurant had officially closed hours ago. Beth's face lit up like a child's when she saw the view, and they were served a variety of French pastries and cheeses on a silver tray.

"*Bonsoir*, mademoiselle. Monsieur." The French waiter smiled at Beth, then bowed his head respectfully to Omar in turn. "Would you like to begin with coffee or champagne?"

"Are you kidding?" she blurted out. "I drink coffee all the time. I'll have champagne!"

As they sipped a very expensive vintage, the servers discreetly disappeared. Beth looked out at the amazing view of Paris, and he looked at her in the soft glow of the flickering candle on their table. The gold-red light moved over her cheek, over the curve of her throat and sensitive corner of her bare neck. Over her collarbone, and lower, to the enticing shadows of her breasts.

"So what do you—" As she turned back to look at him, her voice abruptly cut off. He relished the pink blush that rose on her creamy cheeks. She licked her lips, and he nearly groaned. She swallowed, then said, "So…what do you think so far?"

That I want you in my bed, now, Omar thought. "About what?"

She tilted her head quizzically. "About your choice of bride. How's it going?"

It was going badly, since the woman he wanted was the one he could not have. Though his body was working overtime to convince his brain otherwise. "I must take my time to choose the final five, who will return to Samarqara to meet my council. They will choose the one they feel best suited to be Queen."

She looked horrified. "You don't make that choice yourself?"

"Yes…and no." He looked at her. "I nominally have the final say, of course. But only a fool would discard their advice. Because by the laws of Samarqara, once a child is conceived in a royal marriage, divorce is forbidden."

"No divorce—ever?" Her eyebrows lifted in consternation. "That seems really harsh. Not to mention impractical. What if you—" she hesitated "—fall out of love?"

"Since we will never have been *in* love, that is not a concern." He took a drink of champagne. "The law is for the good of the nation. Half siblings fighting for the throne caused endless wars in the last century."

"Do you have a lot of wars?"

"Not since I became king."

Her eyes went wide. She looked at him with new respect. "Wow."

His forehead furrowed. "Wow?"

"I just realized how much pressure it must be, being king. All the responsibility. Preventing wars. It's not just castles and crowns."

"No. It's deadly serious."

"Where is Samarqara, exactly?"

"It's on the southern edge of the Caspian Sea." His lips curved upwards. "On the old Silk Road, a small kingdom rich with oil and spices, famous for its ancient learning and the warmth of its people."

"Your economy is built on oil?"

"Oil and trade. Our finance industry has also grown in the last fifteen years. But we aren't a tourist destination. Not yet. Not like our beaches and fine weather deserve." He paused. "Though my tourist board estimates that if I marry Sia Lane, worldwide tourism to Samarqara would increase by five hundred percent."

Omar expected her to mock such a practical consideration, to express her horror and disgust at the thought of him marrying the movie star, horror he privately shared. But Beth just looked thoughtful as she nibbled on a sweet *baba au rhum*.

"That's a lot of new tourists."

"Yes."

She sighed. "And I can see how the happiness of your people must matter more than your own." Shaking her head, she said sadly, "In some ways, as king, you're the least free person in your entire kingdom."

Omar stared at her in the shadowy restaurant. No one had ever said such a thing to him before. Of its own accord, his hand reached for hers across the table, even as he said quietly, "It is my birthright."

"I guess, but… Who can you even talk to, when you have problems?" Beth looked down at her small hand wrapped in his. "How do you even have friends? You're the king. By definition, you have no equal." She lifted her head. Her luminous eyes went through him as she whispered, "You must feel totally alone."

A shudder went through his soul.

All the other women today had approached him strategically, like generals with a war to win, as if Omar were someone they had to conquer to achieve their deepest dreams.

But Beth wasn't trying to conquer or convince. She wasn't even weighing the consequence of her words. She had no fear. She wasn't talking to him as someone addressing a king, or even like they were on a first date. She was talking to him like he was just a person.

Like an equal.

She wasn't worried about speaking that way to a king, because she wasn't trying to get him to invest in her research—in fact, she'd totally ignored his attempts to even discuss it. And she'd already voted herself out of the running to be his bride.

Why? he thought suddenly. Because she knew he wouldn't choose her?

Or because she wouldn't choose *him*?

"Sia Lane would make a beautiful queen," she continued sadly. "She's so famous. You're right. Everyone would want to visit Samarqara." She licked her red lips, and his eyes devoured the small flick of her wet pink tongue against the corners of her mouth. "But…"

He met her eyes. "But?"

Beth looked at him. "Shouldn't your choice of bride be based on more than the recommendations of your tourist board? Your council will see that, won't they?" Her gaze fell to his mouth as she whispered, "Even though you're king, you're also a man."

Yes. A flesh-and-blood man.

Looking at Beth across the table of the elegant, empty restaurant, with the flickering shadows of a candle between them and all the sparkling lights of Paris beyond, Omar knew a hunger he'd never known before. He wanted her. Almost more than he could bear.

Gripping the edge of the table, he fought his desire with all his force of will. He wanted to sweep the silver champagne bucket away, throw the dessert plates aside in an explosion of crumbs and push Beth back against the table. All he could think about was how it would feel to have her lips hot and hard against his, her body soft and yielding, to hear her gasp with answering pleasure and desire as he pulled up her gown and took her, pumping into her hard and fast until they both exploded. His body demanded he stake his claim, possess her, with all of the lights of Paris at their feet.

But Omar was king. He could not. It wasn't just honor at stake, but common decency. Soon, within days, he would be an engaged man. He could not seduce a woman he did not intend to wed. It would dishonor them both.

He took a deep breath, then another, not allowing himself to move an inch, except for the involuntary tightening of his jaw as he looked down at her across the table.

Beth's expression changed. Her full, red lips parted. From the corner of his eye he could see the sway of her full breasts, as she took a deep breath and started to lean forward—

Turning, he rose abruptly to his feet.

"The night is late." His voice was low and harsh. "Allow me to escort you back to the mansion, Dr. Farraday."

"Yes," she said, rising unsteadily in her turn. "Of course. I've been greedy with your time."

This time, Omar did not hold out his arm for her. He could not. He was afraid that if he touched her, he might lose his razor-thin hold on his control.

As they descended in the elevator of the Eiffel Tower, they were both silent. She looked at him only once.

"Thank you, Your Highness," she whispered, her eyes full of emotion. "I'll never forget this night."

As the elevator opened, Omar knew neither would he.

Damn it to hell.

Beth's nerves were tight as the chauffeur drove them back from the Eiffel Tower to the royal residence. She was overwhelmed with guilt. She had to tell Omar the truth about her identity. She had to!

No, you don't, she could almost hear her sister arguing. The only reason the king would need to know the truth, Edith had texted her firmly, would be if he were seriously considering her as his bride. *Which is impossible, obviously*, her sister had added.

Beth agreed, even if she thought it somewhat unkind of Edith to point it out. But it was true. Beth was surrounded by nine women who were all better queen material than her. Well, eight, at least.

She was going home tomorrow. There was no way he'd choose her in the top five, not when he was so serious about finding a woman with the skills to reign a nation. Not her, obviously. So why would Beth blurt out the truth now, and tell Omar that she wasn't a world-famous cancer researcher but just a nobody? Even worse, revealing the fact that she'd been lying to his face all this time?

If she told him now, it might briefly make her conscience feel better. But then she'd lose all the good that the two million dollars might do—curing childhood cancer!—when he demanded it back after she confessed her lie.

It was dangerous enough that she'd asked him to call her Beth. Even now, as she thought of how it had felt to hear her own real name on his sensual lips…

She shivered in the back of the SUV. Glancing at Omar out of the corner of her eye, she thought of how gorgeous he was, how devastatingly charming, how rich and powerful. It would be different if she thought he might be actually considering her as his bride. But it was obvious to everyone, Beth most definitely included, that she didn't fit into Omar's elite, sophisticated world.

No. If there was any attraction, it was on her side alone.

So she said nothing as they arrived at the mansion. Silently, he walked her through the residence, his sheikh's robes skimming the marble floor, as he escorted her to her bedroom.

"This is me," she said awkwardly when they reached her door.

"Yes." His voice was low. Electricity crackled between them as their eyes locked. His eyes held such fire that for one moment, she had the wild thought he intended to kiss her.

No. She had to be mistaken. Anyway, he'd be kissing Edith. Not her.

But it had all started to feel so jumbled. He was calling her Beth now, not Edith. His lips would be caressing hers, not Edith's.

He thought of her an amusement, nothing more, she told

herself desperately. Men saw Beth as a pal, someone to confide in about the gorgeous women they actually desired. And hadn't Omar asked her to give him romantic advice about the other potential brides?

But as he took her hand, a strange zing went through her. Her hand tightened involuntarily as she felt the strength and power of his larger fingers pressed between her own. With an intake of breath, she looked up at the dark embers of his eyes. Then her gaze fell to his hard-edged jaw, laced with five o'clock shadow, and his sensual mouth.

He leaned forward, and she breathed in his scent, of sandalwood and spice.

"Beth," he said huskily, "I have a question I must ask. Even though I already know the answer."

Had he figured out she'd lied about being Edith? Was her decision to continue lying all for naught? Her voice squeaked, "Yes?"

Omar's gaze burned through her. Her heart lifted to her throat. Then he said, "Would you ever consider giving up your career?"

Was he—could it even be remotely possible that he—?

"Yes," she blurted out without thinking. "For love."

"Love?" His expression changed. "Is that important to you?"

"What's more important than that?" she whispered, looking at him, thinking how easy, how completely easy it would be, for her to let herself fall.

"Love." His lips twisted. "I'm astonished. You'd give up your research? Your lab? Your life's work? For something as unpredictable as emotion?"

"Love is more than that—" Beth started to protest, then all the air was sucked out of her lungs as she realized she'd answered as herself, not Edith. There was no question that *Beth* would be happy to give up her minimum-wage job working in a shop, for a man she really loved, to raise their children and create a real home. What could be more meaningful than that? She cared about *people*, not work. Her job was just a job. Not a joy.

But Edith wouldn't answer that way. She'd never give up her work. Not for love. Not for anything.

"I'm sorry, I... I misunderstood," she forced herself to say. "I could never give up my work in the lab. Not for any reason. My work is my life."

He gave a single, short nod. As he dropped her hand, his shoulders looked tight. "As I thought."

There was a noise down the hall. Sia Lane, dressed in tight exercise clothes and carrying a water bottle, was coming down the hall, apparently returning to her room after a workout in the residence's private gym.

"Miss Lane," Omar greeted her politely. "Exercising? At two in the morning?"

"I believe in physical activity. At any time," the movie star purred. She glanced down at Beth in her faux fur coat and blue silk gown with a smudge of chocolate at the neckline, and sniffed, "But then, I have discipline."

Her cold blue eyes made it clear that she thought Beth was sorely lacking in that respect. After she passed by, continuing down the hall toward her room, Omar turned back to Beth.

"Well." Silence fell between them, and he said in a low voice, "It was a pleasure to see Paris with you."

Beth's heart fell. This was the end, she knew. She told herself it was for the best. Even if she really had been Edith, it wouldn't have worked out. Edith would never have chosen marriage, not even to a king, over her job. Not in a million years.

Tomorrow, Beth would return to Houston. She'd never see Omar again, except perhaps in news stories. She'd read about his wedding to one of the other women she'd met here tonight.

She took a deep breath, fighting back tears.

Squaring her shoulders, she forced herself to smile and stuck out her hand. "You're right. I guess this is goodbye."

He took her hand. His dark eyes were unreadable. "Goodbye?"

"Good luck with your choice tomorrow." She tried to ignore the sensation of her hand in his. She lifted her chin. "It was great meeting you. I know you'll help your council make a great choice, whether it's Laila or Bere or one of the others. Whomever you choose, I hope you'll be happy together. I hope you fall in love with her."

His lips curved arrogantly. "I told you—"

"Yes, I know. You think love should be no part of it. Just do me a favor." She lifted her gaze. "When you choose your wife, choose from your heart. Not the advice of your tourist board."

Omar looked at her, then his hand suddenly tightened on hers. "Come with me."

"With you?"

"To Samarqara. I want you there. As one of the five."

Beth nearly staggered back from shock. "You—you do?"

"Yes."

"But I'm all wrong to be your queen!"

His dark eyes were grim. "I know."

"Then why?"

He lifted her hand to his lips. "I need you."

He needed her?

Beth's whole body, her whole being, trembled from the inside out as she felt the warmth of his breath against her skin, the brief hot caress of his lips against her hand.

That was all it took—a kiss on the hand. An old-fashioned, chaste gesture. And she felt the world shake as emotion and desire whirled around her like a tornado, leaving her stunned.

"Say you'll come," he commanded.

"Yes," she whispered.

He straightened, releasing her. For a moment, she swayed, looking up at him, still lost in the storm.

"You're an extraordinary woman, Dr. Farraday," he said huskily, cupping her cheek. Then he turned and left.

Beth watched as he disappeared down the hall. A dazed smile lifted her lips.

Then her smile dropped. If he was actually considering the possibility of making Beth his wife…

Oh, no.

Her heart twisted. It meant she had no choice now but to tell him the truth. And Edith would just have to give back the money. So be it. Beth couldn't lie to him anymore. She couldn't risk hurting him—

"So he didn't even kiss you." The voice was a sneer. Turning, she saw Sia Lane standing behind her in the hallway, still in her exercise clothes, her beautiful face incredulous.

Beth wished she would go away. "He kissed my hand…"

"Your hand?" The movie star snorted. "He's a sheikh. A billionaire king. If he's only kissing your hand, it's pretty clear what he thinks of you, isn't it?" She looked over Beth contemptuously. "And who can blame him?"

Pain filled her heart. "Why would you say…"

"I heard you're the only girl he took out to see Paris. Big deal." Coming closer, Sia whispered with vicious satisfaction, "We spent our date in my bedroom. In my bed."

Beth felt sucker punched. "I don't believe you."

She shrugged. "Believe me or not. Men always want me. You and I both know who was born to rule. And who was not." Looking Beth up and down scornfully, the movie star turned on her expensive running shoes, tilting her skinny hip. Gripping her small towel and water bottle like weapons, she said pleasantly, "See you in Samarqara."

Numbly, Beth went back to her own bedroom, closing the door behind her.

Just a moment before, she'd been half in love with him, just because he'd kissed her hand. Because he'd looked into her eyes. Because he'd made Beth feel, for one night, like she was truly extraordinary.

But she wasn't.

She heard the echo of Wyatt's voice. *I'm sorry, Beth. You're just too...ordinary.*

She heard Alfie's, when after six months of oddly chaste "dating" she'd disastrously tried to kiss him the night of senior prom, and he'd flinched away. *I'm sorry, Beth,* he'd told her mournfully. *The truth is, I've never been remotely attracted to you.*

And now this. No wonder Omar had been so late to knock on Beth's door that night—he'd been busy seducing Sia Lane. Beth sucked in her breath. All the time, while she'd been putting on lipstick, brushing her hair, imagining she might be pretty, he'd been kissing the beautiful movie star. And doing more than kiss her.

He's a sheikh. A billionaire king. If he's only kissing your hand, it's pretty clear what he thinks of you, isn't it?

Feeling sick, Beth covered her face with her hands. Of course he'd choose Sia Lane over Beth. What man wouldn't? No matter how mean and rude the woman might be, she was too beautiful and glamorous to be ignored. So Omar had slept with her. Then he'd tried to blame his preference for Sia on the tourist board.

For the love of heaven, the *tourist board*!

A choked sob came from the back of Beth's throat. How could she ever have imagined, even for a moment, that the two of them had forged a connection? That Omar might actually be considering her to be his wife?

She'd been right all along. Omar had never seen her as

a desirable woman, or potential bride. He'd seen her as a pal, just like the rest.

It was for the best, she tried to tell herself for the umpteenth time. But her throat ached with pain. Wiping her eyes, she reminded herself about the extra million they'd get for cancer research after she went to Samarqara. And seeing that Beth was only an amusement for the sheikh, not a real contender, she had no reason to feel guilty.

But that no longer made her feel better. Not this time. Not when she'd just been sucker punched by this final proof of what her heart had always known.

There was nothing special about her. Nothing at all. And there never would be.

Leaning back against the door, Beth cried.

CHAPTER FOUR

BETH DIDN'T SEE Omar at all on the flight to Samarqara the next morning. He'd already left Paris earlier, on one of his other private jets.

"The king must travel separately from us. It's required," Laila al-Abayyi, who'd also been selected as one of the five women for the bride market, told her with a smile.

"Traveling separately? Why?" Beth asked, sitting beside her in the jet's lavish cabin.

"Tradition. But it could be worse." Laila grinned. "In the old days, the king's potential brides had to arrive either by camel across the desert, or by rickety ship across the Caspian Sea!"

Beth returned a weak smile. But her heart felt sad. Even the thought of seeing exotic Samarqara didn't lighten her spirits. All she could think about was how happy she'd been last night, when Omar had kissed her hand and made her shiver, as his dark eyes pierced her soul. *I need you.*

Yeah. He needed her for advice. As a friend. Looking woodenly out the window, Beth took a deep breath. Then she thought again of how hard it must be to be king, how lonely.

Omar al-Maktoun did need a friend, she decided. Setting her hurt aside, she set her jaw. So a friend was what he'd get.

Beth would do everything she could to make sure he ended up with a bride who could actually make him happy.

She heard Sia Lane talking loudly on the other side of the plane about her latest worldwide blockbuster. The two women she was talking to, Taraji, a Silicon Valley executive, and Anna, an internationally known attorney, looked bored.

Beth wished Bere Akinwande, the Nobel Prize–winner, could have been here. But at breakfast that morning, all ten women had been presented with a contract they had to sign in order to be chosen to travel to Samarqara.

The vizier told them tersely. "He requires you each sign, before I can announce the final five."

"And if we don't sign?" Bere had asked.

"Then you won't have even the chance to be chosen," the vizier had said with a smile.

Feeling wretched and a little hung over, Beth had looked at the contract. The language was simple, asking each woman to assert that she had no impediment to marriage, and that she was interested in Omar as a potential husband—knowing that the wedding that would take place within a month, would require the bride to live permanently in Samarqara, and that if pregnancy occurred, would be indissoluble.

There were murmurs of dismay from around the table. "Of course he's gorgeous and I'd love to date him," Bere said, alarmed, "but...marry him in a month?"

"And immediately have children?" Another woman sounded horrified. "I don't care how sexy the man is, I barely know him!"

"And there'd be no escape hatch of a divorce if it doesn't work out!"

The vizier's smile widened. "If you cannot agree, then please do not sign."

Strange, Beth thought. Rather than trying to convince the women to sign, the man seemed almost pleased that so many were backing out.

But others at the table were more eager. Laila al-Abayyi signed it at once, barely bothering to read the words. The lawyer from Sydney was next, followed swiftly by Sia Lane and the Silicon Valley executive. For all their obvious success, they seemed eager to toss aside the daily grind of difficult careers for the fantasy of running away to an exotic land to live in a palace as the bride of a devastatingly handsome sheikh king.

"What about you?" someone asked Beth.

"Only four signed," someone else pointed out.

"Four is enough." The vizier scowled as he turned to Beth. "Dr. Farraday, there's no need for you to—"

Not waiting, Beth took a pen and signed *E. Farraday* with trembling fingers. Her sister's name, but hers, too—*E* for Elizabeth. She had no concern about a quick marriage or pregnancy or the lack of possibility of divorce. Because Omar wouldn't choose her.

She could still remember how she'd felt when Omar had kissed her hand. *I need you*, he'd said. *Say you'll come.* And she'd answered, *Yes.*

For the sake of that promise, she could endure twenty-four hours more. Then she'd go home to Houston with three million dollars for her brainy sister to save the world, and return to being invisible at the thrift shop—forever.

It was all Beth wanted now. All she could hope for. To return to her ordinary life, to her ordinary self, and to never, ever give any man the opportunity to hurt her like that again.

But first, she had to prevent Omar from choosing Sia as his bride. Even if he didn't realize how miserable she'd make him, Beth did. So she'd act like the friend he needed. She'd save him from himself.

Now, sitting on the plane, Beth looked at Sia still talking loudly on the other side of the cabin. She still couldn't believe Omar had slept with Sia. Every time she thought about it, she felt sick.

But she still didn't get it. "Why would Sia Lane sign that

contract?" Beth said slowly. "She's a movie star with the whole world at her feet."

"Because Omar's gorgeous, and a king," Laila replied. She called him by his first name, Beth realized. Her heart twisted in spite of her best efforts. "Besides—" the girl tossed her head "—her last three movies were flops. And she's thirty-six years old. Being a movie star doesn't last forever."

"What about you?" Beth said. "Why do you want to marry him?"

Laila's expression changed. She gripped her hands together so tight that the knuckles were white. "It's my birthright."

Her words echoed Omar's. Beth wondered if the girl was already half in love with Omar, too. They seemed perfect for each other, she thought sadly.

Pushing the pain in her heart away, Beth said brightly, "You should be queen. I'm going to say that when I dance with the king tonight."

Laila looked at her with almost tearful gratitude. "Thank you."

Lulled by the low hum of the plane, or perhaps the unshed tears stinging the backs of her eyes, Beth curled up in her white leather chair and fell asleep. She woke to find Laila gently shaking her.

"Samarqara." She pointed. "That's the capital city, Khazvin."

Looking out the porthole window, Beth was awed by the exotic beauty of the city in the warm golden afternoon light. She saw minarets and domed buildings in sapphire blue, next to squat clay houses, beside new glass-and-steel skyscrapers overlooking the sparkling Caspian Sea.

But after the jet landed it wasn't the view that hit her first. It was the warmth.

Unlike Paris, which was still held by the last gasp of

winter, here in Samarqara there were flowers in bloom, and the sun shone golden in the bright blue sky. Palm trees waved lazily in the softly stirring breeze, redolent of sea and spice, as the five potential brides were taken by waiting limousines through the city to the vizier's gilded palace.

"Welcome to Samarqara," the vizier greeted them, spreading his arms wide. "You will be staying at my palace until the bride market tomorrow. Tonight, there will be a ball, so the nobles of the high council can meet you and decide who amongst you is most worthy."

The women looked at each other nervously.

"What about the king?" the Silicon Valley executive demanded boldly. The vizier gave her a thin smile.

"He will dance with each of you just once at the ball tonight. Then, after the parade of brides through the market tomorrow, he will take the advice of his council and formally announce his decision from the steps of the royal palace."

"So we're just traveling through a market? That's how the bride market got its name?" Beth said in relief. "I was afraid we'd be offered for sale, like candy bars with price tags!"

The vizier looked down his nose. "It's ceremonial, Dr. Farraday. You'll be brought from my palace on palanquins and carried in a parade through the souk—that's the old market square—before being presented formally to the king at the royal palace." He turned to the others. "Welcome to my home. You may choose how to spend the afternoon. Rest and prepare for the ball tonight, or if you prefer, tour the city."

"Rest," four women said in unison.

"Tour," said Beth.

An hour later, Beth was met by a smiling Samarqari tour guide. She spent the afternoon listening to the girl's every word, wanting to learn as much as possible about this fascinating country. She drove through the city streets of Khazvin, sampled Samarqari dishes, listened to the traditional music. She was shocked to learn details about the horrible civil war of two generations before that had wiped out a third of the population.

"And even after the war ended, our country struggled in poverty…" Then the tour guide brightened. "But since King Omar came to the throne, Samarqara has been blessed. Now we await his choice of queen and the birth of an heir, and our happiness will be secure."

Her eyes glowed. Beth blushed beneath her gaze. She clearly thought Beth might have a shot at the title.

After just a few hours looking at the sights, they returned to the palace too soon for Beth's liking. As the driver, accompanied by a bodyguard and the tour guide, drove them back through the city in the SUV, Beth noticed people stopping to stare at them from the sidewalk, peering toward the darkened glass windows.

"Why are they doing that?" Beth whispered.

"They want to see you," the tour guide replied, smiling. "They're curious about the woman who will someday rule them."

"It won't be me, I'm afraid," Beth said wistfully. She looked out at the beautiful city.

"You're too modest, Dr. Farraday. You are the best choice."

Beth turned to her with a frown. "Why do you say that?"

"Because you are the only one who cared enough to see my country," the girl said simply. "And so I shall tell all my friends. Though alas—" she sighed "—they are not on the high council."

After they arrived back at the vizier's palace, Beth lingered in the foyer.

"Please. Just let me try the words one more time."

The tour guide nervously glanced to the right and left

of the grand foyer of the palace. "Are you not in a rush to get ready for the ball?"

Beth snorted. She didn't need to impress the council. She was just Omar's buddy. His pal. She could have worn sweatpants, if that wouldn't have been an insult to both the king and his nobles. But she wanted to have good manners, as her grandma had taught her, and that meant learning the words. *"Please."*

The tour guide sighed and said doubtfully, "As you wish."

The tour guide had earlier tried to teach her a few words of the Samarqari dialect. But learning languages had never been Beth's forte. She'd managed yes—*nem*—and no—*laa*. But the phrase she really wanted to learn, the traditional greeting to respected strangers, *Peace and joy be upon your house*, had made the tour guide look alarmed every time Beth tried to say it.

Now, as Beth attempted the phrase yet again, the young woman gasped. "Honored doctor," she begged, "you must never say that phrase, ever again."

But after the guide left, Beth continued to stubbornly practice the phrase in her mind. *Peace and joy be upon your house.* How bad could her pronunciation really be?

A maid escorted her to her assigned bedroom in the vizier's palace—another truly lavish suite, with a view of slender palm trees and the blue sky over blue water. Beth was ready before she needed to be. She looked at herself in the mirror. Another night, another fancy dress. This one was the fanciest of all, an emerald ball gown, the softest whisper of silk against her skin. She brushed out her light brown hair until it gleamed and put on makeup. She looked at herself in the mirror. Her eyes were sad.

Tonight was the last night. She had to make it count.

Beth was the last to be called downstairs. She saw the other brides whispering to each other in the hall outside the ballroom. Then, one by one, the women were formally presented to the Samarqari aristocracy—including the high council.

While Beth, the Sydney attorney and the Silicon Valley executive were met with courteous, disinterested applause, half of the nobles seemed to go crazy with cheers for Laila, and the other half rooted for Sia Lane, "the most famed beauty in the world!"

Beth wondered ironically how long the nobles would clap for her after they actually got a chance to talk to her. She pushed the thought away. She was determined to have good manners, no matter what.

When Beth was introduced to the five elderly men of the high council, and their wives, she swallowed hard, lifted her chin, and spoke the traditional Samarqari greeting, the one she knew would really impress them.

"Peace and joy be upon your house," she proclaimed proudly in Samarqari.

The eyes of the old men went huge with shock. There was a tinkling crash as one of their wives dropped a champagne glass.

"Beth."

She jumped when she heard Omar's husky voice behind her. With an intake of breath, she turned. And swallowed hard.

In Paris, he'd been sexy, strong, irresistible. But in Samarqara...

Here, Omar was king. His absolute power was like a light shining from the white fabric of his robes. Everywhere he walked, his people looked at him with awe, servants and nobles alike, as if he wasn't just their king, but their greatest hope and joy.

Looking up at him now, Beth's heart squeezed so tight in her chest she almost couldn't breathe. For a moment, in spite of all her vows to think only of finding him a good wife, all she could feel was the fervent, desperate regret that she couldn't be the woman in his arms. Instead, he'd slept with Sia. The last woman on earth who deserved him.

He looked past her, toward the shocked members of the council, then took her arm. "Dance with me."

"Now?" she stammered.

"Right now."

"But—but I was introduced last. The vizier said I'm supposed to dance with you last."

"It's my decision to make," he said grimly, and there was no arguing with that.

Nervously, Beth allowed him to lead her onto the dance floor. Music started, with a haunting melody played by exotic musical instruments. They danced together slowly, barely touching, beneath the weight of all the people watching them.

This was the last time she'd ever be in his arms.

Good, she told herself, trying not to cry. She never wanted to see him again, anyway. Her heart was in her throat as she looked up at his darkly handsome face.

"What are you doing?" he bit out.

"What do you mean?" she whispered, when what she really wanted to ask was, *How could you sleep with her?* or *How could you have ever made me think I might have a chance with you?*

Omar stared at her incredulously. "You gave the high council the traditional Samarqari greeting."

Beth brightened. "Yes. I learned it today—"

"Only you said it wrong, and insulted them with a suggestion about their mothers and a donkey."

Her cheeks colored. No wonder the tour guide had begged her not to say it. "Oh."

Omar shook his head in irritation. "So answer my question. What are you trying to do? Are you trying to *not* be chosen?"

"As if I could be!"

"What is that supposed to mean?"

"We both know I'm just here for moral support. As your buddy. Your pal!"

He looked at her incredulously. "My...pal?"

She nodded, blinking back tears. "It's fine, I totally understand. Even if I'd said the words right, the council wouldn't have wanted me. I'm a failure at everything. I only came here to keep you from making a horrible mistake!" Her skin felt clammy, her heart pounding in her chest as she pleaded, "Don't marry Sia just because you slept with her!"

"What?" Omar stopped on the dance floor. "What are you talking about?"

"You don't have to hide it," she said miserably. "Sia told me all about it. How you slept together right before our date."

His voice was low. "Sia said I slept with her?"

"I'm not jealous." Beth's throat ached at the lie as she whispered, looking up at his darkly handsome face. "I mean, it's not like...not like I thought...you and I could ever be..."

With everyone watching, he pulled her back into his arms and started dancing again. He said in a low voice, "I never touched her."

"She said you—"

He glanced down at her, his expression harsh. "Under the traditions of the bride market, I cannot touch any of you. Not until I announce my choice." Setting his jaw, he muttered, "Though I was tempted."

"Tempted by Sia."

His dark eyes flashed. "Tempted by you."

Intense emotion flooded through Beth. "You—you were?" Then she narrowed her eyes. No. She wasn't going to fall for it again. "You mean as a friend."

He snorted. "*Friend.* I nearly kissed you last night. It

took all my willpower to…" Setting his jaw, he looked down at her. "If Sia lied to you, it's because she feels threatened."

He hadn't slept with Sia? Because he wanted *Beth*? No. It couldn't be true. Could it?

Her pulse was as rapid as a butterfly's wings. "Threatened—by me?"

"She sees what everyone else can see. Except you." He looked down at her. "Why can you not see how beautiful you are?"

She swallowed hard. "I'm… I'm not…"

"You are," he said harshly. His jaw tightened. "But I cannot choose you as my queen."

"No," she whispered. Obviously he couldn't choose the one who'd just insulted all his high council's mothers. The one who'd lied to his face from the moment they'd met. The one who screwed up everything.

But the realization that Omar hadn't slept with Sia—and he'd actually been considering choosing Beth as his bride—was the bitterest moment she'd ever known.

Her heart cried out in grief and regret. If only things could have been different…

But no. The relationship had been doomed from the start.

Blinking fast, Beth said, "So you aren't planning to choose Sia?"

He shuddered. "No."

"Then who?"

"Only three are left." His lips flattened. "The choices are not as—robust as I hoped. My vizier was supposed to have every woman sign the contract before you even came to Paris."

"But we only signed it today. I mean, some of us did."

"I heard." His voice was grim. His dark eyes seared hers. "So what should I do, Beth?"

This was the moment. But Beth found it surprisingly

difficult. It took several seconds before she could force two words from her mouth.

"Marry Laila," she whispered before her throat closed. "She should be queen."

"No."

She looked up at him with stricken eyes. "But she's beautiful and kind and—"

"You have pushed her from the beginning."

"For your sake," Beth whispered. He didn't realize what it was costing her. She took a deep breath. "Because your wife won't just be your queen. She'll be your partner. Your lover. For the rest of your life." She lifted her pleading gaze. "Laila is the best choice—"

"Is that really what you want?" he demanded.

"Yes," she said miserably.

The music ended, and he abruptly dropped his hands. "Then I will go ask Laila to dance." He gave her a short dismissive nod. "Farewell."

"Goodbye," she replied in Samarqari. Omar looked startled, and she sucked in her breath. "Did I say that wrong, too?"

"No." Omar's hot dark gaze crushed her heart. "You said it perfectly."

And he left her.

Omar's heart was full of anger. At his vizier. At Beth. At himself.

He wanted Beth. And every fiber of his being told him that she wanted him. Why else would she have signed the contract that morning?

Yes, her language skills were abysmal and her attempt at diplomacy a disaster. His council already disliked her. But he could have dealt with all that.

The problem was her career. Her research was her life.

She'd never give it up. She'd said it outright. And Samarqara needed a queen, not an invisible scientist in a lab.

But no other woman was Beth's equal. Certainly none who had made the final five.

How could his vizier have made such a ghastly mistake?

It had been one of Omar's only requirements, that every potential bride sign a contract in black and white, stating that she understood the seriousness of the bride market and chose to participate with a free heart. After what had happened in the past, Omar would never again try to take a bride whose heart was not free.

But when Omar had arrived in Samarqara that afternoon, his vizier had informed him of his mistake. Omar had been outraged.

"The contracts were supposed to come first!"

Khalid had bowed deeply. "I am so deeply sorry, sire. And ashamed by my error." He paused. "So do you wish to cancel the bride market?"

"Cancel?" he'd sputtered.

His vizier had met his eyes coolly. "Or you could choose Laila al-Abayyi. She signed. She's ready."

Laila, always Laila. Even Beth had pushed the Samarqari girl on him, when Omar had desperately hoped instead to hear her say she'd consider giving up her career to be his queen. One hint of that, and he would have forced his council to give her another chance.

Instead, he had two unacceptable choices: marry Laila, or let the bride market end in failure and see his culture turned into a laughingstock.

Omar had stared down at Beth on the dance floor. She'd felt so warm and soft in his arms. Her beautiful face was rosy from the heat, her hazel eyes luminous with emotion. And she'd just told him to marry another woman.

Anger had ripped through him.

Setting his jaw, Omar had turned on his heel and stalked

away. He walked past Sia Lane, who was bragging loudly about her films' total cumulative gross to several cornered-looking council members. He glanced briefly at Anna, the Sydney attorney, and Taraji, the Silicon Valley executive, both of whom were watching him with big eyes. But he was sure, any moment now, they'd both wake up from their Cinderella fantasy and wonder what the hell they were even doing here.

That left only one.

Fine, he thought tightly. So be it.

Omar crossed vengefully through the crowded ballroom of the vizier's palace.

Stopping in front of Laila, who was perfectly dressed as she stood talking, with impeccable manners, to the council members, including her powerful father, Omar bowed with a flourish. The Samarqari girl's beautiful face lit up.

"Dance with me," he bit out.

"I'd be honored, Your Highness," Laila whispered, her dark lashes trembling against her cheeks.

Holding out his arm, he escorted her to the dance floor. There was an audible sigh of satisfaction across the ballroom as his nobles watched them. No one was chanting Sia Lane's name anymore.

His vizier's words suddenly floated back to him. *What if all the kingdom united, and begged you to marry Laila al-Abayyi? Then you would do it?*

Omar had never imagined it could happen. But now, seeing all his nobles watching with shining eyes as he danced with Laila, he realized the impossible had just happened. His nobles had united against having a stranger as queen—rejecting any woman who mangled their language like Beth, or who stretched the bonds of civility like Sia Lane.

He'd never thought it could happen.

But Khalid had.

"I am so glad you asked me to dance," Laila murmured,

her eyes lowering modestly as they danced together. "I was starting to fear you never would."

Laila was different from her half sister, he thought. Ferida had been fragile, lost. But Laila had a flash of steel beneath her deliberately demure gaze.

Perfect for a queen, he thought. She left him cold. But if she was the best choice for Samarqara…

Omar danced with Laila, watched with delight by his newly united nobles. But against his will, all he could think about was the one woman he could not have. The unsuitable young woman with light brown hair, watching them from the corner of the ballroom with stricken hazel eyes.

This was what Beth had wanted, wasn't it?

She watched as Omar and Laila danced, smiling together. He leaned forward to whisper something in Laila's ear that made her laugh and her sultry dark eyes gleam.

And suddenly, Beth couldn't bear it.

Turning, she fled the ballroom, rushing back through the deserted palace to her lonely bedroom in the vizier's residence. Shutting the door behind her, fighting back tears, she looked out the window at the silvery moonlight frosting the palm trees. She'd never felt more alone.

Grabbing her phone from the nightstand, she dialed her sister's number in Houston.

Edith had told her she'd stay hidden at the lab while Beth was in Paris, to make sure no one would realize they'd switched places. But Edith hadn't answered any of Beth's messages since she'd left Houston.

That wasn't unusual. Edith never answered her phone. She was always too busy.

Even when their grandmother was alive, Edith hadn't come back once for Christmas at the small dusty ranch in West Texas. Beth had been the one to visit from Houston, to call their grandmother every day, and arrange her funeral after she'd died. She'd been the one to agonize over the paperwork as the bank foreclosed on the ranch. Edith had ruthlessly put her work ahead of everything and everyone.

"I'm close," her sister would always mutter. "So close to a breakthrough."

And yet the breakthrough never came.

Beth always told herself she didn't mind. Edith was a genius, and of course geniuses had to be treated differently from other people.

But now, as the phone rang and rang, for the first time, Beth felt something she'd never felt before. Angry.

All the times she'd been there for Edith—why couldn't her sister be there for her, just once, when Beth's heart was breaking, and she felt so alone?

Hanging up, Beth tossed the phone aside.

She slept badly that night, caught up in dreams. But the morning still came.

Beth was dressed in a traditional Samarqari gown, with long, brightly colored embroidered skirts, robes and headdress. Her eyes were lined with black kohl, her hands dyed with intricately patterned henna.

Following instructions, she left the vizier's palace to find five elaborately carved and painted covered palanquins waiting, in a parade led by royal Samarqari horseguards, at front and behind.

Feeling too sad to smile at the other four brides, Beth climbed awkwardly onto the pillows inside her own palanquin. It was lifted with a lurch by the four burly, uniformed carriers. She grabbed the soft mattress beneath her for balance.

The vizier came to speak to her. "You must not open the curtains until you arrive at the royal palace," he told Beth rudely. "Be silent. Be small." Then he closed the curtains on her palanquin violently.

He didn't seem to like her much, she thought dimly. But

then, could she blame him, after the way she'd insulted the council yesterday?

Beth resolved to remain quiet and invisible from now on. As they left the vizier's palace in a noisy, slow-moving parade, she resolutely tried to follow the rules, as silly as they were.

Beth stared at her closed curtains as they traveled the mile toward the royal palace on the hill. She ignored the voices calling out, pleading for the brides to look, to taste, to come and try this or that. Then she heard children, and she couldn't resist.

Peeking around her curtain, she saw small children following them eagerly. When they saw her face, they cheered. It seemed the height of bad manners not to respond to them.

Her earlier resolve forgotten, she pushed aside the curtains and slid awkwardly out of the palanquin in her elaborate gown and headdress. The carriers stopped with a gasp, holding the palanquin steady so she didn't fall on her face.

The kids came forward, cheering noisily, and so did the other people in the souk. The palanquin carriers looked at each other nervously. Beth wondered if she was making a mistake. Ahead of her, she saw the other four palanquins, all of them with curtains closed as ordered, leaving her behind.

"Hello," Beth said in English—she didn't want to risk another international incident by mispronouncing anything—and smiled warmly. "I'm so pleased to meet you."

"What is your name, miss?" one of the children called in English.

"Beth." She leaned forward. "What's yours?"

As crowds came toward her in the crowded market square, she braced herself for questions. But they didn't ask any. They just welcomed her.

"Try my fig, mademoiselle, we have the greatest figs!" a merchant said, holding it out.

"And this," a plump woman called to her. "My honey pastry is the best in the world."

Beth tried both fig and pastry, leaving her fingertips sticky with honey. She licked it off with relish, to the crowd's delight. As someone asked for a selfie with her, Beth posed with a ready smile. And all the while, people were speaking around her, eager to tell her about their king.

"Miss Beth, if His Highness chooses you, you're blessed."

"King Omar, he has done so much for this country."

"He's sending my girls to college…"

"He saved my son's business…"

"Our country, it is the happiest place now in the world."

And they looked at her, waiting for her reaction.

"I love this place already," she told them honestly. "Any woman would be honored to be Queen of Samarqara."

They beamed at her.

Ahead of her, the other palanquins had disappeared entirely from the souk. The other brides were following the rules. None had even opened their palanquin's curtains.

She heard a loud noise behind her and turned. She gasped when she saw her stopped palanquin had blocked the path of the royal horseguards behind them. One of the soldiers, a scrawny-looking youth, seemed to be struggling to hold back his mount.

Everything happened in a rush.

A toddler, perhaps three years old, ran forward to join the clamoring older children. He didn't notice the nervous horse, a thousand pounds of muscle barely controlled by the young soldier astride him.

Beth heard a woman's terrified scream as the oblivious, smiling child rushed headlong beneath the sharp, slashing hooves—

Beth moved without thinking. She snatched the toddler out of the way, turning her body to protect him as she held up one hand in the horse's line of sight. Surprised, the animal stepped back. Desperately, she softly whispered calming words, as she'd done to the horses back at her grandmother's Texas ranch when they were hot or confused or scared.

For a split second, she saw the animal's bared teeth and hooves and thought she was about to die. Then the horse's eyes stopped rolling. The soldier regained control of the reins, and Beth exhaled, handing the toddler to his mother, who threw her arms around her child with a sob.

"Beth," someone suddenly cried in the crowd.

Within seconds, it turned into a noisy chant. "Beth! Beth! Beth!"

The palanquin bearers looked at each other uneasily.

"Queen Beth," someone shouted.

"This is who we want. Our queen!"

Beth listened with shock. These people didn't know anything about Edith or all her sister's many accomplishments.

They were shouting for Beth. Just for her.

"If you please, most high," one of the carriers bowed deeply, looking at her with new respect.

She looked back at the enormous crowd, now overflowing with people chanting her name. Her throat was dry. Uh-oh. What had she done, breaking the rules? The vizier wouldn't like this at all. And more importantly, neither would Omar...

Hastily, she climbed back into the palanquin and slammed the curtains firmly shut.

But it was too late. As the bearers lifted the weight of the palanquin to their shoulders and started to leave the crowded souk, she could still hear the crowds chanting her name.

Beth peeked out as they reached the grand steps of the royal palace, and was dismayed to see the crowd had only grown larger, following them, still shouting her name.

The palanquin stopped, and then was slowly lowered.

"Welcome," Omar's voice rang out, distant and cold.

The crowds fell silent. The ceremony had begun.

As planned, the brides all stepped out together from their palanquins, in perfect unison. Well, except for Beth, who was a single second behind, getting tangled in her dress and hot with embarrassment at the renewed chant of the crowds behind her.

"Beth! Beth!"

She felt the glowering anger of the four other women, as all five of them stood in a line beside the resting palanquins, looking up at the king standing on the palace's steps far above them.

"Beth! Beth!"

Ignoring the noise, she took a deep breath and lifted her chin. Above her, she saw Omar in full regal robes, standing at the top of the steps, surrounded by his council and honor guard.

Trying to shut out the glares of the other women and the nobles, and the death stare of the vizier, she focused only on Omar.

His handsome face was a furious scowl.

She ducked her head, her cheeks hot. Because of her actions, when he announced his chosen bride—Laila—the moment would be ruined, overshadowed by his people's demand for a different woman.

She'd spoiled Omar's ceremony, simply by not following the rules, simply by being herself.

"Beth! Beth! Beth!"

Omar lifted his hand in a single gesture, and the crowds fell into silence.

"I have chosen my bride."

His deep, husky voice carried on the wind. Beth looked around the royal square, with its palm trees and lush flowers, and burbling stone fountain beneath the blue sky.

"My new queen will be…"

Omar stopped. It was so quiet Beth could hear the plaintive call of a seagull, soaring high overhead. The pause stretched out as he looked from Laila, dignified and still, standing regally beside the first palanquin, past Sia, Anna, Taraji, to Beth at the very end.

Omar's eyes met hers, and her heart twisted. *I nearly kissed you last night*, he'd said. If things had been different, if he'd just been a regular guy she'd met at the thrift shop—

But he wasn't. And no amount of people cheering could make her Samarqara's queen. The council already despised her. How much more would they detest her if they knew Beth had been lying about her identity all this time, and was just a shop girl from Houston? And Omar…he would hate her.

He had to marry Laila. It was the best way this could end. Tears lifted to her eyes. The only way.

So why didn't he just announce Laila's name, already? *Just say it*, she thought fiercely, her whole body tense as she blinked back tears.

"I choose…" Omar took a deep breath. "Dr. Beth Farraday."

She froze, stunned, unbelieving. The crowd behind her screamed with joy.

For a shocked moment, a wave of happiness went through her, greater than she'd ever known.

Then her blood turned to ice, as she realized what she'd done.

CHAPTER FIVE

STANDING ON THE platform at the top of the palace steps, Omar heard his vizier's furious hiss. "Sire!"

Turning, Omar said flatly, "The choice is mine."

Khalid's face was dark with fury. "But the council chose Laila!"

They had. Unanimously. A situation so unusual it was no wonder, even now, that Omar heard the members of the council muttering darkly around them.

He had grimly planned to accept their advice, and announce Laila's name. Though he couldn't imagine taking any woman to his bed, or having any other woman at his side, but Beth.

Looking down from the palace steps, he saw her, and sucked in his breath.

Black kohl lined Beth's eyes, her lips were a slash of scarlet, and her hair was veiled in the traditional headdress. So different. So familiar. She looked like everything he'd ever wanted. He'd felt a sharp pain in his throat as he opened his mouth, trying to force himself to speak a different woman's name.

Then a miracle had happened.

He heard his people shouting Beth's name. Chanting it to the rhythm of the blood rushing through his veins.

"Beth! Beth!" his people had begged.

And his heart had stopped.

Was he king, or not?

Beth was right, he suddenly realized. Whatever his

council advised, he was choosing more than a queen today. He was choosing a wife. A lover.

He wanted Beth. And if the only thing that stood between them now was her career, so be it.

She could keep it.

"Dr. Beth Farraday," he'd heard himself say, and his people had gone crazy with joy.

"Why?" Khalid ground out now.

Narrowing his eyes, Omar said in a voice that would brook no opposition, "Because I want her."

His vizier's jaw tightened. "But she'll never give up her career."

"I know." Omar's voice was clipped.

Khalid's eyes widened in shock. Then he bowed, still radiating resentment.

It was no wonder Khalid was still pushing Omar to marry Laila. After all, Hassan al-Abayyi was a second father to him. Khalid had grown up in their house, after losing his parents.

But surely, Omar thought wrathfully, it would be best for Samarqara if he married a woman he actually wished to bed? A woman who would clearly be an excellent wife and mother? A woman whom his people already adored?

What more obvious sign could there be, than that in just the short time it took for Beth's palanquin to travel through the souk, she'd somehow already made them love her?

Beth stood at the bottom of the royal palace's wide steps, her eyes wide and uncertain as she looked from Omar, to the crowds cheering wildly behind her, then to the rejected brides now simmering with fury—especially Laila al-Abayyi. He could hardly blame the Samarqari girl for being upset. She must have heard of the council's decision, and expected her patience would be rewarded today.

But they could never suit. She'd eventually realize that.

Omar saw Beth whisper something to her nearest palanquin bearer, and the man whisper back, nodding his head toward the palace steps.

Beth took a deep breath. Holding up the edge of her elaborate Samarqari gown so the hem didn't get dirty, she started to climb the stone steps toward him.

When their eyes locked, all of his senses heightened. He heard birds singing in the blue skies, and smelled sweet roses and the soft, salty wind off the Caspian Sea.

When Beth reached the platform, she looked pale and scared. He saw her sway, and reached out and grabbed her arm. Trembling, she looked up at him, her eyes huge.

And he did what he'd longed to do from the moment he'd first seen her in the dark cool shadows of the Paris garden, wearing a too-tight dress as she'd artlessly informed him that no sensible woman would ever wish to be his bride.

Now, pulling her roughly into his arms, Omar lowered his head to hers and claimed her with a hard, hungry kiss.

He felt her intake of breath, felt her shake. But he held her fast, kissing her deeply, crushing her smaller body against his own. Her hands, raised to push against his chest, surrendered and instead wrapped around his shoulders. To the delight of the crowd, she kissed him back, slowly at first, then with a passion that matched his own.

He barely heard the crowd's deafening cheers. With Beth in his arms, he forgot his vizier, his nobles, the other women.

He felt only this. Her.

It was as if Beth were the first woman he'd held in his arms, the first he'd ever kissed. He felt like an untried virgin, kissing her. Excitement electrified his body, turning sinew and muscle and bone to molten honey. He felt dizzy with need. He leaned her back to deepen the embrace, overwhelmed by the ravenous hunger that consumed him—

"Sire," his vizier hissed, and Omar again heard the

shouts of the crowds, and remembered he was holding the future queen in his arms.

Straightening, he pulled away from the kiss. But his heart was still racing as he looked down at her.

Beth's eyes were wide and her cheeks pink. She sagged against him, as if her legs were weak.

"Omar," she whispered. "There's something I should…" Glancing out of the corner of her eye at the council around them, then at the huge crowd in the square, she bit her lower lip. With a shuddering breath, she choked out, "We need to talk."

His eyes, which had fallen to her deliciously red mouth, swollen from his kiss, rose to meet hers. "Talk?"

"You don't—" She swallowed, then said in a low voice for him alone, "You don't know who I am."

"You're Dr. Beth Farraday. Brilliant, a prodigy, one of the most famous research scientists in the world. And the woman I want to marry."

She'd looked scared before. Now she looked sick. "I'm not…" She glanced at the nobles, who'd come forward to listen. "Not worthy of you."

Not worthy? He marveled at her modesty. "Are you worried about your career?" he said quietly. "We'll figure it out. You can move your lab here."

She didn't smile. "My lab."

"Who knows." He gave her an encouraging smile. "As queen, you might lead an explosion of scientific and technological advancement in Samarqara." His smile lifted into a grin. "Even the tourist board will be thrilled."

But she wouldn't smile back.

Was it possible she didn't want to marry him after all?

No, Omar couldn't believe that. She'd signed the contract. And after the way she'd just kissed him—

She wanted him. He'd stake his life on it.

For nearly a thousand years, Omar's ancestors had ruled

this land. He was the last heir. The al-Maktoun line was threatening to die out completely.

But now, as Omar looked at his bride-to-be, he suddenly knew he'd made the right choice. Because he could imagine no outcome that did not involve him getting her pregnant repeatedly. Perhaps they'd have five children. He looked over her face and body hungrily. Ten?

He wanted her so badly he didn't know how he'd manage to wait to bed her until after the royal wedding ceremony, scheduled a month away.

All he wanted to do was get her alone, rip off her headdress and elaborate gown. He wanted them both naked with their bodies entwined. He wanted to push deeply inside her, again and again, until her softly sensual body was rosy and flushed as she screamed her pleasure, digging her fingernails into his skin…

With a shuddering breath, Omar looked at her. His hand tightened on hers, then he held it up high, turning to face the crowd. "In one month's time," he cried loudly, "we will have a royal wedding, and she will be crowned your queen!"

This time, the cheers were so loud the stone thundered beneath his feet. With a final wave, he turned and escorted Beth past the columns, inside the pointed arch that led into the royal palace.

Her hand was unresponsive in his own. As Khalid and his council followed, Omar led her through the grand rooms of the royal palace. But she walked as if hardly aware of their surroundings.

"What happens to the other four?" she whispered. Trust Beth to worry about their feelings, he thought.

He shrugged. "They'll be escorted to the vizier's palace, where their bags have already been packed. They'll leave Samarqara within an hour." He paused. "Except Laila. She may stay. She's, after all, a citizen."

Beth looked relieved. "Good."

He frowned. "You don't need to worry about them. They'll return to their extremely successful lives with three extra million dollars, a new wardrobe and an interesting memory."

Beth seemed strangely intent. "But Laila—"

Omar stopped, putting his hands on her shoulders. "Forget her. I want to talk about you. About us."

He felt her tremble beneath his hands. Then she took a deep breath, glancing back at the glowering advisors and sour-faced vizier.

Following her gaze, Omar said, "Thank you for arranging the bride market, Khalid. It succeeded beyond my wildest dreams." Looking at Beth, he took her hand in his own. "Your service will not be forgotten."

"Sire," the vizier said in a pinched, unhappy voice, "if we could just talk, for a brief moment…"

Looking down into Beth's luminous hazel eyes, Omar's only thought was how to get his bride-to-be alone. He growled, "Later."

"But, sire—"

"Later." He turned to the men coldly. "That will be all."

His advisers bowed and scattered beneath his glare. Only Khalid lingered, his long face tight with repressed anger, before he, too, bowed and disappeared down the wide palace hallway.

"I don't think he likes me," Beth said.

"Khalid is stubborn, but he will soon realize what a treasure you are." He paused, tilting his head. "How did you make the people chant your name?"

A shadow crossed over Beth's eyes. "It was my fault. I knew I wasn't supposed to stop the palanquin, but I couldn't resist…"

As she relayed the story of how she'd saved the child

from being trampled in the market square, Omar stared down at her in wonder.

He wondered how he could have ever considered any other woman but Dr. Beth Farraday, even for a moment. With deep respect, he lifted her hands to his lips, and slowly kissed her knuckles, one by one, allowing the warmth of his breath and lips to linger against her skin.

He felt her shiver. Then she blurted out, "Omar—I have to—"

Three maids walked down the hall, passing them with wide eyes. Omar's hands tightened on hers. "Let's go somewhere we can be alone."

Swallowing hard, Beth said in a stilted voice, "Yes."

Tugging gently on her arm, he led her down the hallways of the royal palace, past the elaborate pointed arches and columns, beneath tiled ceilings soaring high overhead in colorful patterns of lapis lazuli and gold leaf. Omar was proud of offering Beth such a beautiful home. He'd overseen the palace's restoration ten years before, determined to make it even better than it had been, before it had been destroyed by war in his grandfather's time and neglect in his father's.

He led her up past the lavishly restored throne room, the ballroom, the salons. He barely paused to point out a two-story library filled with books, including parchment and scrolls thousands of years old, from the time of the caliphs, containing the history of his country that he couldn't wait to share with her.

Later.

Finally, he led her up the sweeping stairs in the tower to his bedroom. "This is the king's bedchamber."

Beth gasped, looking at the high ceilings, the patterned stucco of the walls. "It's beautiful."

"The most beautiful room in the palace. Except for the queen's."

"Separate bedrooms?"

"Tradition," he said huskily. He cupped her cheek. "There's a connecting door."

But as he lowered his head towards hers, she abruptly pulled away, looking as if she were about to cry. Turning, she walked out onto the balcony.

The air blew in fresh from the sea, making the white translucent curtains undulate in the soft spring breeze. Beth gripped the edges of the balcony, looking out at the sparkling water with haunted eyes.

Omar came up behind her, putting his hands against the balcony railing around her. Directly below the tower were the palace gardens, with trimmed hedges and palm trees, and a profusion of roses in bloom. To the right and left of the palace, he could see the prosperous city, stretching out in old buildings of squat clay beside steel skyscrapers.

"I always see you with flowers," he said huskily. "Like where we first met."

She glanced back at him. "In the garden in Paris."

"I noticed you at once."

She gave a low, rueful laugh. "Because I was stupid. I was the only person who didn't recognize you."

"You spoke to me as an equal," he said. "Not seeing me as a prize to be won."

"My equal?" Beth shook her head sadly. "No. Not at all." A small smile traced her lips. "But I tried to forgive you. I told myself it wasn't your fault you were good-looking."

He gave a low laugh. "Then imagine how I felt when I met you."

She blushed in confusion. "What do you mean?"

Omar looked down at Beth, dressed in the traditional headdress and gown of a Samarqari bride. Electricity pulsed through his body. All he wanted to do was kiss slowly down the length of her naked body. He was hard and aching to claim her as his own. But their wedding was still a month away.

Omar whispered, "You were the sexiest woman I'd ever seen."

Beth looked at him sharply, as if she thought he were mocking her. Then her eyes widened.

Glancing back at his bedchamber, he gave her a crooked grin. "This tower used to be the king's harem."

She snorted. "Harem?"

"The palace is hundreds of years old. It's been built and rebuilt, from the time caravans traveled the old Silk Road. But harems were outlawed a hundred years ago."

"Too bad," Beth said, flashing him a teasing grin. "You could have saved yourself a lot of trouble by just bringing all twenty women here directly."

He returned her grin, then his expression changed.

"But I only wanted one." Pulling her into his arms, he looked down at her, cupping her face with his hands. He whispered, "I only wanted you…"

And he lowered his mouth to hers.

He felt her shock, felt her hesitation when he kissed her.

Then he felt her body rise. Her small arms reached up to his shoulders, and she kissed him back with answering need, as the salty sea breeze whirled around them.

Breaking off the kiss, he whispered against her lips, "I want you, Beth. Now."

He heard her intake of breath, and felt her tremble as she gripped his shoulders desperately, holding him close.

It was all the permission he needed. Lifting her into his arms, he carried her back into the bedchamber, to the enormous royal bed upon which no woman had ever slept. Omar had never brought a mistress here. This bed wasn't meant for any temporary lover, quickly discarded.

He'd decided long ago it would only be shared with his wife. His queen. It was the bed upon which they'd conceive their children. He'd saved it only for her, as a sign of respect.

Setting Beth down on her feet beside the bed, Omar gently tugged off her elaborate headdress. In the light from the windows, her light brown hair shone gold as it tumbled down her shoulders.

Walking around her, he slowly undid the ties that held together her traditional Samarqari gown, allowing that, too, to fall in a *whoosh* to the priceless rug on the cool marble floor.

Beth stood before him in only a simple, traditional cotton shift. His body stirred, and he knelt at her feet, pulling off her shoes. But as he rose to take her in his arms, she stopped him with an intake of breath.

"I can't. We…" She swallowed. "We can't."

Omar drew back.

"Why?" His jaw tightened as he said harshly, "You do not want me?"

She shook her head with a low laugh filled with desperate regret. "You know I do." She looked at her feet. "I never imagined you might choose me, in spite of everything. If I had…"

His heartbeat had recovered from the sickening lurch, and he came closer. "If you had?"

"I never would have come to Samarqara. I…" She took a deep breath, then whispered in a voice almost too low for him to hear, "I'm not who you think I am."

"Why do you persist in thinking so little of yourself?" he said incredulously.

"I'm not being modest." This time, her laugh was bitter. "You think I'm some world-famous genius."

"No."

She looked up at him. "No?"

"You're more," he said quietly. "You're the woman who made my people love you in the space of an hour. The woman who risked her life to save a child. A woman who wants the best for everyone, except perhaps herself." Reaching out, he ran his hand softly through her hair. "The woman who will be my wife, and the mother of my children."

She shivered, her lovely face stricken as she lifted her gaze to his. "How can I even tell you?"

What could be troubling her? Then, looking down at her, Omar suddenly knew.

Gently, he took her hands in his own. "If you're worried because you're not a virgin, Beth, don't be." He snorted. "That's one old custom no one expects. Me least of all."

Her jaw dropped. "What?"

"You're sexually experienced. That's fine. So am I. It doesn't make you unworthy. It doesn't make me want you less." Cupping her cheek, he said in a low voice, "It only makes me want you more."

That was a lie, Omar thought. Nothing in this moment could make him want her more.

Her eyes looked shocked. She looked quickly away.

"Isn't that what you wanted to tell me?" he asked, confused.

She shook her head, her expression anguished. She clasped her hands, twisting them together.

"I...the thing is, I'm not..." She focused on him abruptly. "I'm actually a virgin." Her gaze fell to his lips. "So I couldn't possibly please you in bed, anyway."

Shocked, he stared at her, hardly able to believe her words. "You're a—virgin?"

"Yes. Another reason I can't marry you." Tears filled her eyes. "So call the other women back. Tell Laila you changed your mind. It's not too late to make a better choice!"

As he stared down at her, all he could hear were her words echoing in his brain. *I'm a virgin.*

Unthinkable. In this modern world, his bride would be coming to his bed a maiden? Untouched by any other man?

"How is it possible?" he breathed, searching her face. "Are all the men of Houston such fools?"

Her cheeks burned red. "I've only had two boyfriends in my whole life. The first was in high school. I didn't understand why he never tried to kiss me, until at graduation he announced he was gay. And my second boyfriend..." She looked away. "I had a mad crush on him, but he was never really that into me, I guess. He broke up with me last year because...he said there was nothing special about me. I was too boring, he said. Too *ordinary*."

Her voice was husky with unshed tears.

"Ordinary?" Staring down at her, Omar felt a flood of emotion. He said hoarsely, "That's the last thing you are."

Beth looked at him, blinking fast, as if afraid to believe his words. Taking her into his arms, he felt her body tremble against his.

Then he realized that he was the one trembling.

He'd been wrong when he'd thought nothing could make him want her more.

She was a virgin. *A virgin.*

"But I have something more to tell you." Her voice dropped to a whisper. "Something I...wish I didn't have to say."

Somewhere in the back of Omar's mind came the thought that, now he knew she was a virgin, he had no choice but to wait for marriage before he could bed her. That was the only honorable path. That was the way of the old days.

But how could he wait?

"You have to understand how expensive cancer research is," she was saying. "And how desperate my sister was." She shook her head, running her hand over her forehead. "No, that's not fair to blame her. I also wanted to see Paris."

Omar was bewildered. What did Beth's sister have to do with anything?

He didn't want to talk about their families, or the past.

What did anyone else matter, except the two of them, now? Their life was just beginning…

"Later," he said huskily. He lowered his head to kiss her. His caress was gentle at first. But as he tasted the sweet softness of her lips, his need intensified. His grip on her tightened as he plundered her mouth, teasing her tongue with his own, until she abruptly ripped away.

"Please," she cried, her eyes wild. "*Please.* You don't understand. I'm not who you think!"

Omar couldn't understand. How could such an accomplished woman judge herself so harshly for what could only be some tiny, unimportant flaw?

But he saw in the wildness of her eyes that whatever it was, she was torturing herself over it.

"So tell me," he said huskily. "I want to know every bit of you. Or better yet," he whispered, lowering his head for another kiss, "show me…"

As they kissed, he thought he tasted the salt of her tears. Whatever her imaginary flaw was, he had to show her it didn't matter. He reached around her, loosening the ties of her shift, and the thin fabric fell to the antique rug beneath their feet. Beth stood naked before him, except for white lace panties.

His breath stopped as, still fully dressed in his regal sheikh's robes, he looked down at her full, naked breasts, tiny waist and long hair tumbling down over her creamy virgin skin. Her light brown hair seemed a multitude of colors, tangled strawberry and gold and chestnut. Her big hazel eyes were a swirl of blue sea, green fields, brown earth. The whole world.

He could almost hear the pounding of her heart. Hear the soft pant of her breath as she stood utterly still, her pink nipples tight with arousal. As she looked up at him, her eyes pulled him with their desperate, innocent desire. She was everything in this moment.

Need pounded through Omar so great he knew he could not wait for their wedding next month, any more than a starving man could stand beside a feast without reaching for the food that might save him. Resist? Impossible.

He had to have her. Now.

But Beth was a virgin. Only a selfish bastard would violate that, just weeks before they would wed. Her innocence was a precious, unexpected gift. He had to respect that—and her.

So he'd marry her, Omar thought suddenly. Right now.

CHAPTER SIX

WHAT WAS SHE DOING? Standing here in front of him so brazenly, nearly naked? Did she have no shame? Had she lost her mind?

Yes. Beth had. Her lips were swollen from his kisses. Her body was aching with longing. She wanted more. She wanted—him.

But she had to put a stop to this. Now. Before the impact of her deception became even worse, and he couldn't undo the choice he'd made.

She'd tried to force herself to tell him, to explain. Why was it so hard? All she had to do was say five simple words. *I'm not Dr. Edith Farraday.*

Or six: *I've been lying to your face.*

That shouldn't be hard, should it?

But it was. As Omar stood in front of her in the dappled sunlight of the lavish suite, his dark eyes burned through her. Then they traced slowly, appreciatively, down her body.

She took a deep breath, gripping her hands at her sides. And the words that would end everything caught in her throat.

For the first time, Beth felt what it was truly like to be desired. And by such a man as this…!

Never taking his eyes off her, Omar removed his head covering. His dark hair beneath was rumpled, so soft and wild that she ached to run her fingers through it. Eyes locked with hers, he slowly removed his sheikh's robes.

Standing before her in just loosely fitting trousers, Omar looked down at her. With an intake of breath, Beth stared at the shadows and curves of his tanned, hard-muscled chest, laced with dark hair. He was so powerful, so strong, his shoulders so broad and wide. He made her feel delicate, feminine. He made her feel like the heart of his whole world.

Coming forward, he cupped her cheek and whispered, "I want you, *habibi*."

"Habibi?"

"It means…beloved."

Outside, the palm trees waved against the soft warm wind, dappling the golden light from the windows. Beth froze, trembling with longing she'd never felt before.

Just one night, she thought. One night to know what it was to be desired. One night to cherish for the rest of her life. Then, in the morning, she could confess everything, before any real damage was done. She'd make Edith return all the money. They'd quietly cancel the wedding.

One night in his arms, and then Beth would set him free to choose a different woman to marry. One who was worthy to be his wife, and Samarqara's queen.

The temptation of it was almost unbearable.

Beth licked her dry lips. "This is wrong," she whispered, over the pounding of her heart.

"I know."

Her eyes lifted to his in shock. "You do?"

"You are a virgin," Omar said grimly. Powerful and so masculine, he moved toward her with grace, in spite of his strength and size. "You kept faith with the old traditions. You deserve to be treated as the precious treasure you are."

Her? A precious treasure?

Unwillingly, Beth's eyes traced over the hard muscles of his chest and arms, down the length of his chest, along the arrow of dark hair that led to his taut belly, disappearing beneath the waistband of his loose trousers.

"To make love to you before marriage would be dishonorable. I know this." Cradling her head in his hands, he looked at her hungrily. "But there is only one thing that matters more."

Beth couldn't look away. No one had ever looked at her like he was right now, as if she were Christmas morning and birthday cake and the first sunshine of spring, all at once. "What?"

His dark eyes burned through her. "Do you want me, Beth?"

Did she *want* him?

No man had ever made her feel like this. And she suddenly knew no man ever would again.

Did she want him?

Already, in the short time she'd known him, she'd ridden the greatest roller coaster of her life—joy and anguish and fear and desire.

Did she want him.

Of course she did. But she couldn't have him. She didn't deserve him. If she'd been Edith—

It wasn't fair, her heart cried out. She and Edith were identical, and yet they weren't. Edith had everything, all the beauty and talent, leaving her with nothing.

Couldn't Beth at least have this? Couldn't she feel Omar's arms around her, just for one short, blissful moment? Couldn't she have something, just for herself, a moment she could always remember, before she went back to her ordinary life forever?

"I…" Tears burned the backs of her eyes as she trembled on the edge of the abyss. "I can't."

"You can't what?"

"Want you," she whispered. But as his expression fell,

she couldn't bear it. "But I do," she choked out, searching his gaze. "I want you more than anything."

Omar's larger hands tightened on hers. The expression in his dark eyes pierced her heart.

"Beth," he whispered, then spoke words in Samarqari, kissing her on one cheek, then the other.

"What did you say?"

"If you truly want me, *habibi*, then say my name, and those same words back to me."

Lost in his dark eyes, in the sensation of his hands wrapped around her own, and her trembling guilt for what she was about to do, she stumbled through the words. He was so close to her. When she swayed forward, her bare, aching nipples brushed against the dark hair of his hard-muscled chest. Dizzy with longing, she breathed his name.

His handsome face glowed in the shadowy bedroom, as the soft warm wind curled past the translucent curtains, cooling their heated skin.

"Now kiss me, Beth," he said huskily, his dark eyes burning through her soul. "My right cheek, then my left."

It seemed strangely ceremonial, but all she wanted was to keep this moment, to wrap it up so tight she'd remember it forever. Whatever it took. Whatever it cost. Her heart was brimming with emotion as she stood on tiptoes and kissed his cheek, then the other. As her lips grazed his skin, she felt its roughness, the dark sandpaper bristles.

When she pulled away, Omar's dark eyes were shining.

He lowered his head and kissed her lips, so gently, so tenderly, that her heart nearly broke inside her.

Still kissing her, he slowly pushed her back against the bed, kicking off his shoes, covering her nearly-naked body with his own. She felt his weight, his strength. She gloried in the feel of him against her, a sensation she'd never felt before.

His lips were heaven, hard and soft, as his tongue teased

her, tempting her, swirling against her own. His hands moved from her cheeks, to her shoulders, where her hair spilled in tumbled waves against the pillows.

"You've made me so happy," he whispered, kissing down her throat. She closed her eyes, lost in pleasure as he cupped her full, aching breasts. She held her breath as he lowered his head to taste a taut nipple. He held each heavy breast like a tantalizing sweet to be licked and sucked into his hot, silky mouth. Sensual pleasure swirled around her, drawing her deeper, as a sweet ache coiled low and tight in her belly.

Moving up, he kissed her lips, caressing her body like the precious treasure he'd called her. He kissed her cheeks, her forehead, her eyelids. He ran his hands through her hair and back down her body. He kissed in the valley between her breasts, with a slow lick at each nipple, suckling her before moving downward, ever downward. Slowly pushing her legs apart, he knelt between them on the bed.

The roughness of his cheek scraped softly against the sensitive skin of her belly. She felt the heat of his breath, and then the flick of his wet tongue against the hollow of her belly button. A shiver went through her, but he paused for only a moment, then continued his exploration downward. Exploration?

Seduction.

As he pulled the whisper of white silk lace panties slowly down her thighs, she squeezed her eyes shut, shivering. She felt the bright, hot sun from the open window heating her naked skin. She felt the mattress sway beneath her as he removed his trousers, then knelt between her thighs. His powerful, muscular legs were bare and warm and rough against her skin.

"Beth," he commanded. "Look at me."

She obeyed, and, seeing him above her, kneeling between her thighs, she gasped. His body was tanned, hard and powerful with muscle, so much bigger than her own. And hardest of all…

She looked at his large shaft, standing erect from his body, jutting toward her. She'd never seen a naked man before. She held her breath, lost in equal parts fascination and fear.

Wonderingly, she reached out to take him in her hands. He jolted beneath her innocent touch. He was soft as velvet, hard as steel. She stroked him softly, exploring the full length of him.

He gasped. With a low growl, he grabbed her wrists, pushing them back against the pillow. He kissed her hungrily. Leaning forward, he whispered hoarsely in her ear, "Keep your hands back. Or I'll have to tie you down."

He kissed slowly down the length of her body, finally lowering his head between her thighs. She shivered as she felt the heat of his breath against the most secret places of her body. Then, spreading her wide with his hands, he lowered his head and tasted between her legs with the full rough width of his tongue.

The pleasure was so shocking, she gasped. Inexperienced as she was, she started to reach for him. But remembering his earlier words, she stopped, and forced herself to hold still, beneath the almost unbearable onslaught of forbidden joy.

His tongue moved delicately at first, then lapped her wide. As she started to tense and shake, his rhythm changed. The tip of his tongue twirled against her taut, wet core as he put a fingertip inside her, then another, stretching her.

Her head tilted back, her lips parting in a silent gasp as he worked her with his mouth. She gripped his shoulders with her nails as her hips slowly rose from the bed of their own accord. Her breasts felt heavy, her whole body tight as she started shaking all over. She held her breath. Tighter, tighter. She wanted—oh, God, she wanted—

Then she exploded, and cried out with joy, joy she'd never even imagined existed in the world, as waves of ecstasy shimmered around her.

In that split second, she felt him move, reaching for something in the nightstand beside the bed. Then he paused.

"I've never been with a virgin before." His voice was strained. "I don't want to hurt you."

Beth opened her eyes.

"You won't," she breathed, looking up at him above her, almost dizzy with pleasure.

Positioning himself between her legs, he hesitated. Then, with a deep breath, he pushed inside her, inch by inch.

The pleasure evaporated, replaced by pain. She gasped. But as her lips parted and she started to tell him to stop, he gripped her shoulders.

"Wait," he said huskily. "Wait, *habibi*."

He'd pushed all the way inside her. He now held himself utterly still, giving her time to accept his size. And she realized the throb of sharp pain was disappearing.

As her shoulders relaxed, the grip of his hands loosened. Kissing her gently, he ran his hands down her body, cupping her breasts, biting her lower lip.

And slowly, very slowly, he began to move inside her.

Incredibly, new pleasure started to build, a new sweet tension coiling inside her, deeper than the first. Holding her breath, she twisted her head against the pillow, hair tangling around her. She closed her eyes, lost in sensation.

"No," he whispered, tilting her chin. "Look at me. Feel me as I'm inside you."

Their eyes locked, their souls joined, as he filled her, inch by inch, until she thought she couldn't take any more, then somehow, he made her take more, stretching her deeper still. Pulling back, he thrust again inside her, slowly at first, then faster as he began to ride her.

Harder. Deeper. He pushed her to the limit, thrusting inside her until, to her amazement, she exploded once again, this time, into ecstasy so deep, the whole universe seemed to burst into stars.

From the moment Omar had kissed her, it had been all he could do not to explode.

But she was a virgin. He'd had to go slow. He'd kissed her softly, feeling her naked body shiver as she wrapped her arms around him. As he'd lowered her against their marital bed, he felt the whisper of warm wind against his skin, and the heat of her body against his own. He'd felt the power of her innocent desire for him, and he gloried in it.

He'd desperately held himself back. It had been torture. He'd kissed her soft, sensual body, with her full breasts and curvaceous backside. He'd licked and caressed every inch of her, making her ready.

Then she'd suddenly reached out to touch him, wrapping his shaft in her sensual hands. He'd nearly exploded right then and there. Hence his threat to tie her down. But how else could he keep enough control over his rampaging body, when all he wanted to do was make it good for her?

Forcing himself to go slow had been the greatest feat of his life. Pushing her thighs apart, he'd stretched her wide and tasted the sweetness between her legs, teasing and lapping her with his tongue until he felt her tighten and gasp and explode. Then, with her scream of ecstasy still ringing in his ears, he'd reached for a condom.

Going slow had been torture.

It had been a different kind of agony when he'd taken her virginity. He'd hated hurting her. Holding himself utterly still, in all her exquisitely tight heat, had been almost unbearable. When her pain had abated, and he slowly began to move, he'd still had to keep a tight rein on himself. Making her explode with pleasure once wasn't enough. He'd wanted to bring her to even higher ecstasy. He'd wanted their joy to bind them even closer, as their eyes locked and souls met, as he was buried so deep inside her—

But the moment he felt her shake as she cried out a second time, her body tightening convulsively around him, he lost the last shreds of his control.

Control? He lost his mind.

Her magnificent breasts swayed as he thrust harder and faster, and then he'd exploded, racked with pleasure so intense he almost passed out.

He collapsed over her with a groan, exhausted. Their hot, sweaty bodies remained entwined together across their marriage bed. Then his eyes went wide as he saw the condom had broken.

A chill filled him, even as he tried to tell himself it didn't matter. They were married now. They wanted children.

And yet—

It doesn't matter, he told himself harshly. Tenderly, he kissed her forehead, then pulled her small, naked body protectively against his.

He must have slept, because when he opened his eyes, the shadows across the bedroom had moved, to the slant of late afternoon. His stomach growled. He considered calling for food, then glanced at the clock above the marble fireplace. The lavish dinner banquet, set to celebrate the conclusion of the bride market, was set to begin in a few hours. Perhaps it was better to wait. Especially since he did not want it widely known that he'd already seduced Beth and claimed her secretly as his bride, a month before the formal ceremony.

Though if she were already pregnant, everyone would be able to do the math...

He looked again at Beth, sleeping in his arms, so soft and

warm, and a hunger stirred in him of a different sort. But as he was reaching to wake her, he heard a hard knock on the bedchamber door. He looked up in fury. Who would dare—

The door burst open, revealing his vizier and two guards.

Seeing Omar and Beth naked in bed, Khalid went pale. "What have you done?"

"What have I done?" Omar growled. Beth, blinking awake, looked horrified at having their private moment invaded. He wanted to strangle the vizier with his bare hands. As she covered herself with a sheet, Omar rose to his feet in full, naked fury.

"What is the meaning of this?" he thundered.

"That woman is a fraud, sire!" His vizier's voice lifted a trembling finger to point at Beth. "She's not Dr. Edith Farraday. The real Dr. Farraday is still in Houston, hiding in her lab!"

Omar glared at him. "What are you talking about?" He pointed toward the bed. "She's right here!"

"That's her identical twin, Beth Farraday!"

Identical twin? Omar snorted, shaking his head. "You can't expect me to believe—"

Then, turning, he saw Beth's face. The stricken expression in her eyes.

"I was going to tell you," she whispered.

And Omar's heart went numb. His body changed in a second from warmth and joy to pure ice.

He would have been prepared to fight anything, to defend the woman he'd chosen. But he couldn't fight the look on her face. It almost brought him to his knees.

Staring at her, he staggered back a step. "You…you're not Dr. Farraday?"

Mutely, she shook her head.

"Who are you?"

"I'm nobody," she whispered.

"She works in a charity shop!" his vizier said with malicious triumph.

Omar felt a shot of pain in his throat. Turning on Khalid, he said in an expressionless voice, "Leave us."

The vizier's eyes flamed with impatience. "Sire, I do not think it wise to leave you alone with this *temptress*—"

"Do not make me say it twice."

The guards bowed and obeyed. The vizier grudgingly followed, closing the door behind him with one last venomous look at Beth.

Omar stood naked beside the bed, alone with the woman whose virginity he'd just taken so gloriously as his own.

He felt like he'd just been punched.

The corners of his lips twisted coldly. "At least I know why you asked me to call you Beth."

Looking up at him, she choked out, "I'm sorry."

Sorry. His hands tightened at his sides. *Sorry.* He looked at the bed he'd saved just for his wife. For his queen. Thought of what he'd just done. Because he'd trusted her.

But she'd been lying to him all the while. Lying to his face. Destroying everything he'd tried to achieve.

Fury built inside him, choking him, freezing him from the inside out, as he whispered, "Damn you."

CHAPTER SEVEN

HOW HAD THIS all gone so horribly wrong? Omar was looking down at her as if she were a stranger.

"Please," Beth choked out, "you can't think—"

"Can't think what? That you lied to my face from the moment we met?" His black eyes were hard. "That while I stupidly trusted you, and chose you as my bride, you and your twin sister were laughing yourselves sick at your deception?"

"I wasn't!" Her voice shook. "We had a good reason!"

"Tell me," he cut her off.

Beth held the sheet up higher over her naked body, all the way to her neck. She took a deep breath.

"When Edith—my sister—got your invitation," she said haltingly, "she couldn't leave the lab, you see, but she really needed money for cancer research. So she asked me to come in her place."

Omar stared at her, his eyes cold.

"It was just supposed to be fun," she said weakly. "A chance to see Paris and do some good in the world."

"Do some good," he repeated incredulously.

Beth's cheeks went hot as shame filled her.

"I'm so sorry," she whispered. "If I'd had any idea you might actually choose me—I swear to you, I never would have agreed to come!"

"But you did agree," he said flatly. "You agreed to come to Paris and pretend to be Dr. Edith Farraday. You agreed to be in my top ten. You agreed to sign my contract. You agreed to come to Samarqara in my top five and you allowed me to introduce you to the world, to my country, as my bride!"

Silence fell in the darkening shadows of the king's bedroom.

Grief and regret stifled her. She hung her head, staring at the priceless rug on the floor.

"I'm sorry," she repeated numbly.

Omar turned away. He pulled on some clothes from a wardrobe. Casual ones, simple shirt and trousers.

"Please." Fighting back tears, Beth took a deep breath. "If you'd only try to understand—"

"I do understand." Omar didn't look at her. "You made a fool of me and everything I believe in for the sake of three million dollars."

"For cancer research! Money to help my sister save lives—children—"

"I don't care what it was for." His jaw tightened as he looked out at the open balcony. Outside, the afternoon sun sparkled across the Caspian Sea. There were distant sounds of people calling across the gardens, and the noise of the city beyond the palace.

"You made my people love you," he said in a low voice. "And I hate you for that most of all."

She started to speak, then fell silent. What could she say?

He turned back toward the bed. With his face shadowed against the sunlight, she could no longer see his expression, and for that she was glad. All she could see was the outline of his body, the body that had given her such pleasure. She whispered, "I was going to tell you everything."

"When?"

"Tomorrow."

His dark eyes flashed. "Liar."

"It's true." She looked down at her body, still covered only with a sheet. For the first time in her life, she'd been selfish, and let herself experience the pleasure of his touch. But she was paying for it now, body and soul. "I made a deal with myself. One night with you. Then I'd confess everything."

"Confessing only when it's too late," he said harshly.

She frowned. What did he mean, *too late*?

"Cancer is bad," he mimicked her voice mockingly, then shook his head, clawing back his hair. "I was a fool to think any scientist would say that. Or not immediately explain every detail of your research if you thought you could get more funding!"

Her cheeks burned. She looked away, a lump in her throat. "I should have told you the truth. The first time you asked me to stay, in Paris."

"You never should have come to Paris at all." He stepped toward her, his hands tightening at his sides. "But one thing I don't understand. Why did you let me make love to you? What were you hoping to achieve?"

"I…"

"Were you trying to make me care? To forgive you?"

Looking at him, she blurted out, "No one has ever looked at me like you did. I wanted…a memory. Something I could cherish for the rest of my life, long after you'd chosen someone better to be your bride."

He stared at her, then set his jaw. "Do you even realize what you've done?"

"I'm sorry." Her voice was thick with tears. How many times could she say it? "I'll leave quietly. Just tell your people the truth, that I lied. Your vizier was right. I'm nobody. I pretended to be my sister. She's the genius. I barely finished high school." She wiped her eyes. "I'll take the first plane home and…and I'll make Edith give you the money back." She tried to keep her voice light. "You can marry Laila—"

Omar cut her off with a low, bitter laugh. "It's too late for that."

"Why?"

"We had sex," he said grimly.

As if Beth couldn't still feel that, in every sweet ache of her body! As if she didn't feel that with every wistful beat of her heart! She lifted her chin. "So?"

"You might be pregnant."

That possibility hadn't occurred to her. She sucked in her breath. "But you stopped—I assumed you were reaching for a condom—"

"I did. But it broke."

"Broke?" she repeated numbly.

"I told myself it didn't matter," he said sardonically. "Why should I worry about preventing pregnancy, making love to my own wife?"

A shocked silence fell in the bedroom.

"What?"

"That's right," Omar said in a low voice. "I couldn't wait to make love to you, Beth. But you were a virgin. I couldn't make love to you. Not honorably. Not until we were wed."

Rising horror filled her.

"Those words we spoke," she whispered.

"Yes," he said quietly. "We spoke the vows, followed by the two kisses. In my culture, it is a binding commitment."

"To my sister—"

"I didn't speak the words to her. I spoke them to you."

Beth stared at him in disbelief. They were married? *Married?* She swallowed hard, trying to even comprehend it. "But I didn't know!"

His dark eyebrows lowered like a storm cloud. "And you think that negates the words, after you've already agreed to be my bride in front of all the world? When you've signed a contract stating that you were here seeking marriage? When you told me, in every way possible, that you were mine?"

"But I never meant—" But at his murderous expression,

she took a deep breath. "Fine. So I spoke the vows. No one knows but us. We could just pretend it never happened!"

His eyes were hard. "You might be good at pretending, Beth Farraday. But I am not. I am bound by honor to speak the truth, both as a man and as a king. I do not speak lies." He turned away. "My marriage isn't just a whim. It's about the future of my nation. I chose you over Laila because I thought you could help unify my people. While you were just thinking of fun trips and raising cash—" his voice was tight "—your reckless lie could start a new civil war."

Horror went through her. She gulped.

"So what do we do?"

His jaw was tense as he looked at her. "If you are pregnant, I can never divorce you. It is the law in Samarqara. A king cannot divorce the mother of his heir. Not for any reason."

Beth looked up with an intake of breath. She could actually remain his wife? In spite of the way she'd lied? For a moment, her soul thrilled.

Then she heard the flatness of his voice.

He thought she'd trapped him into marriage. Selfishly. Stupidly. For money.

Her shoulders sagged as she sat on the bed, still naked, covered with a sheet.

"You can divorce me if you want to," she said in a small voice. "I mean, you should. I deserve it."

Omar looked down at her, saying nothing, as the shadows of the room deepened in the late afternoon.

She looked up at him pleadingly, blinking back tears. "Please. Forgive me. I'll do anything."

"Yes," he said slowly. Stepping closer, he looked down at her without touching her. She had the vision of his dark face, his burning eyes. "You will."

Omar abruptly went to the bedroom door. He looked out at the two guards.

"Make sure Miss Farraday does not leave the tower until the banquet." He looked at the vizier, hovering like a ghoul in the hallway. "We have much to discuss."

"Yes, sire." Standing in the doorway, the vizier looked back furiously at Beth, still shivering on the bed. "If I had my way, Miss Farraday, you'd be thrown into prison for the rest of your life."

Her stomach turned to ice. Prison?

"Enough." Omar turned to her. His voice was cold. "Your clothes are in the queen's chambers. The royal engagement banquet is in three hours. Be ready."

"But, Omar," she choked out. "You can't still want me to—"

He left without another word, closing the door behind him.

Alone, Beth stumbled up from bed. Grabbing her formal gown and headdress off the floor, she rushed through the adjoining door to the queen's bedchamber and dropped them on the bed. Going to the walk-in closet, she grabbed the first clothing she saw, a silk robe. Tying the belt, she paced the sumptuous suite, feeling like a prisoner in spite of the lavish surroundings.

If I had my way, Miss Farraday, you'd be thrown into prison for the rest of your life.

Omar might be furious, but he wouldn't throw her into prison.

Would he?

Heart pounding, she went out to the balcony. As the sun lowered to the west, she looked down at the sea and palace gardens. A long, hard drop. No escape there, unless she truly wanted to end it all.

When she thought of the look in Omar's eyes, when he'd discovered her deception... A razor blade lifted to her throat. They were married now. For all she knew she could be pregnant.

There was a quiet knock at the door. Going back inside to answer it, she saw a young girl, perhaps seventeen, dressed in the modest garb of a palace maid. Coming into the queen's bedchamber, the girl bowed respectfully. "I'm Rayah, Your Highness. The king sent me to serve you."

Beth looked at the floor. "You don't want to serve someone like me."

"I begged to be your maid, Your Highness."

She looked up. "Why would you do that?"

"The little boy you saved in the market." Her face glowed. "He's my brother."

Beth stared at her, then a lump loosened in her throat. "Thank you, Rayah."

"Such a beautiful dress," the girl sighed when she saw the traditional Samarqari gown. She carefully hung it up on the door of the walk-in closet. "Now. What do you require first? Some food? A rose-water bath to prepare for the banquet?"

Food was the last thing on Beth's mind. Suddenly, all she wanted was privacy, so she could call her sister. She thought of her handbag, tucked into the closet. "Um…a bath? A bath would be great."

With a bow, the maid departed to the enormous en suite bathroom.

Rushing to walk-in closet, Beth found her phone. She gasped when she saw she'd had ten—*ten!*—missed calls from Edith. Her sister, who never called anyone, had apparently been trying to reach her for the last hour. Glancing towards the bathroom, where she heard the water running, Beth closed the closet door for privacy and dialed her sister's number.

For the first time ever, Edith answered her phone on the first ring.

"What's going on?" her sister cried. "Why haven't you called me back?"

At another time, Beth might have found Edith's question ironic, after her own hundreds of unanswered phone calls. But now, Beth's eyes filled with tears. It was good to hear her sister's voice.

"The king picked me as his bride. Can you believe it?" Her voice choked on a sob. "He announced our betrothal in front of everyone."

"I know," Edith said.

"You—you know?"

"It's all over the news. The lab phone started ringing off the hook. I saw the video of him choosing you in front of his palace. Oh, Bethie, how could you do it? How could you make him love you?"

"Love me?" Beth gasped. Bitterly, she wiped her eyes. "He doesn't love me!"

"Why else would he choose you?"

She thought of the way his handsome face had glowed when he'd spoken her name from the palace steps. The fire in his eyes as he'd kissed her.

"It doesn't matter now," she said soddenly. "He's just found out I'm not you. And now he hates me."

"Come home," Edith said immediately.

"I can't."

"Of course you can. Grab a taxi and head for the airport."

"You have to give back all his money. Please, Edith, you must—"

"Fine."

"Fine?" Beth said in shock.

Her sister paused. "This has all been more trouble than I imagined. I've been sleeping at the lab, like you asked. I've sworn my assistants to secrecy but a colleague saw me this morning."

"Omar's vizier just found out you're in Houston."

"Then it's just a matter of time before the press gets wind of the twin-switch story. Come home."

"I can't. The king's put guards at my door." Beth gave a forced laugh. "I might go to prison."

"Prison?" Edith, always so cool and controlled, gave a curse that made Beth blush. "Forget that. I'm going to send the army and the Marines and even the Scouts to get you out."

What might be an idle threat with some people might really happen with Edith, she thought. Her sister knew people. Powerful ones. "No."

"Are you sure?"

"Yes." Beth couldn't hurt Omar with a diplomatic incident on top of everything else. He clearly wanted to keep this quiet. He'd put guards at her door. Immigration would probably arrest her if she tried to flee the country—which they would be well under their rights to do, considering she'd traveled here under her sister's borrowed passport.

Beth was the villain here. No wonder Omar no longer trusted her. To all evidence, she was a cold, venal, money-grubbing liar, while he'd been honest from the start about his desire to find a suitable bride. He'd even made her sign a contract, stating that she knew what she was getting into. That she was seeking marriage. And that she was Dr. Edith Farraday.

Then she'd slept with him under false pretenses. No wonder he hated her. She deserved it.

"Beth—I'm going to get you out—"

"*No.* I mean it, Edie," Beth choked out. Gripping the phone, she wiped her eyes. "I'm the one who caused this mess—"

"Both of us caused it!"

But Edith hadn't been the one who'd chosen to stay, time and time again. She hadn't been the one who'd slept with him. "I can't just disappear. That would look like I abandoned him at the altar. I don't want to hurt him. Not more than I already have."

"Then what can I do?" her sister said anxiously. "Come and marry him in your place?"

A wrench went through Beth's heart. Her sister was only trying to help. And yet…

Edith? Marry Omar in her place?

A knee-jerk reaction came from deep in her soul. "No."

"Whew. For a second I thought you might say yes!"

"Don't worry." Beth took a steadying breath. "I'll think of something."

Could she?

For much of her life, she'd been the one everyone felt sorry for. Poor Beth, with no talents or skills, overlooked, ordinary, always failing at everything. Poor Beth.

But she didn't need help. She just needed strength. She could do this. Alone.

She'd remain here and be humble and endure, and pray she wasn't pregnant, so Omar wouldn't be trapped into permanent marriage with her.

A strange thing to pray for, when Beth had always dreamed of having a child of her own. Especially strange, because she would have given anything to be Omar's wife forever.

But not like this. Not when he hated her.

For his sake, she would pray she could set him free.

Edith sounded doubtful. "I still think I should…" There was a pause, and Beth suddenly heard muffled noises on the other end of the line, then her sister gasped into the phone, "There are two men outside my lab, demanding I come with them. By orders of the King of Samarqara!"

Beth's blood froze. "What?"

"Get out of here!" her sister yelled to them in Houston, on the other side of the world. "Don't touch me!"

And then, to Beth's terror, the line went dead.

* * *

Omar looked up at the soaring ceilings above the small council chamber. The airy, open space was filled with light. Outside, two birds were singing by the windows. Happy. Free.

"I told you the bride market was a mistake, sire." Omar heard a note of satisfaction in the vizier's voice. He turned to him at the table.

"Your second mistake," he said coldly. "You were supposed to vet the candidates."

Khalid looked pained. "She signed the contract E. Farraday," he protested. "There are few photos of her sister. I believed she'd just gained weight."

Gained weight in all the right places, Omar thought. He remembered the sweet feel of Beth's soft body against his. He'd been so sure he'd found the woman to spend his life with. So sure that he'd immediately married her and taken their wedding night.

Khalid was right. The bride market had been a mistake.

"I don't understand why the banquet is still set to continue, sire. Why have you not thrown her from the palace in disgrace?"

When Omar had told him that he'd married Beth in the old, intimate ceremony, his vizier's howls had been loud. Now he replied, "You know why."

"Yes." The vizier's lip curled. "But why not divorce the American shop girl in private, as you married her? Announce Laila as your queen. The people's hearts will be glad when they see a Samarqari bride, and they will soon forget the other."

Omar rose to his feet, slamming the table with his fist. "When will you understand? I will not marry Laila. She still reminds me of…"

His old friend went pale. "Of Ferida."

Silence fell. Omar looked away, his heart tight.

I belong to another, for as long as I have breath.

He remembered Ferida's tortured note, written right before the desert consumed her.

I can never belong to you, even if you're the king, even if it's the law.

Omar shuddered with pain. After Ferida's death, he'd changed the law so that any woman had the right to refuse to marry, even if her parents ordered it, even if the demand came from the king himself. But he'd never wanted to risk another unwilling bride.

That was what this bride market was supposed to prevent. Instead, it had fallen apart. Because of Beth Farraday's lies.

It was just supposed to be fun. A chance to see Paris and do some good in the world.

He remembered how she'd felt beneath him in bed, the first time he'd pushed into her. How he'd shuddered with the difficulty of self-control, so desperate he'd been to please her. He'd even married her instantly, rather than disrespect her.

And all the while she'd been lying about the most basic thing imaginable: her identity.

Omar had wanted a woman he could respect and trust. Instead, he'd gotten the opposite.

Setting his jaw, Omar looked out the window toward the tall tower, where he'd left her.

I'm sorry, she'd repeated in a small, quivering voice. Had she really expected his forgiveness? he wondered bitterly. When, for the sake of money and a free trip to Paris, she'd carelessly destroyed everything he'd sought to achieve as king?

In spite of his precautions, Omar knew it was just a matter of time before the rest of the world discovered he'd been tricked by the wrong sister. His people would think him either a weakling or a fool. Perhaps they'd decide to get rid of the monarchy altogether, leading the kingdom into chaos.

From the day he'd taken the throne, Omar had tried to bring his people together, and build the prosperity of all. It hadn't been easy. As a boy he'd once dreamed of freedom, of being able to do whatever he wanted, without the chafing bonds of duty. But since the death of his older brother, that had remained just a dream.

Having a solid marriage, a partnership of friendship and trust, was his biggest dream of all. His own parents had hated each other; after his brother died, they'd separated in fact, if not name.

Omar had thought he could do better. Because how could a man unify a country, if he couldn't even unify his own home?

Remembering how happy he'd felt with Beth in his arms, he felt sick. At any point since she'd arrived in Paris—when she was chosen for the top ten, when she made the top five, when she arrived in Samarqara—she could have confessed the truth. Instead, she'd made the choice, again and again, to lie.

And if she was pregnant...

He would permanently have a liar in his bed. As his wife. As the mother raising his children, and the future ruler of his beloved kingdom.

Assuming there even was a kingdom, after it was discovered Omar had defied the unanimous advice of the high council, and rejected the most honored heiress in the land, to marry not a world-famous scientist, but a lying gold digger from Houston.

Hassan al-Abayyi would likely lead the revolt. Fairly or not, the man held a grudge against Omar for the death of his eldest daughter. He would never forgive this second insult.

Omar felt heartsick. He'd been a fool to ever let his heart and body make the choice. He should have let his brain decide whom he would marry, all along.

"Your Highness!"

Looking up, Omar saw one of the palace maids, Rayah, standing in the doorway of the council chamber. He motioned her forward. "What is it?"

"It's your betrothed, sire," the girl said. "She begs you to come to her in the tower. She says it's a matter of life and death!"

So it had already come to this. Omar's eyes narrowed. He'd thought Beth would wait before she tried to manipulate him again. She truly must think her power over him had no bounds.

Tonight, he would show her the error of that belief.

Beth shook with anxiety, pacing back and forth across the queen's bedchamber. She'd already tried twice to get past the guards, to no avail. When she'd shrieked at them about her sister and waved the phone in their faces, they'd simply taken the phone from her. Finally, in desperation, she'd sent Rayah to the king.

"Why did you summon me?" Omar demanded coldly behind her, and in spite of everything, her heart raced as she whirled to face him.

"What have you done to my sister?"

He didn't even pretend not to understand. "What was necessary."

"If you've touched a hair of her head—"

"You think I would hurt her?" Omar stalked forward in his sheikh's robes, his expression dark. He'd showered and changed, and looked handsome and powerful. As if the events of the day hadn't affected him at all.

She held her ground, glaring at him. "I was talking to her when your thugs grabbed her!"

He held up her phone. "Who else have you called?"

"No one—who cares about the stupid phone?" she nearly shrieked. "What have you done with my sister?"

"She's taking a long vacation."

Beth sucked in her breath. "*A long vacation?* Is that a euphemism?" She gripped her hands into fists. "Like swimming with the fishes or pushing up daisies? You *bastard*—"

"Calm yourself." He looked down at her coldly. "A vacation means a vacation. She'll spend a few weeks on my private island in the Caribbean, drinking piña coladas and sunning herself on the beach."

Beth blinked, dropping her fists. "What?"

"Until we know if you're pregnant, you will continue to play the part of Dr. Farraday. Which means the ruse cannot be discovered, as it surely would have been, had she remained longer in the lab. It's a miracle it wasn't discovered before now."

That was certainly true. Biting her lip, she said suspiciously, "Are you telling the truth?"

"I'm not the liar between us." Narrowing his eyes, he held up her phone. "Can I trust you with this?"

"Who would I call?"

"A newspaper outlet, to sell your story? The American embassy, to claim you're being held against your will?"

"It's not a claim, it's a fact!"

His dark eyes burned through her. "Can I trust you to help me undo the damage you've done—to my country? To me?"

Beth hesitated, then said in a small voice, "I want to. But how?"

Omar looked down at her, his eyes cold. "The banquet begins in an hour, and you are not ready. Rayah said she filled a bath for you. Why are you not in it?"

"Seriously?" She lifted her chin. "Your nobles hate me.

Your vizier wants to throw me in prison. There's no way me going to the stupid banquet will help anything. I'm not going!"

"You are."

"Forget it—"

Mercilessly, he pulled her into the gleaming marble bathroom. Outside, twilight had fallen. The shadowy room was lit with flickering candles.

"What's this?" she said, bewildered as she looked around the bathroom, set for beauty and romance.

"Rayah must have done it. I didn't," he said grimly. "Now get in the tub."

Her lips parted. "I'm not taking off my robe in front of you!"

"Get in the bathtub, Beth."

She saw by the gleam in his eyes he wouldn't rest until she was in the bath, one way or the other. Dropping her silk robe she stood before him naked in the candlelight.

His dark eyes flickered as he slowly looked over her naked body, pink in the steamy bathroom. Her cheeks burned, but she lifted her chin defiantly.

He abruptly turned away, his jaw tight. "I will leave you to get ready." His voice was almost strangled. "Come down for the banquet within the hour."

"Why is it so important to you?" Beth was holding back tears. "What can we gain from me pretending to be your future bride?"

"*Pretending?*" he ground out, still not looking at her. "We are already wed, even if no one knows it. The banquet is in your honor. You will respect my people, and your position, by showing up."

His words made her heart hurt. Turning away, she climbed into the hot bubble bath, laced with rose petals. After all the drama of the day, her whole body ached with exhaustion. She leaned back in the hot, fragrant water, giving a soft groan of unwilling, unexpected pleasure.

Hearing a gasp, she looked up. Omar was staring down at her in the candlelight, his dark eyes wild.

Her breasts had risen above the surface of the water. Her skin was pink with heat, her nipples red, surrounded by bubbles and floating rose petals.

Even as she willed her body not to react, her nipples pebbled beneath his glance, every inch of her body suddenly shivering with desire.

No! She could not let herself want him! Not now! Humiliated, she moved the angle of her body so her breasts swiftly disappeared beneath the water.

His eyes found hers. Electricity pulsed between them.

"I never meant to hurt you," she whispered.

"Hurt me?" His jaw clenched, and he turned away. "No. I am merely—disappointed. You made my people love you with your lies. Now, you will make their love for you evaporate."

"How?"

"Be rude. Be unkind. Be a vicious, filthy liar." His lips twisted sardonically. "It shouldn't be too hard."

The big jerk! She swallowed back a retort. "And if I turn out to be pregnant? How can I remain as your wife if I've made everyone hate me?"

"In that unfortunate event, you can easily win back their love. I am the last of my line. If you are pregnant with Samarqara's heir, you will instantly be the most adored person in the land." He gave a cold smile. "By everyone, of course, but me."

"Oh." A lump rose in Beth's throat. He called the prospect of her pregnancy *unfortunate*. Making it clear that any child born of their union would be an unwanted and regrettable burden, forcing Omar to remain yoked to Beth, when he despised her.

And this after he'd been so determined to make love to her, that he'd lured her into unknowingly speaking wedding vows! "What about my job in Houston? I can't stay here for weeks until—until we know. I'll be fired!"

"Fired?" he snorted. "As if you ever intended to go back to work at a charity shop after you collected your three million!"

"That money wasn't for me, I told you!"

"You told me a lot of things. Why would I believe any of it?"

Beth's jaw tightened. She'd tried to apologize. To make things right. What more could she do? "Look, I've already said it's all my fault. I'm trying to fix things. But I'm getting sick of your insults. There's only so much more I'm going to take!"

Omar's eyes narrowed, but as he turned to reply, his gaze fell again to her body, her full breasts peeking above the rose petals and bubbles. Setting his jaw, he looked away.

"In that case," he said tightly, "it's best that we see each other as little as possible until the day you're escorted from my country. May fate grant that the happy day arrives soon!"

He left in a whirl of robes. She thought of a retort too late.

"Mister, I'm counting down the days!" she yelled.

But he was already gone, leaving her alone in the candlelight, her throat choked with unshed tears. Her fury melted away, leaving her shivering with heartbreak in the rapidly cooling bath.

CHAPTER EIGHT

FORTY-FIVE MINUTES LATER, as her maid helped her into yet another beautiful new gown, Beth told herself she felt nothing. Not heartbreak. Because she couldn't love Omar. And she definitely, definitely didn't feel desire. He'd treated her badly and refused to even consider her side. She would never, *never* want Omar again.

A good thing, too, since all she now had ahead of her was the painful task of pretending to be his fiancée, and waiting for Omar to get the all-clear to kick her out of Samarqara, and out of his life.

The thought made her ache inside.

"Is something wrong, Your Highness?" Rayah asked, drawing back anxiously. "Would you prefer a different gown?"

Beth tried to smooth her face into a smile. "No, it's fine. Everything's perfect."

Once dressed, she went down the steps from the tower with a heavy heart, her heavy jeweled earrings swaying in her ears.

When she arrived at the palace's great hall, she was greeted with a coolly polite bow by Omar. Looking at her as if she were a stranger, he introduced her to a crowd of aristocrats as his future queen. They looked no more pleased than Beth at the prospect.

He held out his arm to escort her up to their private table on the dais, in full view of the nobles' tables below. She nervously placed her hand on his arm. Even through his sleeve, she could feel the heat of his skin, the power of his body.

I feel nothing, she repeated to herself desperately. But her body still trembled from the intensity and passion of his possession, just hours before, when he'd ruthlessly taken her virginity and made her world explode with joy.

Now, Omar barely looked at her. As he sat beside her at the table, his hard, handsome face was a polite mask as they listened to speeches, both in Samarqari and in English, welcoming Beth—whom they still called "Edith"—as his future bride.

Beth ate and drank by rote, hardly aware of the taste. She kept her eyes mostly on the floor, and tried to be as invisible as possible. She felt miserable.

She just had to hold on for a few weeks, she told herself, and make everyone hate her. How hard could that be? As soon as she got proof she wasn't pregnant, she could return to her old life in Houston.

Now, Omar lowered his head and whispered angrily, "What do you think you're doing?"

Beth looked at him in surprise. "What?"

"You look like you're facing execution," he said through gritted teeth. "Stop it."

"You expect me to look happy when I'm not?"

"So now, *now* you insist on total honesty?" Omar's black eyes shot sparks. "You've already proven how adept a liar you can be. So yes. Lie. Look happy. Now."

Beth tried. But at every moment, she felt aware of him sitting beside her, and anger and regret churned like acid through her soul. She wished she'd never gone to Paris—wished she'd never even heard the name Omar al-Maktoun!

During one particularly long speech in Samarqari by an older, pompous man, Beth felt Omar's knee briefly brush against hers beneath the table. Nearly jumping in her skin, she moved hastily away. Her eyes fell on Laila al-Abayyi sitting at one of the front tables. She looked utterly comfortable in her traditional Samarqari clothing, dazzling and glamorous.

The vizier, sitting beside Laila, leaned in to whisper to the Samarqari girl. Beth frowned. Something about their body language just seemed—wrong.

As the older man's long speech finally ended, he returned to sit beside Laila and the vizier. The three of them looked sideways toward the king, and for some reason, the way they looked at him made her shiver.

"Beth." Omar's voice was terse. She scowled back at him.

"What now?"

"You're still not smiling."

"How about this?" Irritated, she stretched her face into an uncomfortable rictus of a smile.

He shuddered. "Stop."

"I can't smile, I can't frown—what do you want from me?"

"At least look pleasant."

"Like you?" she countered.

Omar deliberately smoothed his handsome features into a neutral expression that did, indeed, look very pleasant. She was irritated and a little envious that he could hide his feelings so well.

"It's not fair," she grumbled. "You've been trained."

"Trained my whole life," he agreed grimly, reaching for a jewel-encrusted gold goblet. Drinking deeply, he set it down, smiling for the benefit of the banquet tables beneath the dais. "It's how I can sit beside you, pretending to be happy about my choice."

"Do you want me to just leave Samarqara?"

"Leave?" He snorted, glancing at her coldly. "Not before you make everyone despise you as much as I do."

"These people already despise me."

"The nobles might. But not everyone. Not the servants. Not the regular people of the square."

Beth thought of Rayah, and how happy the girl had been to serve her. "You expect me to be rude to them for no reason?"

"I expect you to do whatever it takes, as long as it shows no dishonor to my country or my throne, until I can satisfyingly renounce and discard you."

"What do you have in mind?" she ground out. "Should I rip off my dress and dance naked on the banquet tables?"

His pleasant expression disappeared. "Perhaps later."

Her lips parted in shock. "I was joking."

His black eyes cut through her. "You seemed eager enough to be naked before."

Against her will, her gaze fell to his cruel, sensual lips. Her own mouth tingled. With a shiver, she turned away.

"That was before," she whispered.

"Before I discovered the truth about you."

"No," she said. "Before I discovered the truth about you."

"Which is?"

Beth met his gaze. "That you're a heartless bastard who will never forgive."

"Forgive betrayal?" Smiling for the benefit of the crowd, he took a drink from the golden goblet. "No."

This icy, ruthless king was nothing like the hot-blooded, seductive man who'd taken her virginity—the man who'd lured her with soft lips and soft words.

Blinking fast, Beth said in despair, "What happened to the man I met in Paris?"

"What happened to Dr. Edith Farraday?" was the cool rejoinder.

The rest of the banquet passed in a blur, as she ate food she didn't taste and listened to speeches she didn't want to hear, all about Dr. Edith Farraday's many accomplishments and the glory she would bring to Samarqara as queen.

Beth looked down at her hands clasped in her lap, wishing the torture would end. Because for the rest of the banquet, during all the interminable courses and speeches, she felt Omar's every movement beside her. She felt his every breath. She still felt him inside her. And most of all, she remembered the adoring gleam in his dark eyes when he'd held her, so briefly, to his heart.

All gone. All over. So she forced herself to smile through the pain. Because even though he was her husband, he'd never truly been hers.

Glancing at her face, Omar rose abruptly to his feet.

"My friends, we thank you for your congratulations. Now, my future bride and I must take our leave. She has had a tiring day, and we have much to discuss for our upcoming wedding."

With a slight bow, Omar took her hand, helping her from the table. She pasted a frozen smile on her lips as they departed the hall, hand in hand.

But the moment they were alone, she yanked her arm from his grasp. Or at least, she tried. "You don't need to escort me back to my bedroom."

"Wrong," he said grimly, holding her fast. "How else do I know you won't try to run away?"

"I won't!"

"We've already established I can't trust you." His hand was tight as he pulled her up the twisting stairs of the tower. He hesitated at his own bedroom door, then took her to the queen's chamber. Once inside the elegant bedroom suite, Omar shut the door behind them. His eyes were grim as he faced her.

"Fine," Beth said, wrenching her arm away, desperate for him to leave before she fell apart. She yanked the elaborate headdress off her head. "I'm safely in my room. Now you can go!"

He watched as her hair tumbled down her shoulders.

"Yes," he muttered. "I will."

But he did not move.

Trembling beneath his gaze, Beth leaned her hand against the cool stone wall for support. "Please," she whispered. "Go. Now."

"Yes," he whispered, even as he drew close to her in the shadowy room, lit with dappled moonlight from the open windows. She could smell the faint scent of salt from the sea, exotic jasmine and spices. "I'll go."

He was so close to her. She licked her lips, and he groaned.

"Beth," Omar said hoarsely, "you're killing me—"

And he swept her into his powerful arms, pushing her against the wall as he lowered his mouth to hers in a rough, hard kiss.

Omar had wanted to humiliate Beth. To make her pay.

All night, he'd been simmering. She'd lied to him. She'd made a fool of him—and his country's traditions. And for that, he'd never forgive her. For that, he'd intended to make her pay.

But it seemed hating her wasn't enough. Because he was already doing the one thing he'd sworn to never do again. Kiss her.

With a low curse, he abruptly let her go.

"Why did you do that?" Her big hazel eyes were agonized, filled with both pain and desire. The same way he felt right now.

Everything about Beth in this moment, from her elaborate Samarqari gown to the firm posture of her shoulders, made her look like a queen. He would have been proud to have her as his bride, if she hadn't lied. If things had been different—

Closing his eyes, he turned away.

He took a deep breath, then said in a low voice, "I should not have kissed you."

"No." Her voice was heartbreakingly quiet.

Setting his jaw, he took three steps toward the adjoining door to his own bedroom, then tightened his fists and turned to face her. "This is intolerable. Starting tomorrow, you will do your best to make my people hate you. Until they are begging for me to take someone else as my queen."

"So you said. But how can I be rude?"

He allowed himself a grim smile. "Look at what Laila al-Abayyi does. And do the opposite."

Beth looked miserable. "So you're going to marry her?"

The thought still made him ill. But once the coming scandal of his breakup with Beth erupted across the country, he knew he'd have no choice. "Yes."

She bit her lip. "I saw her at the banquet, sitting beside the vizier. And I noticed..."

"What?"

She paused, then shook her head. "Forget it. It doesn't matter. Good night."

"Good night." Going to the door between their bedrooms, he paused. "Lock this door behind me."

"Why?" she joked weakly. "Are you afraid you won't be able to control yourself?"

"I still remember how it felt to make love to you, Beth. And you were right, what you told me in Paris." He looked at her. "Even though I'm a king, I'm also just a man."

She looked up at him, her luminous hazel eyes full of emotion, her sweet, full lips trembling. It took all of his willpower not to pull her into his arms. With a deep breath, she stepped back, out of his reach.

"I'll make your people hate me," she whispered.

With a stiff nod, he went into his own bedchamber, closing the door behind him. A moment later, he heard the bolt slide with a heavy *click*.

Now all he had to do, Omar thought grimly as he climbed into bed that night, was make himself hate her, too.

For the next few days, he tried to avoid Beth in the palace. He returned to his regular duties as King of Samarqara, while she was tutored in diplomacy, manners and the Samarqari dialect, for her future role as his consort.

But every time Omar saw her, whether from a distance or up close, he felt the same jolt. His feelings were all jumbled, anger and longing and desire. Desire most of all.

The days passed in a blur. As they waited to find out if she was pregnant, Beth upheld her promise, and seemed to try her best to do as he'd commanded. She watched Laila al-Abayyi's behavior, and did the opposite.

Laila was always perfectly elegant, dressed in black and white, either in chic versions of Samarqari traditional garb or designer outfits from Paris. So Beth used the allowance provided to her as future queen to buy cheap clothes from youthful shops in downtown Khazvin, in bright colors and styles, far too tight and with too much skin showing, wildly inappropriate for anywhere outside of Coachella, Glastonbury or Ibiza.

Laila was always formal, speaking only to her friends, her family's employees or wealthy people of her own class. So Beth chatted with everyone, palace servants, strangers in town, even the occasional straggling tourist. She played ball with children in the street.

Laila held lavish charity balls with an elite international guest list, raising money for good causes. So Beth avoided fund-raising, instead spending her free time between lessons and palace duties, to help in Khazvin's homeless shelter. She used her own money to buy crafting materials and bring new computers to the widows' home and schools.

Beth did everything Omar had asked of her. Including avoiding him as much as he avoided her.

And every night, before he went to bed, he heard her carefully lock the bolt in the door adjoining their bedrooms.

Leaving him to many cold showers as he grimly waited out the time. How much longer would he be forced to endure this torture of having her live in his palace? How much longer, until they could know she wasn't pregnant—and they could part?

Finally, on court day, Omar's stamina ran out.

Each month, he held a session in his throne room when his subjects could come to the palace to speak with him directly about problems or issues. When, in the middle of court day, he was greeted by an entire family of seven, he looked at the parents in surprise. It was rare to have children brought to court. "You have business with me?"

"We have business with Dr. Farraday," the man said apologetically. "We wish to thank her."

"For saving our son," his wife said, smiling down at the dark-haired toddler in her arms. "Please, sire, will you permit us to see her? We have a gift for her."

"Of course," Omar said, even as his stomach churned. He nodded toward his guards. "Please ask my lady to come here."

When Beth appeared in the throne room, his mouth went dry.

She looked like sex appeal incarnate. Her light brown hair gleamed, tumbling down her shoulders. Her lips were scarlet red. Her hips swayed as she walked in on six-inch heels. Her curvaceous body was lathed in a tight, totally inappropriate tube dress in red.

But she greeted the family with quiet dignity, with her young maid following her. And though Omar ordered the queen's chair brought beside his, she didn't come to sit on the dais as was proper, as Laila certainly would have.

No. Beth walked directly to the mother, taking the woman's hands in her own. As her maid lifted up the child in her arms, they all spoke together, with the maid translating. They embraced each other, laughing. The parents handed Beth a rough, handmade plaster tile with a tiny handprint in it, and the mother kissed both Beth's cheeks, as the father bowed his head and wept. At the end of it, they were all crying.

Not just the family. Not just Beth. Everyone in court looked teary-eyed, except for Khalid, who grimaced in irritation, and Hassan al-Abayyi, who tapped his foot impatiently. The two men were trying to hurry the end of the court day, so they could return to the small council chamber to begin discussions for a business deal.

Omar realized his eyes were wet, as well. He touched the corner of his eye in amazement, trying to remember the last time that had happened.

Watching Beth, he looked at the kindness and compassion and warmth radiating from her lovely face.

And then—he looked again at the tight red dress over her bombshell curves. He saw the outline of her nipples and realized *she wasn't even wearing underwear.*

Was she trying to make him lose his mind?

Beth hugged the family one last time, then turned and left the throne room. Without so much as looking at him.

Omar rose abruptly from his throne.

"Court day is over," he said.

"Sire," his vizier said in alarm, "you're not leaving? We still have the small council—"

"We have much to discuss," Hassan al-Abayyi said heavily. "Oil companies are waiting to hear if we'll auction the right to drill on our western border—"

"Later," Omar bit out. Hurrying down the steps from the dais, he left the throne room. People took one look at his face and cleared a path. Following Beth down the hall, he soon caught up with her with his longer stride.

Catching her elbow, he turned her to face him.

"You cannot," he ground out, "dress like that."

Still clutching the plaster tile of the child's handprint, Beth looked up at him in surprise. "I know I look hideous. I'm doing it to make everyone hate me, just as you wanted."

Having her sashay into his throne room looking like a sex goddess, when he was already tempted by the thought of her every single moment of the day, hadn't been exactly what he had in mind. "This is unbearable. Are you pregnant or not?"

She stared at him incredulously. "I still don't know."

"When will you?"

"Any day now."

He looked at her breasts, the outline of which were sharply revealed in the tight dress. Were they swollen? He couldn't tell. And just looking made him want to take her, right here in the palace hallway, right outside the throne room on court day. His heart pounded as he clenched his fists at his sides, resisting the temptation. "Go change your dress."

"Why? Isn't it working?"

It was working too well. That was the problem. Everything she was doing was making him want her more. In his bed. As his wife.

And in spite of her efforts, his people didn't seem to hate her. At least not the regular people of the city. He could still remember how they'd chanted her name that very first day. "Beth! Beth!" They loved her now, more than ever.

It was just his nobles who disliked her more. Samarqara's aristocrats watched her scandalous behavior and communicated their scorn to each other, not in open words, but with delicately raised eyebrows.

But that was nothing, compared to the way they'd react once they discovered that Beth Farraday wasn't a prodigy or world-famous scientist at all, but an ordinary shop girl.

If they discovered he'd been tricked, and had chosen such a woman over Laila al-Abayyi—

His hands tightened. He could imagine Hassan al-Abayyi going to war. The man had almost done it fifteen years ago, after the death of his oldest daughter. How would he react to another insult?

If only—

Looking down at Beth, Omar choked out, "I wish you were your sister."

She stiffened, and her lovely face looked stricken.

"I'm not Edith. I'll never be Edith."

Blinking fast, she fled up the steps to the tower.

With a low growl, he followed her to her bedchamber. When she tried to close the door in his face, he pushed it open.

Turning from him tearfully, Beth sat down on the sofa by the window. "Everyone wants Edith," she whispered. "She didn't even have to try, to make them love her. My parents. My grandmother. The world." She paused. "No matter how badly she treats people, she's loved. While I—"

She cut herself off, looking out the window.

"Beth?"

When she didn't answer, Omar stood looking at her. His eyes slowly caressed down her pink cheeks, to her long throat and her luscious curves.

Forcing himself to turn away, he went to the small bar cabinet and poured them each a drink, in golden goblets encrusted with thick jewels.

Sitting beside her on the sofa, he quietly handed one to her.

She looked at it. "I shouldn't."

"Yours is club soda. In case…"

Beth lifted her gaze to his. "In case I'm pregnant with your baby."

His throat closed off as he pictured Beth, ripe with his

child, her breasts swollen and full. His ring on her finger. Her eyes full of love.

No. He cut off the thought. He could not let himself want that. Or the disaster to his country that might ensue.

It was just an illusion, in any case. She'd never had any real feelings for him. None.

Leaning back against the sofa's cushions, he took a big gulp of his own vodka tonic.

"It would be a disaster if I'm pregnant, wouldn't it?" She gave him a sad smile. "You need a queen who is powerful and brilliant and successful. Otherwise, everyone will wonder why you didn't just choose a girl from home?"

He nodded. "Samarqara is prosperous and stable now, but it was not always so. In my grandfather's time, the country was nearly destroyed by war. And my own father was weak. He ignored my mother to chase his mistresses, and did whatever the nobles wanted."

"But you changed all that," Beth said slowly. For a moment, their eyes locked. He felt it again, the twist in his heart, that connection...

Taking another sip of the drink, he forced himself to say lightly, "Did you see Sia Lane in the news yesterday, claiming she only took part in the bride market as research for an upcoming role?"

Beth snorted, and her eyes danced. "She said that?"

"But when the reporter asked what movie it was for, she suddenly couldn't remember."

"Funny. Have you heard about Anna and Taraji?" she said, referring to the high-powered Sydney attorney and Silicon Valley executive.

"What?"

"They quit their jobs, which must have been what they really wanted all along. Anna's bought a vineyard in New Zealand. Taraji's opening a yoga studio in Marin."

For a moment, they smiled at each other. Then Beth's

smile faded. "I don't blame Sia for trying to hide why she did the bride market. She doesn't want people to laugh at her." She looked down at her club soda. "Success is what matters in life. Wealth and power and fame. All things I wouldn't know what to do with, if I had them."

Trying not to look at the tight red dress, which at any moment was threatening to retreat and allow her breasts to fully spring free, Omar said, "There are all kinds of ways to be successful." He took a gulp of his drink. "Look at me. Who am I?"

"A king."

"A job I inherited my job from my father, who inherited it from his father. I told you that a king is like a servant. What glory is there in serving others?"

"Lots," Beth said. "Sacrificing oneself for others is the greatest glory of all. Not everyone realizes that."

Omar looked at her. "You do."

She snorted. "Me? I haven't done anything."

His eyebrows rose incredulously. "That's all you've done since you arrived in Samarqara. Helping others, volunteering, caring." He paused. "It was never about seeing Paris, was it? You pretended to be your sister in the bride market because she asked you. You did it for Edith."

"She's my sister. My parents died in a car crash when we were thirteen. Now our grandma's gone, she's all the family I've got left." Beth looked down at her hands in her lap. "I love her."

Sitting this close to her on the sofa was torture. As Omar breathed in her soft scent of honey and vanilla, he could remember how it felt to have her naked body against his own. Desire pounded through him. It took all of his self-control to look away.

He took another drink from his goblet.

"My experience of family was...very different. After my brother died, my father abandoned us for his mistresses and sports cars. My mother was heartbroken by my brother's death. She sent me off to boarding school in America so she wouldn't have to see my face, and be reminded of the son she'd lost." He turned away. "She rarely left her room. She couldn't bear to. She had to endure all my father's affairs without being allowed to divorce him."

"Oh, no." Beth looked stricken as she reached for his hand. He looked down at her fingers, laced softly through his own.

"When I came to the throne, the nobles were stealing from the treasury, living in luxury as regular people starved. I vowed I would not be weak like my father. I'd rule like my grandfather. Without mercy."

Beth's eyes were huge in the warm afternoon light from the large windows of the queen's bedchamber.

He took a sip of his drink. "I was immediately under pressure to marry, and secure the throne with heirs." He gave a short smile. "I was twenty-one. In my infinite wisdom I thought, who better to be queen than the most beautiful girl in the land? And how better to tame the most powerful noble family, than with an alliance of marriage?"

Omar had never told this story to anyone. He stopped.

"What happened?"

His jaw tightened, and he looked away. "I proposed marriage. The girl accepted. But the morning before I was to marry Ferida al-Abayyi, she ran off to die in the desert rather than be my bride."

Beth gasped. For several moments, the only sound was the cheerful birds singing in the garden beneath the tower.

Omar remembered how he'd waited in the palace that day, feeling at first amused by Ferida's lateness, then insulted. And then—then he'd gotten the news of what she'd done.

"How could she?" Beth whispered.

Staring down at his goblet, he said in a low voice, "She said in her suicide note it was because she loved another."

"Why didn't she just tell you that?"

Omar gave a low, harsh laugh. "It was the law then, that the king could choose any bride, and she was not allowed to refuse. Hassan al-Abayyi assured me his daughter wished to marry me. He insisted Ferida would quickly get over her shyness." He shook his head grimly. "I barely knew her. So I believed him. Because I wanted her."

He couldn't look Beth in the face. Setting his jaw, he said, "Her father wanted her to be queen. But she said in her note she'd already given her virginity to another man. She did not want to betray him. Or marry me under false pretenses, since by tradition the king's bride had to be a virgin."

"That's why you didn't care about virginity with me," she said slowly.

He gave a harsh laugh. "Ferida's death changed everything. When they found her body out in the desert…"

Shuddering, he couldn't go on.

"Who was the other man?" she asked suddenly.

Omar shook his head. "I never knew. Some stable boy, I expect. She was only eighteen." He tightened his hands. "I changed the laws so women could choose their own husbands. And for the last fifteen years, when my advisers begged me to marry, I refused."

"That's why you did the bride market?"

"I had to know my bride was willing. With no secrets."

Beth bowed her head guiltily. "Until I wrecked it by pretending I was Edith." She shook her head. "You never thought of just waiting to fall in love?"

"Love?" he said harshly. "I thought I was in love with Ferida. Love makes you blind." He thought of his father. "It makes you reckless and cruel."

"Not true love," Beth whispered.

He gave a hard laugh. "True love—what is that?"

She looked into his face. "When you care for someone so much, their happiness matters more than your own."

For a moment, Omar caught his breath. Then his shoulders tightened.

"I love my country. There's no room in my heart for anyone else."

Turning away, Beth gently set down her goblet. "It's funny. You don't even want to be loved. While I've dreamed of it my whole life, of being someone's most important person. And someday, after I leave here..." She lifted her chin. "Someday, I'll find someone who loves me. And we'll love each other forever."

Omar felt a sudden sharp pain in his throat. He rose unsteadily from the sofa.

"Then we must pray you're not pregnant, Beth," he said quietly. "So you can find your true happiness."

And he left her in the queen's bedroom without a backward glance, forcing his heart to stone.

CHAPTER NINE

THE NEXT MORNING Omar was in the small council chamber, beginning business negotiations with a multinational oil firm, when he got a panicked phone call from the only person he would have allowed to interrupt—Beth.

"I'm all right," were her first trembling words. All of Omar's senses went on alarm.

"What's happened?"

Her voice choked on a sob. Omar's heart lifted to his throat. Looking at the others in the room, he said harshly, "Leave. Now."

The powerful businessmen looked at him, then at each other. Reluctantly, they left. Only his vizier lingered, listening.

"What's happened?" Omar bit out, clawing his dark hair back as he paced in his Italian-cut suit.

"You know I was cutting the ribbon to help open the new clinic today." He heard the shock in her voice, the tears. "It was all good. Until some men in the crowd started yelling that I wasn't Dr. Edith Farraday, and I didn't deserve to be queen because I was really just a cheap tart who worked in a shop. I didn't know what to do. I froze. And then—then—" Her voice choked on a sob. "They started throwing things at me. Tomatoes at first…then rocks…"

Rage pulsed through Omar as he gripped the phone.

"I'm coming to get you," he bit out, heading for the door.

"No. I'm all right." Her voice broke. "Your bodyguard is driving me back to the palace. But…" She sounded pitiful as she whispered, "The back of your Rolls-Royce will have to be cleaned, from all the tomatoes dripping off me."

"I'll be waiting at the back door when you arrive," Omar said curtly, and hung up.

"What's happened, sire?" his vizier asked innocently.

"Somehow news got out about Beth."

"How?"

"I don't know," he said grimly. But whoever the men were, he wanted to kill them. With his bare hands. "Find out who leaked the story."

"Of course, sire," Khalid said. Bowing, he left.

Omar's whole body felt tight as he strode out of the small council chamber. His hands gripped into fists as he stalked down the halls. Servants took one look at his face and fled. He was still trembling with inchoate rage as he reached the private back entrance of the palace, beside the courtyard and twenty-car garage.

He waited for her car to arrive, pacing beneath the bright sunlight and softly waving palm trees of the paved courtyard. He hadn't waited for anyone since he became king. Others always waited for him. But he waited for her.

Omar couldn't stop thinking about the attack.

Beth had left that morning, not in a tight dress, but something equally inappropriate: oversize white denim overalls over a colorful striped T-shirt, with her light brown hair in a ponytail that made her look like an art student. She'd been excited to help open a medical clinic. She'd practiced her short speech in Samarqari over breakfast, repeating it over and over, anxious to make sure she pronounced everything right and didn't have a repeat of the disastrous donkey episode.

He could imagine Beth smiling and talking to everyone outside the new clinic, holding up a pair of ridiculously oversize scissors so she could ceremonially cut the big ribbon.

And strangers in the crowd had yelled insults at her. Omar paced in fury, clawing back his hair. They'd thrown tomatoes at her. He stopped, snarling out a low curse. They'd thrown *rocks*.

He punched the stone wall of the palace, leaving his knuckles bloody and bruised.

"Sire!"

Omar turned in a rage. Khalid looked nervous, then squared his shoulders and came forward.

"I don't know how her true identity was discovered, but it's all over the news. The people are in uproar. They say if you marry her, you are a weakling and a fool."

"The people?" he ground out.

"The nobles," his vizier clarified. "But it seems the common people have turned against her, as well. How else to explain them throwing rocks?" His thin face sharpened. "What shall I tell the reporters, sire? May I announce that you intend to cast off the imposter, and marry the woman you should have chosen from the start—Laila al-Abayyi?"

Laila. Always Laila! The man was obsessed with her! Omar replied sharply, "I do not know yet if the queen is pregnant."

"You call that shop girl your queen?"

Omar stiffened. "You know she is, until the day I divorce her," he said coldly. "Even if no one else knows that, you do."

Khalid bowed his head. "Of course." He looked up. "But if she's pregnant, you may still be rid of her. She is a proven liar. You do not have to claim the child as yours. You could—"

Omar turned on him with such ferocity, the other man shrunk back in fear. "You think I would lie and desert her and the child? You think so little of my honor?"

"My apologies. I was only trying to—"

"I know what you are trying to do," he said unsteadily.

The vizier paused. "You do?"

"You are trying to serve the throne, as always. And in recognition of your years of loyal service I will forget your insult." Then he saw the Rolls-Royce enter the courtyard and left Khalid without a word.

Before the car had even come to a full stop, Omar was opening the passenger door. He felt ill when he saw his beautiful wife, pale, her cheerful ponytail and white denim now bedraggled and covered in a mess of red splatters that, for one heart-stopping moment, looked like blood.

"I'm all right," Beth stammered. "Truly, Omar, I'm fine—"

He didn't believe her. Pulling her into his arms, he held her tight, until her trembling stopped.

"I'm getting tomatoes on your suit—"

"I don't care," he growled, holding her. Long moments later, he slowly pulled away. "The world has found out about the twin switch."

She tried to smile. "I guess that explains all the television cameras and vans lurking at the palace gate."

He gritted his teeth. "I swear I will find whoever leaked the story and…"

"It doesn't matter," Beth whispered. "I'm fine. Safe."

Safe, he thought bitterly.

"I'm sorry, Your Highness," the bodyguard blurted out, getting out of the front seat of the car. "One moment the crowd was cheering for her, and then—I never expected them to turn like that!"

Omar glared at him. "Send the doctor to the queen's bedchamber."

Nodding, the bodyguard fled.

Beth was still in his arms. Feeling her body against his caused a reaction that Omar couldn't control. For weeks, since the night of the engagement banquet, he hadn't touched her. Not so much as a kiss.

Every night, Beth had slept in the queen's suite, adjacent to his own. Safe on the other side of the bolted door.

Safe.

Omar took a deep breath. He'd never imagined his people could turn on her like that. They'd seemed to love her.

But he knew how violently loyalties could turn. He'd grown up hearing stories of how thousands of people had died, turning family against family, neighbor against neighbor, in the wanton destruction of Samarqara's civil war, barely sixty years before.

Now, Omar anxiously looked her over. "Did the rocks hit you?"

Beth shook her head. "They all missed by a mile." Looking down at her white denim overalls, now splattered with red, she said ruefully, "The tomatoes are another story."

What would have happened if the men had used weapons deadlier than tomatoes and rocks? He shuddered at the thought. "I'm taking you to your bedroom to rest. You'll be checked over by a doctor."

"I'm fine. I was scared more than anything—"

"You will see a doctor," he said harshly. When she hesitated, he lifted her up against his chest and carried her, so she could not defy him.

His heart was still pounding. No longer with rage, but with fear.

What had he done, bringing Beth into his palace? Unlike Laila al-Abayyi, who'd been brought up in a powerful family and understood Samarqara's history, Beth naively believed the best of everyone. What place did she have in politics? What protection would she have, from those who might seek to hurt her, either with weapons, or with words?

None.

When they reached the queen's chambers, Omar gently set Beth down in the en suite marble bathroom. The late morning sunlight shone gold against the silver fixtures.

Turning on the shower to heat up the water, he looked down at her. Her eyes looked up at him, but she didn't say a word. When he put his hand on her shoulder, he felt she was suddenly shivering hard. As if the fear had finally, truly hit her.

Unbuckling the tops of her overalls, he let them drop to the floor. She did not resist as he lifted her arms to gently pull off her T-shirt, then her bra, then her panties. He wasn't thinking about her body. He was only thinking about how to comfort her. How to keep her safe.

He looked anxiously into her numb eyes. "Dr. Nazari should be here any moment."

"A male doctor," she said.

"No, the queen's doctor is always a woman. I'll let her in." He gently nudged her into the hot, steamy shower, and left without looking back. He didn't want to see his wife naked and pink with steam, standing in the glass shower. He could only endure so much.

The doctor arrived a few minutes later.

"Your betrothed is hurt?" Dr. Nazari asked.

"She was scared. So I want you to check. And—" he hesitated "—will you let me know if she's pregnant?"

The doctor looked at him, then slowly nodded. "If she wishes it."

"Thank you." He went into his own bedchamber to wait. He leaned his head back against the wall, exhaling.

If Beth was pregnant…

He wanted that desperately. And dreaded it.

He desired her as he'd never desired anyone. But he could not be selfish enough to keep her. Not when she might be in danger. Not when she dreamed of love. He had to let her go.

Unless she was pregnant.

If Beth was pregnant, he would be bound not just by law,

but by honor, to keep her as his wife. And he would. Even if he had to defy his nobles, his people, the entire world.

Defy them, would he? A voice mocked. He hadn't even been able to protect Beth from his own people today!

And that would always be a risk. If she remained as his queen, she'd have to give up her country, her home, her freedom. And for what? She didn't care about wealth or power or fame. As she'd said, she wouldn't know what to do with them if she had them.

What Beth wanted was love. And Omar could not love her. He did not know how.

Dr. Nazari came out of the bedroom, her gray head bowed.

"Well?" he demanded anxiously.

"The Lady Beth is fine, Your Highness. Just a few cuts and bruises that I have bandaged. It could have been worse." Her dark eyes were kind. "She asks you go in and speak with her now."

With a deep breath, Omar went inside the queen's bedchamber.

The room was dark. The shades had been drawn. He saw Beth's wan figure, now wearing loose pajamas, tucked into the bed. He sat down beside her. Her eyes were downcast.

"The doctor gave me good news. You're not hurt," he said, trying to keep his voice cheerful. "You'll soon make a full recovery."

"I have news for you, too," she whispered. She took a deep breath, then lifted her gaze to his. "I'm not pregnant."

Beth watched his handsome face turning to shock, then something else—grief? No, surely not.

"You—you are sure?" he said hoarsely.

Miserably, she nodded.

She'd been happy the last few weeks. She'd always wanted to help people, and as Samarqara's queen, she'd been able to do that. She'd been trying to learn the Samar-qari language as quickly as she could. She'd loved talking to people from all walks of life—students, workers, elderly people. In spite of her awkwardness, they'd still made her feel welcome. Like she was home.

But it had all ended today.

Beth looked at Omar, sitting next to her on the bed. His handsome face was expressionless. Frozen. As if he didn't know how to react.

He was being kind, she thought. He had to be secretly relieved he could take Laila al-Abayyi as his queen.

She'd seen the good Omar did for the community. His country was prosperous, his people loved him. His gruff, ruthless exterior hid a kind heart, desperate to do right by his people, even if that meant sacrificing his own happiness.

Or hers. So as heartbreaking as it was, Beth knew she had to leave. Because Omar didn't love her, and he never would.

For too many years, she had thought she didn't deserve to be loved. She'd thought she was nothing special, that she was too ordinary.

But now…somehow, after being chosen as his bride, and living here in this place, acting as Omar's queen, she found that something had changed in her. She'd realized she deserved love as much as anybody.

And she would find it. Even if that meant leaving behind a man she could have loved, with all her body and heart and soul. She could easily have given him the rest of her life.

Even now, as she looked at him in the shadowy coolness of her bedroom, her heart cried out to stay.

But she couldn't.

"I'm sorry," she whispered.

"I'm glad." His expression was flat. "You are free now. Just as you wished."

Beth looked down at her tightly clasped hands over the

blanket, willing herself not to cry. Her voice trembled as she said in a low voice, "So, how does the divorce thing work?"

She was proud of how casual her voice sounded. As if they were discussing something of little importance.

Emotion crossed his handsome face, emotion that was quickly veiled.

"It doesn't have to happen immediately. We can take our time." He took a deep breath. "I have no intention of just throwing you out—"

"Why not? More efficient that way." She kept her voice cheerful, to hide how her heart was breaking. "Better for the kingdom to end our secret marriage before the scandal goes any further."

Omar looked her straight in the eyes.

"Beth," he said in a low voice, "is there any reason why I shouldn't divorce you?"

"None." She looked away. What could she do, plead with him to choose her over his country? To make Beth his priority, instead of his duty to the throne? He didn't love her! "I'll leave today."

"At least let me call my lawyers, arrange a fair settlement for you. I don't want you to think—"

"I don't want your money." Her heart was aching. In another moment, she might break down into sobs. If this was the right thing for them both, why did she feel so awful?

"Beth, there's no reason to—"

"Please, Omar," she said softly. She couldn't meet his eyes. "Just let me go."

For a long moment, he said nothing. Then he covered her clasped hands with his own. For the first time, his skin was cold to the touch. As if the fire had gone out.

He repeated something to her three times. Then he said quietly, "Say the same words back to me."

She did, then waited, her whole body trembling with the

effort it took not to collapse, to cling to him and beg him to let her stay and ask why, why, why, he couldn't love her.

Omar took a deep breath, and removed his hand.

"It's done," he said. "We're divorced."

She swallowed. "Just like that?"

"As it started, so it ended. The lawyers will have you sign a stack of papers before you leave, to make it all legal. Once it's filed with the courts this afternoon, it's official."

"Oh," she said dully. "Good."

Reaching out, he cupped her cheek and gave her a trembling smile. "You deserve a life of good things, Beth. Security. Freedom. And love. Love most of all. All the things I could never give you." He kissed her forehead. His voice broke as he whispered, "Goodbye, *habibi*."

And without another word, without another look, he walked out of Beth's life—forever.

Omar felt like he couldn't breathe as he watched Beth leave the palace an hour later, followed by servants carrying her suitcases and bags.

It was for the best, he told himself fiercely, standing in the window of the throne room. Beth was right. Ending it quickly, rather than drawing out the torture, would be a mercy to them both. Now they knew she wasn't pregnant, there was no reason to continue. Not when it was so destructive to his country's peace—and to Beth's.

Yet, as he'd spoken the words to divorce her, they'd tasted like ash in his mouth. And now, as he watched her leave, his body shook. He wanted to run after her, to grab her, to never let her go.

Is there any reason why I shouldn't divorce you?

None, she'd said. *Please, Omar. Just let me go.*

So he did not move. He could not keep Beth here, and watch as her spirit was broken, one tomato, one rock at a time. He could not force her to remain married forever to a man who did not know how to love her, even if he weren't already bound by endless duty to his country.

He could not trap another woman, watching the bright light inside her slowly fade, until, in her despair, she walked out into the desert to die.

His last blurry image of Beth Farraday as she climbed into the Rolls-Royce was from the same window of the throne room, where he'd first conceived of the bride market a few months before.

In spite of her objections, he'd arranged a settlement with his lawyers. An enormous sum would be wired to her bank account, waiting for her when she arrived in Houston. His private jet was already collecting Dr. Edith Farraday from his island in the Caribbean. She would be in Houston to greet her sister. He couldn't bear the thought of Beth being alone.

Someday, I'll find someone who loves me. And we'll love each other forever.

Beth was going to a better life. A better world. Where all her dreams could come true.

And as for him…

"The shop girl's gone, sire," his vizier said brightly behind him. "Shall we discuss your imminent engagement to Laila al-Abayyi?"

Omar didn't move. He'd never felt the chains of kingship more than right now. Or felt so alone.

He shut off all emotion. All feeling. All memory. It was the only way he knew to survive.

Numbly, Omar turned to him. "No engagement."

"But, Your Highness…" his vizier sputtered. "Surely you see that it's necessary. The country needs a firm hand!"

Omar looked down at his hands, which had so recently held Beth in his arms, but never would again. "No engagement," he repeated. "If Laila is willing to be queen, I want the wedding ceremony as soon as possible."

The vizier exclaimed in delight, "Sire!"

"Tomorrow," Omar said flatly. He looked back out the window. "I want this over and done with."

CHAPTER TEN

BETH WAS DOING the right thing.

The only thing.

She repeated that to herself, again and again, on the long flight to Houston. Trying to sleep, she stared numbly out the windows, looking down through the clouds as the private jet traveled over Europe, then the gray Atlantic. She'd done the right thing.

So why did her heart feel like it had been ripped out?

Omar deserved a better wife. A better queen. One who wouldn't be hated by his people and pummeled with rocks. She'd had to let him go.

But when Beth arrived in Houston at sunset, her shoulders were drooping and her heart felt sick. A limo was waiting for her on the tarmac of the private airport. As the driver loaded her luggage—just her rucksack, and a suitcase of cheap bohemian clothes from the funky shop in Khazvin—she wearily climbed into the back seat. Then she saw the person in the back seat waiting for her.

"Beth," Edith cried, holding out her arms.

Just seeing her sister's face, her eyes so concerned beneath her thick glasses, made tears finally flood Beth's eyes. Sobs choked her throat as she threw herself into Edith's arms.

Her sister murmured comforting words, stroking her back, saying, "I'm sorry, Beth, I'm so sorry. This is all my fault. I never should have convinced you to go."

But for her sister to blame herself was absurd. Beth

pulled back, wiping her eyes. "It's not your fault. You're not the one who—" *The one who let yourself care for a man you knew you could not have.* She swallowed hard. "What are you doing here?"

"Your—King Omar sent his jet to collect me. He didn't want you to be alone."

As the limo's engine started, and the driver drove them away from the tarmac, the lump in Beth's throat thickened.

"Bastard," she whispered.

Edith looked confused. "He was just worried about you."

And that was what hurt most. Knowing that he cared. He actually cared.

But he'd still let her go. He didn't love her. Not like...

She stopped the thought cold. She couldn't even think it. She couldn't let it be true.

"How does it feel to be back?" Edith said.

Looking out at the Houston streets at twilight, Beth should have felt pleased to be back home. But all she could think about were the streets of Samarqara's capital city, the scent of salt and spice in the fragrant breezes off the Caspian Sea. She took a deep breath and changed the subject. "You look tan."

"I do, don't I?" She gave a very un-Edith-like grin. "Turns out I don't hate vacations as much as I thought. Especially—" Edith's grin widened "—after I met Michel."

"Michel?"

"He worked as a gardener on the king's estate. He's also a musician." Her eyes twinkled. "And very, very good with his hands."

Beth's lips parted. "Are you saying..."

"We spent lots of time together. We drank daiquiris and danced on the white sand beach by moonlight. It was incredible. So incredible that when I left, he quit his job to come live here with me. In fact..." Leaning forward in the back seat of the limo, looking right and left as if she thought the driver might be listening and judging her, she whispered, "He's waiting for me right now."

"Oh, Edith!"

"I've never been in love before. I always thought love was a waste of time. But now," she said dreamily, "I know when I come home from the lab at night, Michel will be there to play me songs on his guitar. And…" Her cheeks blushed as she gave a girlish giggle. "And all the rest."

"I'm so happy for you," Beth said, putting her hands over her twin sister's. And she was. How could she be anything but happy for Edith, now her sister had finally found love at last?

But the pain in Beth's own heart over what she'd lost—the man and country she'd left behind—was almost unbearable.

As the limo pulled down her street, Beth's lips parted when she saw crowds of television trucks outside her nondescript apartment building. "Has something happened?"

"You," Edith said. "You're famous."

"Me?" she said incredulously. Looking at the terrifying crowds of paparazzi and reporters, she leaned forward to the driver and begged, "Get us out of here." As he nodded and turned a sharp corner, she turned to her sister. "Why would I be famous in Houston?"

"The whole world wants the story of the shop girl who tricked a king into believing she was her twin, and into choosing her as his bride, even over Sia Lane." Edith smiled wryly. "If it makes you feel better, I can't go home, either. Michel and I checked into a hotel. The lab's getting pounded with calls. Television reporters. Newspapers. But it's not my story they want. It's yours."

"No," Beth said weakly.

"They're offering morning show interviews. Book deals. Even a reality show. Check your phone."

Beth turned it on. To her shock, she saw she had forty-one phone messages, and even more texts. She looked at her lackluster social media accounts, which she'd created years before to follow her favorite stars and connect with friends. Her eyes went wide.

"I have eight million followers." She was suddenly shaking. "What's going on?"

"You're famous, Beth. Everyone wants to know you. You're special."

"But how can I work at the thrift shop, with people following me?"

Edith paused. "I don't think you need to worry about that."

Beth snorted. "The forty dollars in my checking account says otherwise. And I'm not selling Omar's story to the press. Not for any price!"

Her sister peered at her as if she was a specimen under a microscope. Then she gave a satisfied nod. "Ah."

"What do you mean by that?" Beth said, disgruntled.

"When your king called me..."

"Omar called you directly?"

"Yes." Edith smiled. "He made it clear that you'll never need to work again. *Tell her to follow her heart. Make her do it*, he told me. He also asked me for the numbers of your bank account." She shrugged. "Easy enough to find. You've used the same password since high school, Bethie. TrueLove1."

"Edith!" she cried.

"Check your bank account."

Glowering, Beth looked up her bank details on her phone. Since all her bills were on autopay, she expected to see she had forty-one dollars left. She'd counted on getting back to work at the shop immediately. She'd been a little worried about next month's rent.

No longer. Her eyes boggled.

Beth had fifty million dollars.

Just sitting there. In her checking account. She had to keep counting the zeroes to be sure she wasn't counting them wrong.

"Why would he do this?" she whispered, feeling dizzy.

Her sister looked at her. "Can't you think of a reason?"

Beth felt topsy-turvy inside. "I'll give the money to you—"

"No." Edith's voice was firm. "He was very clear to me on this point. This money is for you and you alone. But don't worry—" She grinned suddenly, and said in a cheerful voice, "My research has now been completely and utterly funded for the next ten years."

"That's wonderful," Beth said slowly.

But she suddenly faced a life she couldn't recognize. She thought of all the cameras and people outside her dilapidated studio apartment and shivered.

She'd always wanted to be special. But this was too much. And right as she was sitting there in shock, holding her phone, she got a text.

It was from Wyatt, the boyfriend who'd broken up with her because she "wasn't special."

His new message said:

I've made a horrible mistake. Meet for coffee?

"Wyatt wants to give our relationship another chance," she said in a strangled voice.

"Of course he does, Beth." Her sister's voice was soft. "Do you know, I've always been a little envious of you?"

Beth looked up in shock. "You—envious of *me*?"

"I've often wished I could live like you do. With such joy in every day. You bring happiness to so many. I don't think you even realize it."

She stared at Edith. All this time she'd been envying Edith, and her sister envied *her*?

Beth suddenly grinned. "Sure," she said. "And all you do is cure cancer."

"There is that," Edith agreed, returning her smile. Then she sighed. "The truth is, I don't know if I'll ever have that breakthrough. It's always just over the horizon. I might be wasting my life for nothing. And then I look at you. You don't waste a day. You don't waste a moment. Until I met Michel, I never knew how good it was."

"Sex?"

"Love." Her sister looked at her though her thick glasses. "You love him, don't you? This king of yours?"

Love him?

Beth's heart lifted to her throat.

She couldn't love him. He was a billionaire king. She was just a shop girl from West Texas.

She admired him, of course. She desired him. Okay, so obviously she was wildly infatuated, but who wouldn't be?

They were also friends. She cared for him. Respected him. She trusted him. He was the first person she thought of every morning, the last before she fell asleep. All she wanted on earth was his happiness. All she wanted was—him.

Because she loved him.

Beth sucked in her breath, covering her mouth with her hands as it hit her, the thing she'd tried so hard not to know. The thing she'd tried so hard to hide, even from herself.

"What is it?" Edith said gently.

Eyes wide, Beth turned to her in the back of the limo. She choked out, "I love him."

"I knew it," her sister said, then frowned. "So why did you leave?"

Beth's lips parted. "Because…because he didn't want me."

"That's empirically not true. All the evidence clearly shows that he cares for you desperately."

She thought of the emotion in Omar's dark eyes as he'd said in a low voice, *Is there any reason why I shouldn't divorce you?*

Beth swallowed hard. "He's King of Samarqara. He'll always put his people first. And the people don't want me."

"From the stories on the news, that's not true. They're heartbroken you're gone."

"They threw rocks at me. Yelled I wasn't worthy to be queen."

"All of them?"

"Some men in a crowd."

"And you agreed with those idiots, rather than trying to prove them wrong?"

"They weren't wrong!" Beth protested. "I'm not you."

"No doubt," her sister agreed. "You'd be a better queen than I'd ever be. I'm sure you weren't cooped up in a lab, but out in the community, taking care of people. Like you always do." When Beth bit her lip sheepishly, Edith gave a sharp nod. "Right. If you love him, you have to fight."

Fight for him? For a moment, hope lifted wildly inside Beth. Then it came crashing down. "But Omar doesn't love me. He said so. He only loves his people."

"But does he know how you feel? Did you tell him?"

Beth looked out at Houston's passing city lights as twilight deepened. "No," she whispered.

"So do it."

"I can't."

"Why?"

"What if I try, and fail?"

Edith whirled on her, her eyes ablaze. "Do you have any idea how many times I've failed? More than I can count. Failure is part of success. You have to commit. That's the magic. The only magic. You give everything. And when you have nothing left to give, you give some more."

Staring at her twin sister, Beth felt her breath *whoosh* out of her lungs.

"You've never let yourself commit to anything, Beth. Not since we were kids." Edith shook her head. "You didn't want to risk becoming like me, closed off to everything beyond the lab. I was a cautionary tale."

Beth stared at her sister.

"No," she whispered. "You were my shining example. You found what you loved, what you were born to do. And you threw yourself into it, heart and soul. I never committed to anything because I was waiting to fall in love. I never found that." Her eyes went wide as she sucked in her breath. "Until now."

She'd always thought of herself as ordinary, a girl who wasn't particularly good at anything. A mediocre student who couldn't finish a degree or find a real career or attract a decent boyfriend. She'd blamed herself, for not trying hard enough. For not being good enough.

But she hadn't failed. In her heart, she'd never wanted those careers or those degrees or those men.

Then, in Samarqara, when she'd finally found everything she'd ever dreamed of, a man she loved, a job she loved, a place she loved, she'd gotten so used to giving up, she didn't even know how to put up a fight anymore.

Beth lifted her chin, her hands clenching.

Well, that would all change now.

Even if she tried and failed, even if she threw herself at Omar's feet and he scorned her, he deserved to at least know that she loved him. And she deserved to tell him.

All this time Beth had thought she wasn't worthy to be his wife. But she was. Because no one loved him more.

"Take me back to the airport," she told the driver, who nodded and turned the wheel.

"You're going back?" Edith said happily.

"I'm going to tell him. You're right." She hugged her sister. "I'm going to take the first flight back to Samarqara."

Her phone rang. Thinking it was another reporter, she was going to ignore it. Then she saw the Samarqara country code.

Beth snatched up the phone. But it wasn't Omar. It was someone even more startling.

"My lady, it's Rayah," the young maid said desperately. "You must come back to Samarqara. Please!"

"I am—but why? And why are you whispering?"

"I'm calling you from a closet in the tower so no one can hear. It's not even dawn but the king's wedding preparations have already started."

Beth's heart fell. "He's marrying Laila already?"

"I overheard the vizier talking to her in the garden. They are planning to poison the king's goblet in the wedding toast!"

"What?" Sitting up straight in the back seat of the limo, Beth gripped the phone. Her eyes went wide as she heard the details. Blood drained from her body. "You must warn the king!"

"I tried, my lady. But the king's beyond all reason. He's refusing to see anyone."

"Tell the people—have them storm the palace!"

"It would only give the vizier a better excuse for a coup. He's already blocking all access to the king. You're the only one who can get past his guards now."

"When will they do it?" Beth cried.

"The wedding will be private, tonight at midnight in the palace garden. As soon as they're wed, they'll kill him and seize the throne."

"I'm on my way," Beth cried. Hanging up, she tried to call Omar, but it went directly to voice mail. She tried again, but to no avail.

"What's happened?" Edith demanded.

"Omar's in danger." Leaning forward to the driver, she begged him, "Hurry, please hurry!"

Checking her phone, she saw the next commercial flight to Samarqara didn't leave for hours, and had a layover in Europe. She clawed back her hair.

Oh, why had she ever left him? All the thoughts of the future they could have had, if only she'd been brave enough to fight for it, flew through her mind.

"I'll never make it in time!"

"Oh, yes, you will." Edith's eyes, identical to her own, shone with faith. "Now that you know you love him, nothing can stop you."

As the limo drove past the private airport where she'd arrived, Beth had a sudden idea. "Turn here!"

"Not the international airport, miss?"

"No! Here!"

She nearly cried when she saw Omar's huge private jet still on the tarmac. They'd obviously already refueled and were getting ready to leave when she raced up the steps to the open door, Edith behind her.

"You must take me back to Samarqara," Beth panted.

The pilots and flight attendants looked at each other, then at Edith behind her.

"I'm sorry, Dr.—er—Miss Farraday," one said awkwardly. "The vizier said—"

"I don't care what the vizier said. The king's in danger." When they didn't move, she said desperately, "I will pay you fifty million dollars to take me back!"

When they still didn't move, Beth marched into the cabin of the jet and sat down. Nervously, Edith followed her lead.

Looking at the pilots and flight attendants, she ordered, "You will start the engine. Now!"

The pilots and flight attendants looked at each other, then with a bow, rushed to obey.

"I didn't know you could do that," Edith whispered in her ear as the engine warmed up.

"I didn't, either," Beth muttered. As the jet started down the runway, she looked out the window at the wing, wishing she could go out and push it to make them go faster. Because as fast as they were going, she might not be in time to save the man she loved.

Omar paced in the moonlit palace garden where, in just a few moments, he'd be wed in a small private ceremony. There had been no time to arrange a grand public affair, but this was even smaller than he'd imagined. The only guests would be Laila and himself, with the vizier and Laila's father as witnesses. There would be no reception. A small table had been set up for the traditional wedding toast, right there in the garden, with the garden's verdant flowers and a few torches to decorate the ceremony.

"We'll have a more formal public coronation later," his vizier had said brightly. "But for now, after all the...publicity of your last bride—" He'd paused and then continued, "it's best to keep this private."

Khalid had seemed almost *too* happy about it. But he had wanted Omar to marry Laila al-Abayyi from the beginning.

Omar looked down at his formal robes, with a silver dagger at his belt, the mark of the bridegroom. Marrying Laila was a necessary sacrifice. He'd spoken with her that afternoon, and she'd confirmed she was still willing to marry him. He had to marry someone sometime. It might as well be her, now.

So why did it feel so wrong—wrong in every way?

Why did he feel like his vizier was forcing him to wed a woman he didn't even like, let alone desire?

No. That wasn't fair. It wasn't Khalid's fault. Omar was the one who'd demanded the bride market. He was the one who'd chosen Beth, then secretly married and seduced her.

And he was the one who'd demanded the immediate ceremony with Laila tonight. He'd wanted to put some barrier between himself and the past.

Between himself and Beth.

She was gone now. Gone to be happy in Houston, with her sister. Beth was rich now, famous. Special to all the world. But she'd always be more than special to him.

Taking a deep breath, Omar looked at his watch, an heirloom from his great-grandfather's day. Just a few minutes until midnight.

He paced through the dark palace garden. Moonlight frosted the edges of the palm trees sighing above like shadows. He heard the burble of the nearby fountain and, against his will, remembered that other garden in Paris, when Beth had first exploded into his life like a comet.

His heart twisted. He'd let her go so she could find happiness. So she'd find true love. At least he could be proud of that.

But he had to think of his nation. A low, ugly undercurrent of anger had spread across the city at the news of Beth's departure. Apparently, many of the common people still loved her. Whoever had thrown rocks at her in the crowd had disappeared without a trace. Many people said they didn't care if Beth was a scientist or a shop girl. They demanded she return as queen.

"The people are fickle, sire," his vizier had said with a shrug. "Who knows what they'll demand next? But I'll put the palace on lockdown, just in case." His thin lips had curved as he'd said, "They'll soon learn who's in charge."

Who *was* in charge? Omar wondered as he paced the moonlit garden. He stopped. Surely not he. If he were in charge, he would have Beth in his arms right now. He would be kissing her, feeling her soft body against his own. She would be his wife, now and forever.

But he'd divorced her. Set her free. He didn't want her to be trapped in this palace. He didn't want her to be unhappy.

He loved her.

He heard the echo of his own voice from what felt like long ago. *True love—what is that?*

When you care for someone so much, she'd replied, *their happiness matters more than your own.*

Omar looked up with an intake of breath.

He loved her.

"Sire." His vizier entered the dark garden. "Your bride is on her way. It's time."

"I can't," Omar breathed.

Khalid frowned. "What?"

"I love her," he whispered.

"You love your bride? Excellent. In a moment, you'll speak your vows, then we'll toast the future…"

"Not Laila," Omar said harshly. "Beth." His voice softened as his heart soared. Why had he never seen it before? "I love Beth." He started to turn. "I must go to her—"

"You cannot be so selfish, Omar."

His vizier had never spoken to him so harshly. He looked back in astonishment. "Selfish?"

"Would you see this country fall back into civil war? To see our city again become a ruin? To see innocents suffer— merely because you want that shop girl back in your bed?"

Omar took a deep breath. "No. But—"

"You cannot insult Laila like this. Not after what you did to Ferida."

"What I…did to her?"

"Forcing her to marry you against her will," Khalid said coldly. "And now you will scorn and humiliate her half sister? Hassan al-Abayyi will not forgive again. You must know this." His vizier came closer, his eyes gleaming in the moonlight. "You cannot turn back now. You must act like a king."

Like a king, Omar thought dimly.

Just then, Laila walked into the garden, on the arm of her proud father. She looked beautiful and regal in her traditional Samarqari gown and bridal headdress. Omar thought of his kingdom and tried to steel himself for this last, most important sacrifice.

But he could not do it.

His heart was Beth's. He could not pretend otherwise and marry another. For that would be the ultimate lie, the betrayal of his very core. And what kind of king, what kind of ruler could he be, without a heart? Without a soul?

For the first time, he understood why Ferida had fled to the desert rather than wed him against her will. For he was willing to do that now.

For Beth, Omar would set the whole world on fire.

"I'm sorry." He looked between Laila and her father. "I have great respect for your family. But this marriage cannot go on."

The other three looked at each other in astonishment.

Hassan al-Abayyi's face turned red beneath the torchlight as he sputtered, "If you even *think* you can…"

The vizier cut him off with a smooth gesture. Lifting his face into a bland smile, he said benignly, "If the king cannot wed today, then he cannot, and there is no more to be said."

Omar looked at his distant cousin with gratitude. "Thank you, Khalid."

Turning to the nearby table, the vizier poured wine into four golden goblets. "We will toast to the future, and the friendship that will always exist between the throne and the al-Abayyi family." He held out one of the goblets to Omar. "Surely you mean no insult to their honor."

"None," Omar said, relieved they were taking it so well. He took the goblet. Glancing at each other, the others took their goblets from the table.

The vizier held up his wine. "To the future of the kingdom."

"To the future," Omar said. He didn't notice the three pairs of eyes watching him avidly. As he lifted the goblet to his mouth, his mind was already on Beth. He could hardly wait to tell her he loved her. As soon as he'd finished this toast, he'd fly to Houston and offer his heart at her feet—

Smiling to himself, he pressed the goblet to his lips, and tilted his head back to drink.

"No!" a woman screamed, and the goblet was knocked out of his hand.

To his shock, Beth stood before him, her eyes wide with what seemed like panic. She wasn't in Houston as he'd pictured her, but right in front of him now. And he'd never seen anything more beautiful, more wonderful, in his whole life.

"Did you drink anything?" she begged. "Did you?"

Suddenly, there were guards all around them in the garden. The vizier looked at them wildly, pointing at Beth. "Seize this woman!"

But the guards didn't move. They were looking at Beth for their orders, Omar realized.

"What are you doing here?" he breathed.

"Your drink was poisoned." Beth pointed at Khalid, Laila and Hassan al-Abayyi. "They were going to murder you and take the throne."

"She's lying!" Khalid cried.

"Murder me?" Omar said slowly, as the words penetrated the fog of his joy. He looked at Hassan, whose face was red with rage.

"Don't," Khalid said warningly.

But the older man was past all advice. He turned on Omar in fury. "You're ruining this country. All your talk of prosperity and equality for the common people. They need to be ruled with an iron hand, as in your grandfather's time!" He pointed at his daughter and the vizier. "Laila and Khalid know this. They should rule, not you!"

Omar staggered back in shock. He looked at Laila.

"I didn't know for sure they were planning to kill you," she said weakly. "I just wanted to be queen."

Looking at the vizier, Omar choked out, "And you. We've been friends since we were boys."

Khalid looked back at him with undisguised hatred. "We were. Until the day you murdered Ferida."

Omar gasped. "You were the man she loved?"

"And you took her from me," Khalid said tightly. "Just by right of being king. Ever since, I've dreamed of my revenge. I wanted your crown. When you married that shop girl, I thought I'd have to kill you on your honeymoon and seize the throne. Now I'll have to be satisfied," he said in a low growl, "with killing your woman!"

Khalid sprang murderously toward Beth, a knife in his hand.

Ripping his own ceremonial dagger from his belt, Omar blocked his blade at the last moment. They struggled, then Omar threw him forcibly to the ground.

"Take them," he said to the captain of the guard, who nodded grimly. A short scuffle ended with the three plotters being dragged away screaming, all of them blaming each other.

"What will happen to them?" Beth said brokenly, watching as they were taken forcibly out of the royal garden.

"I don't know or care." Pulling her into his arms, Omar fervently kissed her forehead, her cheeks. Emotion ripped through him, as he felt how he'd nearly lost her. Just remembering how Khalid's knife had gleamed wickedly in the light made his body shake. Holding her tight, he whispered, "You came back to me."

"Rayah called me in Houston. She'd heard the vizier plotting but no one could reach you. I couldn't let them hurt you. I..." As she looked up at him, her voice choked, and she turned away.

He gripped her hand, not releasing her. "What?"

"I came to tell you something, but..." Beth lifted her gaze miserably to his. "I can't. You married her. She's your wife."

Omar slowly shook his head. "I couldn't marry her." Lifting her limp hand, he pressed it against his heart and said tenderly, "How could I, when I want only you?"

Her eyes grew wide. "But you were in the middle of the wedding toast—"

"I canceled the ceremony at the last moment. So Khalid suggested a toast to the future." He scowled. "Now I see it was a future where he and Laila would rule."

Beth looked dazed. "How did they intend to claim the throne?"

"He probably intended to announce the wedding and my unexpected, sudden death. Then he'd claim the throne as the only male heir left, consolidating power by marrying the new queen."

"How dare he?" she cried furiously.

"But they failed." Omar looked down at her with tears in his eyes. "Because of you."

Beth was dressed in the same jeans and T-shirt she'd left the palace in, a day and a half before. Her eyes were tired, her glorious light brown hair frosted silver by moonlight. He'd never seen anyone who looked so beautiful, or more like a queen. He took a shuddering breath.

"You burst into my life like a flame," he whispered. He cupped her cheek, looking at her luminous face in the flickering torchlight of the garden. "Like the sun."

He felt her tremble beneath his touch, saw her lips part and her breasts rise and fall quickly beneath the T-shirt. "Omar...there's something I have to tell you."

"There's something I have to tell you, too. Something

I should have said long ago." He met her gaze. "It doesn't matter what your name is, Beth. In my heart, from the moment I saw you in Paris, I knew you were the one."

"You did?" she said faintly.

"You have won the hearts of my people." He straightened. "I offer you the whole city. The love of an entire nation."

"It's not the nation's love I need," she said in a low voice.

The meaning of her words exploded in his heart, and he fell to his knees before her.

"I offer you my love, as well." Taking her hands in his own, he looked up at her. "You are strong and honest and fierce. You are the woman I want. I love you, Beth. And I will strive every day to…"

He looked away.

"To what?" she breathed.

He looked up at her. His eyes were blurry with tears as he spoke the truth from his heart. "To be worthy of you. If you'll just give me a chance to earn your love…"

"Earn my love? You can't." His heart fell to the ground, until she choked out, "It's already yours. I was coming back to you even before Rayah called. To tell you I love you."

A thrill went through his heart.

"You love me?" he whispered, searching her gaze.

Wordlessly, she nodded, smiling though her tears.

Omar didn't remember how he got to his feet. Afterwards, he remembered only the sensation of flying. When he pulled her into his arms and kissed her, he soared.

For the first time in his life, he truly felt like a king.

A year later, spring had finally arrived in Samarqara. Spring, and Beth's sister.

"They're beautiful," Edith breathed, looking down at one-month-old Tariq in Beth's arms.

"The most beautiful babies in the world," Omar agreed,

with his typical modesty where his newborn twins were concerned. He looked down at the baby snuggled in his own arms, Nyah, who was just two minutes younger than her brother.

"Twins," Edith said wryly, shaking her head. "I still can't believe it."

Sitting in a shady spot in the palace garden, beside the newly blooming flowers beneath the palm trees, Beth looked up at her sister fondly. "Think of all the fun they'll have."

"The fun's already begun," Omar said with a grin, stretching his arm along the top of the bench behind his wife. "I thought the kingdom went crazy at Beth's coronation…"

"We remember," Edith said, smiling at her new fiancé, Michel.

"But when the babies were born…" Shaking his head, Omar gave a low chuckle. "A great end for the newspapers. Let's just say the tourist board is very happy."

"Tourist board?" Michel looked confused.

"Tourism is up a thousand percent," Beth told him succinctly. *Take that, Sia Lane*, she thought.

"Oh." The young man looked bewildered, but nodded. "That's good."

Based on her sister's description, Beth had expected Michel Dupree to be a wild, sexy musician, but when Edith had brought him to their wedding and Beth's coronation ten months earlier, she'd discovered a quiet young Haitian, kind and talented, who now worked as a music teacher by day and a musician at night, but whose full-time job was really taking care of Edith.

"He cooks for me. Every night," Edith had confided. She'd giggled. "Then he *cooks*, if you get what I'm saying."

Now, looking at the two of them in the palace garden, Beth saw Michel put his arm around Edith tenderly. Her sister had truly found happiness in love, as well as work, where, as she always liked to say, she was closer to a breakthrough every day.

There were breakthroughs of all kinds, Beth thought. When she'd been brave enough to tell Omar she loved him, everything else had fallen into place. Now, she had a life more wonderful than she'd ever dared dream.

Their royal wedding had been magnificent. Nothing quiet or restrained about it. It had been a full royal affair, with twelve hundred guests from around the world, held in the grand palace. Beth had arrived via horse-drawn carriage, her traditional gown covered with jewels. She'd left on Omar's arm, the crowned Queen of Samarqara.

She still had the actual crown, kept mostly in the vault for special occasions. It was so heavy with diamonds, it hurt her head to wear it for too long. So she mostly didn't.

Beth. A queen. She still couldn't believe it.

The entire kingdom had come out to cheer that day. Even the nobles had cheered, if only to prove they hadn't been part of the attempted coup. Later, three men had shamefacedly come forward and confessed they were the ones who'd been hired by the vizier to throw rocks at Beth.

"We only did it because he threatened our families. We made sure none of the rocks came close to hitting you. Please, we throw ourselves on your mercy, our queen!"

After Beth's pleading, Omar had let the men go with nothing but community service as punishment. But Khalid and Hassan al-Abayyi weren't so lucky. They'd been sentenced to prison for life, their money and estates confiscated. Laila, as an accessory instead of active participant, had received exile. But bereft of her family's fortune, she screamed and begged to be sent to prison, too. "For what's the point of living if I can't live in a palace?"

It was ironic. Omar hadn't wanted the throne. He'd taken it as a duty he was honor-bound to endure. Beth had never dreamed of living in a palace, either. Why would she? The demands of royalty had nearly torn them apart.

But the two of them, by loving each other, had somehow managed to make this gilded cage of a palace into the homey cottage of Beth's dreams.

It was love that changed everything, she thought in wonder. Love could take even a palace and make it a home.

Love, and family.

They'd conceived their twins on their wedding night, in the same bed they slept in now. "I saved this bed only for you," Omar had whispered in her ears. "To make love only to my wife. My queen."

She blushed, remembering. He wanted a large family. He was threatening to get her pregnant a *lot*. Six, perhaps seven more times. And given the way he kissed her, the way he made her body come so alive, she didn't think she'd be able to refuse. Fortunately, a large family sounded just fine to her.

As international media broadcast images of the popular King and Queen of Samarqara, so obviously in love, and now with newborn twins, there was some talk that bride markets—and groom markets—might be the best way to find true love after all. Reading an American newspaper the other day in their bedroom, sitting together near the fire as their babies slept, Beth burst into a laugh. "This article says you're a genius!"

"Of course I am," Omar had told her loftily. "I know everything. That is why you must always obey me, wife."

Then he'd said *ooph* as she smacked him playfully with a pillow.

Now, Beth looked at her husband in the dappled sunlight of the palace garden. As the two of them cuddled together on the shady bench, and her sister and almost-brother-in-law drank mint tea and exclaimed over their tiny sleeping babies, Beth still couldn't understand how she'd been so lucky. What had she ever done to deserve a life like this?

Then she knew.

One thing had changed her life. When she'd found it, nothing could stop her. Not danger, not fear, not doubt. When she'd found it, she'd found her strength. Found herself.

Just one thing: love.

* * * * *

LET'S TALK
Romance

For exclusive extracts, competitions
and special offers, find us online: